ZULU
HEART

Also by Steven Barnes

Lion's Blood

Available from Warner Aspect

STEVEN BARNES

ZULU HEART

ASPECT®

WARNER BOOKS

An AOL Time Warner Company

Aspect® name and logo are registered trademarks of Warner Books, Inc.

Warner Books, Inc., 1271 Avenue of the Americas, New York, NY 10020

Visit our Web site at www.twbookmark.com.

 An AOL Time Warner Company

Printed in the United States of America

First Printing: March 2003
10 9 8 7 6 5 4 3 2 1

Library of Congress Cataloging-in-Publication Data
Barnes, Steven.
    Zulu heart / Steven Barnes.
      p. cm.
    ISBN 0-446-53122-7
    1. Africa—Fiction. 2. Freedmen—Fiction. 3. Imperialism—Fiction. 4. Race
relations—Fiction. 5. Druids and Druidism—Fiction. 6. Aristocracy (Social
class)—Fiction. I. Title.
PS3552.A6954 Z85 2003
813'.54—dc21   2002191004

To my wife, Tananarive Due:
My Nandi, my Lamiya.

Sometimes, one is enough.

ACKNOWLEDGMENTS

Zulu Heart is dedicated to the friends and colleagues who never allowed me to forget either my bliss or responsibilities. This is the life I chose, and no matter how steep the path, one can only climb: for every blister and exertion, there is a commiserate heightening of perspective.

But beyond those stalwarts . . .

To my daughter Lauren Nicole, who has so wonderfully fulfilled her promise.

To Rebecca Neason, Brenda Cooper, Todd Elner, and Tiel Jackson for reading and for comments that helped to clear away the fog. To Toni Young, mother of my child, for both comments and her wonderful maps. Bless you. Once again to Heather Alexander, for permission to quote her wondrous words of song. Readers are again urged to visit her website at www.heatherlands.com for more information.

Charles Johnson and Harry Turtledove, for encouragement.

Betsy Mitchell, who first believed in the dream.

Jaime Levine, my current editor at Warner/Aspect: you demonstrated patience above and beyond the call. This one was like pulling teeth, I know, but you applied what emotional Novocain you could, and were kind.

For Eleanor Wood, my extraordinary agent and friend. How incredibly lucky I was to find you. Thank you for everything, always.

Mad props to Wendi Dunlap for her knowledge of African culture in general and Yoruban philosophy and the Orishas in particular.

More about the wonderful world of Bilalistan can be found on my web page, www.lionsblood.com.

Shall I tell you what acts are better than fasting, charity and prayers? Making peace between enemies are such acts; for enmity and malice tear up the heavenly rewards by the roots.

—THE PROPHET MUHAMMAD

Blessed are the peacemakers; for they shall be called the children of God.

—JESUS CHRIST

If you could get rid
Of yourself just once,
The secret of secrets
Would open to you.
The face of the unknown,
Hidden beyond the universe
Would appear on the
Mirror of your perception.

—RUMI

AUTHOR'S NOTE

Bilalian weights and measures are modifications of ancient Egyptian standards. The royal cubit is here interpreted as about eighteen inches. A digit is about an inch. A kite is approximately an ounce. Ten kites equal one deben, ten debens equal one sep.

The dates given in chapter headings are rendered in both Hijri (dating from Muhammad's flight from Mecca) and Gregorian (dating from the birth of Christ).

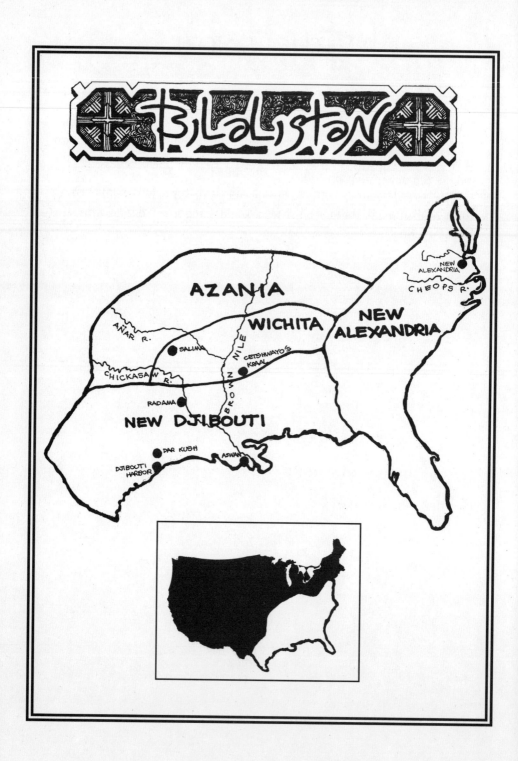

BILALISTAN

AZANIA

WICHITA

NEW ALEXANDRIA

NEW DJIBOUTI

AÑAR R.

SALIMA

CHICKASAW R.

RADAMA

DAR KUSH

DJIBOUTI HARBOR

ASWAN

CETSHWAYO'S KRAAL

BROWN NILE

NEW ALEXANDRIA

CHEOPS R.

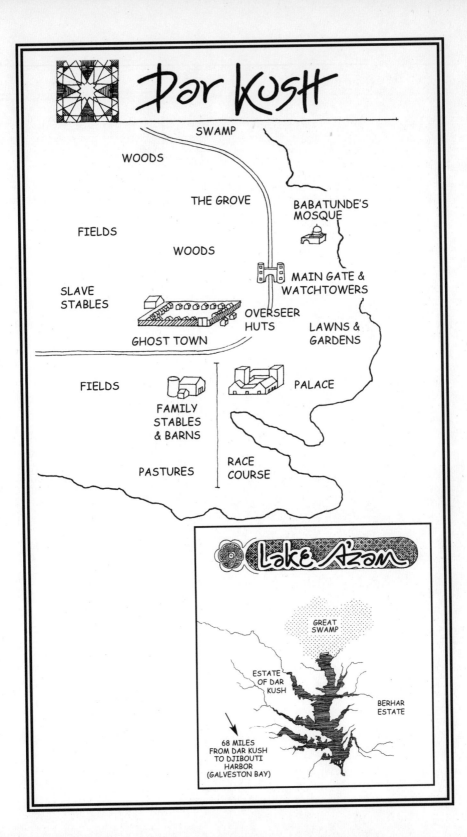

Dar Kush

SWAMP

WOODS

THE GROVE

BABATUNDE'S MOSQUE

FIELDS

WOODS

MAIN GATE & WATCHTOWERS

SLAVE STABLES

OVERSEER HUTS

GHOST TOWN

LAWNS & GARDENS

FIELDS

FAMILY STABLES & BARNS

PALACE

PASTURES

RACE COURSE

Lake Azam

GREAT SWAMP

ESTATE OF DAR KUSH

BERHAR ESTATE

68 MILES FROM DAR KUSH TO DJIBOUTI HARBOR (GALVESTON BAY)

PROLOGUE

Edge of the Dahomy Empire, central West Africa

A.H. 183
(A.D. 800)

IN THE VERDANT GRASSLANDS a brisk hour's run from the coast, close enough for to spice the air with the ocean's foam, thirteen solemn men sat circle, speaking of death.

These thirteen represented the twelve independent Yoruban city-states. Different tribes they were, but a single nation when faced with disaster, whether that grief was occasioned by man or nature. This day they confronted the greatest challenge within living memory: a vast and voracious Dahoman army even now preparing to march against their farms and towns.

Although they had freely elected to lay their lives down for their people, terror and despair gnawed at their hearts. The Dahoman empire had consumed all within its path, offering liberal terms to those who laid down their arms, but destruction, torture, and slavery to any who dared resist.

Negotiation had failed. With the morrow's dawn, the Yoruban forests and plains would churn with battle.

Akintunde, senior war chief and griot of the Yoruba, was a man of fifty rains. Despite his burden of years and scars, he stood as erect as any man twenty rains his junior. His shaven head and torso were intricately tattooed with keloid scars proclaiming Yoruba battles, calamities, and triumphs. Even in silence, Akintunde was his people's living history.

Whatever misgivings the Twelve might have felt, they held themselves straight and strong, eyes locked on the man whose very name meant "courage returns." Akintunde had called this gathering that his people might march to the rhythm of a single heart. His courage would be theirs. As he had done so many times in the past, Akintunde locked his own fear deep within his breast, that only vitality might shine from his eyes, only words of power issue from his tattooed lips.

Each subchief represented many hundreds of fighting men. In peace-time they were farmers, hunters, fishermen. In time of war, they kissed their wives and children good-bye, gave their souls to Chango or Ogun, and marched off to war. This, then, was their final meeting before the morrow's fateful clash.

"Men have faced such odds before," Akintunde began.

"Did they survive?" asked a short, muscular young blacksmith. He squatted on his heels, obsidian face taut with worry. Akintunde knew that Ojo was troubled: his breathing was shallow and high, his posture canted forward, denoting tightness in the gut. During a war-dance hours before, Akintunde noted that Ojo's coordination was degraded by tension. Hunger or fatigue could do these things, but the old war-chief intuited that Ojo yearned for more than food or sleep: Ojo was famished for hope.

"Survival is for the beasts of the forest," replied their leader. "Men are born to conquer and prevail."

Every eye was fixed upon him. Battling desperation, Akintunde scanned his memory for some bit of encouragement he might offer. His chiefs would fight and die if he so ordered them. But if only he could find the words, they might do much more.

If Akintunde was truly worthy of the name his father had given him, they might fight and *win*.

So, steadying his voice and expanding his chest, he began to speak. Not of their own ancestors, who, though mighty and brave, had never faced a challenge such as that the morrow would bring. Instead, it was a tale of an ancient, faraway people, a tale that had traveled with the Abyssinian and Egyptian traders who had plied the coastlines for a thousand years. A tale that lived in the writings of Aeschylus, long-dead bard of the fabled city of Athens, who had raised his spear above a plain called Marathon, and thought that moment of ultimate trial the greatest of his life. . . .

In the days before the rise of Pharaoh Haaibre Setepenamen, Darius, the King of Persia, dreamed a dream that all the world should rest in his bejeweled hands. Between this king and his loathsome vision stood only a tiny group of free warriors who would bow their heads to the sky, or their ancestors, or the Orishas, but never to mortal men.

Darius considered himself more than mere flesh, and vowed to humble the Athenians, or destroy them.

The Persian soldiers were more numerous than ants in the forest. Their mighty warships dominated the oceans. Armor-plated Persian warhorses darkened the horizon. So abundant were Darius's bowmen that their flights clouded the sky. His commanders, Datis and Artaphernes, were demons in fleshly form, beyond human capacity to defeat.

Ten thousand Athenians marched forth, a force that was to the Persians as a stripling is to a blooded warrior. Their tribe, the Greeks, had spawned great Setepenamen, whom some called Alexander.

Unlike the Persians, these Greeks fought not for a distant god-monarch, that his shadow might enfold an entire world. Each fought that his children might live their lives, till their soil, love their women in their own way, and not at the pleasure of a madman who thought himself beyond death and judgment.

Each and every Athenian fought not for gold, but for a dream. No professional soldiers, they were poets, philosophers, teachers, fishermen.

These men had vowed victory, or death in its attempt.

Minds unburdened by the fear of death, they gained the clarity Ogun gifts only those true in every part. They saw not disaster. Instead, the god of war gave them a vision: by meeting the Persians in a narrow place, then stretching their lines out so they could not be flanked, the number of their enemies mattered not.

All that mattered was the absolute courage in each heart, the strength in each Greek arm.

The battle was the crash of waves against a rocky shore. Pitted against a Persian ocean, the Athenian rock did not yield. As the tide retreated, so fled the Persians.

Wise in the ways of war, the Greeks did not pursue. They knew the Persians would send their fleet to Athens, hoping to deceive the city into opening its gates, attempting guile where force of arms had failed. The Greeks sent a runner on ahead, a man of quicksilver tread named Phideppides. Fleet as an antelope, he ran for hours without an instant's rest. Upon reaching his people he cried, "We have won!" and fell, his heart at rest, the ancestors welcoming him home.

When the enemy arrived, the Athenians knew better than to open their gates. For the first time, the Persians knew defeat.

The Greeks won because Ogun smiles upon the courageous, because each and every Athenian was righteous in the eyes of his ancestors, who watched from the shadow world, and were well pleased.

They won because the Persians were slaves of King Darius. He, and the mad King Xerxes who followed him, were weak and arrogant.

The Athenians won because they were free men.

As Akintunde concluded his story, his voice rose to a crescendo. The twelve chiefs stood, pounding their spear-butts against the ground, howling their defiance and battle-fever to the sky. Akintunde was proud, and knew they would give the last drop of blood from their veins, wring the last crumb of strength from their sinews. More than that Chango himself could not ask.

And on that next fateful day, the Yoruba prevailed, inspired by an ancient tale of a long-vanquished people. A tale that, with the passage of centuries, would seem ever more mythic than historical.

After all, Europe was a conquered continent, its children raped and slaughtered, its lands divided among the Africans who washed her soil with blood.

But the Yoruba remembered: once, before the fall of barbarous Rome, had lived the Greeks. And for a single scintillating moment, they had shone as a beacon of light in the diseased soul of a war- and plague-torn continent. On a distant day, Athens had chosen death over slavery, and had been rewarded with freedom. And if her descendants had forgotten that lesson, there were others who held it close.

As a thousand years of monarchies held Africa and Europe in thrall, as emperors clutched the throne of China and the Gupta controlled all of India, as kings and princes of all stripe ruled the islands east of Abyssinia, along with the vast tides of wealth in trade and tribute flowed another current, one carrying not men or materiel, but an idea stronger than either.

Freedom, it whispered.

And one day, though it might take another thousand years, that whisper would become a roar.

PART I

The Wakil

"I have studied for many years," said the student, "and yet have not experienced that of which you speak: that clarity, that connection with the divine. My heart yearns for that food I have yet to taste."

"It is the yearning that sharpens the student," said the master. "And also separates him."

"I do not understand."

"We yearn for what we do not have, so that our minds are there, and here, and there. You seek what was yours at birth."

"Then why do I not feel it?" asked the student.

"Because you have entered the world of men, in which lies are often preferable to truth."

"And in the world of spirit there are no lies?"

"None," said the teacher. "Nor truth. Only Allah."

CHAPTER ONE

Songhai Islands, south of New Djibouti

8 Ramadan A.H. 1294

(Sunday, September 16, 1877)

THE DAY HAD BEEN GLORIOUS. The southern sun gilded the sparse clouds as they frolicked in a fair wind. It was a time of slow delicious sweltering. Now, at last, the day drew to a close. The past seventy-two hours had provided recreation and renewal for the family of Bilalistan's youngest Wakil, Kai of Dar Kush. For those precious hours, duty no longer deviled him.

For now, Kai could release the tension from body and mind, allowing both to dwell only in the fathomless crystal blue of the waters, hands and spirit stretching out for the rainbow of tropical fish fluttering just beyond reach.

He dove deep, suspended as if by the hand of an invisible djinn, hovering above the twisted wreck of a triple-master that had foundered fifty years before his birth. That there was another ship, far more recently scuttled, in the waters east of the islands, he knew too well. The sight of this wreck sobered rather than enthralled. It reminded him of the carnage that his father's gold had, if not wrought, endorsed after the fact.

The sailors' bones scattered in its shattered hull were not the first, nor would they be the last to drift in the depths of the Songhai. The deceptive tranquility of these islands had concealed fierce and deadly battle as the nations of Africa contested for the New World.

Mali had been first to touch Bilalistan's shores, her ships piloted by captains and navigators refused by Abyssinia's royal court. But that kingdom's Immortal Empress had swiftly grasped the potential of the storied land far to the west, and had claimed ownership. Egypt likewise had sent ships and men, as had half a dozen other peoples. Bitterly they fought. As kingdoms rose and fell in the Old World, so did they in the New.

The derelict's barnacled ribs shimmered in twenty cubits of crystalline water, not some heroic singularity but merely another of the rivened husks scattered about the sea bottom like broken birds' nests, once the proud carriages of the bravest sailors the world had ever known. Whether their destroyers' vessels had flown the flags of their origin or slunk through the islands like sharks in the starlight, death had been the same, the watery graves the same, the end the same: northern Bilalistan belonged to Egypt and Abyssinia alone.

Kai resented the fact that such thoughts had interrupted his swim. This was a time for pleasure, not politics. So despite these waters' grim history, or the urgency of a mission he dared not share even with his beloved wife, he paddled about like a boy half his age, reveling in the sun and surf.

Kai of Dar Kush had known war, and loss, and twenty-three summers. He was a tall man, so perfectly proportioned that, in repose, he seemed smaller than his actual height. Beardless and smooth-skinned was Kai, of almost weightless carriage, as easily underestimated as a sleeping cobra.

A solid shadow glided beneath him, roiling the water with its passage. Kai blinked his eyes to clarity, bringing into focus the dolphin's every gray-black digit. Its five cubits of muscle could have shattered him with a flick if it chose, but the creature seemed more inclined merely to float and study him.

On other days the islands' watery denizens had seemed more playful, carving watery loops and curlicues, inviting him to follow if he could. Today the dolphin seemed merely to examine him. Its flat black eyes brimmed with a questioning intelligence. Close behind it, a second, smaller dolphin kept pace.

Trailing bubbles, Kai paddled back up to the surface, where his dhow *Baber Feras,* the "Sea Horse," awaited. Its swooping teak hull bobbed gently on the waves, lateen sails billowing in the afternoon's warm, moist breeze.

His mate Lamiya lay sunning on the hardwood deck with their daughters, Aliyah and Azinza. Lamiya herself was descended from the Afar people on the shore of Lake Abbe in Old Djibouti. A single aged servant, Yohela, had accompanied her on this trip, yet her hair, braided and beaded into the intricate patterns typical of the Afar, never bore the same configuration two days in a row. Four years Kai's senior, Lamiya was in both face and form the most elegantly sensual woman Kai had ever known, and he had adored her since childhood.

Beside her, the small ones waved their pudgy brown arms in his direction, giggling. Azinza, a plump little fireball, had seen four summers, two more than Aliyah. Azinza was adopted, being the daughter of Kai's late uncle Malik. But despite the different circumstances of their birth, the girls couldn't have been closer had they been twins.

As always, the sight of his family filled his heart with joy, but there also remained a trace of regret. Kai loved the water's warm embrace, its ability to challenge his body's endurance and strength. Its potential to wash away sins.

Below the waves lay a world entire, a world more innocent and honest than that above. One he would have shared with his wife, but could not— Lamiya was no child of ocean or lake. Her forays into water were confined to the bath. In fact, except for considerable skills as a horsewoman, Lamiya was more a creature of politics and etiquette than physical exertions.

"Time for another dive?" Kai called.

"Just a few more minutes," his beloved replied. "We'll have dinner ashore."

"Are you sure you wouldn't like to come in? Yohela could watch the children." He arched his eyebrows at her flirtatiously.

She laughed tolerantly, resisting the lure. "Perhaps later, Kai, and closer in to shore."

"I won't let you drown."

"The ocean may have its own plans." She gazed up at the Sea Horse's sails. "A good wind. Will Elenya's ship be on time?"

"If wind fails, her captain will stoke the boiler." He wrinkled his face at her.

She settled back down with Aliyah. "Wave to your *abbabba.*"

"*Abbabba!*" the infant screeched, grinning hugely.

Kai waved back, and then dove, once again seeking the sleek gray masters of the deep. It was they who would attend the voiceless, shattered ships, who might comfort the ghosts of long-drowned sailors. His finned companions' flat black eyes knew him for who and what he was, yet still they accepted him, agreed to be his confessors.

Silently in the depths, they communed.

CHAPTER TWO

GRAND IMPERIAL WAS THE LARGEST of the Songhai Islands, studded with cocoa plantations and shoreside salt harvesting operations streaming revenue north to Bilalistan. Kai owned one plantation outright, and two others in limited partnerships.

Eighteen hours a day Grand Imperial's commercial dock swarmed with workers. As darkness fell, it suffered an almost lycanthropic transformation. After dusk, honest merchants sought shelter in hotels or private homes, and surrendered the sidewalks to the night breed that haunt docks worldwide. They swarmed with pimps and prostitutes, thieves and cutthroats, opium smokers, *bhang* drinkers, and those who ignored the words of the Prophet to seek solace in the fermented fruit of grape, hop, or barley.

While his wife and daughters took their ease in the Grand Imperial's finest hotel, Kai slipped into leather pants, a cotton shirt, and a simple cloak to stride the night in solitary fashion. Tonight he needed no companions. Tonight, he sought a hash den called Al Makman, "The Hiding Place."

Al Makman proved an appropriate title for a reeking hole sandwiched between the slat-walled wreck of a fish-processing plant and a whore-ridden boardinghouse.

Opening the front door, Kai was assaulted by a wave of hemp smoke, the reeking stench of spilled beer, and stale vomit.

He waded through the stink and selected a table where he might keep his eye on the door. He ordered a hookah and spent a few minutes drawing shallowly before spotting the man who had arranged the meeting.

Wearing a yellow scarf as promised, the newcomer towered over his table. Kai looked up into a long sun-beaten face with deep smile lines and bright eyes. "My name is Yohannes," his contact said.

"I am Kai."

"Alabaster."

"Onyx. Join me."

"An excellent notion." Yohannes grunted, and sat, ordering a beer from a sallow, petulant tavern slave. He noted Kai's adverse reaction. "I am Christian," he said.

Kai nodded. "Of course. I've met few black Christians."

"Abyssinia is one of the few places Christians escape persecution," said Johannes.

"I am not deeply schooled in your history," Kai confessed.

Yohannes stretched back into his seat. "Saint Mark the evangelist thought to preach the holy gospel and the good news of the Lord Christ in the great city of Alexandria, and in Abyssinia and Nubia. Through this excellent notion souls were saved, and even the Empress respected those teachings. She gave us shelter when the Pharaoh declared that the Treaty of Khibar did not extend to those Jews who followed Christ. 'Immortal' or not, she is worth the fight."

Beer arrived, foam slopping out of an oversized mug. Kai gave Johannes time to take several sips, taking the opportunity to study Al Makman's net-shrouded ceiling and sawdust-strewn floor. With a single slow sweeping evaluation he noted the drunks and revelers, the whores wiggling on their customers' laps, the cutpurses who eyed his boots and sword, wondering if the stranger might make a profitable night's work and trusting the instinct that said no.

"Have you been to Abyssinia?" Johannes asked.

"Not yet. I hope to visit my wife's family soon."

"An excellent notion. No educated eye should miss the Pillars of the Nile."

"So I've heard." Kai took another small draw on the hookah, then directed discourse to the matter at hand. "Documents found among my father's effects," Kai said, "hinted that a letter would come, addressed in a certain cryptic manner, as did yours. And that I should do as it instructed."

"And gold." Yohannes grinned. "He doubtless spoke of gold."

"So. Not all is patriotism and piety?"

"The three are not mutually exclusive."

Kai handed Yohannes a leather bag. The Abyssinian peered within, smiled, and then hefted it in his hand, nodding approval. Secreting it on his belt, Yohannes then pushed an envelope across the splintered wooden table toward Kai.

Kai examined it, careful to shield it from curious eyes. He looked up, face reflecting the question in his heart.

"The Alexandrian vessel was captured and scuttled," Yohannes said.

"There is more than one way to wage war, and the Lord rewards His soldiers."

"And sailors, apparently."

"An excellent notion." Johannes drained his glass. "We all do what we can, in our own way. Farewell, Wakil. Christ bless you. May we meet again, under better circumstances."

"*Insh'Allah*, and His grace upon you, traveler."

Cavalierly saluting the man he would never see again, Johannes left the Al Makman and strode back out into the mists of night.

CHAPTER THREE

AT TEN O'CLOCK THE NEXT MORNING, the dock thronged with a crowd even denser than the previous day's. Jostling with laborers and merchants for standing room, Kai and Lamiya welcomed the steam-screw *Assannafi*, "The Victorious." This was the second-to-last leg of the journey it had begun in Abyssinia. It had churned the waters of the Red Sea as it rose north, traveled west through the Egyptian Sea, across the ocean and to the Songhais, ferrying Elenya home from university. After the Grand Imperials, it would steam farther north, taking the Brown Nile up to Djibouti's capital city of Radama.

He spotted his younger sibling and her three attendants instantly. "Elenya!" he cried. "How you have grown!"

"Kai! Lamiya!" she cried, and embraced him warmly. Nineteen now, Elenya had grown to within two digits of her brother's height. Her face was heart-shaped compared to Lamiya's gentle oval, although like the imperial niece she wore her hair in tight thin braids. Her gold earrings depended almost to her shoulders. A thin chain linked her gold nose-ring to a mesh cap of wrought silver that dangled over her cheeks and eyes, forming a veil that provided modesty and proclaimed her station at a single glance.

But . . . was that tobacco he smelled on her breath?

Kai directed several sun-bronzed bondsmen to place Elenya's luggage on the Sea Horse.

"Only another few days and you're home," he said. "Miss us?"

"More than I can say. I've been at sea so long I wondered if my legs would still work with dirt beneath them."

"I know!" Lamiya said. "I felt the same way every time I made the crossing."

Elenya looked at Kai curiously. "Why did you decide to meet me here in the islands?"

For an instant Kai's eyes shifted away, and then he answered in a joking tone. "Wasn't it enough that I didn't want to waste a single moment of time with my only sister?"

"Kai . . ."

She had him. "Oh well then, supervising investments for Lion." Truth, if incomplete truth. Lion's Blood was the name of the investment company formed three hundred years before, pooling the monies of several branches of Kai's family into a single driving economic force. By the time a branch opened in Bilalistan it had evolved into a limited partnership, with forty-nine percent of the stock owned by investors, including the Empress herself. Kai's grandfather had chaired its first Bilalian branch. Following the death of Kai's father, neighbor and friend Djidade Berhar had taken the chair, and would hold it until his own death or retirement. This was a blessing: as owner of the largest estate in New Djibouti, Kai was burdened with the duties of Wakil, senator, administrator, supervisor of some six hundred servants, and captain in the territorial guard, as well as those of husband and father. Allah gave a man but two hands, and Kai's were full.

"And importing workers for the salt fields," he concluded.

"I thought Caucasians were too troubled by the sun to be of much use here."

"Greeks are the key," Lamiya said. "They suffer the climate better than those pasty northerners." And worked harder, as well. Bilalistan exported hemp, hardwoods, cotton, salt, teff, and silver. These went to the Twin Thrones in tribute, as well as to trade routes sweeping as far as China herself. Of most immediate importance, guns and steel went to the Northmen who managed the slave trade, guaranteeing a steady supply of labor for the vast southern plantations and estates.

"More expensive, though," Lamiya said. "Quality is always more expensive—oh, boy?" she called to a dock worker. His scarred, shaven head bobbed obsequiously at her call. "Move that below, would you?"

Within the hour *Baher Feras*'s sails were stowed. Her steam engine bellowed its cotton plume as the ship cast off. The emerald waters of Djibouti Gulf embraced them.

"It is wonderful to see you," Kai said.

"And even better to be heading home," Elenya replied.

More than three years had passed since, with the death of his father Abu Ali, Kai had assumed the mantle of Wakil. The office of Wakil was a judgeship with powers of both high and low justice, the second most powerful post in New Djibouti.

Shortly thereafter, he and Lamiya had married. Lamiya had borne him a daughter, Aliyah, named for Kai's brother, who had died a hero during the early days of the Aztec campaign.

"Azinza?" Elenya said to their adopted niece. "I'm your cousin Elenya."

"E-len-yah?" The child giggled, and hugged her cousin's leg through Elenya's dress, refusing to release her. Elenya returned the hug, cooing and cuddling and enfolding herself in the bosom of the family she had not seen in two years, the family which, in a mere two months, she would leave once again. She was no longer a baby, but not yet a woman either, her heart caught in that tenuous place betwixt the two, where the enchantments of the past and the promise of the future balanced delicately, both equally enticing, in a manner that would never exist quite the same way again.

But for now, there was the sun, and the tide, and a joyous homecoming, and that was enough.

CHAPTER FOUR

IT TOOK FOUR DAYS for *Baher Feras* to journey from Grand Imperial to Djibouti Harbor, time that Kai spent in glorious relaxation with the two women he most adored.

They talked, and laughed, and sunned. Together they resurrected the good times; dined on fresh fish, crab and fruit; invented new constellations in the night sky; and played game after game of *satranj*.

In the middle of the third day a crescent of land appeared to the north, slowly resolving into a maze of docks, multistoried brick buildings, and ship berths. Dominating the entire glittering arc was the colossal statue of the Prophet's companion Bilal. The image of the first *muazzin*, the first to call the faithful to prayer, stood astride a tiny island in the middle of the harbor. His visage was grave and wise and titanic, face sublimely noble. One arm was outstretched as if beckoning to a distant horizon. The other held open a bound copy of the Qur'an. The edifice was the second tallest man-made structure in Bilalistan, fifth tallest in all the world. This, then, was Djibouti Harbor, the busiest port in the New World, the economic lifeblood of the southern empire.

"Welcome home, *warsa*," Lamiya murmured. "Dar Kush has not seemed whole without you."

Elenya was walleyed with pleasure. "So much has changed. Look!" She pointed. "New buildings!" Her finger marked out the sloping, half-completed roof of a structure rising above all the others, an inverted arch slightly resembling an enormous saddle. "What is that?"

"The choral house," Kai said. "I'm surprised that you don't recognize the design."

"Beautiful . . . ," Elenya said. "And modeled on the Empress's own!" She spanked her palms together in delight. "Will there be a dome as well?"

"In time. It should be finished within the year," Kai said. "They say Governor Pili will attend the opening!"

They passed the squarish brick building housing the Lion's Blood holding company. It was integrally involved with Bilalistan's primary economic base: buying, selling, brokering, gold storage, management services—any activity that might increase its store of wealth.

The wharf itself was a termite's nest of activity: Bilalian engineers and supervisors directed as servants carried and lifted, the entire process purposeful and planned.

A horse-drawn coach rattled past, driven by a limp-haired man in formal livery. Its silk-shaded windows pulled aside, and Djidade Berhar appeared. Berhar was Kai's neighbor, the father of Fodjour Berhar, his oldest friend. He was one of the district's most prominent men, and if not for Dar Kush's vast riches, he would have been the wealthiest as well.

In youth Berhar had been a muscular giant, but by the time of Kai's childhood that muscle had devolved to corpulence. Further years had collapsed the once-mighty Berhar inward upon himself, so that he had begun to resemble a soft, sun-ripened plum.

The sharp-faced woman beside him was ten years younger, of mixed Masai and Persian extraction. This was Allahbas Berhar, Djidade's second wife and Fodjour's mother. Kai remembered her as an endless font of sweetbreads and handmade toys when he and Fodjour were children. In recent years, he sometimes suspected unnamed woes had soured her, but he was not privy to Berhar family secrets, nor did he wish to be.

Still, a welcoming smile came easily to his lips.

"Elenya!" cried Allahbas. "I had heard you were coming home."

"Madame Berhar," Elenya said warmly. "Sidi Berhar. Good to see you. Perhaps you will make time for a game?"

The old man sighed. "Ah . . . *satranj* takes up little of my time these days. The countinghouse is game enough for me. But still, if it would afford me your delightful company, business be damned."

"If we can contribute to your sister's homecoming," said Allahbas in her husky, musical voice, "by all means let me know."

"Fodjour and I are to play together this afternoon. If there is anything, I'll have him pass the word."

"Good. Well." Berhar patted his waist. "At my age the stomach is a halftrained leopard: when unfed, the claws extend. Coachman!" he cried, and rolled on.

Elenya leaned close to her brother. "Neighbor Berhar appears . . . unwell."

"His health has been a challenge of late. May Allah be kind." Kai watched the carriage depart, lost in his past memories. Memories of Kai, Fodjour, and Berhar swimming in Lake A'zam. Of Berhar hosting parties and riding to the hunt on his magnificent Arabian. All past now. "Well," he said finally, "enough of such thoughts. Let us be off!"

On such a pleasant day Kai and his family decided to take the scenic route home, up the dirt road paralleling the stream leading north to Lake A'zam.

The young Wakil and his sister rode in front of the wagon while Lamiya rode in the back, busying herself with the children she adored. Elenya seemed to drink in the countryside, and whatever cares had weighed upon her seemed to vanish as she did. "There has been so much improvement along the canal since I left," she said. "Yet in another way everything feels exactly the same."

"Your room is as you left it," Kai said with satisfaction. "But things have not been the same."

"No?"

"No. It has not been Dar Kush since you left. It changed. Now, again, it is the same."

She laughed, and leaned her jeweled head against his shoulder, an old, fond gesture, and one dearly missed.

The sun kissed the western horizon by the time they approached Dar Kush's familiar cross-beamed wooden gates. As they did, a gray-haired Irishman tolled the gate's massive iron bell.

"Master's home!" He seemed not to believe the evidence of his rheumy eyes. "And young mistress! Tell the house; tell the fields! Young mistress come home!"

Elenya leaned over, smiling at the familiar, white-haired figure. "Abdul. How are you?"

The old man flashed a gap-toothed smile, helping her down from the coach.

"Oh, fairly, mistress. Me back is a misery, but aside from that, Allah been good. Blessed saints, it's good to see you."

Kai paused as the gates closed behind him, allowing a moment's pause to absorb the sight of his ancestral home. It was ludicrously easy to take such splendor for granted, and he had sworn never to let this happen. Too much blood and sweat had been spilled to create this elegance, and after three generations, his were the shoulders upon which the responsibility chiefly rested.

The estate was one of two sharing the waters of Lake A'zam, famous for boating and fishing, with tributary streams running south to the Azteca Gulf.

Some said Dar Kush's manor was the finest in all New Djibouti, and Kai found no flaw in that judgment. Banners fluttered from the turrets above the main house, displaying Dar Kush's flag: Bilalistan's moon and lion, with the lethal arc of *Nasad Asab*, Kai's treasured *jambaya*, beneath. The castle had been disassembled and shipped stone by stone from Andulus five decades earlier. Its hundred rooms, three stories, vaulted Moorish ceilings, six rose-lined fountained gardens, miniature date palms, and thousand-pillared hallways were the envy of any fortunate enough to explore her.

To others it was a museum, or a monument. To Kai, it was simply the only home he had ever known.

CHAPTER FIVE

SENSATION HAD FLED Yohannes's arms and legs.

Suspended from the naked ceiling beams of his cell by leather straps, arms and legs spread-eagled, the Abyssinian couldn't clearly remember what had happened to him. What he *did* know was that his chances of ever again seeing the Pillars of the Nile had diminished to something very near zero.

He remembered meeting with the Wakil, and then pulling a blanket under his chin in the cheaply rented room next to Al-Makman, but nothing further until awakening suspended above the clay floor. That had been days ago. How many he did not know: too many cycles of torture and unconsciousness had intervened. Agony had the tendency to distort time.

His body sagged toward the ground. If there was a square digit of his body that had not suffered indignities, he could not locate it.

For the moment, he was alone. He turned his remaining eye toward the door. They would return, the men who had brought him to a place where death seemed preferable to life. Even if he was rescued this moment, he thought that the man who might descend from the bonds was not one who would wish to live. It would be a man with one eye, and a single unruptured eardrum. A man with toes on neither foot, and worst of all, a man whose *abalä zär* had been burned with hot pitch.

Jesu, take me, he prayed. He could feel it—there was a breaking place for all men, and that awful void beckoned him. If the good Lord he loved could not aid him, he would have to aid himself.

If he did not . . . then ultimately, he *would* answer the questions that the men had put to him. Ultimately, he would do anything to stop the agony. Even if that meant betraying his oath and mission. As a result of his weakness and stupidity the Immortal Empress herself might well fall. The Abyssinians had been kind to her Christian children. Betraying his mission meant betraying his brothers and sisters in Christ. And that he would not, could not do.

But . . . how to end himself? His arms and legs were not free. He felt a pain in his lower back, the muscles of arms and shoulders exhausted from hanging. . . .

And there, and in the thought of his lord Christ, Yohannes had his final excellent notion.

The men who entered the cold, black-tiled room had seen death before, often enough that it held neither allure nor mystery. It was merely a fact: thus-and-so-many sep of cooling meat to be disposed of. They were Persian, or Africans who had been trained from youth by Persian tutors. They were of a forbidden Islamic order who, long ago, had sworn allegiance to an outlaw cleric named Hassan. Shaykh Hassan had transformed them into a fabulously lethal tool, famed from China to Bilalistan as spies and killers on a par with any in the world, a group whose very name had entered the common lexicon. They had taken that name from Hassan, and not, as some ignorant and slanderous enemies supposed, from the name of a drug allegedly used to convert the weak-minded.

Only the strong entered the ranks of the Hashassin.

The tallest of the three men was the first to enter the room. Therefore, his were the eyes that first spied Yohannes suspended with his arms and legs crossed, and his distorted face sagging toward the ground. The Christian's eyes were open and sightless, his tongue swollen and protruding from his mouth.

"Damn! Cut him down at once!" the tallest bade them. His name was Omar Pavlavi. The blood in his veins was as noble as any in the Persian Empire, but his father had been a bastard, disowned by the pompous noble who had seduced and disavowed his own fourteen-year-old cousin. Omar had had few choices in life, and accepting the way of the Hashassin had been the best.

His men did cut Yohannes down, but the Christian was already beyond resuscitation. Grudgingly, the tall one admired the Abyssinian's commitment and courage. Through horrific exertions the Christian privateer had managed to dislocate his shoulders, turn himself over in midair, so that he crossed the ropes at wrists and ankles, and was suspended downward, waist sagging toward the floor. In that position, his pectoral muscles had quickly tired, suffocating him.

"Much like his Esu," Omar said in a flat, cold voice.

"And now, Omar? What now?" one of his men asked.

"We need the list: who was in Grand Imperial that day? Every commercial vessel's registry must be searched. Every hotel guest list scrutinized. Work backward. Find everywhere Yohannes went, everyone he spoke to. Send our current information to the Pharaoh immediately, by the next ship."

"What if the contact arrived by private boat?"

"The docks will have records," he said. "I want to know. The man who received those documents was powerful. Probably military. Wealthy, or with access to wealth. He will leave a trail. We must follow it. We will find the man we seek. And when we do . . ."

"What, sir?"

"We will send him west." That last was an Egyptian, not a Persian turn of phrase. In ancient days, it meant to send a corpse to the embalmers who lived on the west bank of the Nile.

Still, in this miserable land of mongrel cultures, Omar found the expression apt.

CHAPTER SIX

KAI'S FINGERS STUNG, and his ears rang with the percussive slap of palm against drum as it echoed back from the dome of the Berhar solarium. Hands a blur of motion, he luxuriated in what could only be called rhythmic bliss.

One of the few respites from his economic, military, and political duties was *djembé* practice. Of all his companions, Fodjour and Mada Berhar practiced with him most often. Fodjour had considerably more drum skill than Kai, a fact his friend mentioned at every opportunity. Kai, in turn, exacted vengeance at sword strokes. In that more martial practice, few of his companions cared to contest with him. In truth, in all New Djibouti there simply *was* no swordsman at Kai's level. But Fodjour's ego seemed as impervious to the embarrassment of consistent, predictable defeat as Kai's was to Fodjour's dazzling polyrhythmic exhibitions.

Conversely the willowy Mada often seemed to have no ego at all. Fodjour's thirteen-year-old half brother was blessed with the ability to submerge himself in any activity at hand with equal enthusiasm if not facility. He was not particularly gifted at drum or sword, but was a sturdy workman in his intellectual studies. And more than that, what Mada possessed in plenty was a child's sheer, exuberant joy in living.

Kai had laughed and played with his friends for the better part of an hour now, the white-domed solarium reverberating with their music, be it improvised or traditional. The solarium itself had been constructed twenty-five years earlier by Fodjour's father as a wedding present for his second wife, Fodjour's mother Allahbas. It was a place of exotic scents and sights, bristling with a hundred varieties of tropical flowers and plants. There, it was easy to imagine that they were not in arid Djibouti but instead in some palatial Malian or Yoruban home. Although Fodjour had adjusted his pace to allow Kai to extend himself, all three drummers were glazed with sweat.

Years before, in traditional fashion, beneath the discerning eye of a wizened, impossibly ancient drum-master, Kai had hand-carved his goblet-shaped *djembé* in one piece from a hollowed-out tree trunk and covered it with a shaved goat skin. Over the course of the ensuing month he had delicately adjusted skin tension and shaved wood to alter the resonance and pitch, until his teacher had finally smiled toothless approval and declared the instrument complete.

Traditional African music was a standard part of a young gentleman's education. The *djembé* was played with the hands, unlike the more sophisticated Abyssinian *lelit samäy*, a fifty-four-key choral accompanier. The "Night Sky" could, in combination with its eight tonal membranes, produce an almost infinite variety of rhythms and melodies, earning its name when a delighted eighth-century Empress declared that it could create more sounds "than there are stars in the night sky."

The *djembé*, a far simpler Malinké instrument, achieved its aural spectrum through diverse hand positions and the intensity with which a musician struck the skin. Response varied from a deep bass achieved through a strike at the center, to a middle "tone," to a light, metallic "slap" created in response to a strike at the edge.

Every *djembé* player developed his own style, but Kai's was informed and influenced by a lifetime of sword practice. Fodjour was precisely the opposite: in swordplay, he was excessively fond of flamboyant rhythmics, sometimes at the cost of efficiency. While Fodjour's musical exertions were motivated by pure pleasure and expression, Kai's mind was always partially occupied with thoughts of varying timings of martial engagement. When lost in the music his blood rushed with the imaginary clash of swords or hands, his body swayed in response to the complex and challenging spontaneous invention that was Fodjour's delight and forte.

For those hours, he was not Wakil, nor husband, nor even loving father. He had no name: he was merely a drummer among drummers, following the lead of a master musician, lost in the energies and textures of the music he loved. Together they re-created and explored the land that birthed their people, although that continent was a world away, more a thing of dream and imagining than experience.

For an hour after practice, the three drummers broiled themselves in the Berhar *hamam*, a form of steam bath loved in the Islamic world for a thousand years. The *hamam* was another domed building built separately from the main house. There, languid servants served cakes and tea, offered vigorous massages, and played music on flute and lute. Steam was pumped in from well-stoked boilers, temperature controlled by a cunning series of valves.

Sweat streamed from Kai in glistening rivulets, carrying away the toxins of exertion.

"For years I had wondered," Fodjour said. He arched back to allow a mild gout of steam to play over his broad, thick torso. "You're such a fiend for drumming that it sometimes seems you're trying to kill yourself—and me along with you. Now I know you're just trying to get to heaven."

"Punish the body to save the soul." Mada grinned.

"The younger brother grasps subtleties that entirely escape the elder," Kai murmured, melting into the heat.

"Hah," said Fodjour, without the slightest trace of humor. "Hah. Hah. Seriously, Kai: slow down a bit. You might improve." He considered for a moment. "Not that you'll ever be as good as *me*, of course. . . ."

"One day," said Kai, "when you have students of your own, you will think back on these conversations, and smile."

Fodjour grimaced as a servant adjusted a valve, and steam gushed into the domed room. "Will I now?"

"Oh, yes," Mada said. "You will make a wonderful shaykh one day."

"I'll leave the spiritual path to Kai. I am quite content drifting in the shoals of finance." Now, finally, he smiled. "But I do feel Allah's call when I clasp a mare's flanks between my knees and spur toward the horizon." Eagerness touched his voice. "Perhaps we could ride tonight?" Fodjour was almost as fine a horseman as a drummer. During the Aztec Wars, those equestrian skills had saved every man in the Mosque of the Fathers.

"We could ride now," Kai said. "A race around the lake? I must be back for afternoon court, but no reason I can't enjoy the trip. Mada?"

"Mother needs me in the topiary garden," he said. "Perhaps tomorrow."

"A plan. So. Once again, it is Fodjour and Kai, racing for . . . let me see. Shall we wager?"

"Of course. The prize?"

"The loser writes a poem praising the winner."

"Arrgh. Sharpen your quill, villain. The race is on!"

Ordinarily, Kai held court on a weekly basis. He preferred to conduct business in a canopied section of public gardens, northeast of the main house. Although not so refined as the mansion's solarium, the gardens were the result of fifty years of expert cultivation and were renowned as a haven of balance and poise. When dispensing justice, Kai craved all of these qualities he could muster.

The wealthy and powerful flocked to Dar Kush, hoping for a favorable settlement of feuds, debts, or contracts. These he generally found boring, mere applications of legal codes studied for hours every week. But the day's fourth case brought something different to the docket. It was a sharelander named Sallah Mubutu who bowed humbly before him.

"Please." Sallah trembled. He was short, round-faced, and elephanteared, with a straggly mustache that threatened to overwhelm his mouth. His clothes were overly patched but clean. It seemed all he could manage to keep from crumpling to his knees. "Mercy, *Sidi*."

"Who is he, and why is this man before me?" Kai asked. He broke the seal on the scroll his friend and assistant Kebwe D'Naan handed him, and began to read. "I would think that the local constabulary could adjudicate these matters."

Kebwe leaned closer. "Sallah Mubutu served in the Aztec campaign, Wakil. His family pleads that you hear his case." Kebwe was Ibo, his people from Oturkpo in western Africa. Kebwe was a staunch friend and comrade, another veteran of that western conflict that had claimed so many good Muslims and sent so many Aztecs howling on the road to hell. Kebwe was sergeant of his brother Ali's regiment Djibouti Pride, and now a member of Kai's guard. He was blue-black and heavy-limbed, but deceptively lithe enough to have earned the nickname "Little Frog" as a child.

"Very well." Kai sighed. "Who is the arresting officer?"

A broad hearty man with three parallel scars on each cheek stepped forward. "I am, sir. Constable Mamady."

"And who has seen this case?"

"Justice Asab."

"A good man. Stern man. And his judgment?"

"Guilty of theft," Mamady replied.

"Mercy!" the poor man shrieked.

Kai ignored the outcry. "I see. And the complainant?"

"I, sir, Abu Hassan," said a man in varicolored robes, a tall, knobby fellow who had watched the proceedings with barely disguised contempt.

"Ah," Kai said. He leaned to Kebwe and whispered, *"Father had dealings with this one."*

"And he is?"

"A knife with two edges and no handle." Kai cleared his throat and addressed the complainant. "So you came personally?"

"To see that justice is done to this wretch."

Kai raised an eyebrow slightly. Even if his father had not warned him, something about Abu Hassan set his skin acrawl. "A worthy goal. Please. Relate the circumstance."

Hassan harrumphed and began. "Sallah farms on my property, and has done so for seven years. In the four years since his return from the mosque, he squandered his half-Alexander—"

"Sir!" Mubutu protested.

The constable clapped his meaty hand on the poor man's shoulder. "Silence!"

Kai spoke more softly, but with no lesser degree of authority. "Your turn will come," he said.

He turned to Abu Hassan. "Continue."

The richer man gestured with a bony arm, continuing as if his right to public audience had been prescribed by the Almighty. "His family has not made its break-even, so I carried them for the past two years, hoping that this good-for-nothing would put his back to it. And how does he reward me? By stealing my prized Egyptian chickens. What does the Kitab say? 'And as for the thief, his hand should be cut off.'"

"Chickens?" Kai glanced at his assistant, amused in spite of the situation's gravity. "Chickens. We are in mortal danger here. Why are this man's ankles unshackled? Very well. The defendant may speak."

Sallah Mubutu's wife and three children knelt humbly to the side. He moaned on the ground, misery apparently negating his capacity for speech.

"The defendant may address the bench," Kai repeated.

"Sayyid, I am a poor man. . . ."

"This," Kai said, as kindly as he could, "is evident from your raiment." Most who appeared before him wore their best, seeking to curry favor. The man was poor indeed, and the gap between their stations made his use of the honorific "Sayyid" understandable if a bit improper. Most correctly, this was only applied to descendants of the Prophet, Peace Be Upon Him. "Please continue," Kai said.

"Ask him if he stole my chickens," demanded Abu Hassan.

Kai's irritation increased. "You had your chance to speak. Does he not deserve the same? Fair is fair. It is, after all, his hand at risk." His gaze returned to Sallah. "Continue."

"I stole them," said Sallah, "but my family was hungry!"

"They say you squandered the gold you earned in the Aztec War. Is this true?"

Sallah tried to straighten his shoulders. "Not squandered, sir. I purchased implements with which to begin a new business."

"And what business is that?"

"Toolmaking. My uncle was a shipbuilder, and I apprenticed in the harbor. I have a talent for engineering."

"And your father was . . . ?"

"A farmer, and his father before him, and fine ones. He fell into debt through no fault of his own. I simply do not have the way of it in my bones, but yet attempted to carry my father's debt after his death."

Kai empathized with the little man more than he cared to display. A son's burden could be heavy indeed. "A worthy goal. And what happened to your business?"

Sallah's face fell and shoulders slumped. "My landlord went to his neighbors and advised them against dealing with me. I could find no customers."

Kai's hands fisted in his lap. He turned to Abu Hassan. "He speaks truly?"

Abu Hassan squared his thin shoulders and spoke with no hint of embarrassment or apology. "This man is a scoundrel. I merely wished to protect the righteous from his deception."

It was well that Abu Hassan could not see the fire seething in the Wakil's eyes. "I see. So. And why was his family hungry? This same sloth?"

Kai stepped down from his platform and extended his hands to Sallah. After a pause, the poor man extended his own. Kai examined them carefully, eyes and fingers tracing every blister, tear, and callus. Sallah had thick skin and clean, broken nails. "The hands of a lazy man?"

Abu Hassan merely grunted.

"The soil is poor, sir," Sallah moaned. "Abu Hassan will not let a third of it lay fallow, nor did his father, and the land is exhausted."

Abu Hassan was pitiless. "Another excuse!"

Kai folded his fingers together. "And so when he ran out of food, rather than redouble his miserable efforts, he stole chickens."

"Exactly!"

Kai leaned toward Sallah. "Abu Hassan is correct when he says that the thief's hand should be cut off."

Sallah Mubutu rolled in the dust beneath his feet and sobbed. His family wailed and tore their hair.

Abu Hassan was exultant. "Yes! You see? Your efforts to embarrass me have availed you nothing."

"A moment," Kai continued, raising a single slender finger. "The Book further states: 'but if the thief is repentant, then Allah will forgive him.' Sir," he said to the prostrate Mubutu. "Are you repentant?"

Abu Hassan sneered. "He would say anything."

Kai had grown dangerously quiet. "Please, do not interrupt. Sir, are you repentant?"

"I regret being poor," Sallah said. "I regret working my entire life to pay debts that are not my own. How can I regret trying to feed my family?"

"Indeed," Kai said. "It is, in fact, your sacred duty. Hmmm." He leaned back, growing more thoughtful.

"I regret troubling the great Wakil," said Sallah. "I do not know what justice is. I only know that for pain of hunger, my children cry in the night."

"Loudly?" Kai asked.

"Yes, sir."

He turned to Abu Hassan. "Truth?"

Hassan rolled his eyes in his great sun-weathered face. "Oh, I suppose they wail that their father is such a wretch. I have a hundred sharelanders, as did my father before me. If they have a bad season, I advance them seed, tools, food."

"As you did to his father."

"Yes."

"Are many of these sharelanders in debt to you?"

"Many of them, yes."

"Most?"

"Perhaps, yes."

"All?"

Hassan looked away. "I think not."

"I see." Kai drummed his fingers on the desk. "Our laws allow such systems, which in essence place our humbler citizens on a level with whites. Would you agree with that?" Kai studied his fingernails carefully.

"If they sink so low, I suppose," said Abu Hassan.

"There are obligations," Kai said. "Servant to master, master to servant. What are *your* obligations?"

"Why, to deal with them honestly," quoth the pious Abu Hassan.

"By the law of the land. Yes. But more, as well. You, sir, have the obligation of charity. This man works your land. His hands are blistered with toil, to make you wealthy. Sallah is correct—it is his responsibility to feed his family. However, it might also be said that it is *your* responsibility to look out into the world and find those who are in need, and respond to that need."

For the first time, Abu Hassan's smile faltered. "That is not the law."

"Yes, it is," Kai corrected. "Sacred, not secular. You opened that door by quoting the Qur'an. You are devout?"

"Of course," Hassan said, allowing a tremor to enter his voice.

"Then you should know charity is one of the five great obligations. The Ulema has gone so far as to say it is the second most important, excluding only the obligation to proclaim the singularity of Allah and His messenger." True enough. The Ulema, the college of scholars who debated and interpreted both the Qur'an and Hadith, was considered the most important contemporary source of sacred law. "This man stole chickens, but he found himself in that position because he attempted to clear his father's debts. That he failed in his efforts does not change the intent, and it is the intent that led him to this place."

Abu Hassan's eyes narrowed. "What is your meaning, Wakil?"

"I will pay for your chickens personally. I declare this man's debts to you canceled."

While Hassan sputtered, Sallah's family wept uncontrollably. Kai leaned forward. "You are a toolmaker?"

"Yes, sir," Sallah replied.

"A good one?"

"On my life, it is the greatest skill I possess."

There was a path, a thread of justice in every case. Where the early phases were often a confusing compendium of law and custom, suit and countersuit, claim and defense, there came a moment when Kai could see the path that wound narrowly between law and morality, and could set his feet confidently upon it. It was these moments that made all of the formality worthwhile. "There are jobs in the Djibouti shipyard. You will go to a man named Maputo Kokossa, and tell him that I sent you."

The little man wiped his tear-streaked face, gazing up at his benefactor. "Ko-Kokossa? *The* Maputo Kokossa?"

"Oh?" Kai said dryly. "You know of him?"

"Who has not? You would do this for Sallah?"

"No," said Kai. "This I would do for the one God, who lives in you. You stood with me at the mosque, and there proved yourself a man. Rise, and be one once again."

Kai then turned the full measure of his scorn upon the astonished Abu Hassan. "And as for you, who feel no charity toward those who have profited you, I say it was as much your responsibility to be aware of genuine need among your people as it was Sallah's to feed his crying children. One might say that you forced him into his current condition. That by forcing him to his knees before me you stole from this man his pride. If this is true, then *you*, Sidi, are the thief."

The assembled murmured in response.

By now, Abu Hassan had completely lost control of his temper. "How dare you, you Sufi whelp! Your father would never have—"

Kai stood, breathing deep in his belly to quiet the adrenal fire flaring in his veins. During his father's life, Abu Ali had been sensitive to local conservative prejudices against Sufism, requesting Babatunde to keep a low profile. Since Kai's ascendance to the office of Wakil, the nasty whispers had continued, but lacked any legal or political weight. The term "Sufi" had been used pejoratively before, but never in Kai's own court! He stood. "You ask how I dare? Who am I to dare? I am the Wakil, empowered by law and custom to be the court of appeal for men like you and the men bonded to you in service. You dare quote scripture to me, and conjure my father to serve your purpose? Then know this: I place you on notice. Within the month I will inspect your sharelanders. Their homes and your books. And if I find that either of them are in disrepair—if I find that you have abused the laws of usury in any way—then it is your wrist that will bleed."

It was possible that never in all Abu Hassan's adult life had he been so publicly upbraided. If a sword had been close to hand he might well have leapt forward with murderous intent. "How . . . how dare . . ."

At that instant, Kai considered lending this toad a *shamshir*, that Hassan might fulfill his apparent fantasy of challenging the master of Dar Kush in his own home. Such conflicts he found cleaner, more honest. More swiftly resolved.

"I will appeal to the Governor!"

Kai's smile was cold. "Yes. Do. Let us both go before the governor. And the Ulema. And ask them to interpret the law for us, with your financial records for the last ten years presented in your defense."

Abu Hassan was stunned. He sagged like a deflated waterskin. "You . . . why would you do this, Wakil?"

"Ah," said Kai, seating himself again. "So I am once again Wakil? No longer the upstart son and nephew of dead heroes?"

Defeated, Abu Hassan lowered his head. "I meant no offense."

Kai snorted, unable even to acknowledge Abu Hassan's polite lie. "It is in the memory of my father, and in the shadow of the Kitab that I proclaim so."

Abu Hassan's eyes searched the courtyard, as if searching for support. There was none. "I . . . a thousand apologies, Sayyid." Kai almost smiled at the slip. Truly, fear was a leveler of men. "I deeply regret any actions that may have, however inadvertently, contributed to . . . this action."

"The theft of chickens. Yes. Small things can have large consequences. It would be good for us all to remember this."

"Yes, Sidi," several of the witnesses agreed.

"Next?"

CHAPTER SEVEN

THE GARDEN'S MYRIAD LEAVES and flowers rustled as the prior complainants retreated down the narrow tiled path, and a pair of new entreators advanced.

To Kai's surprise and immediate interest, two identical sword-carrying women entered the courtyard. "Who are these?" Kai asked of Kebwe. Both women were tall, muscular, and of mirror visage: two souls with but a single face. They carried long-bore muskets and wore heavy, unbleached, undyed cotton skirts over some kind of dark leggings. The skirts fell to a few digits below the knee. Their blouses were crimson silk, with front buttoning, similar to those worn by Hausa Muslims.

Their necklaces were tightly beaded, colors and shapes repeated in intricate mathematical patterns. Their faces were strong and square. Unpainted and unadorned, still they were of noble character and almost masculine beauty. Almost. Despite the relative harshness of their garb, there was something indefinably feminine about the two, some inexpressible aura of sensuality that could not be hidden or disguised.

Fascinating.

A black ink crocodile was etched on each of their cotton skullcaps. Their leather sandals cradled strong feet with square-cut toenails. Their carriage and alertness would have shamed most of his own guard, challenging enough to send a tiny jolt of alarm coursing through his veins.

"Dahomy warrior women," Kebwe whispered. "Forty in number, who arrived in this district yesterday. These are their leaders."

Kebwe consulted a sheet of paper. "Their names are Yala and Ganne."

"Warrior women? Twins? Dahomy?" Kai said in delight. Not only warriors, but comely as well. He wished that Babatunde was there, knowing his tutor's hereditary distrust of all things Dahoman. Suddenly, the day seemed brighter and far more interesting. "How shall I tell them apart?"

"Why would one wish to?" Kebwe whispered. "On a dark night, an honest mistake . . . one sister as ripe as the other . . ."

Kai *tsk*'d and fixed his magisterial expression back into place. "Very well," he said. "Approach."

They moved with focus and discipline as well as grace, and Kai hazarded that they could use those swords with lethal facility. Although delightfully womanly, their bodies carried no excess padding: muscles in their arms bunched and released like oiled chains.

"I am Ganne," said the one on the left. Kai saw that she had two thin scars on her cheeks, while the identical woman beside her bore but one. "And my sister is Yala. Our farms in Deregget are suffering." He knew the district, a southern parish of Wichita whose Amharic name literally meant "to lay the foundation."

"We lost our crops," Yala agreed. "After council, we decided to fall back on our grandmothers' ways."

"You have raised sword and shield?" Kai asked.

"And gun, yes. You understand?" Yala said.

"No," he replied. "But I empathize."

"You are a warrior, Sidi." said Ganne. "What if you had been born a woman?"

"I would not be a warrior."

"But what if you were?" she insisted, not a kite of deference in her manner. "What if that was your heart? We cannot change our natures—they were given to us along with our blood and marrow."

Kai leaned back thoughtfully. "And you propose to sell your swords. I must tell you frankly—I have little love for mercenaries. You would kill for money?"

"We would prefer to act as guards, or even a roving patrol, but will take any honest work offered. Your Honor," Ganne said, "you said in your own court that it is a parent's obligation to feed her children. Ours were hungry. The hiring of a sword arm is more palatable than the sale of our bodies. Our culture does not offer many choices to such as we."

On his desk, a long-necked vase held a single cut rose, just that morning pruned from his private garden. He leaned forward and inhaled deeply.

"Here," he said to the twins. "Scent."

Yala of the single scar did so, briefly, then stepped back. "It is very beautiful."

"Your women appreciate such things?"

"Of course." She bristled.

"And swords as well. Delightful. Please," he said. "A bit of your history to illumine a dreary day."

Yala commenced without hesitation, as if she had told the story many times. "Once upon a time," she said, "there was much corruption in Dahomy, many traitors, much intrigue. But a troupe of woman hunters had served the King well, and were recruited to the palace as guards."

Kai held up a finger, asking for silence, and turned to Kebwe, eyebrows raised in a quizzical arch. Kebwe inclined his head slightly. *Affirmative.* So, his old compatriot had heard these stories as well, perhaps from Makur, a friend and comrade of Dahoman ancestry. He turned back to Yala and Ganne. "Continue, please."

"Those grandmothers were sworn to celibacy, and kept from things feminine. Still, they were women, and the more ferocious for it."

"Oh?" Kai asked, using his mildest voice. "Are women fiercer than men?"

"Yes," Ganne said. "They must be. Men fight for land, or honor, or gold. Women fight only for their children."

"And these bodyguards? They were mothers?"

"The King is the life of the country," Yala explained. "Without him there is war, and the children die."

Kai shadowed his mouth with his hand, pleased with Yala's answer, but unwilling to reveal it. In her pride, beauty, and physicality, she reminded him of . . .

Nandi.

Once begun their ruminative journey, it took a powerful effort to tear his thoughts from that path. "More of your history, please."

Pleased with his interest, Ganne continued for her sister. "Of course. These first became the seed of a great army, an army of women who marched, trained, and fought beside the men, and often outperformed them."

So Kai had heard, although he had to confess that he had assumed the stories to be mere fables. Politely, he kept that assumption to himself.

"Time passed," Yala said, "and the monarchy gave way to a parliament. The women's army became more, hmmm . . . symbolic than practical. First we were allowed to marry—then encouraged, and finally ordered to do so. It became illegal to practice our martial arts, or pass them on to our daughters."

"Although you did, behind closed doors."

"Of course."

Kai could no longer repress his mirth, and laughed openly. "Do continue."

Encouraged by his reaction, Ganne continued. "At that point, many of us immigrated to Bilalistan, where we might be free to raise our families and conduct our lives as we saw fit. For two generations we have been farmers—"

"But we continue to teach the skills of archery, spear, and rifle to our girls."

Kai raised one dark eyebrow. "Not your boys?"

"No."

In all his young life, he had never heard anything so absurd! "A world upside down, indeed. I would not care to be one of your sons."

Yala's answering smile was shaded with mischief. "Perhaps we could adopt you as a daughter."

"Yes!" Kai roared, and slapped his hands upon his desk. "Stay on my land a time. Seek employment as you will, but I must have you as my guests."

"Will you commend us to your friends?" Ganne asked eagerly.

Kai glanced at Kebwe, who shook his head. "I cannot—" he answered. The sisters grimaced, but held their tongues.

Kai continued on. "—without testing. Perhaps we can arrange a demonstration of your skills. If they are as you say, I *might* write a letter in your behalf." He was delighted to hear Kebwe's soft, sincere groan of protest.

The sisters bowed. "We could ask for no more."

"Well then," he said, blood quickening. "Let us retire to the field." He turned to Kebwe, and noted how his sergeant ground his teeth in irritation. Delightful. "It seems this day holds greater promise than I anticipated!"

With a general murmur of pleasure the court adjourned.

Kai's training dome and outdoor training arena lay a few hundred cubits southwest, between the great house and the lake. Drum servants had summoned Kai's personal guard, a rough-and-ready lot, battle-hardened all. They seemed almost offended to be asked to contest in such a fashion.

What began as a great joke evolved into something considerably more serious and fascinating as Yala and Ganne chose five of their followers to compete with five of Kai's. While not as tall and strong as the sisters, all five Dahomans possessed that oddly appealing combination of strength and allure.

From the first engagement, the Dahomy performed well beyond his expectations. Their archery rivaled Kebwe's and as horsewomen they might have tested Fodjour's mettle. With musket, their speed of reload was slightly below his standard, but their aim at the midrange was superb.

Only at swordplay was there a gap in skills. Here, his men's superior strength exerted itself, and one after another of the Dahomy were disarmed or touched upon the armor. Only Yala and Ganne held their own at blades, with sufficient blend of litheness and speed to counteract strength of arm.

Kebwe had watched it all, declining to participate in the impromptu matches. Kai could sympathize.

"I see skill here," he was finally forced to admit.

"Will you write a letter of recommendation for us?" Yala asked eagerly.

"Well . . . we will see. I have my own curiosity."

"About?"

"Never have I crossed blades with a woman," he confessed. Kai drew his *shamsir.* Its forty digits were but ceremonial steel, hardly the superb Benin man-killer he had carried during the Aztec wars. And his father's blade *Ruh Riyâh,* Soul Wind, would be the master of either, or both. Lighter than either of those swords, the ceremonial blade was more comfortable to carry. No weapon to protect home and heart, its very inferiority made the coming bout more exciting. He would have to be careful to keep single-scarred Yala from finding effective leverage. . . .

Yala took a step back. "And if I win?"

"I will hire you myself."

"Sayyid!" she screamed in delight, and slid steel from scabbard.

Kai advanced half a measure, saluted with guard to forehead, and extended his arm. Their swords crossed. Her initial touch was feather-light; then metal rang sharply upon metal once, twice, three times—high, low, and then slightly off-center—Kai deliberately creating an opening to test Yala's reflexes and aggression. She was quicksilver itself, a woman in visage but a hawk in combat, of superior will and keen mind. But, thought Kai as he countered a lovely quarter-beat attack, she was entirely too eager to prove herself. He deliberately blocked too widely. When Yala went for the bait, Kai dropped his elbow to increase leverage; corkscrewed his blade, catching hers against the pommel; and disarmed her.

Yala lowered her head in shame. "I . . . I have failed. May my sisters forgive me."

Kai chuckled, happy with what he had learned in their brief exchange. "Not at all. You lasted twelve seconds." He paused, then added, "I can disarm the sergeant of my guard in ten." Kebwe clenched his teeth and looked away. Life was good! "I think I can find work for you."

CHAPTER EIGHT

WITH SERVANTS COAXING SONG from fiddle and pipe for their masters, the owners of Dar Kush savored a leisurely dinner of *Doro Wate* chicken and lentils. Even in months other than Ramadan, Kai generally fasted during the day and then ate massively in the evening. His custom was to begin with vegetables and salad, then to gorge on meat, and lastly satisfying his appetite with all the rice or bread he could eat. When he felt more thirst than hunger, he would stop, drink a glass or two of water, and relax. If and when hunger called again, he would eat another meal.

Because they had fasted all day, for once Lamiya and Elenya wolfed their food as avidly as he. As Kai dismembered and devoured his second chicken, Elenya was cutting the first strips from her third. "And what do you hear of war?" he asked her.

"There is talk and talk," she said between mouthfuls. "The boys of how brave they will be, the girls of how canny the Empress has been."

"Canny?"

Elenya spread her hands. "The thought is that the Pharaoh hopes to lure the Empress into rash action: violation of treaties with Persia, interference with Egyptian colonies in Europe, threats to blockade the Nile. So far, she has succumbed to none of his provocations."

"Bravo," Kai said in a soft voice.

Lamiya dabbed at her mouth with a napkin, then leaned forward. "And how is my aunt herself?" Kai was surprised she had waited so long to ask that question. Marrying Kai had placed Lamiya in the Empress's ill graces. She was a *feqer näfs*, a "soul mate," promised to Kai's older brother Ali. The exquisite Lamiya was one of those girls whom the Empress, in dream, might declare the perfect partner for this or that wealthy and powerful merchant or potentate, thereby strengthening and enriching her empire. Governor Pili himself had married one of the Empress's nieces.

But more than love had motivated Lamiya's action. Practicality and compassion were also factors. When Ali perished at the Mosque of the Fathers, tradition dictated that Lamiya return to Abyssinia and enter the

Steven Barnes

nunnery. Her mission, upon which all her life's preparations had rested, would have come to naught. Marrying Kai saved Lamiya from a cloistered life and also gained Dar Kush's resources for Abyssinia. Unfortunately, her marriage had also cast doubt on the entire *feqer näfs* system. For how could a single woman be truly bound to multiple souls?

"I hear she is well," said Elenya. "I was presented to her, of course, and have been to court twice, but we have never really conversed."

Lamiya nodded understanding. "What hear you from her courtiers?"

Elenya pondered. "It is said that she lacks materiel, but her position is strong. She controls the sea routes to India and China, and could defeat Egypt in a naval war . . . at least that is the talk."

Kai nodded. " 'Egyptian blood has no salt,' " he said, quoting the ancient Abyssinian mariner who had taught him to hoist the Sea Horse's sails. There was truth to the saying. The very Nile that had made Egypt the world's first nation also prevented her from ever becoming a true thalassocracy. Early Egyptian mariners had had it too easy: Traveling north, one merely rode the current. Travel south, and use the prevailing winds. With such advantages, why learn true sail craft?

Kai pulled his mind out of those speculations. "And on land?"

"Again, strong. She controls the center of the board. But the Pharaoh has powerful allies among the Masai, making the Empress vulnerable to envelopment, I think."

"Thus speaks the *satranj* wizard." Kai paused for a moment, considering. "Tell me, have you played at court?"

"Yes, a challenge match with one of the junior officers." She brightened a bit at the subject.

"And?"

"I won three of five, but his endgame might have been stronger than mine, had I not outpositioned him in the midrange."

"Keep your eyes open," Kai said. "Play many games. If possible, play them with Egyptian officers. You may learn interesting things."

"They rarely speak of politics."

"No, that is not my meaning. Men reveal themselves in game," Kai said. "Their courage, intelligence, gift for strategy . . . *satranj* is not a game of ivory pieces. It is a game of war. In playing with Egypt's warriors, you may well gain insight into her plans."

"Brother!" Elenya exclaimed. "Dwelling on worldly matters in such a fashion. Shall I be shocked or pleased?" Her teeth worried a fleck of chicken away from the bone. "Perhaps both."

War was no idle threat. For hundreds of years, Europe and Bilalistan had been carved into colonial fiefdoms, looted for land, slaves, and raw materials. Over ten million European men, women, and children had been carried off, east or west across the seas, sold to China and India. European slaves toiled in Bilalistan and northern Africa, in Egyptian, Abyssinian, and Zulu mines in South and Central Bilalistan. Bilalian natives had traveled east to labor in Africa's warmer, wetter climes: Europeans had proven too frail for the work.

Uncounted tons of minerals and precious goods had been stripped away, carted by the boatload back to African conquerors, fattening their coffers and children as Europe starved and the Aztecs transformed into the last viable resistance to the armies of Egypt, Mali, and Abyssinia.

In Europe, whites who fled to cooler climes were often savaged by eastern barbarians, and often captured and sold into slavery by the Northmen, whose trade with the Africans brought them guns, medicine, and steel.

The two most ardent competitors were Egypt and Abyssinia. Once upon a time these colossi had contested for influence in Africa. Egypt had had the best of it until the fabled Black Barges ferried disease and death to her royal house, twelve hundred years ago. As Alexander's bloodline withered, the Empress gathered the reins into Her immortal hand. For a time, Mali and Benin had successfully challenged Abyssia, buoyed by Bilalian gold. Other coastal nations tried European and Bilalian colonies as well, with varying degrees of success. The cycle had turned again, however. Now, as in the beginning, Pharaoh and Empress stood supreme.

The *Nasab Setepenamen,* "The blood of the Pharaoh Alexander," was a spiritual/political commitment between the Twin Thrones. It had led to a thousand years of educational, economic, and technological development in sub-Saharan Africa, resulting in unparalleled wealth and opportunity, and the rise of advanced nation-states all along the coast.

But truly, it was the New World's promise of limitless riches that provided the truest test for the bonds of blood.

It was customary for Bilalistan's noble daughters to return to Africa for education and presentation at one or both thrones. In a month, Elenya would return to complete her education, and in all probability, find a husband.

"Enough of this talk!" his sister cried. "That is all far away from us."

"Not so far as you might think," Kai said.

"Well, far from me right now." She sniffed. "You haven't asked about my social life. I begin to think my brother cares for nothing but politics these days."

Lamiya laughed, happy that the conversation had lightened. "Well, then—what of your social life?"

Elenya leaned forward eagerly. "I think . . . I really think that I may have met someone. An officer—"

"Of the Royal Marine?" Kai finished for her. An excellent candidate, if he was of good blood, and that was a given, if one of the Empress's Royals . . .

"Yes!"

"That *satranj*-player, perhaps?" said Lamiya, while Kai mused.

Again, Elenya flushed, and glanced away. "Perhaps."

Lamiya pretended to busy herself with her veal. "Ah. Well. You may well have the stronger endgame, but watch your opening as well."

Elenya started, eyes wide, outraged and delighted. "Lamiya!"

Kai's mind had wandered, lost in thoughts of a possible future wedding. "What? Did you say something?"

The two women giggled and looked as innocent as newborns. Lamiya donned her gravest expression. "I merely reminded Elenya that at court, every game is played for higher stakes."

After their meal Kai and Elenya adjourned to the mansion's central courtyard, amid the fragrant leaves and blossoms of Dar Kush's largest private garden, to enjoy a game of *satranj*. As usual, she spotted her brother Sultana's knight. As usual, it affected the outcome not a jot.

"I notice you are spending more time with Fodjour," she said as he studied the board.

"He is a good friend." Hmmm . . . did he detect a weakness in her mamluk formation?

"Even more now that Aidan is gone, eh?"

Kai looked at her sharply. "Not a thing to say publicly." Damn! It was true: he had sought out Fodjour more frequently in the three years since Aidan O'Dere, his former slave and best friend, had left Dar Kush to seek his fortune to the north. And Kai was certain that that was a sore point with Fodjour. Even worse, as his mind wandered, he found it difficult to remember the exact weakness he had seen in her position.

Ah. Wait. There it was. Not now, but in two moves . . .

"And how go things with Lamiya?" she asked innocently, and Kai's vision of the board blurred. Cursing under his breath, he moved Sultana's knight, hoping that he had not blundered.

Elenya nonchalantly moved a mamluk toward the center of the board.

"We are happy," he finally answered.

"When we were children," she said, "I think you imagined that her love would make you the happiest man in the world."

"I remember."

"Well?"

"I have her hand. More than that no man could ask."

"And her heart?"

"You have grown talkative since last we met," he said in irritation. "What have they been teaching you, beside the technique of tobacco inhalation?"

"A great many things," Elenya said, refusing even to protest her innocence. "The Academy is quite progressive. But it is philosophical as well. We are told to listen to the silences."

"Indeed? And what do these silences tell you?"

"That your heart is happy, but not entirely full."

Kai was taken aback: only the most acute ear could find silence so instructive. "The house is mine," he said, "but is so empty now."

It was Elenya's turn to smile. "Remember how vast it all seemed when we were children?"

"Yes," Kai said. "But in an odd way, it is even larger now. . . ."

She studied the board, then reached out to take his hand affectionately in hers. "You still play hesitantly, Brother," she said. "They are mere pieces of ivory!"

He laughed at himself. "To you. To me, they are men on the field. I hate to see a mamluk die."

"Then you will continually fall prey to Fazul's Gambit. When I know what you hold dear, it is easy to threaten you." She put action to her words, moving her Sultana's vizier on its diagonal to threaten his Sultan. "Check?"

He studied the board dourly. "Well, it may be that, and it may be that my sister is simply brilliant. I concede."

Already, Kai ached with Elenya's absence. The memory of the time when she used to follow him about like a kitten made their inevitable separation rankle all the more.

There was something poignant about the effort that they put into having fun together, as if each understood that childhood was far behind them, and that nothing could ever truly be the same if an Abyssinian won her hand. Yearly letters could not compare to daily hugs.

"I don't know about this officer," Kai said, "but I know Father always thought that you'd find a husband there. And if that happened, you would be Abyssinian, not Bilalian."

"You'll always be my brother," she said, comforting him as if she were the elder.

"I know." He gestured vaguely. "There are just ways that I feel . . . disconnected from the world. As if very little bonds me here. I miss you."

"You have your daughter. Both daughters."

"Yes," Kai said. "Praise Allah."

She pretended to study the board carefully as she replaced the pieces to their starting positions. "There is one thing that surprises me."

"And that is?"

"You have yet to mention Nandi."

"Nandi?"

Her voice was teasing. "Yes. Daughter of Cetshwayo? Niece of Shaka Zulu? Princess, buffalo hunter, mischief-maker? You know, Nandi."

Kai scratched at his chin. "I seem to recall the name, yes."

"I am surprised to see that the great Wakil has but a single wife. Is it not shameful to so besmirch Bilalian manhood?"

Kai had no answer for that at all, shaking his head in confusion.

Elenya chuckled. "That aside, I imagined her people would have come to you by now."

Kai turned away from her, suddenly finding it oddly difficult to speak. "I've heard nothing from them in three years."

"Zulus have long mourning times."

"We have all had much to mourn," he said.

She finished placing the last *satranj* piece onto its square. "Then again"—she grinned—"they might have been respectful of the new marriage." Elenya leaned forward. "I wager that Nandi steams by now."

Allah preserve them both, these modern girls were a handful! The last of Elenya's childish aspect was evaporating like yesterday's shadow. Soon only the beautiful woman would remain. Already, it seemed she understood things that he himself kept from conscious awareness.

Doubtless there was humor in the situation, but he had yet to find a way to embrace it.

Time and patience, Kai, he thought to himself. *Time and patience.*

And with that thought, southern Bilalistan's youngest Wakil went about the happy business of losing his game.

CHAPTER NINE

Kai navigated the merry chaos of two dozen guests as they milled through Dar Kush's main reception hall: at the fireplace composing impromptu poetry in celebration of Elenya's return, admiring the statuary, discoursing on the recent kite-fighting tournament, or swapping hunting tales. He spotted a willowy, silver-haired man of East African blood and picked out his patient, erudite voice a moment later: Maputo Kokossa, one of Bilalistan's most celebrated inventors, and the father of Elenya's dearest friend, Chifi.

"And where is my old nemesis Babatunde?" Kokossa asked, observing Kai's approach. The inventor and Kai's Yoruba Sufi master loved to butt heads intellectually. Kai regretted that the scholar was away. It was vastly entertaining to watch the two mental giants contest. He cherished the memory of a debate concerning the value of modern transportation. Babatunde never trusted anything that moved more swiftly than a man could walk, while Kokossa's machine shop had produced gear prototypes essential to the production of the wheeled, cargo-pulling iron monstrosity known as a "steam dragon."

"Gone to the capital," answered Kai. "I will meet with him in some days. Do you miss your arguments?"

"I miss everything about him," the inventor said. "It was he who wagered I would never get the gear shaft working properly—he owes me a supper." Babatunde would indeed have to pay up. In the last months track had been laid east and north of the harbor, and even through a northeastern strip of Dar Kush.

Kokossa punctuated each word with a thump of his fist against the table. His braided hair gleamed in the candlelight. "Have you seen Chifi?"

"Here she comes now," Kai said.

Chifi entered on Fodjour's arm, followed by the customary serving girl/chaperone. Chifi was a slender girl whose jaw was too square, her nose too prominent for her narrow face. Nonetheless, she possessed animation and energy, and the sort of secretive smile that made one suspect unfathomed depths of heart and mind. Her hair, uncut since infancy, was knotted and braided together, hanging down her back in the fashion of unmarried Dagon women the world over.

Fodjour, dashing in his dress whites, led her to the banquet table, maintaining a continuous line of casual conversation. "Have you tried the goose liver? It enchants."

"No," Chifi replied. "I haven't had the pleasure. Would you serve me?"

"My honor."

Kai and Kokossa watched, tickled. "Ah! Young Fodjour again!" said the older man. "I have seen them speak several times. Am I an old fool, or do I sense a spark?"

"You're no sort of fool at all," Kai said. "And it would seem the most natural thing in the world for Fodjour to fall beneath her spell, Maputo. She is a prize."

"In a father's eyes, yes." He leaned close enough to whisper. "In truth I worry for her. She cares more for the workshop than the parlor."

Kai chuckled, made a polite excuse, and began to circulate. He glided between the guests, murmuring a greeting here, a compliment there, as his father had done on countless occasions.

He joined a line of guests in the preparation area between banquet hall and kitchen, where a few liveried servants offered a dessert of shaved ice. Through one of the front windows he could see Ghost Town, the village where Dar Kush's white servants lived and raised their families. As a young man he had occasionally sported there, but since marriage and ascension to the office of Wakil, had rarely ventured past its wooden gates.

He accepted a cup of ice and honey-sweetened lemon, savoring the taste as it melted against his tongue. If material things were capable of conferring joy, Kai of all men should have been utterly content.

Kai's life was good, but filled with specters. Regardless of his efforts, duties, and entertainments, a hole gaped in the fabric of his world.

Despite steadfast Fodjour and Kebwe, there remained a gap that only male relatives—or the most intimate of friends—could fill. Father, brother, and uncle were gone forever, and it was misery even to consider the depth of his affections for them.

But some who had touched his heart remained alive. In truth, the living human being he missed most was not family. Not even of African descent.

Truth be told, the living face he most longed to see was that of an Irishman named Aidan O'Dere.

Ghost Town's denizens flitted about the estate, obedient and obsequious. He accepted their groveling but simultaneously found it oddly distasteful. Despite their protestations of loyalty he found himself wondering what truth lurked behind their servile smiles, burned behind their politely averted eyes.

"Olaf," he said to the scarred, grizzled man shaving at a block of ice as tall as his hip. "How go things in the village?"

Olaf One-Ear was one of the district's few free whites. A veteran of the Aztec Wars, Olaf had chosen to remain at Dar Kush despite emancipation, even maintaining a billet in Ghost Town. But as a freed man, Olaf had greater choice of duties than any servant, and sometimes sold his services to surrounding landholders, pocketing the profits.

"Oh, mighty well, sir," Olaf said, bobbing his head. His left ear had been sheared away during the abortive rebellion that had cost Kai's father his life. In point of fact, Kai had done the shearing himself, but that particular bit of history was never discussed or mentioned. "We be right happy these days."

"What do they think about the grove's replanting?" The prayer grove had been a sacred place to the servants, one destroyed in punishment following the uprising that had claimed Abu Ali's life and Olaf's ear.

Olaf's smile was bright and glassy. "Oh, they happy, sir. Everybody thinks that just fine."

Kai felt himself running up against a wall, but that merely motivated him to redouble his efforts.

"I heard from Master Berhar that you've been seen over at his estate, and not just handymanning about. Have you been visiting that woman Morgan again?"

Olaf hid a smirk, but looked down at the ice, refusing to answer.

Kai tried again. Once belonging to Dar Kush, Morgan had been sold to the Berhar estate years back. "Now, now . . . I heard she got married, or close to it. Is that really wise?"

"Don't know what you're talking about, sir," he said flatly.

"Olaf," Kai said in frustration, "after you returned from the mosque, for a short time it seemed that when I spoke to you, and you spoke to me, we really *saw* each other."

Olaf's expression changed not a whit. "Don't know what ye mean, sir."

"I think you do," said Kai. "And month by month, I watched that slip away."

For just a moment, there was uncertainty on Olaf's face, a flicker of a different man beneath the placid mask, like a bird glimpsed flitting between palms. Swiftly sighted, swiftly gone. Olaf scratched at the stump of his ear. "Oh, ye know, sir. Day-to-day life just has a way of flowing in, coverin' things up. But everything's fine, sir. Fine as it ever was." A beat. "Would that be all you're needing, sir?"

"Yes," Kai said, resigned. "I suppose it is."

Kai looked out over to Ghost Town. Distantly, he heard the simple, pleasant strains of Irish music. A faint smile shadowed his face.

Olaf looked at his master—his *employer*—with concern. "Are ye all right, sir?"

"Yes. Fine. You're a good sort, Olaf. It's not fair to ask you to be something you're not."

"Sidi?"

"Never mind, Olaf. Just a stray thought. Be about your business."

That annoying blankness descended over Olaf's face, and he turned to Fodjour's half brother Mada, the next guest in line.

Kai stepped out through the kitchen and through the back door. Evening had only recently fallen. The sun's legacy still lingered in the air. The contrast between the lemon ice and the air's warmth tantalized. Even the chills as the first cool breezes gusted from the west merely added to the agreeable sensations.

Life is good, he thought, *but so is memory.*

CHAPTER TEN

THE SAME GENTLE MOON that cast its reflected radiance on Kai shone over all Dar Kush. Its bounty did not stop there: those rays silvered the rolling hills and lakes and rivers, even those farther north.

It was the same partial moon that shone four hundred miles away, northeast over the mountains of Wichita province. Those mountains were a symphony of shortleaf pine, blackjack and post oak, downy serviceberry and winged elm. Little of it was currently under cultivation, but what there was had given bounty to the Ouachita tribes who had once flourished. Now these lands provided groaning tables for farmers black and white.

Here the influence of Africa and Egypt, of Islam and the sands of the Middle East seemed to wane. Here, the seeds of a distant, almost fabulous eastern isle blossomed and bore fruit.

Here, far from Dar Kush, Aidan O'Dere and his wife, the former Sophia de Meroc, had established a small village and begun their life together, with a dozen other formerly bonded families.

Similar to the village of Aidan's youth, it was built as a crannog, a man-made island constructed stone by stone from the lake's bottom. Although not fully complete, it was based on the same defensive concepts.

The completed section was craftily positioned, with good stout walls and rifle portals. A single wooden bridge connected it to the land, a bridge easily destroyed in time of siege.

There was good farming aland, but many of the former slaves busied their days with fishing or hunting.

White-hot from the furnace, steel rang against the anvil of the crannog's smithy as he struggled to reproduce the fabled work of Damascus, if not aspiring to that of fabled Benin. In other roofed shops, freedmen carved, whittled, and nailed, constructing doors, cabinets, and the circular fishing boats called coracles.

The inhabitants were not all Irish: they were former bondsmen from across Europe. Any white man or woman with a strong back, freedman papers, and the willingness to build community was welcome.

A squat, tunicked German yellow-hair named Hans hefted his toolbox and headed off through the narrow road toward the forest.

"Hans!" another freedman called. "Off to see the black folks again?"

The little man bit his thumb, the universal symbol for money. "Need silver, Mfumi. Reckon to get a piece of land, other side of the lake."

Mfumi chuckled. "I know ye. Ye'll work five year and then lose it all on a throw o' the bones."

Hans replied to that with an appropriately obscene gesture and swung off down the road.

Many of the men had skills of wood or metalcraft. Some rented their labor to local black farms, or worked in the neighboring township.

Despite their sometimes precarious circumstances, the land that had once belonged to the Ouachita was truly a bountiful stretch of woods and mountains, streams and a silvered lake teeming with fish. Immediately west roamed tribes of red men, and farther west than that, more black homesteaders, but few black townships of any note. A thousand miles west or north the Nations began, the zone in which one found no blacks at all, and in which the various native groups who had once dominated this continent made peace or war with one another and lived their separate lives.

The natives were curious about the whites, but not hostile. Mixing of blood was inevitable when people of different races lived in proximity. Already a Ouachita brave had taken a Roman wife. More than one former slave woman had coupled with a native or black townsman, so that her children might enjoy the advantage of mixed blood. Pure-blood whites might never have real power in Bilalistan, but the slightest drop of dark blood opened doors. Women shaded and braided their light hair to make it seem more African. Men worked in the fields until the sun had broiled them, seeking to add a few precious shades of bronze. Sometimes they tinted or painted their skin to achieve the desired effect.

In their precious free time, the crannog's males also practiced military arts under the instruction of Aidan O'Dere himself. The forest rang with their cries and the sharp clack of stick meeting stick as men barely accustomed to freedom pretended to have at it with pike and sword.

Aidan O'Dere was a rugged, long-limbed, yellow-haired Irishman. His bright blue eyes gave little hint of the terrible price he had paid for his dangerous skills. It was a rare night indeed that did not include the horrid visitation of old and dire memories, phantasms of his homeland's destruction. A thousand nights he had awakened screaming, and ten thousand times he had sworn that no such slaughter would ever happen again.

"Hold that stick tight, Mbuti," he roared to one of the smaller, slighter men in the skirmish line. "Dammit, hit! Hit!"

"I ain't ready for this," the little Scot squealed, the cudgel wobbling in his hand. "It's all too damned strange."

Aidan came close to him and whispered. "Mbuti, listen close now. Yer not just fightin' for your own miserable arse. It's your wife's. Yer daughter's. Already, your eldest swings her hips at the shadows, dreamin' of easy silver. Nothin' easier than layin' on her back, ya? If her da is weak, she'll cross that focking line. Do ye want that?"

The tears welled from Mbuti's eyes and ran in rivulets down his pale cheeks. "I just can't."

"Yes," Aidan said patiently. "Yes, ye can. Not a human bein' on this planet doesn't have the urge running in its blood. The bastards worked hard to rip it out of ye."

Weeping, Mbuti turned his back. Aidan grabbed his shoulders and swung him around.

"Face me," Aidan roared. "Face me!" He had seen this dysfunction again and again: the longer a man had been in bondage, the harder it was for him to imagine ever fighting back. Mbuti was a third-generation slave.

"I cain't," Mbuti blubbered. "Jus' cain't. Is all easy to you, with yer black man's clothes and yer shadow talk. Cain't fit all that in me head!"

Some of the other men had begun to stare. "What are ye looking at?" Aidan snapped at them when they stopped to stare. "Which of you is stronger or faster than this man? Back to your practice."

The others gawked, but then got the message and left them alone.

"You pick that stick up, boyo. You do your best. Be a man, damn ye."

The freedman did as commanded, then wandered back to the line. Wiping the water from his eyes, Mbuti again commenced the business of thrusting and parrying.

A sharp, familiar whistle from the sidelines snapped Aidan around. To his pleasure, the whistler was his wife and love, Sophia.

Although her olive skin betrayed Africa's grasp upon Andalus, most of Sophia's heritage was European. She had suffered years of training in one of the world's finest slave houses: Egypt's Dar Hudu, the House of Submission. Every sensual art was hers to command. In Aidan's considerable experience, her mastery of those arts was sublime.

Tall, graceful as the dancer she was, with full promising lips and dark eyes. Though of Andalusian blood she was dressed as a good Irish woman: a rope-cinched dress of raw, unbleached cotton, and a thin woolen shawl about her shoulder. She wore none of the elaborate brooches, armlets, and necklaces in which the women of his childhood home had delighted. One day he hoped to provide her with those pretties.

Her belly was swollen with their second child. He rested his hand on the gentle convexity, mirroring a gesture his father had made to his mother long ago, in another existence.

"Kettle's got a good boil," she said. "Been cooking most of the morning. By lunch, I can promise you a feast."

"Oh, darlin'," he sighed. "You know just what I need to hear."

"How goes the training?"

"Slow." He rested a hand on his chest. "But you put fire in my heart, darlin'. And that makes it all aright."

Later, as the day cooled, Aidan, his firstborn son Mahon, and his friend Donough Boru fished the lake in their handmade coracle, the round woven-walled fishing boat of distant Eire. In peacetime Donough was a mild-mannered giant. In war he transformed into a screaming crimson whirlwind, a colossal veteran of the action at the Mosque of the Fathers. He was also Aidan's oldest friend, the only denizen of long-lost O'Dere Crannog he had ever met in Bilalistan, and therefore a precious reminder of past happiness.

Mahon was quite another matter. Four years old, the boy might have been the mirror of Aidan's own youth, impossibly long ago in another world. Pale-haired and freckled, of boundless energy and curiosity, the very sound of the boy's high, thin voice evoked memories of a better, simpler time.

"Water's cold." Mahon trailed his hand down onto its silvery surface.

"That it is," Aidan said.

"Why?"

"Reckon it comes down out of the hills," he said. "At least, it did back home."

Donough grinned at them. "This ain't home, but still a sight better than it's been."

"An undeniable fact, on the face of it." Aidan paused. "Still have dreams?"

Donough's vast face tautened. "Time to time. Fading now. That's one of the sad things."

"How do you mean?"

Donough considered. "You hope that you can take the things you love with you, in here." He thumped his chest over his heart. "Or here." He tapped his head. "But days come and go, and slowly, it all just seems to drain away. Not sure I'd recognize me own mum, if I saw her dancin' down the street." His slablike shoulders sagged. "And that feels like I'm killing her all over again."

Aidan searched for something to say. In business or farming, Donough moved and thought slowly, but in matters of the heart, he sometimes rose to a strange and almost poetic clarity.

"Uncle Donough," Mahon said, clutching at Donough's thick, sun-bronzed arm with one small, pale hand. "Don't be sad."

Donough pressed his lips together. "No, little man. Happy to be here." He looked out over the trees and lake, and inhaled sharply. "This ain't me land, but it is me family, and that's for sure." He smiled, and tousled Mahon's fair hair.

Trust a child to know what to say, Aidan thought. *Jesus in heaven, he's so like me. Ma, Da . . . if only you could see.*

Suddenly, Mahon's attention was caught by a tiny figure standing at the shoreline. "Look!" the boy said.

Aidan shaded his eyes. "Who's that?" Whoever it was, they were waving their arms at the coracle.

"Can't see," Donough said, squinting.

"Snow Elk," Mahon said, and clapped with glee.

Snow Elk was a Ouachita brave from a neighboring valley. Aidan glared good naturedly at the boy. "Me sight can't be fading just yet," he muttered, and began making his way toward the shore.

Donough craned his head. "Who's with him?"

Aidan looked at Mahon. "Little eagle-eye?"

"Looks like a white man," Mahon said.

Aidan paddled toward the shore. "Don't see the Ouachita as much as we did even a year ago. These black folks won't stop until they drive the brown men into the western sea."

"There's another sea?" Mahon asked.

Donough stood and craned his head left and west, as if searching for the other body of water, rocking their boat comically.

"Sit, you great lumbering oaf. You'll drown us all."

Donough sat, chuckling. "Tell us about this western pond."

"This land goes on for two thousand miles. Maybe more."

"No!" Donough and Mahon said at once, and then shared a laugh.

"And on the other side of it, there's an ocean. I've just heard of it. It's wide and wild, and there are yellow men camped about."

Mahon shook his head. "Yellow men. Brown men. Black men. White men."

"Who knew the good Lord had so many colors to paint with, eh, boyo?" Donough said.

Pulling hard, they reached the shore in a few minutes.

Aidan signed a clumsy salutation. "Snow Elk. Greetings."

"*Wasaamu Alakum,*" Snow Elk was bronzed by sun and blood to a tone halfway between white and black. His skin was thick and wrinkled, especially around his dark brown eyes, those wrinkles appropriate for a man who had seen at least forty winters—a withering burden of years given the harshness of his life.

"*Waalaykum salaam,*" Donough replied.

Several warriors accompanied Snow Elk, and they brought forth a quavering white man in ragged, stained pants. His chest was bare and scratched, his back bore half-healed lash tracks. His ragged, shoulder-length black hair was streaked gray with mud.

"And who is this one?" Aidan asked.

Haltingly, Snow Elk answered. "He came to our village, begging food. We fed him. The shadow men offer reward for turning him in. We do not like the shadows."

"More about these Ouachita to love," Donough whispered.

"Will you care for him?" Snow Elk asked.

"He is our responsibility now," Aidan said. "I thank you."

Snow Elk took a step, and then turned around. "Be careful," he said. "The shadows do not like your village. There may be war."

Aidan shook his head as Snow Elk and his people retreated into the forest. "Takes two armies to make a war," he said. "Otherwise, it's just a killing."

"Then we better make us an army," Donough said.

"Been tryin'," Aidan replied. "Come on," he said to the refugee. "Let's get you fed."

With an hour's notice, a formal council was convened in the crannog's longhouse, with one main question to answer: what to do with the runaway?

The refugee might have come from as far as Wichita City. He was frightened, hungry, and exhausted. "Please," he pled, kneeling before them. "Help me."

"What is your name?" Aidan asked.

"Me mother named me Simon. Me master named me Kufu."

"Here, we'll call ye Simon."

Sophia's face was compassionate but unyielding. "We can give you food, and shelter for the night—but not here. There is a place we can take you."

"But why?" asked Simon. "Ain't ye my people? Help me."

"We cannot," Sophia said. "The townsfolk would love an opportunity to bring us low. And if we helped you, and were discovered, some of us would be returned to slavery. I'm sorry. Food, and shelter, and a map to Vineland. And that is all."

"Take 'im for food and drink," one of the others said. "This needs talkin'."

Simon was removed. Sophia turned to the man who had spoken. "So, Eric. What do you need to say?"

"We can 'elp him more than that. I'm not so sure it ain't our duty." Some of the others murmured assent.

One of the other men stood. "There's the *river*, if you understand me meaning." Indeed they did. His inflection lent the word special significance. In this context, the term *river* meant no body of moving water. Rather, it was the escape route north or west to the unincorporated territories, maintained by black abolitionists and free whites. Or at least so it was rumored. An absolute condition of its use was silence as to the particulars. The few whispers Sophia had heard detailed blindfolds, clandestine meetings, frantic escapes, bribery, and occasional violence against the ubiquitous slavecatchers. Any black found guilty of abetting the escape of slaves could be jailed. Whites could be executed.

"Do you know where to find the river?" she said in challenge. "If not, don't talk about it. There's nothing positive to be done, and loose talk hurts us all."

An older Irishman named Niad stood up. "I denne understan' why we canna keep 'im. Blend 'im in. We all look alike to the stinkin' shadows anyway."

"Because we're out here alone," said Aidan. "We already have problems with our black neighbors—"

"Fock 'em! We ain't slaves no more!"

"No," said Sophia. "But this man is. Would you dare our neighbors to fall on us with all their guns and soldiers? It would be difficult to imagine something that would cause us greater grief."

"But we are strong!"

"Sophia is right," Aidan said. "We are strong so long as we remain *within the law*. If they 'ad a single reason to attack us, they'd tear us a new hole faster than ye can say 'jump.' "

"There are tales," Sophia said, "of other freedmen's camps burned to the ground, its members returned to slavery, on mere *suspicion* of harboring a runaway."

"This is the truth," said another of the men. "I came here from Azania, and I tell you that there was a settlement there where every man, woman, and child was returned to slavery for harboring. And worse, it was a 'belly did 'em in."

"What?"

"It's the truth. Renegade whites—not Irish, I'm proud to say." He spat on the ground. "Deliberately set out to trap freed slaves, for gold. Hellish thing, but real. Seen it with me own eyes!"

Niad grunted. "I heard such, but never thought it true. Damn!"

There was a great deal of muttering and low cursing before order was regained.

"Even if it weren't true," Aidan said, "just the rumors keep us in line. We haven't much, but we have each other. In time, we'll grow, and maybe one day we'll be strong. Right now, we have to be careful as mice in a cat barn. Not forever, but now."

And that was, for the time being, that.

Aidan crept up behind Sophia as she and one of the other women sang to the children at fireside. The evenings were generally a time for stories and fables: "The Children of Lir," "The *Llanfabon* Changeling," and "The Sea-Maiden" were all favorites.

Tonight they sang of one of the terrible creatures of this alien land, the hunting apes called thoths, which the Irish equated to the *gruagach* of legend. Not for the first time, Aidan reflected that those titillated by horror were least likely to have ever experienced it personally.

> *Deep within the forest dark*
> *Lies a beast with baleful bark*
> *Feasting on an infant's soul*
> *Cross its path and pay the toll. . . .*

When they reached the familiar refrain, the others joined in.

"*Aire!*" they cried. "*Gruagach! Aire! Gruagach!*"

What amazed Aidan was the fact that despite Sophia's personal encounter with the abominations, she still managed to wear a mask of playful terror, imagined dread. Such a feat would have been beyond him. He had no idea where she locked away that horror, how she could make light of images that still gave him night terrors.

He remembered what the apes had done to Brian McCloud, once the handsomest man of Dar Kush's tuath. For the sin of desiring freedom, his golden face had been ripped away.

> *Pass not through the village gate*
> *Sun has set and day is late*
> *If you walk alone at night*
> *You meet black and gray and white. . . .*

He wanted to leave, but found himself hypnotized by his woman. He had a glimmering of how she did it, that deep within her heart there was a room where she had been taught to hide her feelings and emotions, proper training for a pleasure slave. And if such a place existed, then it was difficult to imagine the manner of horrors crouching there in the darkness, awaiting her inspection.

An incredible skill, purchased at unspeakable cost. He knew some of that penalty, what she had paid to be the remarkable spirit she was.

What price they *both* continued to pay.

> *Run, hide, stay inside! Listen unto me!*
> *Dark sport is the court of the Unseelie!*

The children were laughing, giggling with delight at the horrid images. Aidan was simply transfixed, lost in memories, admiration, and sadness.

Sophia was bringing her song to a conclusion and had slowed her pace, every image generating a different dancer's posture, so that one solitary woman seemed an entire company of mimes.

> *I have saved these words for last*
> *Learn them well and hold them fast*
> *Never venture from your bed*
> *Else your very soul is . . . dead!*

As the stars crept from cover that evening, Aidan and Sophia returned to their own home. In many ways life with his dearest was sweeter than he had ever known. Already, his son was abed. She served his dinner, and they ate in silence. She knew her man, knew his moods and expressions, and his silent withdrawal did not offend her in the slightest.

"I wonder what Kai would have done," he said finally.

"You still miss him?" she asked.

"How could I not? He was my brother." He tore a fistful of fresh hot bread from the loaf and bit it in half.

"He was your master."

"Aye. And the truest friend I'll ever have." He wiped the remaining hunk around the edge of his stew bowl and groaned with pleasure as he chewed. Simple fare, but a feast of plenty. "Some of the burdens we carry haunt us."

"Kai?"

Aidan nodded his head.

"Nessa?"

He flinched. The mention of the twin sister ten years gone never failed to savage his emotions. Time healed some wounds. Small wounds. It seemed the larger ones never healed at all. "Still," he said, and peered into the fireplace. The logs crackled, but the fire's warmth seemed to stop at his skin. "Sometimes, not often, I wonder what life might have been like, had I stayed on at Dar Kush."

Sophia turned away.

"No, darlin'," he said quickly. "It's different if you were raised there. Children expect to be controlled. Not until you become a man do you truly understand what it means to be a slave. At times life was good. At times, Ghost Town was the best home in the world. When I forgot about Eire." He paused, considering. "Not many of those moments, but they existed."

She looked at him with startled curiosity. "How could you have ever forgotten?"

"I wouldn't have. But if things had been different, if I had decided to stay . . ."

"If *we* had decided."

"Yes. We."

"I couldn't have remained, Aidan," she said, chewing slowly. "Too many memories. You weren't forced into . . . some of the situations I faced."

"No." He closed his eyes, hoping not to resurrect the evil memories. "I don't know how you survived them, and still had heart enough to offer me."

She reached for his hand. "How did *you*? All those years of companionship with a 'friend' who could buy and sell you."

He gazed at her with a face that was younger, and more naive, than that she kissed at night. "I loved him, Sophia."

"So did I, a little." She gazed at him across the table. "But not as I love you. I knew you would come. I had to believe it. I saved my heart for you."

He came to Sophia and embraced her. She cringed, then tensed and gasped, turning partially away. He cursed to himself, instantly recognizing his mistake. "Sweet? I'm sorry."

She pushed her closed fist against her mouth. "No. I'm sorry. So sorry."

This hurt bitterly. Malik's sexual domination of Sophia had made their own lovemaking a very fragile thing. Aidan could not simply approach his woman. Rather, he had to wait for Sophia to come to him. And as frustrating as that was, it was not so terrible as once it had been, when her eyes might go dead and cold in the very midst of passion. The old wounds were healing, but never fast enough for him. Never.

"Still," she said. "Not always."

He sighed. Rarely did he initiate discussion of this aspect of the past, but here it was before them, and he was unable to avoid asking a question that had been asked before, answered before, in a dozen different ways. "It was very bad?"

"Not that he hurt me. *Physically,*" she clarified. "Malik was not an evil man. But . . ." She seemed to be choosing her words carefully. "But I was first raped when I was fourteen, Aidan. I was trained to hide myself away, and I did. Until I met you."

He stroked her shoulder, and she relaxed a bit.

"And with you," she continued, "I glimpsed the girl I might have been, had I never been kidnapped. Never forced against my will. I began to feel again. Really *feel*. And when they took me away from you and gave me to Malik, I tried to hide."

"And couldn't?"

She shook her head. "No." A tiny voice. "I couldn't. I tried. He tore through my barriers. It wasn't until I started fighting back, when I seduced him to aid the rebellion, that I regained any scrap of control. I couldn't wait for him to initiate. I had to be the aggressor, Aidan. I had to arouse him, to force him to sex me on *my* terms, not his. And when you were taken away, when you went to war, for those weeks Malik and I were engaged in a battle of our own, with my soul as the prize."

Aidan considered. "When I saw him last . . . before Kai killed him, he seemed . . . not wholly himself."

Sophia set her jaw. "No. I found his weakness: pride. He became obsessed with mastering me. Malik forced his body to perform more than it should have. Many times a day. I believe he used herbal potions to force erection."

It was Aidan's turn to wince.

"I am sorry, my love," Sophia said, and stroked his face with the back of a smooth hand.

He caught and held her hand. "No. Please continue. I need to know."

She nodded. "He was broken inside. What he had seen and done in the name of country, of Allah, of personal honor, had made him brittle. I used his own pride to attack him. Pride in . . ." She groped for a word.

Without thinking, Aidan offered, "His sword?"

She gazed at him, and then somehow, impossibly, they began to laugh, melting into uncontrollable guffaws until tears streamed down their cheeks. They held each other so tightly they could barely breathe. "My love. All wounds heal, in time. I will heal. Every day I feel it to be more true. Be patient with me?"

"We have all the time there is," he said, and kissed her.

CHAPTER ELEVEN

THE DYING FIRELIGHT DANCED shadows against Aidan's closed eyes. At length his lashes fluttered a bit, and a few breaths later he began to moan. . . .

Memory's mirror had clouded.

Occasionally Aidan dreamed of fishing, and returning to O'Dere Crannog. In night-fantasy's lens it was always empty and dust-swept.

In slumber-play he was a grown man, striding the streets of his childhood. "Ma?" he called out. "Da?"

Never was there an answer.

He looked down at his hands, which had transformed into a child's hands. Small. Soft. Boyhood, sweet and terrifying, had returned. "Anyone here?" he called out, voice high and thin.

At last he glimpsed golden hair and broad shoulders, a familiar lanky, confident gait. His father, Mahon, best fisherman and fighter in all the crannog. The desperately beloved figure was striding away from him, growing smaller at every moment. "Da!" he called.

Mahon looked back over his shoulder without apparent recognition, then began to walk faster. Aidan ran through the streets, glimpsing his father at each turn, until finally cornering him.

His father turned.

Mahon O'Dere had two mouths: one beneath his nose, for speech and eating and kissing. The other grinned beneath his chin, gifted him with a single golden knife stroke by a bear-headed Northman.

There seemed reproach in his father's eyes, sadness, an emotion verging on anger. And Aidan was shocked to realize that, without a word being spoken, he knew why.

Then that uncanny psychic bond was rendered irrelevant. The dead man spoke. Not with tongue, but with the ghastly lipless maw of that second, lower mouth.

"Nesssssaaa . . ."

*   *   *

Clutching at his blanket, Aidan sat erect with a sudden, sharp exhalation, choking on the scream lodged in his throat. His beloved lay drowsing beside him, her every silken exhalation a reassurance. Aidan ran his palm over his hair, then hers, and lay back down. Although he feared that slumber might never come again, within minutes his snores had once more intertwined with hers.

After slow sleepy hours the eastern horizon began to blush, sending night's starlit canopy into retreat. Slowly, the village responded to the increase in light and warmth, stirring from their beds as the forest flowers opened to the dawn. Irish and German, Scot and Greek, they emerged yawning from their houses and commenced their daily tasks.

In one little shack to the west of the central fire pit, Sophia conducted classes. Most of the children, and some of the adults, were there. Few of the crannog's adults could read or write, but their strength and skills were necessary for farmwork. Books were as precious as gold.

"Well," Sophia said, "who will spell *caliph* for us?"

A girl rose and walked to the rude board against the wall. With a piece of charcoal, she spelled the word out in Arabic: *halifa-t*.

In the back of the classroom sat several adults, also learning to read and write. One of them was Konso, a stout, grizzled, freedman whose freckled face seethed with anger.

"Why I got to learn this shyte?" Konso complained. "We free now! We should go back to our own talk—"

Some of the other former slaves buzzed with agreement.

"And what language would that be?" Sophia asked. "Irish? German? Latin? There are too many of us, from too many different places."

"Then we make up new words." He glowered. "Anything's better than this A-rab double tongue."

Sophia understood his pain completely, but could not allow the part of her that agreed with him to find voice. "What if we created a language, and then taught it to our children. How do they speak it to the blacks who control this land?"

"To hell wit' the shadows!" Konso shouted, slamming his fist against the wall hard enough to shake it.

"Yes," Sophia said. "To hell with them. But with us, too. I didn't want this world, but it's the one I live in. And my children, or my children's children, are going to have their chance to benefit by my sweat and blood. If you can't speak Arabic, if you don't understand the men who rule this land, you'll never get your piece of it."

"Who the hell wants a piece of it? I just want be lef' alone."

Sophia walked back between the rows until she stood over him, balled fists set on her hips. "Then go. Go on; be alone, or take with you whoever is of like mind. But I believe that things will change. I don't know if I'll live to see it, but my grandchildren will, and they will know that their grandmother prepared them for *that* world."

She walked back to her place at the head of the room, anger and pain and other long-repressed emotions wrestling in her heart. She knew what Konso wanted, and it wasn't terribly different from what she herself desired. A home! A place to call hers, where she would not be forever an outsider, an interloper, a quasi-human oddity given freedom revocable by any black with a grudge.

"We study this," she said, measuring each word carefully, "so that we can have our own world, where we can be left alone." Konso was watching her now. Listening. Like the others, he wanted to believe. "Where we can raise our children and preserve the ways of our people." She leaned forward and pronounced each word with firm emphasis: *"But we have to speak their language to do it."*

The others looked back at Konso. He raised a thick, gnarled hand and scratched at the bare spot above his frizz of hair and then shook his head slowly. "All right," he said, and jutted his jaw at her. "You teach. I learn."

She turned back to the board, sighing with relief. As she began to write, her mind buzzed. *How will I get us through this?* She asked herself a dozen times a day. *How do I unite these fragile twigs into a bundle strong enough to stand? Because if I cannot . . .*

If we cannot unite . . .

We are doomed.

In the early part of the day Aidan usually made repairs, but this morning he walked the narrow, muddy streets with the intent to meet Donough and see if they couldn't wreak a little havoc on the lake's aquatic population.

"Aidan! *Guten Morgen!*" called Hans, one of the newer arrivals.

"*Wie geht es Ihnen?*" Aidan answered, those six words comprising half his German vocabulary.

"*Kalimera,*" called another, a stocky former mine slave from the Egyptian Sea. By great good fortune, this man had apparently earned his freedom by saving his master from a cave-in within two years of his date of capture.

"*B'teke Araby?*" Aidan asked. *Do you speak Arabic?* The man, whose name was . . . Stavros. Yes, that was it. Stavros pouted a bit, and then began a painfully clumsy greeting in the tongue he hated.

Donough clapped Aidan on the shoulder. "Och," the big man said. "Another wonderful day in O'Dere Crannog."

"Don't call it that," Aidan growled.

"But it is," Donough said reasonably enough. "This is O'Dere Crannog, sure as you're living." He clapped a bearlike hand on Aidan's shoulder. "We have a real, genuine O'Dere right here, and I say yer fathers are smilin' on ye." He paused. "O' course, that Simon cursed us a bit when he left this mornin', but that's only natural. I guess he wanted a bit more than food and water and a map to the Nations."

"So would I," Aidan said, but relaxed a bit. They had done the right thing. Perhaps the nightmares could recede after all. "Maybe. Maybe you're right." He thumped his friend's solid gut.

"Now," Donough said. "Let's not keep the fishies waiting, shall we?"

"It would be rude."

"Aye," Donough said, grinning. "And if I've learned any lesson at all, it's to be anything but rude."

"Kill them, yes. Insult them, no," Aidan agreed.

Donough chuckled. "We *are* talkin' about fishies, ain't we . . . ?"

PART II

Radama

"So often in the affairs of men," said the student, "we must come together in groups, to accomplish those things beyond our individual strength."

"This is true," said the teacher.

"I know I can trust Allah. My family. My tutor."

His teacher inclined his head modestly.

"But how do I trust strangers?"

"Trust them not. Instead, rely upon them."

"What?" said the student. "This I do not understand."

"Rely upon men to do what is in their best interests."

"Appeal, then, to their higher natures?"

"No. Many are unaware they have such a thing. Instead, appeal to their greed and fear. That net is wider, and catches all."

"Even the wise?"

"Yes," said the master. "Even the wise, who are greedy for knowledge, and fear Allah."

CHAPTER TWELVE

20 Ramadan A.H. 1294
(Friday, September 28, 1877)

BY GHANJAH-STYLE FLAT-BOTTOMED steam-screw, Kai and Fodjour traveled the Brown Nile north to Radama, capital of New Djibouti, a four-day trip for Kai to take his place in the Territorial Senate.

The steam-screw's deck rocked mildly in the river current. The river-banks to east and west were dotted with cottonwoods, sycamores, and tiny human figures waving greeting as the mighty ship passed. Skiffs and canoes drifted with the tide, crowded with fishermen pulling at their nets. The occasional heliograph relay tower flashed its messages toward the horizon.

With faithful Fodjour at his side, Kai wandered close to a knot of men who stood at their ease, sipping coffee. He pretended to gaze at the river-banks as he eavesdropped on their conversation.

"Word has come," the first said. "Tensions increase between Abyssinia and Egypt."

"Why?" asked the second, silver-bearded gentleman.

"Fighting over European colonies, trade routes . . ."

The second man persisted. "War between the Twin Thrones is no longer merely possible—it is inevitable."

"The better to increase tensions already dire. North and south have lit-tle enough in common now. We hold the Empress close to our hearts, while the north licks the Pharaoh's backside."

"And what if war came?"

The first man clenched his fists. "We would fly to the Empress's aid. The Red Sea would be red with blood."

"It is not so easy."

"Things never are."

The second man pressed his point. "By treaty and law, Bilalistan is an Egyptian colony. To violate that treaty, to war with Egypt, would negate millions of Alexanders in trade agreements, worldwide. Allah alone knows the chaos it would cause."

"Millions? Surely you exaggerate."

"I fear not." The silver-bearded one turned, his eyes widening with recognition. "Greetings, young Wakil. I am Al-Hakir." The man was older and something of an oiled and perfumed dandy. His shirt was of Chinese silk.

"Kai ibn Jallaleddin ibn Rashid." Kai bowed politely.

"Of Dar Kush. A pleasant day, yes?"

"Yes."

"If only all days could be so placid."

Kai nodded, waiting for Hakir to conclude pleasantries. "Indeed."

The silver beard fluttered in the breeze. "I find it likely that these will be more placid than those ahead."

"Truth?" He could almost hear his father's whisper in his ears. *Take care, my son. The spider spins his web.*

Hakir leaned close enough for Kai to smell the rose oil in his beard. "I was your father's . . . *friend*."

Kai's smile remained in place, but inside he went cold. Hakir's emphasis was clear, his intent clearly political. Had Kai not known that there were code words to be exchanged, he might have relaxed his guard. Or would he? A closer inspection of Hakir suggested that there were indeed clues to warn the cautious. The silk shirt, for instance. The stern Abu Ali would never have condoned such effeminacy among his confidants. "He never spoke of you."

"There was much he could not speak of," said Hakir. "Much you should know. Come to the meeting, tonight. Bilalistan must be free!"

And with those words, Hakir retreated.

Kai watched after him. "What does he want?" he asked, wondering what Fodjour would make of it.

Fodjour laughed without humor. "Little save your money, your power, and your name." *Well said.* "Faith! How do you know who to trust?"

A fine question, one to which Kai had no immediate answer.

Fodjour grunted. "Was your father truly involved in this movement?"

Kai shrugged. "He never spoke of it to me."

"I notice you haven't answered my question."

Kai laughed. If the mantle of Wakil had graced Fodjour's shoulders instead of his own, his friend might have excelled. "Very good. I will say instead, then, that I believe he was very interested in the future of this nation, and never thought that Bilalistan would remain an Egyptian protectorate."

Fodjour cocked his head to the side. "Were there no papers among his effects?"

"A few things. I assume he was involved, but could not swear either way." Again, an evasion, but this time Fodjour didn't seem to notice.

"Then you must take care. Evidence of your father's involvement in a Bilalian freedom movement could cost your seat in the Senate."

"Who would press for such a thing?" Kai's puzzlement was genuine.

"Governor Pili, for one."

"But why?"

Fodjour looked at his old friend as if he were addressing a child. "He opposed many of your father's policies, but Abu Ali and Malik were a mighty team, both politicians and lauded soldiers. For the governor to stand against them—when he himself has never lifted sword in battle—would have seemed cowardly."

Again, well reasoned. "But my own war record is less than golden."

"To some. But make no mistake: to others, you are a hero. You received your captaincy after your return, so some of those admirers are in the military council." His face went soft, eyes questioning and dreamy. "Kai, men such as we, men of destiny . . . we never really know who we are. But then, after we are dead, historians will argue endlessly about who we *were*."

Kai thought for a time, and then nodded. A river's breeze and an honest friend's conversation. Both were cleansing to the mind. "I know who you are," he said. "And you know me. And that, for now, is enough."

21 Ramadan A.H. 1294

(Saturday, September 29, 1877)

Radama was a frontier capital, with all of the energetic and occasionally slapdash architecture that that implied. Most of the city was a maze of brick and adobe buildings, few taller than three stories. Where more space existed, for instance in the affluent section of town, one found gardens and estates built more in the round, with symbolic structures fashioned in circles of stone or mock-stone obelisks as tall as two men, reminding Kai of light-paintings of Zimbabwean architecture.

The steam-screw nested its curved stem against the dock just after noon. Kai and Fodjour hired a cart and relaxed as bustling bondsmen took control of their luggage and persons, delivering both to the most luxurious hotel Radama had to offer, a three-storied guest mansion with an Asian flavor. Malagasy perhaps? It was those sailors who had established sea routes to China, returning with both material and cultural riches.

After a quick bath and a pause for prayer, the friends found their way to the Senate building, which held both the Round and a less formal meeting hall, where provincial delegates milled and debated the day's issues.

Bilalistan was governed by the Caliph, through appointment by the Pharaoh. He was certainly the greatest power in the land, the only real rival being the Ayatollah, who led Bilalistan's spiritual college of scholars, the Ulema. While having no direct legal power, the Ulema's religious proclamations and interpretations of both the Recitation and the life of the Prophet held great sway, and could be ignored by no leader who wished to keep either title or head.

While the Ulema was the voice guiding a Bilalian's inner life, the Caliph controlled the reins of secular government. Beneath him was the military council, composed of the highest officers in army and navy, and the forces composing the territorial guards, of which Kai himself was an officer.

The landowners controlled the Senate, their seats conferred by appointment and subsequent inheritance. The National or "Grand" Senate was composed of delegates from the Territorial or "Lesser" Senates, one of which was held yearly, or upon demand. The system had worked for two hundred years, and might for a thousand more. . . .

Or might not.

The Senate was an exhilarating experience, and Kai had found it so since his first visit there, the year after his father's death. Then he had merely observed, but had received a standing ovation, honored both as the son of a dead senator, and as a hero in his own right. But this time was different; this would be his first active participation, and he was pleased to have Fodjour along as friend and advisor.

One of the things he most enjoyed about the Territorial was the fact that, by custom, the delegates wore clothing and headdress honoring not only Bilalian traditions, but their ancestors on the mother continent.

So, intricate Fulani beadwork, veiled Tuareg men, wigged Danakil, and feathered Kikuyu sat side by side with formal military dress and Indian-style coats and trousers.

It was late afternoon before the Zulus made their entrance. Four of them, wearing leopard skins and golden bangles, haughty and imperious, as if they were foreign dignitaries instead of settlers of a territory owing allegiance to the Caliph.

Kai shrank back into a shadow as Cetshwayo and his entourage passed. He was not yet ready to deal with Shaka Zulu's younger brother.

Behind him, a delegate asked, "If there was war, for whom would the Zulu raise his spear?"

A second delegate shrugged. "It is hard to say. They are wild and independent. Most likely, they would wait for both sides to weaken, and then strike for their own land."

Kai admired the man's clarity: that was exactly what he himself would suppose a perfect Zulu strategy.

"I think it may well depend upon the side which offers them the best terms," said the first. "One ought not count on family ties where there are none, or loyalty where it has never been displayed before."

"Come, Sidi," said the second. "They fought in the Aztec Wars."

The first delegate gave a low chuckle. "The Aztecs threatened to attack Zulu homelands. Our frontiersmen were merely fighting a war on another's territory, always a sound strategy."

"So cynical!" the second chided.

"They are not Muslim, nor do they owe fealty to Pharaoh or Empress. Draw your own conclusions."

Kai moved away before he could be trapped into the discussion, or indeed, one of them noticed his eavesdropping.

In the past years he had studied Zulu history in depth. The first major wave of Zulus left Africa following a war of succession some four generations earlier. Discontents, fortune-seekers, and families seeking cheap fertile land and empire had been immigrating ever since.

Shaka kaSenzangakhona, *Inkosi*, or hereditary chief of the Zulu, had immigrated from Africa in his mother's womb. Although he never returned to the land of his conception, he had considered himself a Zulu first, Bilalian a distant second.

It was certainly possible that this sense of loss of his identity—along with the loss of right of royal succession, had warped Shaka.

Kai was not the only one who pondered these things, but none of these thoughts were ever shared in the presence of Zulus, who were seen as wild-card allies at best, and at worst, potential threats to the social order.

"Kai!" one of the delegates called.

Kai turned, mortified that his given name had been shouted. Perhaps foolishly, he had entertained the notion of slipping quietly from the room, but that hope was now as dead as Shaka. He bowed slightly to the speaker, a man perhaps ten years older than himself, with speckles of gray lightening a sparse beard. "Sidi Akmed. *Salaam Alakum.*"

"*Waalaykum salaam*. Peace be unto you and yours." Akmed was a rotund man of mixed African and Persian blood, like Fodjour's mother Allahbas. He owned extensive holdings in Wichita and had placed Bilalian cotton, teff, and wheat in successful competition with Egyptian goods. Kai admired his boldness. "Tell me, my friend. You, more than any of us, have had congress with these Zulus. What do you think of them?"

Kai considered before answering. "Phenomenal warriors, stout allies. Fearsome enemies."

Akmed meditated on this for a moment. "And your impression of their Shaka?"

Kai tried not to let his distress manifest in his face. "He was . . . singular."

"And died in the assault on the mosque?"

"So I hear," he replied. "But no outsider was invited to his funeral, so I cannot say."

Akmed watched his eyes carefully. "Your brother died in that same assault, didn't he?"

What does Akmed know? Surely, nothing. "Yes. Shaka and my brother died on the same day."

"Two great warriors," Akmed said without apparent irony. "Allah called them home."

Indeed, Shaka was said to have died in the assault on the Mosque of the Fathers. Because Kai had always maintained that his brother died in that battle, and had never told anyone that it was a Zulu *umkhonto*, not an Aztec's war axe, that had slain Ali, no one had ever imagined there to be motivation for Kai's own murderous act. So far, he had gone unaccused.

There were only three living witnesses to that dread day's events: Kai, Fodjour, and Kebwe. And those three had sworn secrecy.

Shaka's younger brother approached Kai. Cetshwayo's limp, the result of an old hunting injury, was more pronounced than it had been just three years before. Regardless, the man remained an onyx wedge. Kai steeled himself. Cetshwayo seemed both distant and polite. "*Salaam Alakum*."

"*Waalaykum salaam*. It is good to see you."

"And you. My condolences on your losses since last we met."

"And mine to you on the death of your brother."

"Yes," Cetshwayo said. "We have both lost brothers."

"They died as warriors."

The Zulu prince displayed little emotion. "Yes," he said. "We speak again, later." Then he turned away. Kai watched him, uncertain of how to respond to this borderline rudeness.

Before he could decide on a response, one of Cetshwayo's liveried slaves approached him with a note. The thin-lips bowed deeply, then backed away. The note read: *"The Wakil's company is requested tonight at suite 107, Plains Hotel."*

According to conversation after conversation, as the Caliph fielded Egyptian requests for ships, guns, gunpowder, and men for the upcoming conflict, New Djibouti, Wichita, and even parts of New Alexandria fought to stay out of the looming conflict. This increased the very real chance of separation between north and south, the probability of secession, and the possibility of civil war.

Even now, Egyptian ships floated in both Djibouti Harbor and the mouth of the Brown Nile. However benign their stated purpose, the implicit threat was obvious.

One of the Caliph's most powerful allies, Admiral Amon bin Jeffar, was present at the territorial summit. Respected by both the Senate and the military council, bin Jeffar traced his descent directly from Alexander and the Abyssinian princess who had given him sons.

Bin Jeffar's retinue appeared: two lieutenants; a male secretary who appeared to be of Egyptian-Afari extraction; and rather surprisingly, a striking blond slave woman.

Kai turned to a delegate, a supple man a bit taller than himself named Negash. "Bin Jeffar arrives."

"Indeed. One-third of the Triumvirate." Negash made a spitting sound. "Triumvirate" referred to the three most powerful men in New Alexandria: the Caliph himself, bin Jeffar, and an industrialist named Dosa. "They will drag us into this mire, no doubt about it."

"Still, his reputation is—"

Before he could develop his theme, bin Jeffar himself approached them. He was slender, a bit paler than Kai, with high cheekbones and slanted eyes. Unusually dark-skinned for an Egyptian. The blond slave woman followed him a respectful step behind.

"Captain Kai ibn Jallaleddin ibn Rashid," the delegate said, "allow me to present the honorable Admiral Amon bin Jeffar Sephenamen."

Kai bowed deeply. "Your bloodline beggars any compliments I might offer. Allow me to say simply that it is an honor."

"I knew and admired your father," bin Jeffar said mellifluously. "No empire easily sustains the loss of such men."

"Thank you, Admiral." Despite his natural caution Kai liked the man immediately, then reminded himself that the Admiral was a professional politician. It was bin Jeffar's gift to make himself plausible. Kai took an emotional step backward.

"I am certain," said bin Jeffar, "it would be his fondest hope and dream that you exceed him."

"You ask too much, I am afraid. I am a simple scholar, more at home in books than in the Round."

One of the admiral's dense eyebrows arched. "Or on the battlefield? No modesty, please. I read both your report and the official inquiry into the events at the mosque. You performed commendably. These are dire times. The strong must stand and bear their share of the load, or the nation suffers. I think I will see more of you, Captain." A delegate on the far side of the room had raised his hand, attempting to catch bin Jeffar's eye. Finally, he succeeded. "Pardon. I must conclude an earlier conversation."

"Of course."

Bowing, bin Jeffar excused himself. His entourage followed. With the conversation ended, Kai had an opportunity to appreciate the woman who had followed bin Jeffar at a proper distance. She wore a checked *kalasiris* sheath dress, with broad shoulder straps and a collar studded with semi-precious stones. Her pale hair was tinged with strawberry, a shade he had seldom seen. In turning, she displayed unusual grace and poise, a suggestion of strength of spirit that, in combination with her well-proportioned face and form, aroused his curiosity.

"What do you think?" delegate Negash asked.

"Most impressive. Statesman, mathematician, historian, naval commander—is there anything at which he does not excel?"

"Keeping ghosts from his bedroom?" Negash glared at the girl. "She is pretty enough in her limp-haired way." He sniffed. "It is still distasteful the way he parades his weakness in public."

"Who is she?" Kai asked.

Negash shrugged. "A pleasure slave, probably." He leaned closer. "I hear that she actually accompanied bin Jeffar to court. Quite the scandal, really."

"Why do you ask?" another guest queried, cruising closer to the conversation.

"She just . . . looks familiar. Never mind. What do you know of the admiral?"

"The Pharaoh's bloodline, that much is certain. I believe he has ambitions."

"A fancy one," said another guest. "He's written books on numerical theory, apparently invented a gun-sight and a table for calculation of munitions trajectories." The subject seemed to have its own fascination. "He has a vast estate south of Azteca: cocoa, and a silver mine, I believe. Quite the polymath. Some think the Pharaoh chose the wrong Caliph."

"Hmm," Kai said, mind still drifting in other directions. "Humor me. Would you know if that woman was born here?"

The second guest stroked his beard. "I heard she was a wild ghost, born in Germany or Eire. I forget which. Does it matter?"

Kai shook his head. "She seems good breeding stock. I thought of making an offer."

"Lavish attempts have been made and rejected," the second guest said. "He will not sell."

"True? Ah, then, best forget the wench." Kai spoke the words, and the other guests appeared to accept them at face value, but his eyes followed the girl carefully.

CHAPTER THIRTEEN

KAI'S HOTEL NESTLED between a clothing shop and a silver smithery in one of Radama's trendier sections. The sun was far enough beyond its zenith to cool the air without threatening immediate darkness. Kai strolled the clay sidewalks, enjoying the sights and sounds when he heard the universal call of tradesmen in the market.

His heartbeat quickened. Like most Bilalians, he loved a good marketplace, a place where fruit, fowl, meats, leather goods, pottery, honed steel, and a thousand other delights were offered to passersby, with the bargaining as great an attraction as the eventual purchase itself.

A rag-swathed wretch sat on the street corner, shaking his wooden begging bowl at passersby. "Alms. Alms," the mendicant cried.

Two pedestrians tossed coins into the bowl, pointedly avoiding eye contact with the small grubby man stumping for their gelt.

"The blessings of Allah upon you," said the beggar. "Alms. Who will give me alms?"

Kai watched, and smiled in recognition. A second's visual search spied a tiny, well-appointed café across the street from the beggar's corner. This month, their day traffic would be lighter than usual, and Kai had no trouble finding the ideal table at which to sit and watch.

A waiter approached him. "Yes, Sidi?"

"Coffee, please. How long has that beggar been there?"

"All week," said the waiter disapprovingly. "Should I have the filthy rogue beaten?"

Kai almost smiled at the thought. "No. No. Just the coffee, please." He sat, watching.

"Alms . . ." the small man called.

As the afternoon waned Kai sipped his coffee, mind drifting with the flow of the traffic. Most pedestrians walked around the tramp; others dropped coins. A discourteous few hissed at him. Finally, Kai settled his bill and walked across the street.

"Alms?" the mendicant asked.

"Here." Kai dropped a small rectangular coin into the old man's cup.

The beggar didn't look down into the bowl, but heard the sound of silver against wood and smiled. He continued to chant. "Blessings upon you. Alms . . . alms . . ."

Kai walked on, took up a position on the next block, and continued to observe.

Finally the shadows deepened, and the streets emptied as the faithful journeyed home to break their fasts. The old man picked himself up, sorted through the change in his bowl, and dumped it into a prayer fountain. He approached Kai.

"El Sursur," Kai said to Babatunde.

"Young Wakil." The two embraced.

Nearing sixty, Babatunde was the son of a Yoruban prince and a shepherd girl of Yoruban and Turkish extraction. Denied palace comforts and tutors by reason of his tainted blood, by the age of twenty he was renowned for his poetry and scholarship, and holder of a spiritual lineage at least forty generations old, extending back through Nur Addin Qwami and Jafar al-Sadiq to Bilal and ultimately, to the Prophet himself.

Tiny enough to have been nicknamed "the Cricket" by Kai, Babatunde had been tutor and companion to Lamiya almost as long as the Wakil could remember. That this stern teacher would become Kai's master in esoteric Islam was a surprise. That he would, with the death of Kai's entire male clan, become like a second father could never have been conceived at all.

"So . . . I know you have no need for money. Why were you begging?"

His tutor smiled. "Why, for them, of course. And for you."

Kai shook his head. "If I ever live long enough to understand you . . ."

"Hah! We should *both* live so long. Well, what are you waiting for?"

"What?" Kai asked, genuinely puzzled.

"Aren't you going to buy me supper?"

"The best in town."

Babatunde took Kai's arm. "I know just the place."

"This should be memorable," Kai said that with a glance at Babatunde's clothing. And a quick sniff of the air that had grown more pungent in the Sufi master's presence.

More important than memorable, this promised to be amusing.

* * *

"Wakil!" Their eager Fulani restaurateur bowed his skeletally tall frame low. "Welcome to our humble establishment."

Then in the next moment, the server saw Babatunde gliding in behind Kai, and paled. "Ah! Guard! Another of the street people has wandered in." He spanked his skinny palms together. "Remove him!"

"He is my guest," Kai explained, concealing his smile as he awaited the explosion.

The restaurateur seemed torn. On the one hand, a wealthy customer with a jangling purse. On the other, his haughty clientele might well bolt to a competitor at the distressing sight of this street wretch. "Ah . . . but . . . I . . ."

Feeling merciful, Kai slipped a gold rectangle into the owner's bony hand. "A sensitive and resourceful man can arrange these things."

The man's fingers rose halfway to his mouth before it paused, as if realizing that to bite the coin would be an insult to his benefactor. "Perhaps a private booth?"

"Very private," agreed Kai.

The server clapped again. "The Wakil has great understanding. At once!"

Babatunde looked up at Kai guilelessly. "Is there a problem?"

"Nothing gold cannot solve."

Swiftly, and no doubt wishing that they could have sheltered the newcomers with a rolling curtain, the waiters escorted Kai and Babatunde to a darkened, *extremely* private booth in the back of the restaurant. Guests glared from both sides and covered their noses with handkerchiefs as they passed. In his heart, Kai wasn't certain what he enjoyed more: reuniting with his tutor, the prospect of a meal, or the discomfiture of the other guests.

Ah well, he supposed. *I'll finish maturing one day. But not quite yet, merciful Allah. Not quite yet.*

Despite the meal's shaky beginnings, their table now groaned beneath the weight of a feast of lamb in various configurations: kabob, pastry, wrapped in grape leaves, cubed and set in a bed of long rice. Kai's gustatory habits changed little with the coming of Ramadan. Babatunde himself had suggested and refined Kai's regimen as a means of increasing physical and mental powers. As he had phrased it: "To use this method is simple: one has air for breakfast, prayer for lunch, and two or three bountiful dinners."

Babatunde himself declined to embrace such a severe regimen, but he was blessed with the sort of inner fire that allowed him to eat all he wanted of almost everything and never gain a kite.

Kai had already finished his first meal and had now slowed to picking at his second. He watched Babatunde as his teacher feasted on lamb *sambusa* pastries. "So . . . ," he said as his appetite receded. "It has been eight weeks since last we supped. I wonder if I should ask of your adventures since last we met."

"Awful," said the Yoruba. "Just awful. As you recall, I came to see an old colleague before he left for the Continent. After his departure, a week remained before you would arrive. Boat, horse . . . ah! Whenever men try to move faster or farther than they can walk, there is travail."

"Have you seen the steam dragon?" Kai asked. "I hear that it has a spur from New Alexandria almost down to our capital. Another is under construction traveling inland from the harbor. They say it can travel at forty miles to the hour!"

Babatunde looked almost ill. "There will be a reckoning, I swear to you. But no, my days have been fairly peaceful. . . ." He regarded Kai shrewdly. "But you, my boy. What has been happening with you? I know my pupil. Something troubles you."

Kai smoothed Cetshwayo's invitation on the table between them. Babatunde examined it, read it, examined it again.

"Ah," he finally said. "Well—it was only a matter of time, wasn't it?"

"Still a surprise."

"But a delightful one, I would think." He nibbled at the corner of his pastry and then chewed thoughtfully. "But I doubt a bridegroom's jitters could furrow your brow." Babatunde's gaze was steady. "Would you like to talk about it?"

"Yes," Kai said. "I would. More than I can say . . . I'm just not quite ready yet."

Babatunde nodded. "Very well, young Wakil. Age has taught me nothing if not patience. To my room then, and a bath." He sniffed his underarms. "I stink!"

"I'm glad you'd noticed." Kai considered leaving an additional sum, but knew he had already paid enough for five such feasts and decided against it. Drawing as little notice to themselves as possible, they left.

Immediately after they vacated the booth, a small squadron of waiters descended, cleaning, swabbing, and scenting the air with perfume . . .

And gathering napkins and tablecloth to be burned.

The Zimbabwe hotel represented two-storied functional elegance at its finest. Nonetheless, as Kai's guest Babatunde's appearance attracted little overt attention until the slave boy opening their room door wrinkled his freckled nose. "Bath in dere."

"I think I can find it," Babatunde said, mustering his full dignity.

"Please," Kai said.

"Is this how you treat your elders now?"

"Whenever possible. I will see you in the morning?"

"And considerably more presentable."

"A thousand noses thank you."

Kai closed the door, leaving Babatunde chuckling behind him.

However cavalierly he might have presented himself to his tutor, Kai allowed his genuine emotions to emerge only when locked in the quarters he shared with Fodjour. There, he paced anxiously and related the day's events, glancing at the clock every few seconds.

"Cetshwayo wants to see me privately in his suite," Kai said. "Hah! I can imagine why."

"His purpose?" asked his friend.

"Most likely strangulation."

Fodjour managed a wan smile. "If he had wished you dead, he would have sent assassins to Dar Kush."

"Perhaps it is a Zulu custom of some kind: the death of a brother must be personally avenged. Damn! You are probably right, but I just don't know!"

"Guilt clouds your logic. Seek counsel. Ask Babatunde."

"I cannot," Kai said, throwing his arms up in despair. "I have never been able to tell him the truth of that day."

"Not even the Cricket?" Fodjour asked, incredulous. "I did not know."

"In the end," Kai said, standing, "a man is alone with his fate. I go."

Fodjour gripped his shoulder urgently. "Allow me to accompany you. Two blades are better than one," he said.

"I believe the intention is clear: I am to go alone." Kai swirled his cloak around his shoulder.

"I don't understand. As your friend and second I could champion you in a duel, but cannot accompany you on a social visit?"

"The invitation was for one. To do otherwise is insult." Kai did not deny his anxiety, but remained insistent. "I am the holder of my father's seat. In my role as Wakil there are things more important than my own safety."

"But—"

Voice kind but firm, Kai said, "This time, I go alone."

CHAPTER FOURTEEN

IT TOOK A QUARTER HOUR for Kai to reach the luxurious hotel suites occupied by Cetshwayo and his men. With every step in that direction his anxiety flared to new and higher peaks, and he began to resent his own mind for the manner in which it nattered, throwing one disastrous scenario after another up to plague and torment him.

He stood before the ornately carved door with hand raised, suddenly wary of knocking.

What should he do? Of course, in all probability this was a trap. It was far more difficult to determine what in the world he should *do* with that knowledge. Complain to Cetshwayo that the Zulus had abandoned the Shrine of the Fathers? The Zulus had been questioned on this very topic. They had calmly explained how, upon Colonel Shaka's death, battlefield command had reverted to another officer, who had chosen to deploy forces more dynamically until support for the mosque could be guaranteed. They claimed to know it could not be held, and that the only outcome of a sustained battle would be the mosque's destruction, which had indeed occurred.

Technically speaking, the Zulu had been allies, not subordinates. The Bilalian high command had been forced to accept this answer. Three years later, it remained a sore point.

Should he even mention the past at all? Cetshwayo was the most powerful political leader among Bilalian Zulus, even if he hadn't Shaka's military authority. If Kai did not speak with clarity regarding crucial topics, mightn't Cetshwayo consider this evidence of cowardice or guilt? But if he did, mightn't he be thrusting his sword into a hornet's nest?

Wiser to choose a middle course, finding ways to praise Zulu courage in battle, and to offer further condolences for the death of Shaka, without accepting or implying personal responsibility.

After all, Shaka had struck Ali first, and from a familial point of view Kai's actions might be considered justifiable. From a military standpoint, on the other hand, they had been within Shaka's chain of command at the time, and Kai's actions might well merit execution.

Things were equally confusing from a political perspective. The Zulus owned much of Azania as private or corporate holdings, but had the legal responsibilities of any other Bilalians. Owing fealty to any but their own rankled the intensely proud Zulus, who wanted little other than their own homeland. They enjoyed living in their own way and had little respect for external protocol. While they would wish to avenge Shaka's death, they stood to gain more by affirming their connection with the wealth, power, and prestige of Dar Kush.

Might Cetshwayo know *exactly* what happened at the mosque, and expect Kai to intuit that the subject must not be mentioned? Or might that merely be what he wanted Kai to think, while his actual intent remained murderous?

But how could Cetshwayo know with any certainty what had happened? There were no witnesses save Kebwe and Fodjour, and surely neither of *them* . . .

The door opened, and all conjecture ceased. He steeled himself, but much to his surprise, Cetshwayo's massive arms enfolded him heartily.

"Kai!" he roared, boisterously enough to rattle the windows. "It is good to see you, out of the sight of the others. There is much for us to speak of."

Kai was taken aback. "Y-yes," he stammered. "Of course there is. . . ."

Cetshwayo bared his teeth in a grin. "And life has been good for you? Sweet?"

"Yes."

"Enjoy it." The Zulu beamed. "There are so many things in life that cannot be anticipated. This leg!" He slapped his damaged right limb. "I never dreamed that I would lose a part of my body! But so life goes. Things we hold dear can vanish in a twinkling."

"Yes." Ar-Rahman preserve him! What manner of game was this?

"But enough of this talk. We have both lost, but now we must put mourning behind us, and move forward with life."

"Move . . . forward?" Kai's head swirled. He felt behind himself for a chair, and sat, staring up at the Zulu prince.

"My emissaries will call upon you. It is time to negotiate ceremony and brideprice."

Kai sat very very still. "For Nandi?"

"Of course!" the Zulu roared, and slapped his knee. "Hasn't she been patient enough?"

Kai was beginning to feel like an animal with one foot caught in a trap. "More than anyone could ask."

"Ah," Cetshwayo rhapsodized, grin splitting his great dark moon of a face. "What a day that will be! I am certain that none of us will ever forget it."

Kai swallowed. "How could we?"

"A shame that your father, and your brother, could not be here to see it."

"Yes," was all that Kai could think to say.

"And Shaka," said Nandi's father. "It was not in his nature to say such things, but I am sure he thought you and Nandi should be together. I am quite certain that he will be watching."

Kai couldn't handle the conversation turning in that direction. "When will your people call?"

"Soon," the older man said. "*Very* soon. I think that would be best, yes?"

"Of course." Kai felt callow, and small. And trapped.

"Who will be your second in negotiations?"

That required but a moment's thought. "Babatunde, I think."

A bit of light ebbed from Cetshwayo's smile. It remained tolerant but noticeably cooler. "I have not spoken of this before, but it is unseemly for a man of your stature to have a mixed-breed so close to his ear. He is one-quarter white!"

"Turkish," Kai said thinly.

"Bah! They are all the same." He placed his arm around Kai's shoulder. "Your father, a fine man, a great warrior, is dead. Nothing would give me greater pleasure than for you to think of me as your father, now that with this marriage, our two houses become one."

"I am honored to share such noble blood," Kai said.

"Then let your new father give you a piece of advice: One drop makes you whole, Kai. Babatunde is polluted, and you should ban him from your affairs."

Kai gathered himself. "I understand the Zulu attitudes toward these matters, and respect them. But our law says that one 'darker than dusk' is automatically a free man."

"A weak law," sniffed the Zulu.

"But the law, nonetheless."

"Such half-breeds generally do not mix in polite society. They head to the frontiers." He clucked derisively. "An exception is the effeminates of New Alexandria. They revel in their mixed blood as they do their sexual perversions—as if they think that their taint places them above either black or white."

He paused a moment. Then, with a surprisingly teasing tone said, "What think *you*, Kai?"

Kai kept his most immediate thoughts strictly to himself. Did Nandi know the truth about Shaka's death? If so, then what was the actual intent here?

Damn it! Kai felt as if he had drained a cask of hemp beer! There were entirely too many mixed emotions involved. His relationship with Lamiya was loving and intense, but memories of Nandi were enough to boil his blood. Kai could sense that, despite his intellectual rigor and physical vitality, in recent months lethargy had cloaked his spirit. The thought of Nandi, and the night she had initiated him into the curiously chaste ecstasy of *ukulobonga*, awakened him.

"I respect the ways of the Zulu," he said finally, "but Dar Kush is my home, the home where your daughter will soon be mistress. Our ways are different, and must be respected."

He held his breath as Cetshwayo seemed to build energy like a thunderhead. Then the giant pealed laughter. "Very good!" he said. "Any less manly an answer, and I fear that my precious *ntanami* would eat you alive."

He slapped Kai's back nearly hard enough to make him cough blood. Then the two men talked, drank tea, ate biscuits and preserved mussels, shared hookah, and talked until the very early morning.

And not for a moment did Kai allow his hand to stray far from the hilt of his *shamshir*.

CHAPTER FIFTEEN

ON RETURN TO HIS ROOMS, Kai was reluctant to make Fodjour privy to any of his speculations. "And what was their concern?" his neighbor asked.

"They want the marriage to go forward." He shrugged, yielding to the seemingly inevitable.

"Ah . . ." Fodjour scratched at his beard. "As your father intended. I suppose it would be a good thing. Yes?"

"I hate politics. Cetshwayo calls the New Alexandrians 'effeminate.' Doubtless he calls us 'barbaric.' He plays both ends against the middle."

Fodjour chuckled. "Would you do otherwise, were you he? He clearly respects your position, at least; otherwise he would never offer you his daughter."

His friend might as well have been listening in on the evening's conversation. "I suppose," Kai said. "I am tired. I will rest, and then . . . there is no end to these damned parties. Let me just close my eyes for a moment. Please."

Fodjour watched Kai, curious but allowing him his privacy.

And he could tell just from the sound of Kai's breathing that his friend was troubled indeed.

22 Ramadan A.H. 1294

(Sunday, September 30, 1877)

The following evening, an elegant delegate party was held at a private Radaman residence. Behind closed gates and doors, discussions raged in every corner. The major topic: If and when war came, would the south have any chance at all?

Governor Njau Pili, a soft little man of Kikuyu extraction, approached Kai. "Come, Kai. Take my arm." Kai knew him to be a man of pretentious bearing but impeccable blood.

"With pleasure, Governor," Kai said.

"Njau, please. Walk with me." The two of them strolled.

"What brings Your Excellence to this gathering this evening?" Kai asked.

"Would not the promise of music and companionship be enough?"

"Your Excellence is far reputed for his own parties. Certainly your meanest would beggar our poor gathering."

Pili laughed. "You give me too much credit. This is a fine feast."

"Still, I think there is a purpose."

The Governor's small eyes twinkled. "How sharp you are! Delightful. Tell me, Kai, how do you find the responsibilities of office?"

I flip over a flat rock, and there they are. "May I speak freely?"

"I would expect nothing less."

"I do not enjoy them," said Kai. "I do not know how men such as yourself manage to swim in such waters and keep your robes clean."

"Family secrets, Kai. Family secrets." His laugh was not entirely convincing, as if he wondered if Kai had delivered a subtle insult.

"Why do you ask?"

They had strolled as far as the gardens. The Governor bent to sniff a flower. "Do you know this blossom?"

"Abyssinian lotus. It grows in the Diredawa Valley."

"Very good! You are a young man of culture and breeding, as well as a war hero. . . ."

"Some would consider that assessment entirely too lenient."

"Not to your face, and that is all that matters."

"So?"

"I believe that you could go far, young Wakil. Why limit your ambitions to a provincial little parish, a few thousand scratch farmers—"

"Fifty thousand," Kai corrected.

"That may seem like the whole world to you now, but it is nothing. The capital needs men like you."

"Radama?"

"New Alexandria."

Interesting. "Ah. New Alexandria. Well. If you speak of the Grand Senate, then you must hold the possibility of war in low regard."

"If I did not, would I have invited Admiral bin Jeffar to address our assembly? Men talk and talk of fighting, but when it comes down to it? We would rather tend our gardens, and enjoy the fruits of commerce and statesmanship."

"I have heard that said."

"Kai," the Governor said. "You are of a great bloodline, and in marrying the Empress's niece have secured for yourself international stature. It need not end here."

Ah, Father. Where are you when I need you? "No?"

"No. If . . . *when* the Continental unpleasantness is concluded—"

"And what do you think the conflict's outcome will be?"

"It matters not to me. There are always wars, and after them come the arbiters with armloads of scrolls and Alexanders for eyes."

"And do you see us in this conflict?"

The Governor leaned close. "Not if we are clever. This union, this Bilalistan, was made by men, and can be unmade the same way."

That was a surprise. "You suggest dissolution?"

"Secession. Of Wichita, Djibouti—and southern New Alexandria."

Kai inhaled sharply. There, the words had finally been spoken, and by a man with the power to see it through. "And you think that the Caliph would merely stand by and see this happen?"

The little man's shoulders drew back. "I think he has no taste to war against his own—he may lose a state, but gain a trading partner. He is, at his core, a merchant."

"You underestimate him."

Pili smiled indulgently. "Kai, you are inexperienced in these matters. I wish that your father had lived, that I might have conducted this conversation with him. I hope you will accept my mentorship." He extended his palm. "Take my hand, Kai. Say that the wealth and status of Dar Kush supports me in this matter, and I promise that you will never regret it."

Kai looked at the Governor's hand for a long while before he spoke. "You would have me tell my people that we will leave the union, and nothing will come of it? That war would rage in the Old World, without spilling over onto the New? That our sons will not bleed, nor our wives and daughters weep? I can take your hand in friendship, and gladly do. But I cannot accept that grasp if you would have me lower my sword." Kai raised his hand. "In what spirit do we clasp, Governor?"

Pili lowered his hand. Anger danced in the darkness of his eyes. "You have made a mistake," he said coldly. "Great things are afoot, young Wakil. I do not extend my hand again to be rebuffed. When you have seen the error of your ways, come to me humbly, and in remembrance of your father, you may still find me a friend."

Kai strove to change the subject. He weighed his options and decided to take a risk. "Governor. You have heard rumors of . . . certain scrolls?"

He sniffed. "The Alexandrian scrolls? Supposedly stolen from one of the Pharaoh's ships? A myth."

"I believe they are no myth," Kai said. "I believe further that they came on the market recently, and may have been acquired."

Pili raised his eyebrows. "And they say . . . ?"

Kai sighed. "As yet unknown. The code has not been broken."

"Coded scrolls. Privateers. Secret meetings. This is the stuff of yellow-sheets, not diplomacy."

Kai bored in. "Why coded, unless to conceal intent? What intent more grievous now than to conscript our sons into battle?"

"Oh, now you possess a crystal ball?"

"Already," Kai pressed on, "the Caliph's ships blockade the Brown Nile."

"Nonsense. The Aztecs threaten our plantations in the southern hemisphere. Ships mass for attack."

Kai tried again. "Warships are at anchor in our own harbor. Storm clouds gather, sir."

The Governor was scornful. "The Caliph has personally guaranteed a peaceful intent."

"If we do not prepare, Governor, we will be caught unawares."

Pili's eyes narrowed. "You would have me stir my nobles to alarm, to . . . to *treason*, to raise their levies to equip an army we need not, a navy we need not, on the strength of a phantom scroll? You know less of the world than I thought, young Wakil. Perhaps I am mistaken about you. Perhaps you are not the man I had hoped."

"Don't you take the Empress's part in these matters?"

His chest puffed out indignantly. "You dare question my loyalty?"

"Neither loyalty nor lineage. Sir, she will call you. Call *us*. We must be swift to the mark."

For a moment they held each other's gaze. Then an assistant appeared. "Governor Pili! The reception awaits you."

Kai bowed. "Governor."

"Excuse me," the little man said coldly, and walked away.

When Kai rejoined the party, the same discussions were in the air.

"The most important question is," said one guest, "if war came, how many weeks would it take to beat the northerners back?"

"The Egyptians have no taste for war," proclaimed another. "They are dominated by their women, are too decadent and soft even to properly control their slaves."

Another added, "I have heard northerners speak of emancipation."

"Easy talk," said the second. "Easy talk. They made their money *selling* slaves, knowing we build our economy on their pale shoulders. Now they want to preach morality, knowing it would cost them nothing. Feh!"

"The Prophet hated slavery," Kai offered.

"But did not *forbid* it. His soul communed with the Almighty, but his feet trod the same dust as common men. A majority of our wealth is tied up in slaves and the crops they are needed to work."

"Still," said another guest. "As slavery vanishes from North and South Africa, there is pressure for Bilalistan to move in the same direction."

The first guest snorted. "How the northerners agonize over the order of the universe! I've heard of men who voluntarily sell themselves into bondage, so that their masters can buy them and then set them free, thereby gaining favor with Allah."

They laughed heartily, one tall bluff fellow loudest of all. "Truth," he crowed. "I heard of one such who did this a dozen times before his last master sold him again to a rice farmer in New Djibouti."

"Akmed," said the man closest, "do you not have a rice farm in Djibouti?"

The tall one laughed. "Indeed. He works there in the paddies still, and claims he has a fortune in an Alexandrian bank!"

"Surely he would ransom himself . . . ," said the first.

"I have no need for his money." Akmed laughed. "It is amusing to have an arrogant pigbelly slogging through the muck. He rants and barks at the moon."

Several of the men enjoyed a good laugh, and then to Kai's relief they settled back to political subjects.

"If it comes to a vote," Akmed offered, "the north can control enough seats to force a change in the colonial accords."

"Long before that happens," another guest concluded, "we would leave."

Kai nodded vague agreement and moved on to another conversation. He found it swiftly.

"If our country remains whole," said a fourth guest, "make no mistake: our sons will fight on Abyssinian soil, against the Empress."

"That would never happen," a fifth offered. "My family traces its bloodline back as far as bin Jeffar's but in the service of the Immortal one. I would rather have blood in the streets and be done with it. Captain!" he said, recognizing Kai. "What do you say?"

Kai smiled. "I say these are dangerous times. My father wanted to keep our economy and armed forces whole."

"Easier said than done, I think," said the fifth. "And your view of emancipation?" At this question, several new faces turned toward him.

Kai weighed his words carefully before answering. "I would think my possession of three hundred slaves speaks for itself."

With relief, he noted that Babatunde had entered the room, resplendent in his varicolored, striped robes. He excused himself and fled to his teacher's side. "I was not prepared for this," he whispered.

"In many ways, your father shielded you," Babatunde said. "Ali was prepared, but not young Kai. Allah has a sense of humor."

"A pale one. They think me a bumpkin."

"You are."

Kai looked stricken.

Babatunde plucked a sweet from a passing silver tray. "A dear, clever bumpkin."

Together they strolled until they reached the edge of another group, where a speaker of Kai's age addressed a cluster of avid listeners. "The north has a much larger navy than the south," he lectured. "If New Alexandria blockades Djibouti Harbor, they could strangle our economy."

"They wouldn't dare, Kaleb! It would mean war!"

The speaker, a slender young man with shaven head and a hawk's eyes, seemed to warm to his subject. "Already, the Pharaoh has promised reinforcements for a raid on the Aztecs. His entire western fleet is headed our way."

"You are saying that those ships are a threat to us?"

"I am saying they are a demonstration. A demonstration of Egyptian force."

"The Empress's navy is stronger than the Pharaoh's," said another guest. "We could appeal to her for help!"

"But if they have more factories, more manpower . . . ," said a third, older man, "if their alliance with the Pharaoh proves greater than ours with the Empress—what then?"

Kai chose this moment to speak. "We have a fighter's chance—if courage does not fail."

The hubbub quieted, and they turned to look at him.

"The young Wakil," Kaleb said quietly.

"There is more to war than numbers," Kai said urgently. "There is also heart—and mind."

"I am sure that the Shrine of the Fathers taught you much, Sidi."

Another guest whispered loudly enough to be heard. "But we may wish to leave some of our institutions intact."

There was muffled laughter, and sharp glances. Kai ignored both. "It is my belief that we are at the end of the time when swords or even rifles decide wars. In New Alexandria one can find the beginning of a new era in human history—the time of the machine."

"The machine?"

"Some of these devices will be tools of war," Kai said, warming to his subject. "And the first to make use of them will control that new world—and their fate within it."

"What kind of machine?"

"You know that the Senate supports the work of Maputo Kokossa."

"A madman!" Kaleb said.

"But a brilliant madman," said another with awe.

"Brilliant, yes; mad, no," said Kai. "He has developed designs for advanced cannon, for ironclad warships, and even for a submersible."

"Submersible? It swims like a fish?"

"In a manner of speaking."

"And how would such a vehicle display its colors?" There seemed general agreement on the question's validity.

Kai responded. "The purpose of a submersible would be to compensate for an unfair numerical advantage, reinforced by secret treaties and—" He stopped himself, loath to tip his hand about the existence of the scrolls. Instead, he raised his voice. "Southerners!" He sharpened his voice, drawing attention from some of the other attendants. "Be not deceived: the north holds a terrible advantage over us in industrial capacity. Our strength is our freedom of spirit, the heights to which noble blood might spur the mind, that we might see farther into the future than those of more mundane inclination. Should we not use it?"

Kaleb jutted his chin, and Kai suddenly remembered comments he had heard about this one: Kaleb was a duelist, a quarreler, of wealthy family and questionable appetites. "Are you quite sure that there is no other motivation?"

"Excuse me, Sidi?" Kai asked, choosing to dissemble a bit. "Do I know you?"

The man bowed deeply. "Kaleb al-Makur, at your service."

"And your question?"

"Sidi," Kaleb said gravely, "the display of colors is an accepted part of civilized warfare, ensuring that civilian vessels are not fired upon. A military gentleman has certain duties, including the obligation to declare his affiliations."

A reasonable assertion, and one deserving an answer. "Was it cowardly when New Medina's patriots disguised themselves as Algonquin to rout the Northmen?"

The onlookers murmured in agreement.

"This may be truth in fact, but it was hardly a gentleman's conflict, sir."

"Still," insisted Kai, "it points to the need for unconventional tactics at unconventional moments in history."

Babatunde drew closer. "Wakil . . . perhaps that lesson on Setepenamen we spoke of?"

Kai brightened at his friend and tutor's words. More and more guests drifted in their direction. Just behind them was a large pond, where bobbed several model ships: triremes, steam-screws, and dhows, painted in blue and red. Kai peeled a branch from a nearby mulberry bush, shucked its leaves, and divided the ships.

"Now watch," he said. "In the battle of Alexandria, the Romans had every reason to believe they could repel Hannibal aland and simultaneously win a battle at sea. Their navy was superior to Egypt's—or so they thought."

"They certainly regretted that estimation, Sidi," said Kaleb. "They were destroyed!"

"Yes. Abyssinia's eastern trading route had provided the necessary technology. Specifically, the Malay sail, which proved more maneuverable. But, Sidi . . ."

He pushed another ship forward. "Think what might have happened if the Romans had been able to move a ship into position without the Egyptian alarm rising, close enough for Greek Fire?"

Kaleb scoffed openly. "You are speaking of Maputo's 'submersible,' no doubt. Fire from beneath the water? Absurd!" His comment was generally accompanied by laughter and not-so-gentle mockery.

Refusing to rise to the provocation, Kai kept his voice and manner mild. "There are other ways. I have seen Kokossa's design for a mine at the tip of a lance, moved into position on the lead ship, to strike next to its powder magazine."

"Thereby blowing themselves to hell!" Kaleb yelled, striking the water with his riding crop, rocking the ships and sending a great gout into the air.

"Kokossa is a genius," another guest averred. "Not a man here doubts that. His variable gear made the steam dragon possible."

"And his experiments with electricity!" crowed another.

Kai leapt in, sensing the tide of opinion flowing in his favor. "I tell you that with genius such as this on our side, we need fear nothing."

"And I say that you are dreaming us into the grave!" said Kaleb.

Kai paused. There was something in the air that he had not sensed before: expectation. Men glanced from Kai to Kaleb alertly. Something had happened here, something of which he had insufficient knowledge. His nerves burned with warning.

Kaleb continued on, his posture clearly confrontational. "I say that your words are those of one who would strike from darkness in the name of honor. Who would destroy a mosque to save a few miserable doghairs."

Kai gnawed at his lip. He softened his gaze, as Malik had taught him long ago, until he could take in almost two hundred degrees of arc. Judging by their posture, these men had already allied themselves with Kaleb. This was an attempt to force a confrontation. A merely verbal confrontation? No. Kaleb fancied himself the finest sword in the south. Well, then . . . Kai was supposed to rise to the challenge and defend his honor. Instinct told him that this situation would swiftly spiral out of control, that no mere wounding would satisfy Kaleb. His adversary intended to kill or cripple him. If duties of office prevented Kai, then by social convention Fodjour would be allowed to duel in his stead. During that defense, he or his second would probably be slain. In either case Kai's Wakilhood would be damaged.

Would death come by fair means or foul? There were too many ways such a scenario might play out. Kai fought against the red tide of anger rising behind his eyes. *No, Uncle . . .*

He raised his palm in a placating gesture. "It is regrettable that you view my words in such a light. With your permission, gentlemen." And he backed away from the group.

"War hero," Kaleb said derisively as Kai left the field.

Babatunde studied his student as they retreated. "I am surprised that you take no offense," he said.

Kai grimaced. "Oh, I take offense. But I will not let such a man dictate my battlegrounds. He has a purpose. Let him reveal it. Are you disappointed?"

"Pleased, actually."

It seemed probable that Egypt and Abyssinia would war, then, largely over the status of European colonies, which had been divided up between African nations for hundreds of years, their resources looted and populations dominated.

Kai himself had read dozens of yellow-sheet novels as a youth. Lurid things: tales of fantastic adventure in the wilds of Europe. Black queens of primitive druid tribes, tales of gold and jewels. Mythical creatures lurking in the shadowed forests, worshipped by naked, painted cannibals.

All quite incredible, but stirring in a childish way. Some of his acquaintances had hunted in Germany. Some had even brought back light-paintings of themselves astride dead bears and wild bulls.

Seeking diversion, Kai wandered into the central garden. There, in a makeshift arena, the Caliph's champion was engaged in a demonstration match with a huge red-haired slave.

The champion was a battle-scarred, black-maned German. He was barrel-chested and grotesquely thick through the arms, with short powerful legs and heavily callused hands.

The German was said to have an unbroken winning streak—that for the last four years, the brute had kept the Caliph's gambling coffers full. His appearance in Radama was obviously an attempt to stimulate interest in wagers and competition.

Regardless of the daunting history, the guests laid their silver and gold down enthusiastically. Kai watched, distracted. The champion fought twice, with only five minutes' rest between victims. Both times he performed in precisely the same fashion. He balled his fists and waded into his hapless foe, hammering from all angles. There was a limit to what flesh could bear, and the German's blows simply conveyed force beyond that threshold. His opponent's efforts at defense crumbled before the onslaught.

"He punches as if swinging an axe," Kai said.

"It seems effective enough," a guest countered as the second man was hauled senseless from the sand.

"Against fools or trees, yes," Kai said, and turned away.

CHAPTER SIXTEEN

23 Ramadan A.H. 1294
(Monday, October 1, 1877)

THE TOWN NEAREST AIDAN'S crannog was called Salima, after a famed Sudanese oasis. If an oasis was a place of nourishment and comfort, Bilalistan's Salima did not deserve its name. It was a dusty, ugly place of clapboard, brick, and clay, home to perhaps eight hundred souls.

Every few days, Aidan brought his catch in for sale and trade. Many of the townsfolk shunned the whites entirely, and some others welcomed them with smiles and cheating hearts. Fortunately, a few were open to trade with any honest man regardless of his color, and for these Aidan was ever grateful. Akii-bua was one such, a mallet-fisted Kikuyu shopkeeper in his fifties who wore a patch over his left eye, souvenir of some youthful military adventure. "Hey, Irish," he said. *"Wasaamu Alakum."*

"Waalaykum salaam, Sidi."

The big man leaned over his counter. "And what have you for me today?"

"Fresh fish, and pelts," Aidan replied.

The shopkeeper rubbed his meaty hands together briskly. "Excellent."

Akii-bua examined the catch. Two other customers entered the little shop. They sneered openly at Aidan, but the Irishman kept his back straight and his face forward.

"I can give you cash," said Akii-bua. "Or credit."

"I'd prefer to take it half in cash, the rest on account." The storekeeper spat in his hand, and extended it to Aidan. Black and white palms pressed.

"Have you picked out the items?"

"Doing it now." Aidan cocked his head to the side. "Tell me, Akii-bua—some of the others in town won't deal with us. Why do you?"

The storekeeper grinned his gap-toothed grin. "It's business, and the first obligation of a good Muslim is to support his family."

"But you have no family," Aidan said.

"Not yet. But when I am rich," he crowed, "ah-hah!"

Aidan grinned and shouldered his bag. "Well, thank you. You're a good man."

The customers had retreated toward the back of the shop. Akii-bua noted this, and seized the opportunity to speak more seriously. "Be careful, Irish. As you've probably noticed, some of mine hate some of yours."

"Story of my life." Aidan grunted.

"I've been out to your village," the shopkeeper said. "What is that word you call it?"

"Crannog," Aidan said.

"Yes. Well, you work hard out there on your 'crannog.' Allah loves blisters. I guess slavery served you well, eh?"

Aidan managed not to flinch. "Some say."

"Well, you people are willing to do any honest task, work long hours. Some of the black folk hereabout don't work as hard, or as shrewdly . . . and frankly, aren't doing as well." He ran his fingers through his generous beard. "Jealousy is a worm that eats its own tail. You watch yourself, Irish."

Entering or exiting Salima from the south, one traversed its most elegant section, a double row of single-story brick buildings: stores, a tiny mosque, and a hotel. A coffeehouse served both liquid refreshment and hashish, with a back room in which men could find more fleshly comforts. Aidan knew that white women often earned extra coppers servicing townsmen in the darkness, but fought to keep the vile images from his mind. Salima also had posts for trading with the Ouachita, crowded with government agents and private land brokers feverishly swindling the natives out of their remaining land.

"I don't like this place." Donough sniffed the air.

"It's not so bad," Aidan said. "Seen worse."

"Where?"

"Little town I passed through with Kai, years back." He dug in his memory, trying to remember the name. What was it? *Addis Ababa.* That was it. A real piss-trench, filled with blustering blacks and beaten-down slaves.

"Smaller'n this?"

"No. Bigger. But nastier, I think."

"Ah," his companion said. "These folks'll get nasty enough, when it suits 'em."

There was painful truth to that. Already, Aidan could see the inevitable end of the conflict to come. As Bilalistan's population increased, the Ouachita and other natives would be driven off the continent, or perhaps into perpetual war in frosty Vineland with the vile Northmen. Or the natives might eventually join the Aztec Empire, which of course might lead to troubles for Bilalistan.

Once or twice Aidan had even seen strange-looking *yellow* men, said to be from the continent's west coast. Called *Chinese*, they were colonists from an empire as formidable as India's. The yellow men seemed to be moving east. The past had seen skirmishes between the empires, but ultimately there would be greater conflict there as well; he needed no seer or dream interpreter to guess the end of *that* clash. Inevitably, they would be crushed beneath Africa's heel, as the black men's ravening lust for land and power ground to splinters everything in its path.

Aidan and Donough were on their way back out of town when it happened. A haughty face-veiled black woman recoiled as Aidan brushed by her. "You dog-haired bastard!" she screamed. "You touched me!"

"I? No!" he protested, only belatedly grasping his danger and lowered his eyes. "But if by some mishap I touched the lady, I beg pardon."

The man accompanying her snarled. "Are you calling her a liar? Cheeky *muzawwar!*" He drew back his hand as if to strike.

Without thinking, Aidan slid to position a porch's wooden support beam between them. This potential disaster had to be defused at once. "I merely feel she is mistaken. I mean no harm."

A white-haired, street-sweeping bondsman sidled closer to whisper to him. "Sidi Aidan?" he said. "You don' talk back to black folks. Jus' 'pologize and back away, quiet-like."

Aidan seethed, but managed to bank the fires burning within him. He'd risked life and limb to be "free" and still had to lick his neighbor's black ass?! Still, survival warred with ego and won. "I apologize for any offense. Please forgive."

Despite his humble tone, the woman was not mollified. "Well, that's not enough!"

Some of the other men bristled and began to gather about. A rotund, muscular constable plodded up. "Here now! Here now! What's all this?"

The woman drew herself to full and formidable height. "Constable Oba. This *hinzr-batn* tried to tear my veil," she said.

"And who witnessed this?"

The men grumbled, but none of them stepped forward. "Well, now, I don't know, *hanam* Nunz . . . ," one of them began.

A searing look from the woman silenced him.

"My word is enough." Her tone left no room for question.

Holy shyte, Aidan thought, collar growing hot and moist. *Is this* gruagach *the banker's wife or something? I'm focked!*

The bulky Oba wasn't a bad sort. He had introduced himself the first time Aidan and his people had ventured into town, warning him against mischief. He was no white-lover, but the law was Oba's life, and Aidan had seen that he held it above all else. Oba studied the scene as if trying to re-construct what had happened. "*Armala-t* Nunz, I tell you what. You file a complaint, and we'll look into it. And as for you—" He turned to Aidan and dropped his voice. "I think you'd better get back to your village, Aidan. I know where to find you if I want you."

Aidan's anger gnawed at him. This wasn't fair, dammit. It was more than anyone had the right to ask him to bear. "But I didn't *do* anything."

Oba's eyes narrowed. "That remains to be determined. Take your leave, boy. While you can."

Despite his ire, Aidan and Donough took Oba's advice and retreated without further delay. The danger haunting Salima's streets was painfully real, fed, he thought, not merely by hatred and a sense of frustrated enti-tlement, but a terror that their former slaves might attempt to seek re-venge. The best defense was always an attack, keeping the freedmen off balance with continuous intimidation and accusation.

His massive friend kicked at the dirt as they walked beside their horse-drawn cart. "Swear I can't 'andle this no more. Some ways, it was better bein' a slave. At least then we knew where we was. Now, they say we're free, but still treat us like shyte. Where's the justice in that?"

Aidan sneered. "Don't look for justice in life, just leverage."

"What?"

"All we're lookin' for is a little piece of land, and a little peace."

"When I was chained," the giant said, "I knew proper that there wasn't nothing I could do. Now my hands are free, and they're itchin' to wrap those skinny black necks."

Aidan lost himself for a moment in pleasantly lethal speculation. "Why didn't you when you were a slave?"

For a long moment Donough was silent. Then: "Don't know. But during the mosque . . . all that fightin'. I guess maybe I really learned what killin' was about. Watched the shadows die, and what do you know? They cried and screamed and shyte themselves like any other men. Found out that killin' wasn't so hard, if you don't mind the nightmares."

"And you don't?"

Something dark and glittering surfaced in Donough's eyes. "Fact is, kind of like 'em," he said softly.

To that Aidan had no response. Donough didn't seem to notice the uncomfortable moment and went right back to his discourse. "An' one other thing."

"And what was that?"

"Not bein' afraid of dyin'. And once that don't twist yer tail, you don't let nobody push ye, nobody hurt ye."

Aidan smiled. *Well done, old friend.* "One day, they might discover it was a mistake to teach us to fight. They tried to hold back, but we could figure out what they didn't give us."

Donough hammered his fist against a tree trunk. Bark chipped. "Why don't we fight *now?* Ain't so many of 'em here."

"No. There aren't. But they have all the armies of the east at their command. If we fought against them we'd just attract soldiers, and more soldiers, and more, until we were crushed and dead—or slaves again. Do you want that?"

Donough hung his head, so angry he could hardly dare trust himself to speak. "Don't know how long I can hold onto it."

"The day will come," Aidan swore. "I'm sick of it meself. Fugitive slave gangs. Feh! Any 'belly can be grabbed, clapped in chains, and returned to masters who never owned 'im in the first place."

It was true. Whites could be pressed into service on labor gangs, patching roads or picking seasonal crops. Wakils earned more money for declaring a white a slave than for setting him free. Whites were not allowed to testify in their own defense, or against a black man.

Azanian Zulus sometimes traded in Salima as well, and they were even bigger arseholes than the Muslims. They strutted about as if every black heart pumped royal blood.

The day will come. The day will come. Aidan *had* to believe that. There simply had to be a way out of this trap. He could control his rage as long as he believed that there would be an ending, if not a reckoning. That his son Mahon might enjoy the same freedom and hope that he, Aidan, had taken for granted as a lad.

The day he ceased to believe that was the day he might go berserk.

He *had* to believe.

CHAPTER SEVENTEEN

24 Ramadan A.H. 1294
(Tuesday, October 2, 1877)

AFTER DAYS OF DEBATE AND DISCUSSION, New Alexandrian admiral bin Jeffar himself took the Round's central podium to answer questions from the assembled. His short white hair contrasted sharply with his unlined face. In the Egyptian custom, he wore a false white beard attached with a chin strap. He seemed at the same moment both old and young, both terribly wise and dangerous and somehow beseeching. It was easy for Kai to believe that this man hated the prospect of war, and was hoping for any honorable means of averting that possibility.

"It is said," began a Yoruban senator from Wichita, "that even now, communications speed between our capital and Egypt, with the intent of bringing Bilalistan into the coming war."

"An unfounded rumor!" bin Jeffar protested.

"And would you tell us if it were true, sir?" probed the senator, his twin manhood scars making his face as angular and confrontational as any fighting bird's.

Bin Jeffar gave a rueful sigh. "Any direct answer to that question leaves me vulnerable. Instead, I say that my record speaks for itself. Every man in this room knows my word is my bond."

"Making you," said the senator, "the Caliph's perfect agent."

"Please, please," said Kaleb, the representative from a non-Zulu section of southeastern Azania. "The Senator is correct—his record is impeccable. He would not have been invited here otherwise. There is another answer."

"And that is?" asked the first.

"That bin Jeffar does not know all that his masters plan." On the surface, Kaleb Al'Makur seemed the very voice of reason, but Kai did not miss the insulting use of the term *masters.* "After all, the Caliph might well feel that bin Jeffar's interests are not his own."

9

Zulu Heart

This comment drew an answering murmur of agreement from the assembled.

"Clever." Bin Jeffar stroked his faux beard. "Inviting me to salvage my reputation at the cost of my usefulness as a negotiator."

Kaleb then attempted a more soothing approach. "Is it not true that the Caliph would lose power if Bilalistan severed ties? Between the two of you, who welcomes independence the more?"

"And what form of independence?" cried another. "I have heard talk of abolishing the aristocracy."

"And replacing it with what? Democracy? Bah!" Kaleb sneered. "The peasants are a lazy, uneducated rabble. My ancestors did not establish this land to hand it over to the commoners! The Greeks tried that nonsense, and look what happened to them! The only decent civilization Europe ever spawned, dead and done!"

Bin Jeffar attempted to be conciliatory. "Now, now—whatever the future brings for our good land, Senator, I assure you that your ancestors' contributions will never be forgotten. But at the same time, this 'common man' that you speak of does most of the working and fighting and dying in Bilalistan. If his voice is not heard, you may believe he will find another way to express his will."

A low angry rumble answered bin Jeffar's suggestion.

The Caliphate had similarities to the office of Wakil: both were initially appointed; both could be inherited by descendants, assuming appropriate service had been rendered. The Caliph would certainly use any and all means to hold onto his position, not merely for his own sake, but for the sake of generations to come. He would certainly lose power if Bilalistan severed its ties to Egypt. Such a precariously placed politician might very well fear the wave of democratic thought. Kai thought it odd that the Yoruban Senator did not raise his voice in defense of the concept: his people had profitably experimented with democratic principles for a thousand years.

"And the young Djiboutan Wakil?" asked the first senator. Heads turned toward Kai, who sat in the Round's first row with fellow landowner Fodjour Berhar. Perhaps, just perhaps, the Yorubans were waiting to see how much support Kai could rally before committing themselves.

"I say that honorable peace is preferable to war," said Kai, choosing each word with care. "But that peace should not merely reference a possible war in mother Africa. It must relate also to our Alexandrian brothers."

Kaleb was swift to the attack. "Woman's talk," he said. "The Egyptians must learn that the south fears neither lead nor steel. They have no taste for honorable war, and would fold their tents within a fortnight. But this would require courage that some of our honored representatives seem to lack."

For the second time in twenty-four hours, the theme of cowardice had arisen. Abu Ali would wish his son to be cautious indeed.

Kai regarded him carefully. "I cannot control how the honorable gentleman interprets my words. I have bled for our country and our faith, and would again if summoned. Nonetheless, I would labor at almost any price to save my fellows from the lessons I learned in that process."

"Yes," said Kaleb scornfully. "You learned how to obliterate mosques!"

That withering witticism triggered another rumble among the nobles.

"Kai," rasped Fodjour. Already, he had clasped his hand to his sword. "You cannot allow such a statement to go unchallenged."

"Even if offensive," Kai whispered, "it is truth. This is no time for pride to lead to violence." Despite the soft words, Kai's blood boiled, and his heart hammered in his chest.

"Then I will." Fodjour began to stand.

Kai grasped his friend's arm, holding him in place. "No. Kaleb is one of the finest swordsmen in the south."

Fodjour's hand tightened upon the hilt, but he sank back into his seat. "You think I cannot match him?" Fodjour's lips were tightly pursed.

"It is not a matter of wins and losses," Kai whispered. "We need both your swords."

Kai bowed to the assembled and raised his voice. "I apologize if my presence offends," he said. "Perhaps it is time I retire for the evening." Kai and Fodjour left the Round, amid murmurings and protests both from those who had sought to hear his counsel, and those who wished blood on Kaleb's sword.

Barely had they exited into the hall when Fodjour exploded with anger. "I can understand why you, as Wakil, might hesitate to bloody your blade in duel. But to deny your friend the chance to strike blows in defense of your honor—this I do *not* comprehend."

"Fodjour—"

"Unless," he said, more slowly now, "in truth, I am not the one you love most dearly."

An uncomfortable pause followed that remark, as Kai searched for some palliative word. "Kaleb wants war, knowing that in such a cauldron rapid advancement is possible, and fortunes shift mightily. His father Uthman

Al'Makur imports iron from Vineland—and would grow fat on the blood of soldiers."

Fodjour didn't seem to hear him. "Tell me, Kai," he said. "Would you have let Aidan strike in your defense?"

And there it was, the wound that had bled life from their friendship for a decade. Kai did not, could not, meet his eye. "No. Your arm might match Kaleb's. Aidan would have been slain at once."

Kai's answer, optimistic as it had been, did nothing to dampen Fodjour's ire. "But if Allah had seen fit to combine my arm and his heart, what then?"

Why was Fodjour so upset? He should have been relieved that he was not required to match swords with Kaleb . . . unless of course he was relieved, and ashamed of that relief. And was hiding that shame behind a mask of anger. Kai looked at the ground, searching for words, but it was already too late.

"You have answered me already," Fodjour said, and stalked away.

Kai called after him. "Fodjour!"

His boyhood friend stood still. Then, without looking back over his shoulder, he said, "I will take in the night for a time." He laughed bitterly. "Fear not! Even if the fog devours me, you will have lost little of value."

CHAPTER EIGHTEEN

25 Ramadan A.H. 1294
(Wednesday, October 3, 1877)

THERE WAS TALK AND TALK in the Senate chambers, but unlike a formal session, here no vote was called, and there was nothing to transform heated speech into rash action. When most had spoken their mind, the session was dispersed. Some went to late dinners or other diversions. Others broke into small groups to continue discussions.

In one of the local hotels, less luxurious but more private than that housing Kai and his entourage, Kaleb son of Uthman Al'Makur held council with his sword master, !Ting.

"Damn him!" the younger man snarled. "I thought certain that I could force a clash."

His Xhosa sword teacher laughed. "He has better sense than to test your blade, young sir. He knows your father, and knows my teaching. Whatever he was able to absorb from Malik before murdering him could be no match for you."

Kaleb drew, slashed the air with his blade, and returned it to his scabbard all in one flawless motion. "Tell me, !Ting. Some say the Wakil was Malik's best student. What then?"

The big man was thoughtful. "Dar Kush's art is great indeed, but a frontier art, no match for the Royal House. My fathers plied their craft teaching the way of steel to Caliphs and the Pharaoh's guard, and are the finest in the world."

"So what would have occurred?"

"Death. As we will see tonight."

Kaleb seemed to shrink. He heard the intent behind the words, and even one possessed of his own lofty ambitions quailed at the thought. "You would dare?"

"I dare. I, and my son."

A short, solid, very dark young man stood from his couch. His wrist flickered. A sword's deadly stalk sprouted in his hand.

"If the young Wakil will not fight for honor," said !Ting, "then he will fight for his life instead. *Ndiyavuya ukudibana nawe* . . . pardon. I do not understand how such a coward could have slain Malik."

"And if he will not fight when challenged directly?"

!Ting's black eyes gleamed. "Then it is best you be seen in a public place this evening."

Kaleb's own eyes widened. Hurriedly, he wrapped his cloak around his shoulders. "I . . . believe that Radama has an excellent brothel. I feel a sudden need to bury my cares in flesh."

"As have I," !Ting said. "We both have pinking to perform. I daresay mine will be the more pleasurable."

Shivering, now fearful of what his ambitions had placed in motion, Kaleb said *"Ulale kakuhle,"* one of the twelve Xhosa phrases at his command, and left the room.

How Elenya would enjoy that dress, Kai thought, peering through a clothier's front window. How many shops were available here, and how delightful it would be to plan a shopping trip, with all of his ladies: Lamiya, Elenya, Azinza, and Aliyah, all together to enjoy the town.

Buoyed by such happy thoughts, Kai walked the streets of Radama. Despite his years of study, his wealth, or his protestations to Babatunde, in many ways he really was a country bumpkin, one who immensely enjoyed the challenge of a new and vibrant city. He needed to clear his mind. There was much going on for which he had no instinctive understanding, and in the jungle of politics, the instinct to rend or aid, to ally and deceive, ruled all.

He turned into an alley and found his way impeded by two men, both broader and thicker than he, one half a cubit taller. They stood in postures of martial challenge. Kai felt no fear, only a cool inevitability. Politics was strange to him. This, on the other hand, was utterly familiar, and he breathed a fervent curse that these two fools had given the most feared part of himself an excuse to walk the night. His father the peacemaker receded from his heart, and in his place strode forth Malik, lord of war.

Kai stepped sideways, still sufficiently in control to attempt an avoidance of hostilities. They bracketed him.

"I am !Ting," said the larger man. "Sword master to Kaleb al-Makur. And this is my son."

The younger threw his own cloak to the side. "I am Xsiam."

"What do you want?" Kai asked. *Strange,* he thought. *Those words were spoken in a deeper, fuller voice than my own.*

!Ting bared his teeth. They were black-stained, perhaps from the chewing of betel nut. "Are you a fool, to ask such a question? *Ndiyavuya ukudibana nawe,* Wakil." *It is good to finally meet you, Wakil.*

Kai thought to try more words, to cajole or to bribe, but already it was too late. That *thing* inside him was alive, and loose in the night, and it was pleased. He felt the corners of his mouth pull upwards into a cold smile. Malik's smile.

For just an instant !Ting was taken aback, as if Kai's response had been different from that expected, both in words and posture. But expected or not, things had gone too far, and the two swordsmen moved forward, steel in hand.

Kai swept his cloak back with his left hand and drew his *shamshir* with his right. Despite their life of experience, neither of the Xhosa could have anticipated what next occurred, nor did they have time to adjust either thought or action.

In a blur of sword feints and low sweeps, Kai floated so quickly from one position to the other that father and son were marginally hesitant in response, fearful of striking one another. The night was shadow and steel, grunts of effort, soft sliding footsteps and the sound of pierced flesh, and then . . . silence.

The younger swordsman lay facedown in his own blood. For a moment !Ting's son braced his arms as if trying to perform a push-up, trembling with the effort to rise and rejoin the fray. He spasmed and relaxed into death.

The elder Xhosa sank back against the wall, dimming eyes wide. "Where . . . did you learn that technique?" He coughed. Blood dribbled from his lower lip, staining his beard. "That is not Dar Kush!"

Kai said nothing. He merely stood with shamshir at the ready, watching dispassionately, as if calculating how much blood a man had to lose before collapse.

"*Ndilahlekile.*" *I am lost.* "We were wrong about you," !Ting gasped. "You are not a coward. You are a devil."

"A small one," Kai granted. The corners of his mouth lifted, exposing teeth. "Salute the greater, in hell." And he swung his sword in a great, scything arc.

Joi, owner and manager of the Odalisque, was a middle-aged gentleman of Fulani extraction. He hunched over his desk, documenting the evening's financial gain. Business was good: an informal Senate was in session, and such a congregation of respectable men invariably filled the coffers of brothels and hashish dens to overflowing.

The Fulani were a pastoral West African folk who often formed insular religious communities if forced into the cities. Doubtless if his grandmother knew his current activities, she would tear her hair and wail. But men had physical as well as spiritual appetites, and what was the harm in providing a clean, respectable establishment wherein such hungers might be slaked?

The crackle of breaking glass in the foyer pulled Joi's attention from his self-congratulatory thoughts. Feeling more curiosity than concern, Joi climbed from behind his desk, thinking that perhaps a clutch of rowdy senators and statesmen had invaded his place of business.

The Fulani did not recognize the handsome young man who stormed in. Judging by his garments, he knew the invader to be wealthy. A blood-stained leather sack swung at his belt, large enough to hold a dead cat, perhaps, or . . .

"Kaleb!" the newcomer screamed. "Where are you?"

Joi waved his hand nervously at a eunuch, who tried to halt the intruder. The guard took an evil-looking punch to the stomach and sank gagging to the ground. A second eunuch, this one a massive shaven-headed Roman, attacked the intruder next: a house guard was one of the few whites who could lay hands upon an African, but the sight remained jarring. The young noble seemed not even to move: their figures merged for a moment, and the eunuch smashed into the wall. Joi was thunderstruck. He had paid good Alexanders for the pair, and had seen them clear the room of a half dozen men. What the hell was *this?*

"Kaleb!" the invader cried. He turned and locked eyes with Joi, and the Fulani quailed. The man was younger than Joi had initially thought: perhaps twenty-two or -three. Clean-shaven and slender, Joi might almost have thought him effeminate. At this moment, gazing into the fire blazing in those brown eyes, the invader seemed both more and less than human.

The owner pointed a single quivering finger upstairs. The intruder stalked up the stairs, disappearing from sight. A muffled shout. Joi watched, aghast, as the last of his guards tumbled bonelessly down the steps, coming to rest at the bottom as devoid of consciousness as any opium smoker in the Odalisque's back room.

Kai slammed open two doors before finding the man he sought. He stormed into the third room in time to see Kaleb withdraw his glistening member from a small, thin Greek girl-child, black hair flagging her shoulders, her breasts still but promising buds on her narrow chest. "W-what is this?" Kaleb stammered.

" 'Are you mad, to ask such a question?' " And with those borrowed words Kai tossed the bloody sack onto the floor. It bounced across the room before rolling to a halt just digits away from the curtained bed. "I found it in the gutter."

Kaleb eyed his sword, just within arm's reach.

"At your service," said Kai, then added, "if you survive this night, I suggest replacing your manservant, who sold me your location for a silver."

For a few seconds Kaleb sought to hold Kai's gaze defiantly, but at last was forced to look away.

Kai studied the girl, who sat staring at him. No shame, no embarrassment. No feeling at all. Her olive skin gleamed with oil. The mingled scents of perfume and sex soured the air.

"How old are you, child?" he asked.

"Thirteen," she murmured, eyes wide and staring. A baby.

He turned back to Kaleb. "You will leave this place, this city, pederast. Tell those who would rush to war that the House of Kush will not kneel to such as you."

He tried to keep his attention on Kaleb, but his eyes flickered back to the nude girl. Her eyes were darker brown than those of most ghosts. He wondered if there wasn't some African blood in her. She stared at him, unblinking. A kind of feral awareness smoldered deep within her eyes. She saw him. Knew who and what he was: just another man who would pay to use her and throw her aside.

Kai's sword flickered. Blood erupted from Kaleb's nose, gushing down the young man's cheeks and over his lips. Kaleb made a wet squealing sound, covering his spurting, sliced nostrils with one hand while he gripped the covers with the other.

"If ever I see what remains of your face, I take the rest of it."

Two new guards appeared at the door, swords in hand. Stern and challenging at first, they quailed at the sight before them. Joi appeared behind them, peeking past their shoulders.

"Sir!" said one. "What is the meaning of this?"

"This man sought to murder me. My business here is concluded," Kai said. His shamshir disappeared into its scabbard. He took a step away. Turned to leave, but found another painfully vivid image of the girl, passively accepting Kaleb's ravishment.

And tomorrow there would be another Kaleb. Or later tonight. And every day, for the rest of her childhood. Until she was a haggard young crone, with little resemblance to anything that had ever been human.

When did you become the champion of hapless ghost? Malik laughed. *You can't save them all.*

No, Abu Ali said. *But you can save this one.*

He glanced again at the girl, who was unable to meet his gaze. "What is her name?"

"Tata," said Joi.

"And her price?"

Seeing money, the owner abandoned thoughts of vengeance. "Two silvers—"

Now she leered up at Kai, a faux-seductive grimace on her painted face. "No," he said sharply, turning away from the child. "Her *price*."

"Sir," the owner said. "I would expect to earn . . . over the course of her career . . ."

Career? Allah preserve him. Before his marriage he had used pleasure slaves, but they were always *women*, not mere children. Always, he had felt that they enjoyed their . . . duties. Hadn't they? "What did you pay for her?"

"A half-Alexander, sir!"

"You lie," said Kai. A typical male slave could be purchased for a half. A child usually sold for a quarter. "Half that, I think. But no matter: Here is a half." He threw the owner a thin gold rectangle. "She is mine." He scribbled a note on a piece of cardboard and handed it to the proprietor. "Deliver her to my hotel within the hour, or I will be back." He closed his eyes, forcing himself to relax. Then he turned to Tata and in a softer voice said, "I mean you no harm."

She looked away from him, little body shaking uncontrollably. For some reason that he couldn't fathom, he noted that her shoulder was freckled.

Then, trembling with rage and some other emotion he could not name, Kai turned and left.

CHAPTER NINETEEN

26 Ramadan A.H. 1294
(Thursday, October 4, 1877)

FODJOUR PACED A TROUGH in the deck during the following day's trip south along the Brown Nile. Babatunde seemed more concerned with the hazards of river travel than the possibility of reprisals. Of the three of them, Kai seemed most detached, a man devoid of emotion, staring out over the shallow waves without apparent pleasure, anticipation, or fear.

"They say Kaleb's sword master and his son were slain last night," Fodjour ventured.

"Bandits, no doubt," answered Kai. He had not slept. His veins still burned with the previous evening's fire. What had begun as righteous anger and then flared to bloodlust had cooled to a more manageable, but less definable quality. As if he were a machine that burned blood.

He had thought he had made his peace with slavery, with the institution that had built his family's fortune. After all, the servants of Dar Kush were well fed and decently housed, they were allowed their culture and even religious festivals. No overseer touched a white woman without risking dismissal and the lash. And Kai felt that he had done his part.

But . . . what difference did the conditions of Dar Kush make, when it was absolutely inevitable that children like Tata would become the playthings of men like Kaleb? That slaves seeking freedom would endure torture and suffer death? In supporting the institution, was he not giving tacit approval for such murderous abuse? And what would he say of these things when, one terrible day, he stood before Allah Himself and attempted to justify his life?

"There is much danger about these days," said Babatunde, at their sides. "The same death that came for them might well come for you, young Kai."

The water stared back at Kai without expression or comment. "I think I might prefer death to life," he said. "An hashassin would be doing me a favor."

Tata huddled against the rail, watching her three strange benefactors with the eyes of a small, wounded animal. Kai studied at her without expression.

"Sah," she said. "Will you be wantin' me tonight?"

"Not tonight," he said, not looking at her. "Not any night. You will work on my estate. It is hard work."

She reached out with one pale soft hand, and stroked his. "I don't know things like that," she said in voice nauseatingly younger than her years. "But I can make you happy."

He grabbed her shoulders, trying to think of something to say. Her eyes regarded him blankly, as if she were sedated. To Fodjour he said, "Take her below. See she's fed."

His friend nodded. Kai leaned against the rail, watching the water pass beneath them.

Babatunde joined him. "There are many kinds of slaves."

"As there are many roles in life. They say it is all part of Allah's design." *Allah preserve me.* How many times had he heard his uncle speak those very words?

"How fortunate that Allah's design so carefully fits the needs of men like Kaleb."

"If another man had said that, I might accuse him of blasphemy."

"If another man had mouthed your words, I might have accused him of myopia." And then without another word Babatunde left his side.

Kai watched the river as it healed with the steam-screw's passing, and thought of the waters of the Songhai, so peaceful and deep, and the smiling dolphins frolicking within. They seemed more than a world away now. That had been another life, before blood money had changed hands, and while he could still imagine himself untouched by the corruption his father had tried so hard to keep from his younger son.

Three days later, Kai turned the girl over to Maeve, Ghost Town's eldest grandmother. "This is Tata," he said. "She has no one."

Maeve examined the girl closely, noting the swarthy skin and dark hair, she ventured, "one of your orphans, sidi?"

The siege at the Mosque of the fathers had merely begun the Aztec campaign. Thousands of men spent the next year beating them back, ultimately forcing the lords of Azteca into a fragile peace. The stream of corpses heading east from the frontier spawned a growing population of widows and orphans. Even at the beginning, Kai had known that would be the case.

So at his behest, the Lion's Blood trading company had funded two orphanages in Djibouti Harbor, with a total of four hundred beds. In addition to room and board, a stipend for each child guaranteed education and the acquisition of a suitable trade.

Every day around Dar Kush, fifty or so of these children could be seen, working with the Kikuyu and the herds, or even mending fences and engaged in other forms of common work.

So efficient were his eager young charges that acquisition of new slaves had dropped by sixty percent over those three years. Several of the orphans had shown an interest in studying the martial ways and had become students of staff and empty-handed combat. If they were of good family and carriage, a handful of them even spent a few hours a month waving wooden swords about.

But these children were all black. The white waifs were absorbed into Ghost Town's families. Maeve had made an understandable error in supposing that Tata might be a quarter black.

"No, she will stay here," he said simply. He was exhausted, had slept little for the past days, but felt a deep and gnawing compulsion to complete this business. "Find her lodging. Warn the men away from her. I want no messing. *Ever.* You understand?"

Maeve was bent but unbroken, an aged weaver who had given great service to Dar Kush and was now pensioned with her own plot of land and vegetable garden in Ghost Town. She nodded her gray head. "Yes, Master Kai."

She took Tata's unresisting hand. "Come, child," she said, and led her away. Kai felt a bit of his burden lift. Maeve would break Tata in carefully, finding her a home, seeing that her first week's duties were light. Doubtless she would learn where he had obtained Tata, but that would not work against the girl. Slaves had no choice of duties.

It was what made them slaves.

Kai slept for ten hours, and then began an effort to pick up the pieces of his home life. As always, he sought to stay above local and territorial politics while watching the circling vultures carefully.

He knew he had left a Radama abuzz with rumor and speculation: the dead, decapitated swordsmen in the alley, a disfigured young noble, a violent intrusion into a pleasure den. Such things were the stuff of legend.

And the worst part was: he hadn't intended to maim Kaleb. Hadn't wanted to. But !Ting's attempt on his life, and Tata's naked vulnerability still plagued him, and he knew that if Kaleb was in front of him today, *Ruh Riyâh* would run with blood.

What had been done . . . what *Kai* had done in that brothel could not be undone.

And both father and uncle were proud of him.

But the days passed, and no riders arrived at the gate, and the heliographs flashed not with demands that New Djibouti's youngest Wakil be brought to justice. In time, he began to relax.

As the days passed, Cetshwayo's words, and thoughts of Nandi remained with him. Why had she touched him so deeply? He had certainly been no virgin, and in truth she had not actually accepted him into her body. But there had been something both proud and yearning about the Zulu princess. There was danger here . . . but also opportunity.

The subject had to be broached with his First, and accordingly he finally approached Lamiya.

A true child of the Twin Thrones, she would understand. Lamiya had been raised from birth to know that she would likely share her husband with other wives: wives chosen for political or financial reasons, widows taken under protection, perhaps even fertile women chosen specifically to bear heirs.

On the other hand, Kai was obliged to consider her wishes in this most delicate of decisions. If she rejected the idea of Kai's marriage to Nandi, regardless of the stress it might cause with the Zulus, Kai was honor-bound to demur.

Lamiya did not know the full story of the tragedy at the mosque. All she needed to know was that there was political value in unity with the volatile Zulus.

Fingers folded carefully in her lap, Lamiya said, "Kai, in these matters you must be careful to observe all protocol and procedure."

"Agreed," he replied. "I wish I had a week to spend reading Zulu wedding-custom scrolls."

She smiled. "It's not as bad as that. In truth, your father had worked out all of the most important details years ago. Didn't you know that?"

"Well, yes . . ." His mind raced. Yes, it was almost certainly true that Abu Ali and Cetshwayo had filed initial wedding contracts when Kai was no more than seven or eight. No wonder his father had been impatient for him to cease his whoring and brawling! There had been a contract to fulfill, two lives to meld into a single shining destiny.

"Make your arrangements at once, Kai," she said. "The Zulus have waited three years. This meeting in Radama was the first chance Cetshwayo had to speak with you informally, without making his family vulnerable if your answer was negative. A face-to-face meeting was the only way to do this. Past hesitation can be forgiven. Failure to act swiftly now would be a grave insult indeed."

Kai thought back over her words and found them convincing. He found them also to be curiously devoid of inflection. Lamiya had weighed the pros and cons as if discussing the market price of teff. He thanked and left her, not certain whether to be relived or annoyed at her reaction.

Later, Lamiya took counsel with Babatunde. Her brothers and uncles were scattered about the world, and her father had died when she was twelve and away in Bilalistan. The little Sufi was the only male with whom she might have intimate discussions. "I know that I was raised to such a fate, but things have changed. . . ."

"Things always change, my dear."

Bitta, her shaven-headed Ibo bodyguard, smiled silently.

"They changed when I changed. When I bore Aliyah in my body, I grew selfish. I want everything for my child—all of his wealth and power, all of his love. To be forced to share that with a stranger . . ."

"Nandi is not a stranger," Babatunde reminded her.

"Yes. I met her, twice. Once when she was a child, and once again at the engagement party. But I do not *know* her."

He covered her hand with his. "In time you will."

"In time . . ." She seemed to ponder his words. "Still," she said finally, "it doesn't matter. This is my fate. I will make my peace, and find ways that the arrangement will be to my advantage."

Babatunde studied the girl he had virtually raised. "Why so cold?"

"I received a note from my eldest brother," she said.

"This is very good! How is Ghana?"

"He did not say. He said little, save that his family is healthy, and that the Empress's advisors tell her that by marrying Kai I have weakened the *feqer näfs* system."

"One might have hoped that that would not be true—you have, after all, married the Wakil, which is what the union to Ali was intended to accomplish."

"Yes, but the *feqer näfs* system rests upon the belief, deeply held by millions, that the Immortal Empress can see into the inner heart, and find a perfect soul mate. She is, of course, in the business of creating political unions: *but that is not the veil she draws across it.*"

"Ah," said Babatunde. "It is not the reality that is threatened, but the illusion which supports the reality." He shook his head. "I'm afraid that I must side with Kai on this: politics are a necessary insanity."

Lamiya smiled wanly. "So. If my aunt's advisors are to be believed, her daughters and nieces are no longer such untarnished gold, and I have been the agent of diminishment. I am, they say, a scandal."

Babatunde sighed. "Perhaps love ought not be bartered in such a manner."

"To be simultaneously so naive and so wise requires prodigious gifts." She was smiling as she said that, but it was not a happy smile.

"Hmmm," mused her tutor. "To think I once bounced you on my knee. Once again, wisdom's seeds have fallen on barren ground."

Lamiya bent her head. "I pray I have done the right thing. I have made such prayers countless times. And my brother hints—indirectly, of course, that the Empress wishes to reach out to me."

"If war truly comes, you may be of greater aid on this side of the ocean."

"I pray so," she replied. "I would like to see my mother again. My brothers and sisters. Save for a few short notes sent through intermediaries, they have turned their backs upon me."

"They had no choice."

"Perhaps," she said. "But still, part of my heart remains in Africa. That gives me less to offer my husband, and weakens our union."

Babatunde hesitated. "Do you love him?"

She paused as well before answering. "Can you love someone you do not understand? The heavens do not sing when I gaze into Kai's eyes, but he has a good heart, and I am happy in his arms. I wish to understand him. He has never spoken to me of what occurred at the mosque, and I long to know. I think something happened there, something that keeps his heart from me."

Interest flickered sharply in the tutor's eyes. "Something? For instance?"

"I know not. It is said that Malik killed too many men, and fell into the darkness. Perhaps that is all I sense, that Kai's sword sent too many men to hell, or Paradise. Perhaps Kai's own spirit is suspended between the two, unable to choose."

Her tutor bored in. "Two, yes. But not heaven and hell. It is Abu Ali and Malik who contest for Kai's soul."

"How will he save himself?"

"His heart. It may seem hidden now, but what if he truly offered it to you? All of it? Would you be strong enough to love him, weakness and all, when your heart does not sing for him now?"

She lowered her eyes. "Sometimes, it is easier for a woman to love when she senses a gap in the armor, a place where her softness might enter and comfort. At the beginning he needed me. Now . . . I just don't know." Her hands fluttered. "I think. I hope." A pause. "I hope."

She looked out the window. Below her in the lawn between Dar Kush and the public gardens, Kai was giving two-year-old Aliyah a riding lesson on her Zulu pony.

"I should have given him a son," she murmured.

"You are yet young," Babatunde replied.

CHAPTER TWENTY

2 Shawwal A.H. 1294
(Wednesday, October 10, 1877)

ALIYAH AND AZANIA TODDLING AT HIS SIDE, Kai walked with his daughters through the hall of ancestors, a passage connecting the first floor's main library with the central atrium. In much of the Muslim world, images of human beings and animals were discouraged: those of the Prophet and his family forbidden. But Fatimite Islam as practiced in Bilalistan had a fine tradition of graphic and statuary art.

Here in the hall were exquisite portraits of his mother, Kessie; his father and grandfather; his Uncle Malik and brother Ali.

"Who was that?" Azinza asked, pointing up at a woman's portrait seated next to that of Kai's father. Round-faced, with full smiling lips and bright eyes, although of Ethiopian blood she wore a Yoruba-style headwrap of gold cloth that perfectly crowned her face. The artisan had managed to imbue her with a sense of serenity and great vitality, so that the eye was powerfully drawn.

Kai never saw that painting without some shift in his mood. Today, thankfully, it lifted his spirits.

"Your grandmother," he said. "She died when I was a little boy, not much older than you."

"Beautiful," said the little girl.

"More than you know," Kai replied.

"What happened to her?"

It was the first time Azinza had asked a question about death. Instead of answering directly, he said, "She knew how the world began. Would you like to hear?"

"Yes," Azinza and Aliyah said at once, and Kai told them a story that he had heard from his mother. He had been only five when she died, and might have forgotten, but his nurse had recited it a hundred times, and told him that his mother herself had heard it from her own Kikuyu nurse. . . .

On the first day, God created the light. From the depths of this light, God created the souls of every person who would ever live. First, souls of the prophets were created, then the souls of holy men and women. After these, the Lord fashioned the souls of ordinary people. Angels, too, were woven of this light. Because their bodies are transparent, they contain only purity, and their only need or desire is to worship God and to help His children.

After the light, God created seven other great things: the Throne, the Canopy, the Book, the Pen, the Trumpet, Paradise, and Hellfire. The Canopy is like a tent above the Throne upon which God lives. The Book contains all the events that will ever take place. The Pen reaches from sky to earth and writes, day and night, the fate of all people. The Trumpet of the Last Day will announce the world's end and God's final judgment over all the souls He created. God then created Paradise, where good and obedient souls will live in eternal bliss. Finally, God created Hellfire, as a place for the wicked to repent their sins.

Beneath His Throne, God fashioned a giant tree, the Cedar of the End. On this tree's branches are millions of leaves, some fresh and green, others old and withered. God writes a name on each and every leaf. When he wills it, a leaf comes floating down, but before it reaches the earth, the Angel of Life reads the name on the leaf, and tells the Angel of Death who is ready to leave the earth.

At the end of the day, God created the Earth out of one ocean, and also the sun to rise above it. The warm sun made the mists rise up and form themselves into clouds that travel from one end of the sky to the other. Then God called the continents to rise out of the ocean. Next, he called the islands, and they rose up quietly in the midst of the foaming waves. God caused green vegetation to sprout. Trees formed forests, grasses decorated the hills, and palm trees waved along the seashore.

When God made the sun set in the west, He painted the sky red and gold. He filled the night sky with bright lights, which He called stars.

Next, God created animals in four classes: those that swim, whose king is the whale; those that creep, whose king is the python; those that fly, whose king is the eagle; and those that walk on four legs, whose king is the lion.

Four classes of creatures with intelligence were also created; angels woven of light; djinn or wind spirits woven of air; evil spirits woven of fire; and human beings woven of the earth.

All of the Lord's creatures are born, and so they all must die, for nothing will live forever except God.

"Nothing?" Azinza asked, her dear little face shining.

"Nothing," Kai said.

"Papa no go," Aliyah said, and held Kai's leg.

"Not for a long time," Kai said. "Not for a long, long time."

Kai wondered why had he told that particular story to the children. Certainly the idea of death would trouble them, would lead to painful discussions in the days and weeks ahead. Certainly, he might have waited until they were a bit older. But no, Kai had opened his mouth, and the story had emerged.

You heard that story as a babe. Knowing death makes you strong.

Did it?

After putting the children down for their naps, Kai went alone to the family graveyard northwest of the main house, as if in this place he could actually confer with the spirits of his dead father and mother, brother and uncle.

As in times past, once there he knelt against the cropped grass and bowed his head. After a few moments of silence, he spoke. "I have tried to keep true to the values you taught me," he said to his father's spirit. "To protect the wealth and power I have inherited. Men envy me, think that I came into this station cheaply. Some are callow enough to wonder if I rejoice in the deaths of those I hold most dear."

His voice shook; his fingers furrowed the earth. "But they do not know that I would abandon all of this, all the luxury and privilege, if I could but spend one more hour with any of you.

"Father. Your only failing was to think that we would have more time to spend together, that the time you spent with Ali to my exclusion would strengthen our house. How could you have known?"

He paused. The whispering wind stirred the trees behind him until they rustled like a restless audience. "Ali," he said. "You were my idol. You were best at everything—despite the single time I beat you at horses, or that Malik claimed I would one day surpass you at swords. Ever you extended your hand to me, like the stronger climber reaching out to the lesser. Gratefully, I took it."

Again he paused. "Malik. There is nothing for me to say. I draw breath today because you spared me. Men wonder if I know this truth. I know, more deeply than they ever could, that I am not worthy to *carry* your sword, let alone clash with it. You are within me, more deeply than anyone except Father. Please: help me be strong enough to channel your fire."

He turned to face the fourth of the simple granite headstones. "Mother. I am shamed to say that if not for your portrait, I would no longer remember your face. But still, your voice is with me, and always will be. That, and your touch."

Kai's eyes brimmed, spilled. "Why did you leave me so soon? In dying, you gave us Elenya, in whom we are justly proud. But if Allah had granted you more summers, perhaps I would have found a flaw in you. In your smile, your walk, the clarity of your mind. Without that flaw, how can any woman compare to you? And if none can, how can I ever open my heart as Father opened his? After you, there was no woman for him, nothing but the hope of a life swiftly and honorably passed, that he might hold you once again, in Paradise."

He waited, but the wind held no answer. "They say that those we love sometimes come to us in dreams, and speak to us of things unfinished. If you can, please do. Any of you. I need you. I feel so alone."

Overwhelmed with sorrow, he lowered his head to the ground, and there he remained for a time, his weariness of spirit and body more than he could bear.

Kai turned his head, blinked, and for a moment a familiar visage seemed to be standing before him. A muscular, bearded man of proud carriage, with a predator's piercing eyes. "Father?" so alike the brothers were! "No! Uncle! Is it you?"

Malik's full lips curled in anger. "Did I die for this?"

"What?"

"That you might weep like a virgin on her wedding night, regretting all that you have done, all that you have earned?" His scarred dark face radiated scorn.

"Earned? I earned nothing!"

"Save such talk! You deserve everything you have! Do you think you are a being alone, a tree without root or seed? No!" In Kai's ears, Malik's voice rolled like thunder. "My blood flows in you, as it once flowed over you. Your father's blood mingles with yours! And our father's, and back unto the beginning! If I had known you would wail so, perhaps I might have thought less of your life's value, and perhaps *I* would wear the title of Wakil, not a coward who kneels and begs the forgiveness of spirits." He came closer. "But then, you've always had a weakness for ghosts, haven't you?"

Kai recoiled. "Uncle," he pled. "Please . . ."

"You *killed* me, Kai!" his uncle roared in a voice that seemed to issue more from sky and earth than any mortal throat. "Shall it be said that Malik was slain by a weakling, or by a man great enough to carry his father's sword? Did your father and I die for nothing, or for the future of our blood and land? Tell me, now. At once!"

Now, at last, Kai was able to raise his head. "For . . . the future."

"Aye," said Malik, and nodded his head. Kai could see now: that head was not substantial. Trees bent in the wind behind that furrowed brow. "Weep no more. All that has happened is as it was intended. I am at peace, young Kai. You slew my body, but I live on, in you."

Malik began to retreat. "Uncle . . . don't leave."

Now at last the apparition smiled. "You have all you need, young Kai. Allah would not be so cruel. Your father gave you his seed, but you are *my* son. *I* live in you. Let other men trust their hearts." A pause, and then the thick lips curled in a smile. "You may trust your sword."

And with those words, Malik was gone.

And moments later, Kai awoke, alone in his bed, staring up into a ceiling barely dappled with the first soft glow of the new day.

CHAPTER TWENTY-ONE

Fragrant fir and spruce trees around the Ouachita crannog were chopped down, their stumps pulled so that their land expanded every week. When cleared, the land was seeded with mulch and cow dung until ready for planting. It was hard, honest work, and to his surprise Aidan found that he actually enjoyed it.

They had spent the morning digging and pulling, Aidan and Donough and some of the other men harnessing their horses to the stumps, cutting and hauling until the earth surrendered and the remnant ripped free of the ground.

The wood went into the walls, into the fire pits, into their boats and houses and sheds. On the land, they raised their crops. The arable land had increased threefold in their years there. In decades it might spread out so far a man could not walk its circumference in a day.

As they worked they sang old songs, timing their efforts to the happy sounds. They had just finished a story of King Roth's three sons, and were raising their voices to another song brought recently by a Scottish ex-slave.

> I will go as a wren in spring,
> With sorrow and sighing on silent wing,
> And I shall go in Our Lady's name,
> Aye, till I come home again. . . .

They all sang, exulting in the simple glorious effort and the strength of the sun beaming down on them. Every song sang and shared knit them more closely together, and it buoyed Aidan's heart to hear them, helped him to forget the problems in Salima.

He had not been to town since, and had allowed others to conduct trade for him. Upon return, their stories said that the mood in town was ugly, with fewer shopkeepers willing to trade. There had been more shoving and cursing, as if a slow thunderhead were assembling. But so far the constable had kept a lid on things, and he hoped that the energy would dissipate.

> *Then we shall follow as falcons gray,*
> *And hunt thee cruelly for our prey,*
> *And we shall go in the Good God's name,*
> *Aye, to fetch thee home again—*

And then he heard a scream.

Donough ceased his prying at the stump, his eyes growing huge as he spied what Aidan saw next:

A black-haired white man stumbling out of the woods, stripped to the waist, body crisscrossed with whip marks. His hands were lashed behind him.

Stavros, the Greek. Aidan was running toward him, as others ran from the crannog's gates. Stavros managed another few steps and then collapsed into the dirt.

Gingerly, Aidan turned him over. Stavros's nose was smashed and bloody, one eye swollen shut.

"What happened?" he asked. "Who did this to ye?"

He had to bring his ear close to Stavros's bruised mouth to hear the answer. "Mob," he whispered. "Caught me just out of town. Said this was just a warning. Said they wanted you. Said they'll get you, Aidan. . . ." Then he managed to smile, "I . . . I broke a few teeth of me own . . ." And then he passed out.

Donough tenderly lifted Stavros, hefting him as if he were almost weightless. The giant cradled the Greek in his arms like a baby and carried him back to the crannog.

Suddenly, and despite the sun's warmth, Aidan felt chilled to the bone.

CHAPTER TWENTY-TWO

THE WORLD TURNED, days passing like sparrows before clouds. Life continued on Dar Kush. Kai rode the extent of his domain, from rock quarries to lake fishery, from teff fields to the vast herds where itinerant Kikuyu guarded Kai's stock from any theft but their own. With Lamiya he supervised the social calendar, receiving guests and supplicants. He walked a thousand miles in the gardens with his children and Babatunde as the little scholar taught them the names of each and every flower.

"What is this?" Kai said to Aliyah.

"Fig," she said, toddling beside Kai and her cousin.

"Sour fig," Azinza corrected.

Kai laughed. "Well done!" He turned to Babatunde. "You see? Genius runs in the family." Kai crouched next to Azinza. "And do you know what it's used for?" The flower had narrow purple leaves and a fluffy yellow center.

Azinza screwed her little face up. She shook her head no. "Tell me," Azinza said.

"The Khoe-Khoe of the western Cape used this plant for ointments." Babatunde said. "If a person is stung by an insect, it can help the swelling go down."

"Khoe-Khoe," Azinza said, and rubbed her arm as if she had just been bitten. "Owww. I want Khoe-Khoe."

Kai laughed, and hugged her, saying, "First, let's see if kisses will work just as well."

Late in the day, Kai was poring over household records at his desk when Babatunde and Lamiya entered. "El Sursur," he said in pleasure. "And she who holds my heart. Give me a bit more time," he said, scratching his head. "These records are crystalline to you, but a labyrinth to me. I have no idea how you reconciled the last month's expenses with the report from the trading company. Magic. Are you a witch, as well as . . ." His playful, puzzled words wound down as he noted her tense expression. "Yes, my love?" he said.

"A letter," she said. "From Alexandria."

That caught his attention, tore him from the world of balance sheets and numbers. "New?"

"Old," she said. Her face was curiously strained.

He put his quill aside. "Who is it from?"

"Elenya." Her tone carried a spine-bending load of anxiety.

"Egypt?" he said weakly. "That cannot . . ." He seized it from her hand, tore it open, and fumbled out a rectangle of parchment. The almost mechanical clarity of penmanship announced it Elenya's slightly florid hand, each word crafted as if by an artist. At first he read to himself, and then as if sharing made the burden more tolerable, read aloud.

"Dearest brother," it read. *"I write this letter in sadness. The vessel returning me to court was intercepted by Egyptian privateers, and Captain Fazul forced to turn me over. Please do not hold him accountable. I am now a guest of the Pharaoh, and will remain so until certain matters can be resolved. I am well, and will so remain unless you take actions against Egyptian interests. Please remember that I love you, and all that we shared during my visit. I hope to play* Satranj *with you again, soon. Affectionately yours, Elenya."*

He paused, unable to speak or move. Almost unable to breathe.

It was Lamiya who first regained the power of speech. "Brave girl," she whispered.

Kai's voice was a deadly hush. "How dare they!"

"He is the Pharaoh," said Lamiya.

"I care not if he is the angel Azra'il! This is my family! Why would he do this?"

"Leverage," said Lamiya. "You are Wakil, second only to the governor in authority. You are a war hero, a wealthy man, and married to the Empress's niece. This is preemptive action. She will be well treated—so long as there is peace."

Babatunde studied Kai with concern. "I know that expression," said his tutor. "This is not a time for rash action."

"Yes," Kai said. "It is a time for caution—but also courage."

"You dare not," Lamiya whispered.

They might not have been in the room at all. "All I wanted, more than anything in the world, was to be left alone to live my life and raise my family."

Lamiya and Babatunde exchanged a glance.

"Apparently," Kai continued, "this cannot be."

Babatunde's voice was low and reasonable. "We have spoken many times over the years, Kai. There is always a price—for either action or inaction."

Lamiya touched his arm. "Lives will be lost."

"Life lasts but a few days. Principle is eternal. I must act."

"You must *think*," she insisted.

He wheeled to face her. "Why do you discourage me?" Kai said. "It is your wish that the house of Kush support the Empress."

She met his gaze squarely. "I wish also to see Elenya alive and safe."

He managed a shallow smile, a bit of warmth breaking through the frost. "I did well taking you to wife. Do not fear; there is a way."

Babatunde tried another tack. "What do you think *Elenya* would want?"

"She would want me to act, even if such action placed her life in jeopardy."

Lamiya seemed doubtful. "How do you know this?"

Kai grinned wolfishly. "When she mentioned and capitalized the word 'Satranj,' that emphasis was intended to remind me of our last chess game. The master of her ship was Captain Kwazi, not 'Fazul.' "

"Then what was her meaning?" Babatunde asked. Then his eyes widened. "Ah! Fazul's Gambit?"

Kai nodded approval. "Yes. It works only against players who care less for position than materiel. She chided me on just that point during our last game together before she left. She said I must love my mamluks less, and my Sultan more."

"Kai," said Lamiya, "Allah gave man arms to raise a sword, but also a mind to think."

"Yes," Kai said, but already his eyes had drifted elsewhere.

"I plead with you to remember that there are times when inaction serves a greater purpose," Babatunde said.

Now Kai faced his teacher. "I have done little these past three years—" When Babatunde made as if to interrupt him, Kai raised his hand. "No, hear me out. After the mosque . . . after Malik's death, I imagined I could withdraw from the world, fulfill my duties, but no more. Raise my family. Find some measure of peace. Now I see that even if I do not seek the world, the world will seek me, and mine. I must act."

The three, family in a sense greater than blood, shared a moment of silence.

Again, it was Lamiya who spoke first. "Yes. I see that this may be true. But Kai, if you are to place Elenya's life in peril, you must be very certain that the effort will not be wasted. You must decide exactly, *precisely* what you will do, and *when* it is best to do it. You must conceal your hand until the last possible moment."

"Agreed," said Babatunde. "You must determine with great clarity: what is the minimum action that might have the maximum result? Motivating others to take action while remaining in the background would be ideal. Make no speeches, and be very certain of your allies."

"But what action?" Kai mused aloud.

"Motivate the other nobles to prepare," his wife suggested.

Kai chewed at the inside of his lip, and then turned and pressed a panel on his wall. A compartment opened, and from within it, he withdrew two scrolls. He handed one to Babatunde.

The Yoruban scholar studied it, and then blanched. His finger traced a crimson wax cartouche depicting a pyramid with the sun above its apex. "This is the Caliph's seal. How did you obtain this document?"

Kai shook his head. "From a Kushi privateer in the Songhais."

Lamiya glared at him. "So that was the true purpose of our 'vacation'? The reason you decided to intercept Elenya's ship?"

"A small deception, I hope," he said, sounding uncomfortably contrite. "I had no wish to involve you. Two months ago there was a very heated meeting in the Caliph's home. Do not ask how I know, but I know that a message was dispatched to the Pharaoh concerning its outcome."

"Spies? In the Caliph's house?"

"Let us just say that from time to time a little information makes its way to me, and that this informant was insistent that something of importance had occurred."

"I see. . . . But it doesn't explain—"

"No, it doesn't. Seven weeks ago one of the Caliph's ships was taken, and these scrolls found in the captain's cabin. I received a letter offering to sell them to me, which included a code phrase my father's will had warned me to expect. He was, indeed, part of a movement pressing for secession. I determined when the doomed ship left New Alexandria, and realized that there was a chance that these scrolls were minutes of that very meeting."

Babatunde unrolled the scroll. It was covered with Egyptian hieroglyphs, abstracted images of birds and snakes and such. "The high speech," he murmured. "But this is gibberish!" He glanced at Kai, suddenly comprehending. "Coded?"

"Yes. I can be certain that they were intended for the Pharaoh, but beyond that, can say nothing."

"I know little of ciphers," said the Sufi, "but if necessary, would accept the challenge."

"While in the capital," Kai said, "I made inquiry. In all Bilalistan there may be no more than two devices capable of decoding that message."

Lamiya traced a finger down a row of hieroglyphs, both horrified and fascinated with the danger the two documents represented. "And where are these 'decoding machines'?"

Kai seemed to ignore the question. "Every instinct tells me that these messages betray the Caliph's intent, else they would not be encoded. Else the captain and crew would not have sold their lives so dearly—"

"Kai!" Lamiya said, alarmed. "Men died?"

"They always do," he said.

She seemed to bite down on her emotions, repressing her response. Finally she said, "And if this letter proves the Caliph intends to betray us?"

"I believe the landowners would accept a deeper levy, that we might raise our ramparts higher. Without this, I fear we will not be ready, and failing readiness, will fall if the northerners attack."

"Be very careful, Kai," his tutor warned. "Your decisions will affect Elenya, the Empress, the fortunes of Dar Kush, and the fate of your nation. Pray for wisdom."

"So should we all," said Kai. "As the Pharaoh should have, before he took my only sister hostage."

All night they talked of politics and possibilities, espionage and war. Lamiya had been to New Alexandria, and helped him refine his thoughts, and gave her husband new ideas that might never have occurred to him.

And when the sun began to rise, she asked him, "And afterward. How do you get them out?"

"I have an idea about that," Kai said. "The two of you have done most of the thinking this night. I am glad to make a contribution of my own."

He smiled at Babatunde, and the little Sufi's answering smile was, Kai noticed with interest, creased with tension.

"Yes indeed," Kai said. "I have a fine idea."

CHAPTER TWENTY-THREE

OFTTIMES, Kai prayed for the souls of the dead at Babatunde's mosque, a small brick hutch east of the main house and gardens. Tonight, he wished to pray that their plans would not trigger a disaster. He had thought the mosque would be empty this evening, but as he entered he spied a human figure crouching in the shadows.

Male, bone-thin, white. Shivering in the darkness so that his teeth actually rattled together. The man stank with terror.

The young Wakil pretended not to notice. Babatunde entered behind him, and seeing the huddled form, quickly ushered Kai back out into the starlight.

"Come," said his teacher. "Let us take in the night. There are times Allah's canopy of stars is a better theater for prayer than any wrought by the hands of men."

"They are beautiful, indeed," Kai said, and allowed himself to be led away.

Babatunde sought to comfort him. "You are plagued by doubts. Questions about whether you are the man your father would have wished to inherit his mantle."

"Yes," Kai said softly.

"You are your father's flesh, and no finer blood runs in this new land," Babatunde said. "And he could wish no better son than he who holds his office."

"But it was Ali he prepared to be Wakil."

Babatunde shrugged. "How could he do otherwise? Ali was the eldest."

Kai brooded. "All the times they spoke of war, and I crept about the outer edges of their company, listening. . . . Ali saw me, knew I was there, but let me spy. I sometimes suspect he knew this day would come." He glanced at his teacher. "Why did my father shield me so?"

"He thought that one brother might live in the world of men, and the other in the world of spirit, and that together, they might rule Dar Kush with greater wisdom. The world of men, of politics," said Babatunde, "is not absolutely corrupt, but is often corrupting."

"Why?"

"Where there are two men, there are two ways of looking at the world. In a world of millions, no common view of the physical world can be forged without compromise."

"And of the spiritual?" Kai asked.

"Tell the Sunnis and the Shi'ites," Babatunde said. "Or the Fatimites who control our own Ulema. No, there may be one reality, but there are as many roads leading to it as there are men to traverse them. This is why we say that every man must make his own way to Allah—the Prophet, Peace Be Upon Him, could not shoulder that burden for us, as the Christians seem to believe the Christ suspended it for them."

"How do I do this?" Kai asked.

"To be *in* but not *of* the world? I think you already know, Kai. Keep your eye on Allah, and with every action and thought, prepare yourself to kneel before him and justify your actions in this world."

"I struggle."

"As do we all. But I think your struggles will bear sweeter fruit than most. Kai . . . your father may have shielded you, but always you were his son. And he would expect you to act as lord of this house."

"And if I err?"

"Then you err. Only Allah is perfection. The rest of creation can but strive toward that unreachable goal. You will do your best. That is all your father would ask. All anyone who loves you would ask."

He held Kai's hands and gazed into his student's eyes. "And all you may ask of yourself." He chuckled. "Otherwise, you would be like a Persian rug weaver, deliberately leaving a flaw in your work, that you might not approach that perfection found in heaven alone. You have no such ego. And that, my boy, is both blessing and curse."

"Will you pray with me?" Kai asked.

"Forever," his mentor replied.

CHAPTER TWENTY-FOUR

4 *Shawwal A.H. 1294*

(Friday, October 12, 1877)

HUNDREDS OF MILES AWAY, across the border from New Djibouti in southern Wichita, another world existed.

A Zulu world.

Cetshwayo's kraal, although smaller than his brother Shaka's Azanian holdings, remained a place of power and majesty, home to vast herds of cattle, thousands of square miles of grasslands, and hundreds of internested wood-frame houses. Zulus preferred wood over stone or adobe. When appropriate timbers could not be harvested locally, they were imported for the sake of tradition.

A line of horsewomen rode west along a low ridge overlooking the grounds, from which they could peer down on a series of fences. There they watched a small group of Zulu men training a pack of ridgeback hounds.

The dogs were almost fifteen sep apiece. Black, lean, and long-muzzled, they ran and jumped with the alacrity of small horses. From birth they were taught to fight and obey commands even unto death.

The head trainer was called Chalo, a handsome young man, lean and sharp as his *umkhonto*, with perfect white teeth in his gleaming smile. He was, of course, a blooded warrior, tested in the Aztec Wars under Colonel Shaka. Although in Islamic Bilalistan a dog trainer would be a position of low status, among the Zulu Chalo was celebrated as a lord of the hunt.

At the moment he was completely immersed in the business of training, inviting his formidable charges to attack him. When they lunged for his throat they grasped instead his leather-wrapped arm. Man and hound strained together, and it was here where Chalo's superlative strength and balance came to play. A lesser man would have been forced to the ground and savaged. Instead, it was Chalo who wrestled his four-legged adversaries one after another into the earth. He would control their heads, and gaze into their eyes until they quieted, and they adored him for it.

On the ridge above them, the first woman in line winced as Chalo torqued one of the great ridgebacks on the axis of its neck. The dog crashed to earth paws-up, a feat that required not mere strength and speed, but absolute coolness of mind to wait until the very last instant. "He is very brave."

"Yes," replied the woman behind her. "And handsome, too, don't you think?" As Cetshwayo's eldest unmarried daughter, Nandi was the focus of more attention and speculation than any woman in the Zulu nation.

She was tall but not slender: this was a full-hipped, broad-shouldered Zulu woman in her prime. She wore no makeup or facial paint, and needed none. Her eyes were wide and deep and filled with laughter, her nose generous, her lips full and generally curled in a secretive half smile. Her cheekbones were high, her ears small and delicately shaped.

A single golden braid surrounded her neck: no multiple strands, no gems or strings of other precious metals, just that single braid, as if any further ornamentation would draw the eye away from the perfection of her face and form. Although she had spent nearly her entire life within the confines of her father's kraal, the finest tutors gold could buy had educated her in both traditional Zulu herbology and Greek and Egyptian medicine and animal husbandry. If she were not a princess with a royal destiny— had she been, say, a *man*—her intellect might easily have found a place for her at any university, or indeed in private practice. But those potentials were less important than her status as bargaining chip in nuptial negotiation. She knew it, her mothers and father knew it, and for a thousand miles in all directions, every father with an eligible son knew it as well.

But it was to the younger son of the Wakil Abu Ali that she had been promised, and to that fate she had reconciled herself. To find herself so enormously drawn to Kai had been an unexpected blessing. To be set aside for long years as her intended played out some morbid Muslim mourning drama was a torment almost beyond bearing.

"I might think that," said her chaperone. "But you cannot. What of Kai?"

Nandi waved her hand in a dismissive gesture. "Oh, away. It has been years; my father has heard nothing. I'll be an old maid like you if I don't take matters into my own hands."

Her chaperone's eyes widened. "Mistress! You have not met this dog trainer alone?!"

"No," she said with a faint, contemplative smile. "Not since we were children. Even when we trained IziLomo, we were chaperoned. I have never met with him." She paused, then added, "But I might."

Chalo stood, and looked up at her, and waved. Nandi guided her horse down to him.

"Mistress!" her companion implored. "This is improper!"

Nandi grinned. "Yes. Isn't it, though?"

She rode down to where Chalo trained the ridgebacks, sitting high in her saddle, conscious of her every motion and her impact on any and all who might be watching.

"Good morning, Princess," Chalo said.

"Good morning, Chalo," she said brightly. Chalo himself was descended from a noble line. Man or hound, it took generations to breed a champion. "How goes the training?"

He grinned broadly. Nandi's retainers twittered a bit, scandalized but also delighted.

"Well indeed." He squared his shoulders and expanded his chest. His shirt, of thin pressed and beaten leather as malleable as wool, swelled under the pressure. "None of these are as fine as IziLomo, but they'll do. We hunted this morning."

"Successfully, I assume?"

"My gift." With a flourish, Chalo pulled a tarp back from a shadowed hump. Beneath lay the mauled form of an enormous brownish-black bear. Its eyes stared vacantly, and upon them insects crawled already. The carcass must have weighed fifty sep. The scent of blood was a sudden perfume.

Nandi inhaled that heady scent sharply. She was trained in biology, of course. As a people who measured wealth in cattle, Egyptian ideas of classification and analysis had swiftly taken root among the Zulu. The animal sciences, the understanding of human and beast on every physical level, became a specialty of Zulu academies. The others, of course, were war and jurisprudence.

To read of exotic medical procedures or beasts is one thing: to see and smell them, to taste with the mind, remained an almost overpowering exhilaration. "Magnificent," she said, gazing into Chalo's eyes.

"Truly, one of a kind," he replied. "She was well worth the hunt."

Their eyes kept contact for a moment longer, until Nandi's youngest chaperone said, "Mistress. We should return to the house. Your father is home soon."

"Princess," Chalo said. "I will have my experts prepare and skin the carcass. It is your wall hanging, and a token of my esteem."

"I thank you." Nandi's eyes sparkled. Again, their gazes linked and smoldered. Then the princess turned and guided her horse away.

After a hard day's riding, Cetshwayo and his men had finally returned to the gates of his kraal. This was his pride, inherited from his father, who had homesteaded before most of the Zulus had expanded into the Azanian Purchase, the vast tracts acquired with Zulu gold in hope of creating a separate nation. Such hopes had not yet been realized, but the coming time of crisis might prove to be just the leverage the Zulu nation needed to become a geopolitical entity. While Cetshwayo possessed extensive Azanian holdings, it was the Wichita kraal that truly stirred his heart.

Immediately after turning his stallion over to a servant Cetshwayo went to the house of Munji, his second, and favorite, wife.

As Zulu custom dictated, Cetshwayo had no house reserved for himself alone, nor did all wives live beneath the same roof. Rather, each lived in a separate house, the seven houses arranged in a circular ring in the center of the kraal, protected by a ring of warrior's barracks without. His second wife Munji lived in the eastmost building. A round stern woman with the most beautiful eyes he had ever seen, Munji had noted his approach from a window, then vanished so quickly that the curtains were still swinging after her back had turned.

As he had expected, she awaited him with a somewhat formal demeanor, but Cetshwayo sensed that behind the reserve lived a reservoir of almost giddy expectation.

Munji wore a tan beaded headdress and several ropes of small, densely stringed pearls. Her voluminous orange cotton dress was cinched at her ample waist, and her small and shapely feet were shod in fashionably thin leather sandals. "Is it done?" she asked, her plump hands folded before her.

No need to ask her meaning. "Yes. Soon it begins. I would speak to my daughter."

Although she had four, and knew that Cetshwayo had twelve more by other wives, Munji required no clarification. Without a word she led her husband upstairs, then stood aside as he knocked on his daughter's door.

After a short pause, the door swung open, and Nandi stood before him, eyes cast slightly downward.

"Daughter."

"Father," she said, and tiptoed to kiss his cheek. "How went your trip?"

"Well," he said. His eye cast about for the great lump of shadow that usually crouched at her side. Where? He looked to the right, and there, hidden in shadow, hunched IziLomo. A five-year-old Zulu ridgeback in the very peak of its power and senses, IziLomo was fourteen sep of black muscle and bone, a fearsome hunter who was affectionate only with Cetshwayo's daughter, who had raised him from a pup. Quiet and respectful IziLomo might well be to family members and Nandi's friends, but the beast was utterly protective, and the Zulu prince himself hesitated to raise his voice in its presence.

IziLomo seemed naturally to seek the camouflage of shadow, so that in any room one entered, it was necessary to look twice to make certain the monster was not lurking about. So watchful was the dog that he was often restrained when visitors arrived, for fear of an unfortunate incident. This was no idle concern: when but a year old, IziLomo had been running alongside Nandi's horse Bejane, "Black Rhino," when the unfortunate beast threw her. Before anyone could intercede, IziLomo had torn Bejane's throat out.

"If not for this leg of mine," said Cetshwayo, "I would have found it all to the good." He sat heavily at the edge of her bed.

"Truly?" Despite herself, she could not restrain a touch of eagerness. "Tell me, Father. Tell me *everything*." Nandi had never traveled to Radama, and probably would not until and unless taken there by her husband. However much she loved every hollow or blade of grass in her father's holdings, she yearned to be her own woman, forging her own life path with a great warrior and statesman at her side.

Their trip, four years ago, to New Djibouti on the occasion of Ali's engagement and that Abyssinian witch Lamiya's return had been her most recent extensive sojourn. Since that time, she had been kept in a kind of frozen time, awaiting decisions beyond her influence.

As a loving father, Cetshwayo regretted these things.

As Shaka Zulu's younger brother, and inheritor of his political power on the other hand, there was no choice at all.

Nandi suddenly seemed to remember her restraint and reined her excitement back in, dropping her eyes again.

Cetshwayo yawned massively. "This accursed leg condemns me to the chair or canter, but in truth I prefer the thrill of the hunt to the world of politics." He paused. "In that sense, I believe I am similar to a certain young Wakil."

Now her eyes sparked. "Oh?"

He nodded. "I believe we can play each side against the other." His generous mouth split in an open smile. "If we conduct ourselves with care, our homeland is all but secured."

She knelt before her father, gazing up at him. "Tell me more of this young Wakil."

IziLomo's ears had perked up, and he made a snuffling sound, as if aware that his young mistress's interest was engaged. But neither that nor Nandi's eagerness wrought any change in Cetshwayo's manner. "Oh, he is a bright young man, thought to have excellent prospects."

"Is he a family man?"

"Indeed. Married to the imperial niece, although there, too, is a scandal."

"And why is that?"

"It is said that she was intended for his brother, who died in the Shrine campaign three years ago."

She sniffed. "She should have returned home, to live her days in a nunnery."

He neither agreed nor disagreed with this sentiment. Lamiya could be drowned in the sea, a cloistered virgin, or bride of a Celtic Druid—any of these would have suited his purposes. But her marriage to Kai made the situation far more complex. "She chose to stay. Some say she saved the Wakil from madness. Some say that their 'Immortal' Empress has disowned her, others that it was under that Lady's clandestine orders."

"And you think . . . ?"

Cetshwayo shook his head. "I doubt there was time for a message to travel from Bilalistan to Abyssinia. Either contingency plans were preexistent, or the two reached some new arrangement."

Nandi seemed to ponder that one. "Extreme circumstances call for extreme actions. Father, brother, and uncle all died within a span of weeks. Their house must have been greatly disarrayed."

"Yes," Cetshwayo said calmly. He paused, as though listening to music above her range of hearing.

The tension was unbearable. Finally, she broke the silence. "And how fares the young Wakil now?"

Cetshwayo considered for a moment. "Healed, I think. And ready to find his Second."

Nandi's face was perfectly composed, hands resting on her knees, eyes relaxed and focused on her father's. "And . . . ?"

"This is your time, Daughter."

Nandi's face remained steady, but her eyes were bright and hot behind the mask of restraint. Whether joy, anger, or anticipation it was hard to say. Even her own father could not be certain. How strange that he could know this child since birth, and still be uncertain of the emotions burning in her breast.

"Are you prepared?" he asked.

"All my life," said Nandi.

"And these three years?"

Her full lips thinned. "Harder than I will say."

Cetshwayo nodded. "They made you wait, my child. Can you control your anger?"

She inhaled sharply, then let the breath out far more slowly. "I am your daughter."

"Never forget that," her father said. "For our time is at hand. If you will but trust me now, and follow my advice and command . . ."

She half lowered her lids. "Have I not, always?"

Her father studied her intensely. "In your way. In these recent years you have masked your heart, even from me."

"Really, Father?" she asked. "Never was that my intent. Why would I have reason to mask my feelings from you, Father, who have given me nothing but love all the years of my life?"

Cetshwayo was quiet. He knew, and she knew, that his children were as much political instruments as the nieces and nephews of the fabled Empress. Knew further that he could not deal with them merely as a father who loved his twenty-five offspring. What, then, was her statement's meaning?

In that instant he wondered if Nandi was even stronger than he had suspected. By sky and sun, if only she had been a son and not a daughter!

"Have I not done everything I could to please you?" she said.

"In your way."

"Did I not open my heart to the one you chose for me?"

Now it was Cetshwayo's turn to remain impassive. "At the least."

Her eyes flashed fire, although the rest of her expression remained the same. He had misjudged. That last comment had hurt her, and her rage was but thinly veiled. IziLomo sensed the mood shift as well, and gave a low rumbling sound. Cetshwayo's hand slid a digit closer to his *umkHonto*.

"I did what I was born and bound to do," Nandi replied. She was so still that Cetshwayo felt as if he were peering into the eye of a hurricane. "I was to be first wife to the son of a famed Wakil. Then came the slave uprising, the Shrine, and all of its ugliness. And the death of my uncle, great Shaka."

She paused. When she looked at him again, her eyes were piercing, and he actually had to fight the urge to look away. "This is no longer politics, is it, Father? I am no longer a bridge, a means of joining. You no longer see me as a daughter. You see me as a spear."

Cetshwayo broke eye contact. "You are a princess of your people. You are all things. And I, a loving father."

Her smile was cold. "Yes. Well, then, loving father. I will be loving daughter, and do as you say, as I have always. Tell your obedient child what you would have her do, now that your plans have come to fruition."

A chill swept through him, although whether motivated by temperature or tension, Cetshwayo could not say. He suspected the latter: something had just shifted in that room, some subtle sense of mass or energy.

Then Nandi's face softened. But was this a mask donned or removed? Her smile was radiant. She rose. Without a sound she leaned forward and pressed her lips against his.

"A daughter's kiss," she said, retreating again. "How few remain. Soon, Father, I will no longer be of your house."

"You will always be of my house, and of my heart."

"Always of your heart."

He nodded. "And when the ceremony is past, the Zulu blood will run still in your veins, and you will remember the things I say this night."

"Always," she said.

Then, after a short silence, he began to speak.

CHAPTER TWENTY-FIVE

ALTHOUGH ONLY THREE-QUARTERS the size of Dar Kush, because less of the Berhar estate was devoted to farm land, it actually had more raw, undeveloped, recreational acreage. It was also less dependent upon slave labor: most of the Berhar fortune came from business concerns at home and abroad, rather than from agriculture.

Still, they maintained more than a hundred slaves, and half as many free laborers and supervisors.

There were small dwellings scattered across the entire estate, and it was toward one of these that Allahbas Berhar was led by her boss slave Olalye. Olalye was an ugly tree trunk of a man with limited intelligence but great capacity for both work and loyalty. Years of honest toil had been rewarded with his current position, which not only meant a better cabin and more meat, but which had won him the hand of one of the prettiest little sluts on Dar Berhar, a red-haired hussy named Morgan.

He was a happy man now. And if Allahbas suspected that Morgan was not entirely faithful, and that the object of her lust happened to be Kai's man Olaf, well . . . that was slave business. And slave business didn't reach the main house. What was her business was her suspicion that Morgan's constant demands had induced her boss slave to steal from his owners. Silverware and rare spices had come up missing, and whispered accusations indicated Olalye. If this turned out to be true, punishment would be severe indeed. But for now . . . she watched and waited.

Olalye bowed to her, and said, "Here he be, ma'am."

"Thank you, Olalye," she answered without a hint of her ugly thoughts, and entered the hut.

There in the darkness sat an olive-skinned Persian, face bent in shadow, form cloaked in a vertically striped robe.

"Omar Pavlavi," he said, and bowed in his seated position.

"Allahbas Berhar," she replied, sitting across from him in a straight-backed chair. Never before had they met face-to-face, but Allahbas knew the Hashassin by more than their lethal reputation. In fact, once upon a time she had made excellent use of their deadly skills. She felt no fear in his presence, only an intense heightening of awareness, as one might experience in the presence of a leopard. Such a heightening would be interpreted by most as an unpleasant sensation.

Unless one were also a leopard.

"I am glad you have come," said Omar. "I wish conversation on business that might enrich us both."

"I dealt with your people ten years ago, and that interaction was both successful and profitable," Madame Berhar said.

"More profitable for you than for my predecessor," he said, "but I have no reason to complain. The contract was fulfilled, and you became First."

She nodded. "If this day's conversation proves as profitable as that, you will find me receptive."

"I come to you on behalf of the Caliph of Bilalistan. Some weeks ago, an important message was stolen, and we believe that it found its way to the Wakil of New Djibouti."

"Kai?" she asked.

"Yes. The son of Abu Ali. We wish for you to observe him, and report back to me."

She pondered, and then phrased her reply carefully. "I must respectfully decline."

"May I ask why?"

"Certainly. I am aware that your master seconded you to the Pharaoh, doubtless to gain some trade or political negotiation point favorable to Persia."

"True."

"I assume that the Pharaoh, in turn, lent you to the Caliph."

"True, again."

"The Caliph's concern is the subjugation of the south, and therefore our interests are not his."

"You are a secessionist?"

"Do I speak to you as an agent of the Caliph, or as a cousin?"

Omar considered as carefully as she. "It does no dishonor to my master to say that you may speak to me openly, protected by the Queen's blood we share, however distantly."

"Good. I feel nothing but love for my mother's land, and would do whatever I could to further her aims. But I cannot stand against southern Bilalistan without risking all I have spent a lifetime in building. My husband will die soon, and my son will inherit. At that point, my conduct present and past must be beyond reproach. I cannot supply you with information: the nature and character of any observation invariably hints at the observer's identity. A thousand pardons, but I cannot do this thing."

She lowered her eyes. Omar watched her with care. Finally he nodded. "Very well. It is in both of our interests to keep this conversation, and the nature of our connection, secret."

"Indeed," she said, and looked up as Omar started to rise. "Hold."

His pale bearded face was expressionless. "Yes?"

"I cannot do the service for you, but I can profit you still, and in a manner that does nothing to compromise your mission."

He sat back down. "I am interested."

"I wish you to destroy the Wakil."

"You wish him dead?"

She shook his head. "No. No need for that. I have watched this boy since childhood, and in truth, have a certain affection for him. If he had been my son instead of Fodjour . . ." She paused, and then shook her head. "A pointless speculation. At any rate, it is sufficient that his power and credibility be destroyed."

Omar considered. "And if it is, you believe your son would be chosen?"

"Yes. I have sufficient power and influence to guarantee this."

"This idea . . . does not conflict with my mission. In fact, in effect if not intent, it might well satisfy the Caliph. I will consider it." He paused. "Have you a plan in mind?"

"No," she said. "Not yet. Major changes develop in Kai's life. I have little doubt that an intelligent observer will, during the next weeks or months, find a path to our common goal."

Omar nodded. "Let us speak more of this," he said, and sat once again.

CHAPTER TWENTY-SIX

9 Shawwal A.H. 1294
(Wednesday, October 17, 1877)

FOR THE PAST TWO WEEKS, Salima had boiled with resentment, fueled by arguments in the back rooms and frequent beatings of the hapless slaves unfortunate enough to live in town.

Constable Oba had kept his word, tried to keep emotions and actions within a peaceful limit. The lack of a corroborating witness made the widow Nunz's accusations impossible to prove or disprove, and legally, Aidan O'Dere was a veteran and a free man, and even a landed black woman's solitary word was not enough to convict.

Legally.

But in the hashish den, and in the back rooms where wine was served in defiance of the Prophet's edicts, day-by-day resentment grew, until it became an unreasoning thing, needing no greater reason than hatred, having no greater purpose than death.

On most days, Sophia O'Dere awoke before dawn, rising to stir her family's breakfast porridge. Mornings she taught, and early afternoon was generally occupied by cleaning. In midafternoon she administrated work crews patching the fences or weeding in the fields. As the afternoon heat began to wane, kneaded dough entered the communal ovens, emerging just in time for dinner.

The teff loaves had just begun to brown when Donough called from the wall: "Visitors!"

She didn't see her husband, and thought that he might even be out on the lake. Well, then, best she see to this. Sophia climbed up to the top of the barricade, shifting the awkward pregnancy weight carefully as she rose.

From the top she could peer down on the land bridge connecting the crannog to their little farm.

A dozen black men stood below her, bristling with rifles and pistols, in postures of anger and confrontation. Their leader was a man known to her as a corrupt, ambitious fop: Hamed was his name, and it was their bad fortune that he was Salima's assistant constable.

"Who goes there?" she called down.

Hamed's hair and thin beard looked as if they were oiled and combed on the hour. "Send out the yellow-hair you call 'Aidan,'" he called up.

Sophia bit back a harsh answer. She could not allow fear to motivate her to rash words or action. "What do you want with my husband?"

Hamed declined a direct answer. "He will be given justice."

Sophia's answering laugh was shrill and derisive. "Justice? Like last year, over in the Dell? That boy was nailed to a tree two hours after they gave him up. Is that justice?"

White teeth gleamed in a black face. "What know you of law? Left to your own device, your kind gnaw each other's bones and rut with each other's children. Best send him out, *qahba-t.*"

"Where is Constable Oba?" she asked.

That triggered a wave of grumbling among the assembled. "An old man needs his nap," Hamed said. "No need to wake him for this. You send Aidan out now, and I swear he'll be treated fairly."

Fairly. Even if intended as truth, who could say what Hamed meant by that? "What say we wait until the Constable arrives?"

"Do not test my patience," Hamed answered. "I give you half an hour to decide."

Shaken, Sophia climbed back down from the wall. To her relief, Aidan had arrived. His feet were wet. She reckoned she was right in supposing that he had been upon the lake.

"What do they want?" he asked.

"You, but if it was legal, Oba would be here," she said to Aidan. "I know in my heart that they aim to crucify you."

Aidan clenched his fists. She knew her man, knew that he was considering the welfare of the entire crannog, not merely his own precious hide. "I can't put all of you at risk," he finally said.

Before she could reply, Donough snarled, "Shyte upon that! Ain't for you, there'd *be* no fockin' village."

Another freedman gripped a hoe as if it were a club. "This ain't your concern alone, Sidi. This is all of us. If they can take you, they can take any man here . . . or any woman. Ain't there no law a black man has to obey?"

"They *is* the law," someone muttered.

"That's the fact of it," said Donough.

Sophia scanned her people. Every citizen of Aidan's crannog was there. Hard men, proud women, and small, fierce children, they were his in heart and hand.

She knew that he would die before placing the crannog at risk, but something had happened here. Aidan was not merely the man who had planned and laid the foundations of their village; he was its very core. Turning Aidan over to Salina's vigilantes would destroy the crannog more certainly than a thousand torches.

She watched his face change as he came to realize the truth of that. "Then that's the way it is," Aidan said.

Despite the danger, this was a moment worth savoring. This was no mere collection of refugees. They were a people, united not by blood but history. These were Aidan's people, as surely as if they had drawn sustenance from the rivers and streams of his youth. They were not a rabble: they were a village.

Aidan climbed to the top of the ramparts and addressed the posse. Sophia watched through a spy hole on the lower level.

"We've decided," her husband called from above. "I'll surrender myself to Oba."

Hamed twisted his beard and clucked. "Allah has dimmed your hearing as well as your wit. I said that Oba is napping. You wouldn't risk an old man's health, would you? Come on now . . ."

He suddenly, savagely grinned. Sophia tensed, knowing that things were about to get uncomfortably honest. "Or we'll burn you out," Hamed concluded.

Her belly knotted.

"You have no legal right," Aidan called down, in a voice too obviously weakened by distress.

Hamed's answering laughter was ugly. "I need no doghair quoting laws and rights. When you've learned to read, perhaps we'll talk. Ghosts! Best obey your betters."

"What guarantees do I have?"

"Guarantees?" Hamed's men chuckled. "The promise given to all men: only what Allah wills can occur." His expression lost any semblance of good humor. "Unless you would rain fire upon every man and child in your filthy mud hole, *open your fucking gate.*"

Sophia saw the same identical intent in every black face, every brown eye. "No," her husband said.

Strangely, Hamed seemed satisfied, as if he had secretly hoped for that answer. "Then—let it be upon your own heads. Fire it is."

One of the townsmen pulled his arm back, threw a torch. It tumbled, raining sparks, then bounced off the wooden walls.

"Fair warnin'," Aidan called. "The next man throws a torch gets shot."

Shot? Sophia thought. *Oh, Aidan, if we kill one of them, we're lost.*

But if we don't fight, we're lost as well.

Hamed seemed almost to have read her mind. "For every dead man of mine, I'll see five of your men, women, or children nailed to the tree."

The second man pulled his arm back. Aidan aimed carefully, and shot him in the shoulder. The black man howled and clutched at the wound, the torch tumbling from his grip

Donough peered out, and then clapped Aidan's shoulder. "Good shot— you only wounded him."

" 'Good shot' my arse," Aidan spat. "I was aimin' dead center."

Shots rang out from the woods, rattling like a string of firecrackers. The villagers hunkered down behind the fence.

"Make every shot count!" Aidan called. Then more softly to the man beside him: "Pass the word. If you can, don't shoot for the head. The fewer dead, the better off we are."

"We ain't got no chance," one of the villagers moaned.

"More than you think," said Aidan. "If this was righteous, they'd have brought Oba with them. If we can hold them off—"

The villager looked at him incredulously. "You're hopin' for help from a black man?"

"It wouldn't be the first time," he muttered.

It would have been bad enough if the attack had been constant. Oddly, it was the pauses *between* attacks that were the hardest to endure. Evening had fallen fully before the next wave began.

"Here they come!" Donough screamed.

The villagers snapped back as the townsfolk crept up to the bushes and fired a volley. Donough picked his shot carefully, and fired. A black man reeled back, limping.

"Ali's wounds!" one of the townsmen screamed. "Damn 'bellies, I'm hit!"

An answering volley, and more garbled curses. Sophia covered her ears with her hands, too hypnotized to pull away from the sight. Then there was silence. Then:

"Ghosts!" the assistant constable called. "You hear me?"

There was no answer from above her.

"The only hope you have is to send your Aidan out. Send him out, and we'll leave you alone."

"He's lyin'," Donough said without a trace of resentment. "They jest want the gate open."

Donough scanned every man and woman near him, his flat, square face utterly bland and serious. "They'll kill every one of us."

"You hear me?" Hamed called. "I'll wait an hour for your answer."

He motioned to his men, and a third of them disappeared into the shadows.

"What they doing out there?" Donough asked.

Aidan grunted. This was far from over. "If he's got half a brain, he'll keep our attention to the front, while he flanks us."

Donough scratched his head. "Like Shaka?"

"Just like Shaka." Aidan motioned to several of his men. *Watch the perimeter.*

"Look at the sides. Expect someone to try to come in from the lakeside."

"Aye, Sayyid" said a freedman. Several of the women stood guard along the wall as well. A shot gouged a chunk of wood right next to Donough's tiny, sharp-faced wife, Mary. She flinched back, cursing, scrubbing at one sunburnt cheek.

Almost immediately, a derisive voice sounded from the forest. "How can you hide behind your women in such a fashion? What manner of cowards are you?"

One of the other blacks laughed. "Yellow bellies to match the yellow hair. Not a drop of true blood in the lot."

"We'll see their blood, soon enough. The *gruagach* are on their way." The voice grew louder. "Hear me, slaves? The *gruagach* are coming! They smell your flesh, and grow hungry, and thirsty."

Aidan felt his bile rise, longed to smash their faces, and knew that their talk was calculated to elicit a rash, ill-considered response. The men beside him muttered and cursed. "Don't answer them," Aidan said. "Don't feed it. They talk to distract, to make themselves brave . . . and to buy time."

"Time? Why do they need time?" asked a freedman.

"To get into position," Aidan explained. "To get reinforcements."

The slave bowed. "Sayyid! You are wise indeed. Where did you learn such things?"

"On the killing ground—watch out!"

Two flaming torches arced over the balustrades and struck a hut. Sparks flew.

"Buckets!" Sophia screamed below him. "Bring water *now!*" He was comforted to hear her voice, but simultaneously wanted to tell her to retreat to safety. And could not. Every calm voice helped to hold his people together.

Like mice scurrying from a cat's questing claws, the freedmen rushed about to well and shed, filling buckets. They slopped water against the smoldering wood until the fire was extinguished.

More hours crept by, until they had reached and passed midnight. Waiting was agony, and then . . .

Thickly cloaked in early-morning shadow, two black men waded through the lake's cold, drear water, until they drew within striking distance of the crannog walls. Invisible as spirits of the dead, they held unlit torches over their heads.

The shorter of them held his torch steady, while the other squeezed a twist of fire paste onto its wadded bark and moss. In a few seconds it sputtered, then smoked and popped into flame.

The taller snarled, "They take the best fishing, best hunting . . . we'll show them!"

"Burn them out," his companion whispered. "I'll bet we can find a runaway in the bunch. Cancel their papers, put them all back into chains where they belong. . . ."

"And send a few to Jahannum!"

The torch finally flared into life. "Good!" the first townsman yelled. He used the first torch's fire to ignite the second, and then hurled. The brand twirled end-over-end through the blackness, shedding sparks as it tumbled. It arced up and landed on the far side of the barricade. They taller man wound up to throw the second—

A single shot rang out from the crannog's ramparts.

The taller torch-man reeled back, clutching his belly. His scream was horrific but cut short as he flopped back into the water. His companion struggled to keep him above the surface.

"Akim is dying!" the shorter man screamed.

"You all heard!" Hamed called. "It's murder now!"

"Murder my arse!" Donough growled. "Even a 'belly 'as the right to defend 'is home."

"This won't do," Aidan worried. "There's no one to help us. No reinforcements or cavalry like at the mosque. The longer this takes, the worse we are. If we sit here, they'll just take their time and burn us out."

Several of the freedmen hunkered around, looking at him worshipfully. "Aidan. What do we do?"

He peered carefully out of the fence. Their sheds aland were in flames. Their little teff and carrot gardens were being rooted up by hooting townsfolk.

In the darkness beyond the edge of the light, metal clanked.

"Remember these?" crooned a voice without a body, rattling chains. "They remember you. Come out, come out, and wear them once again. Sleeping on straw is better than sleeping in the dirt."

Behind Aidan, a young freedman stood, ready to leap down from the balustrade and die killing his enemies. "I can't stand it!" he called.

Aidan yanked the boy back out of harm's way. "That's what they want," he said softly. "Just wait."

Out in the woods, the townsfolk had begun to grumble. "They're keeping their wits about them. Strange for slaves," one said. "I'd have thought they'd beg for mercy by now." He paused. "That's been the way of it, until tonight."

The assistant constable spat. "That Aidan's the one holding their guts in."

Another townsman shifted uneasily. "What is so special about this dog?"

"He shed blood in the Aztec campaign," the assistant constable said. "Thinks he's some kind of soldier."

Despite his obvious disdain for the besieged, the townsman seemed impressed. "He fought with Shaka?" The man straightened his legs, as if wanting another view of the besieged compound. When he did another shot rang out, and he jerked backward, blood spraying from a shattered shoulder.

"Damn! Ah, damn!" the injured man screamed, rolling on the ground. "Those devils!"

Hamed pulled at the others. "Get down! Down, damn you."

"What do we do?" another townsman asked. "You said that we'd have the infidel nailed up by dawn. You know Oba will put an end to this!"

The assistant constable seemed baffled. "I thought they'd hand him over." He scratched at his oiled, thinning hair.

That thought seemed to shake him out of his lethargy. Filled with new determination, he crawled to safety back behind a tree and then stood. "All right, then, if that is the way of it—they can put out one or two fires, but we'll build a barricade, get close enough to give them a proper taste of hell." He pointed to a pair of tool huts not yet burning. "Tear those doors off. Lash them together. We'll get close enough to slather that wall with pitch. Then we'll roast their bones." He pointed to the shadows north and south of the crannog. "We'll position some riflemen to pin them down. If they try to escape in boats, we'll pick them off in the water."

The townsmen scurried to their places. Hamed used torchlight to check his timepiece. *Good.* Five hours remained before dawn. Plenty of time to bring this to a conclusion. Still, he felt a nagging doubt: this Aidan was a strange one, unlike other whites he had known. He might be trouble.

Ah well, all the better to end this now, tonight, before their little village could grow, before they could grow strong, before . . .

Somewhat to Hamed's surprise, he realized that he felt a bit of fear. And somehow, that was the most disturbing thing of all.

CHAPTER TWENTY-SEVEN

DESPITE MASHED THUMBS and frequent, painful splinters, Hamed's preparations for the siege engine were very nearly complete. In its construction, several of the crannog's shed doors had been taken apart and lashed together as makeshift barriers. The result was ugly, unwieldy, and hopefully, deadly as Satan's forked tongue.

"It begins," he said. "The sight will curdle what little blood flows in their miserable veins." Despite his bravado, he felt as if he had aged years in the hours since he had set out from town.

"I'd like to see some of that blood," said a townsman. "That was my cousin they gut-shot. I fear his wife is soon a widow."

"You'll see all you want, and more," Hamed promised. "Are you prepared?"

They began to move the shield toward the village. The crannog loomed up before them, night-black, crawling with early-morning mist.

"Nothing," said a townsman. "This is not to my liking."

"I'll wager it's hemp's kept their courage up—and like enough, they're sleeping that off by now. They'll wake soon—and wish they still were dreaming." They had crept out of the gardens and onto the bridge connecting the crannog to land.

Without warning, shots rang out from the forest *behind* them.

One of the men crouching behind the barricade was struck low in the back. "Camel *biraz!*" he screamed, and collapsed.

Several rifles opened up on them from behind the stockade as well. With rifles on both sides the townsfolk were horribly vulnerable.

Hamed loosed an inarticulate stream of blasphemies, then managed to get hold of himself. "We're trapped!"

As they crouched behind their now achingly insufficient makeshift stockade, bullets ripping at them from both sides, it was hard to disagree with that judgment.

The assistant constable ducked as a bullet slammed splinters from wood mere digits from his head. "They must have snuck men to shore while we were building. *Biraz!*"

The townsmen trembled, and then broke. "I'm getting the hell out of here!" one screamed.

"Wait—" yelled Hamed. Then, a bullet gouged his leg. "Damn!" he yelled, hobbling. "Wait for me!"

He limped as fast as he could, crouching, zigging and zagging. The rest of the townsfolk were running now, dragging their wounded, all thoughts of courage and victory at least temporarily abandoned. Bullets smacked the ground around him. One man stumbled and fell but was helped up, and the rout was complete.

For a few minutes there was silence: the wounded had been carried off.

Then slowly, pale-skinned men began to emerge from the forest, cradling their rifles. Very cautiously, more like hunters than soldiers, they entered the clearing, and then retreated to the gates. Women rose up from the top of the barricade, rifles in hand. Hesitantly and then with greater spirit, they began to cheer.

Donough peeked from behind a tree a little narrower than his own shoulders. "We did it! We rightly did it!" he screamed and waved to Aidan, up on the ramparts.

Aidan waved back, weary but satisfied. "Let's not celebrate just yet," he called soberly. "They may return."

"Not tonight, love," said Sophia, taking her place beside him. "They are afraid, and it will take time to gather their courage again. Let us hope that Oba is a good man."

"You are far too optimistic." Aidan stretched and yawned. He covered his mouth. "Sorry."

"You've been up since dawn yesterday. I say you need some rest."

"Let me make sure everyone's fed," he said. "And get a rotation going, and then we'll see."

"And where did you learn that?" She smiled. They both knew the answer.

"What?"

"To not surround them. To leave them a route of escape."

"Guess," he said, and laughed.

She slipped her arm about Aidan's waist, and hugged. "And wouldn't he be surprised to see the use you put it to."

"Maybe. But maybe not."

"I'll get your meal ready," said Sophia. "And then sleep?"

"Bed first. Then food. Then sleep."

Sophia giggled with delight. "Oh!" And she went off to their home. Aidan turned back to his men.

"All right now!" yelled Aidan. For the first time in a day and a half, he was beginning to feel that underappreciated emotion called *hope*. "Steady does it. . . ."

CHAPTER TWENTY-EIGHT

BECAUSE AIDAN KNEW that only his presence and reputation had held his men together, he was loath to take rest until sunrise brought a new day and the possibility of Oba's intervention.

So despite deep and numbing fatigue, he remained on the crannog's ramparts. "See anything?"

Donough peered out into the mist. "Not yet—wait! What is *that*?"

Another freedman shifted restlessly. "The blacks have demons at their command. I know. My brother saw them." He paused in painful memory. "Before they tore his eyes out."

"No demons," Aidan said. "Animals they are, called 'thoths.' Trained to hunt us, and keep from our sight. We burned them to death in my day."

"Really?" the freedman looked up at Aidan with awe.

Donough pointed toward the woods. "Look!"

Stirring at the edge of the trees, torches cast wavering light. In the borderland between light and shadow capered monstrous figures.

"Send him out!" cried a wavering, phantasmal voice. "Send him out! We cannot long hold back the *gruagach*!"

"I knew it!" cried a young mother, her infant in a sling at her breast. "They'll call demons, and slay us all."

From deep in the darkness a light flashed, a sound like a whiplash cracked, and Hans fell back, clapping his hand to his head. "*Gott!*" he moaned. Instantly, a pair of women ran to him, dragging and carrying him to safety and care.

"Stand fast!" screamed Aidan. "Demons don't need rifles; men do. And men bleed."

"We don't stand a chance!" one wild-eyed Roman yelled. "This is Aidan's fault! Give him up, says I—"

Donough swung a fist like a rock and caught that man a thunderous blow over the ear. The coward fell to the ground, bleeding, too stunned to do little save cradle his wounds. "Next man—or woman—talks such trash gets 'is neck broke," the giant growled. "We fight!"

Aidan took cold satisfaction from his old friend's actions. Most of his men and women stood strong, but cowards and children whimpered in the shadows. He could empathize. More than empathize. For three years he had feared this night's coming. The entire affair triggered long-dormant memories: the fall of his father's crannog, terror and murder in the night, of Northmen masked like animals, those masks concealing men more dangerous than any beast.

Fear could paralyze, but it could also vanquish fatigue and body ache. Instead of retreating to his bed, Aidan remained at the barricade, directing fire and keeping his men alert.

For long hours they watched, changing positions so that sharpshooters could not draw beads on them, spying from knotholes and then popping up to take their shots, cheering when their efforts were rewarded with a curse or groan.

And before the morning rose over the eastern woods, the blacks began to retreat, no longer laughing or daring to caper and taunt. It was the townsmen who lost their nerve, not the men and women of the O'Dere crannog.

"Done well, Aidan," Donough said, when an hour passed without a single hostile sound from the forest.

Aidan clasped his arm. "You were at my side all the way."

"World's a strange place," the bigger man said. "I'm startin' to think we might be better soldiers than fishermen. Ain't that a thing?"

That was a strange comment, and one that mirrored ideas long since stirring in Aidan's own mind.

"Or am I just being stupid again?" asked Donough.

"No," Aidan said thoughtfully. "You might be right. I just don't know what to think about it."

"What's that mean?"

Aidan considered. "There are some things you can know about yourself, and never act on. But what happens if you think you're one kind of man, and you turn out to be another? That can turn your whole life around."

Donough nodded. His blue eyes were still crisp and clear. The night's exertions seemed to have had little effect on him. "That it can."

Aidan heaved himself up. "Enough o' this philosophizin'. This fight isn't over yet. There'll be more souls set free before it's over. We ain't started to see ugly yet."

CHAPTER TWENTY-NINE

DESPITE THEIR FEARS, morning came without further incident. Aidan, utterly exhausted after almost two days without sleep, had finally been persuaded to bed.

The fog seemed to seep upward from the earth itself, wreathing garlands along the grass.

A mixed team of men and women guarded the crannog's ramparts. One man's head lolled, and he appeared to be dozing off. The settler to his right flat-handed him across the face in reprimand. He jerked upright, shaking himself, not certain exactly what had just happened, but head stinging from the effects nonetheless.

The chastised man peered out, and saw nothing but the morning fog. Then his eyes opened wide.

"Townsmen!" a freedman cried. "They're back. They're back!"

Like centaurs emerging from a primeval glade, a line of horsemen trotted in out of the fog.

One of the wall guards ran across the village, stumbling across a sleeping dog. He found Aidan's hut, and rapped plaintively at the door.

After a moment, Aidan answered, yawning and cinching up his pants. "An attack?"

"Horsemen, sir."

Sophia appeared behind him, belting a gown around her waist. "Soldiers?"

"We'll see," said Aidan. He pulled a shirt on and grabbed his rifle. He sprinted for the wall in a loose-hipped gait that belied his anxiety.

The Irishman vaulted up the wall, and then peered out. At first his expression was one of concern, but then he began to grin.

"Sir? Sir?" asked a freedman.

"Open the gates."

Donough jerked his head around in shock. "What? More townsmen?"

"Not with horses like those. These are highborn, and . . . God above, the banner! See the banner? *Dar Kush!*" The flag of Bilalistan was a crescent moon and lion upon a field of red: that of Dar Kush consisted of these two images, plus that of *nasab asad*, the ancestral fighting knife passed down for generations in the Wakil's family.

Aidan felt weak with relief.

"Dar Kush?" Confusion creased Stavros's bruised face. "What is this?"

"Blind me twice, it's Kai!" said Aidan, leaping down from the barricade. "Open the gate!"

Stavros was aghast. "But . . . they're black!"

"Nobody's perfect," Aidan said.

Aidan unbarred the gate himself, and threw it open. He walked out on the little bridge that connected the crannog to the land. The gate swung open, and Aidan stood in the middle of the opening, Donough coming to stand at his side. Donough held a spear, Aidan a rifle.

Approaching were a line of magnificent Arabian and Zulu mares. Seated upon them were a squad of fierce, lightly armored Moorish knights, armed with swords and rifles.

Watching from the battlements, the freedmen were mesmerized by the sight.

At the front of the line was Kai of Dar Kush. His dark, smooth face was neutral, but Aidan knew him well enough to know that the expression was a mask disguising a mind that had already absorbed everything in the environment. He rode perhaps the finest horse Aidan had ever seen, a black mare so alert and aware he would not have been surprised to hear her speak. From hoof to mane, bit to tail, she was as perfect a physical specimen as gold could buy. Aidan shook his head in admiration. Nothing but the best for his old friend.

Although the men following Kai sat erect and terribly formal, their keen eyes noted the unmistakable signs of battle, and were at the alert.

Kai's expression was neutral as he approached. His horse stopped. "*As-slaamu Alaykum.*"

"*Waalaykum salaam.*"

"I come in peace. Might a weary traveler find water for his horses and comfort for his men?"

Aidan inclined his head gravely. "I welcome the exalted and honorable Wakil of New Djibouti to my humble abode. Come, sit and share bread with us. We haven't much, but what we have is yours."

"A thousand thanks," Kai said, and dismounted.

Kai examined the makeshift battlements, the torn earth, burned buildings. He bent, and plucked up a bit of furrowed earth, rubbing it between his fingers. It was tacky with blood. "Well, Aidan, from the look of things I'd say you haven't kept as far out of trouble as I might have hoped."

"You know me. If there's a fight around, I've just got to have a piece of it."

He and Aidan circled each other, noting clothing, weaponry, and trimness of waist. Finally Kai chuckled. "Still ugly as ever, I see."

"And apparently," Aidan replied, "among your people effeminacy remains no barrier to power."

There was a pause, a long moment in which the two regarded each other almost as if they were afraid to break the silence or close the distance. Then they could restrain themselves no longer, and embraced heartily, smacking each other with rib-rattling buffets about the back and shoulders.

"Al-Muqit be praised!" Kai cried. "It is beyond wonderful to see you again."

"Kai, Kai . . . ," Aidan said, shaking his head. "If yesterday I had had any idea how soon I would see you, it would have rolled a stone from my heart."

Aidan turned and addressed the onlookers, who stared. "Let it be known by all that this is he of whom I have spoken, the Wakil of New Djibouti, my brother, Kai of Dar Kush. Let every courtesy be extended to him, and to his men."

"What happened here?" Kai asked. He gestured toward the field as he spoke.

Aidan grimaced. "A little problem with the local townsfolk."

"Was the law involved?"

Aidan nodded. "They waited until the chief constable was abed. His assistant was here, but this was an unofficial party."

"I see. Kebwe?"

Kebwe looked down from his mount. "Yes, Captain?"

"Take a third of the men, and go to town. I want this matter sorted out."

"Murad!" Kebwe called. "Azul! Follow me!"

One of the freedmen sidled up and took the opportunity to whisper to Aidan, "This man will side with us against his own kind?"

"This man will uphold the law," Aidan said. He paused, considering. "Or the right. Whichever is higher."

He called to his people. "Food! Drink!" He paused, shaking his head. "Ah, to hell with it: *Festival!*"

*　　*　　*

Within an hour, a joyous party had bloomed to life. Kai's men ate and drank (water) and admired the pretty Celt and Frankish girls. One of his old compatriots, the flat-faced Dahomy archer Makur, groped out, calling to a pale-skinned wench who danced enticingly just beyond range.

"Mind your manners," laughed Kai.

"But she smiled at me!" protested Makur. The Dahomy was a lieutenant in Djibouti Pride, the military regiment that had once belonged to Kai's brother and now rested in Kai's hands. Unlike Kai's guard, who were employees of Dar Kush, Djibouti Pride consisted of young men of good breeding and education, officers all. In civilian life they were lawyers, merchants, heirs to industrial empires. At least three times a year they gathered to drill, but aside from those times, or war, they lived normal lives.

Makur had stood with Kai at the Mosque of the Fathers. Although seriously involved in his father's construction business, Makur had leapt at the opportunity to take a week's travel with Kai and his guard.

"We are visitors here, upon an errand."

The lieutenant nodded reluctantly. "Yes, Captain."

A pale hand appeared before Kai's face. "More milk, sir?" asked a familiar voice.

"Yes, I—"

Kai turned to face Sophia, who smiled at him radiantly. He had not seen her in the half hour since entering the crannog, and had been too polite to mention the fact. It was, of course, possible that she might deliberately avoid him, at least for a time. Their personal history was regrettably complex.

Kai held his cup out in a rock-steady hand and had never been more grateful for the appearance of calm.

"Yes?"

"Sophia," Kai said. Her name had not passed his lips in months.

"Kai."

He shook his head in admiration. "You look radiant." She had been his first true lover, the first to teach him the arts by which a man truly pleased his woman. Her teaching had been a bewitchment.

"Thank you."

"I think that this life suits you well."

She inclined her head graciously. "And you yours. I heard that you and Lamiya are joyously wed."

"And a child!" Kai laughed. "A beautiful daughter, Aliyah. With the grace of Allah, she will resemble her mother in all things."

Their eyes locked until the contact grew a bit too intense, and she lowered her eyes. She smiled shyly. "It is very good to see you, Kai," she said. "I hope life has been kind."

"There is reason to all things. If life has seemed sometimes cruel, Allah has been merciful enough to allow me, from time to time, to glimpse His design."

Sophia's voice dropped. "The design that brought us all together?"

"Yes," he said. "And Aidan. A more tangled web than any of us could have known."

Sophia shook her head. Her black hair was shorter than he had last seen, and lay carelessly about her shoulders. Lack body or strength it might, but he still found it oddly attractive.

And so, he remembered, had other men, notably his uncle Malik. Because of her . . . because of the world they lived in, Kai had been forced to make a terrible decision. On the one hand, family and law and custom. On the other, honor and his immortal soul. Allah grant he never be forced to make such a choice again.

Sophia seemed almost to be reading his mind. "I am sorry for any pain you suffered because of me. Of us."

"Allah does not give a man a load exceeding his strength, however heavy it may seem. It remains for each of us to find the way to bear it."

"Kai," she said, "if it is any consolation, Aidan and I could not love you more were you flesh and blood. Mean it may be, but any house of ours is your home."

Kai searched her face, perhaps seeing reflected in her eyes a younger, less complicated man, one he missed terribly, one who might, for a few precious hours, now return to him.

Kai remembered:

The shadow of Malik's castle clutched at them, every one. Kai, shamshir in hand, faced his fearsome uncle, the greatest swordsman in New Djibouti and, some said, all Bilalistan itself. A bloodied Aidan, spent and exhausted in his futile effort to best Malik, had all but collapsed. "By right of arms," said Kai, "by all that is holy, I say that this man and his family are under my protection."

They could see that Malik had no wish to hurt Kai, but it seemed that all the threads of all their lives had spun out to lead them to this single, inexorable moment. Kai and Malik knelt in prayer, knowing that they would never meet again, this side of Sirat, the bridge to Paradise.

And then, the duel began. It was a fearsome explosion of steel and nerve, eye-baffling flurries of riposte and counterparry driving sparks from the blades. Still, despite the feroc-

ity of engagement, it was obvious to all that these two men loved each other more than they
loved their own lives.

And then he accessed yet another moment, his mind not quite spinning
the memories out in temporal sequence, but seemingly more according to
their relative emotional weight.

Kai held his dying uncle in his arms.

*"I remember your first step," Malik rasped. "Your father . . . your father . . . how
proud . . ."*

*And then Malik sagged, his fierce spirit finally at rest. Kai wobbled upright, weak from
loss of blood and emotional overwhelm. "By right of combat and inheritance, I declare myself lord of this manor. Is there one who would challenge me? Is there . . ."*

Then, strength spent at last he fainted, and collapsed to the ground.

Sophia watched Kai carefully. Impossibly, she seemed to intuit where
he had gone during that brief interlude. "Your home, Kai," she repeated.

Kai gazed at her. Her shy response was an acknowledgment that a
thread of something precious extended between them. "If my brother's
mate might be considered my sister, that would warm my heart."

Sophia smiled, that mere curl of her lips an act of magic. "Oh, Kai. That
was done long ago." She stood. "Dance with me?"

Kai looked around, embarrassed. "That is not my people's way."

Aidan clapped his hand on Kai's shoulder. The Irishman grinned. "You
are among *my* people now. This is *my* home. The mistress of the house has
asked you for a dance. Would you insult her?"

Mousetrapped, Kai stood. His men gawked at him as he did, but he
merely scowled at them and offered Sophia his arm. A beautiful flame-
haired fiddler struck a tune, and several of the freedmen began to dance.

The fiddler sang:

"My home used to be on a faraway shore . . ."

Clearly, this was a village favorite, because the mere beginning of the
song drew a crowd, and several sang the refrain following the first line:

"Sit ye down laddie and tell us your tale . . ."

The fiddler seemed to grow more confident with that response, and
bore down more seriously on her bow.

"I fear now forever I'll see it no more."

And the gathered answered:

Fresh hops and hemp truly make a good ale.

The fiddler went on, the crowd answering her calls in a ritual that went beyond the needs of a particular song, and gave Kai a brief glimpse of what life might have been like in their primitive Irish villages.

I serve under masters not cruel but not kind
Sit ye down laddie and tell us your tale
Of my health and hardships they pay little mind
Fresh hops and hemp truly make a good ale. . . .

Then all of them joined together in chorus:

Brown red or pale
Hearty and hale
Fresh hops and hemp truly make a good ale.

The melody was strong, but the rhythm seemed halting. Still, Sophia guided him, one small warm hand resting on his side, the other on his shoulder.

My family and kinsfolk are far, far from me
Sit ye down laddie and tell us your tale.
But I wish them good fortune wherever they be
Fresh hops and hemp truly make a good ale. . . .

Again they sang the refrain, and he was surprised to find himself whispering the words as they did:

Brown red or pale
Hearty and hale
Fresh hops and hemp truly make a good ale.

Kai did not drink, had not tasted alcohol in four years. There had been a short time, earlier in his life, when he had hoisted a cup as eagerly as any tavern brawler, and could empathize with the thirst for the magical potion that salved the ills of both body and heart.

Dancing in this way was a completely new experience. For once in his life, Kai the master swordsman felt clumsy and clubfooted.

> *I miss my good children, I miss my fair wife*
> *But I'll make what I can of this poor servant's life. . . .*

The world whirled around Kai, and he found himself able to relax a bit, just enough to ask himself how he might have felt, how he might have dealt with the twin burdens of slavery and ignorance. As much as Allah might have blessed him by making him a member of a superior race, there had also to be blessings in being of European blood. Surely a merciful God would not completely abandon the children He had created from clay. Adam and Hawaa, whom Christians called "Eve," were names that literally meant "black" and "brown" in Arabic. The first humans, created by His mighty hand had, therefore, been Africans.

But however far from Allah they might stand, these whey-skinned folk seemed of unbreakable spirit. And that was one of the blessings of submission, which all men must ultimately accept. Submission unto Allah, the one true God, submission unto His laws, and for some, submission to those whom Allah had created first and raised high.

> *One day I'll be lucky, my freedom to win*
> *Then I'll roam through this country to find kith and kin.*
> *As a free man I'll wander far to the west sea.*
> *And what service I do will be service to me. . . .*

And there was a fine dream. A fantasy of freedom and travel, placing the cares of the world at your back, seeking strange new horizons. This was a familiar reverie. Despite his riches and power, he had often indulged in it himself. Kai sometimes dreamed of climbing onto his horse and simply riding west, away from everything, into the Nations, there to find adventure, peace, or death. Everything that he had done in the last three years had been an attempt to postpone the very actions he now undertook, a full engagement with the responsibilities of Wakil. The responsibilities of the only surviving son of Abu Ali.

> *As a free man I'll purchase a house of my own*
> *Made of good wood and good thatch and good stone. . . .*

Sophia's hand was warm and soft on his back, and he closed his mind tightly, refused to let it wander to a time that those hands had been more intimate, more giving. The time when Sophia's every secret had been his to command . . .

Or so he had imagined.

> *As a free man my days will be pleasure to keep*
> *I'll live my life gently and pass in my sleep. . . .*

A sentiment for a slave. There could be no freedom without responsibility. He hazarded that Aidan, now a leader of his people, had come to understand that. Kai depended upon that understanding, and cursed himself for that dependence. In a better world, it would be possible to accomplish great feats without placing those you love in jeopardy. But this was not that world. Perhaps, if he gambled well, he could help create such a place, a world of honor and faith, rather than one of wealth and power.

> *But I work a long day and I sleep a short night*
> *So this mug full of beer is a comforting sight*
> *Pray talk with me friend while I finish this brew*
> *With a few more like this I'll be in a good stew. . . .*

Kai was uncomfortable with his men's good-natured hooting, but Sophia's smile was welcoming enough to thaw his reserve, and he fell beneath the music's spell.

He felt his way into the rhythm, and the steps that Sophia used to wind her way through it, until finally the final refrain arrived and the tune itself came to its harmonious conclusion.

"Done!" said Kai, somewhat relieved. "And wondrously so."

"Your people do not dance?" said Sophia. "But I have seen them!"

"Men do not dance with women," he explained, "except their wives and fiancées."

"Ah." Her eyes twinkled. *And others who are special, yes, Kai?*

"But what a gift!" he cried, breaking eye contact. "And I have gifts for you as well. Makur!"

The tall, thin Makur led a pair of pack camels to them. Both blacks and freedmen crowded about as they unburdened the animals.

"Rifles, Aidan!" a villager exulted, tearing a crate open. "Two of 'em!"

"Unless Kai has changed," said Aidan, "they are the best. Let me see!"

The freedman tossed Aidan a Benin breech-loader. Kai noted his friend's effortless catch and smiled in approval. The Irishman's coordination had always been superb, and now, for once, that would be of critical importance. Aidan examined the rifle with increasing relish, running his hands over the stock's fine dark grain, the barrel's cool gray-black metal. "Yes!" Aidan crowed.

"It meets your approval?" Kai asked, already knowing the answer.

"Exceeds it by far."

"Aidan!" a slave said eagerly, inspecting a keg half as tall as he. "Beer!"

Aidan hoisted an eyebrow. "This wouldn't be . . . ?"

"Hemp beer, yes," Kai said. "And I seem to remember that you enjoyed hemp itself—or at least its fumes. There is leaf and seed in that bag."

"We'll make you an honorary Irishman yet," Aidan said.

"I'm not certain I could survive the revels," Kai said.

The other villagers gathered around the pack animals, distributing *this* copper pot and *that* bolt of spun silk, laughing and sharing almost as if the previous night's horrors had never occurred at all.

With a new lightness in his step, Aidan led Kai around the crannog, pointing out the village's myriad features.

"And how did you seal the logs?" Kai asked, peering closely at the fence.

"Clay—the lake banks have a good quality."

"Do you remember Dar Kush's brickworks?"

"Indeed. I worked there a month, once upon a time."

"Mixing straw with your clay, and then baking, would produce an even stronger wall."

Aidan nodded. "You're right, I'm sure. None of my people know how to do this. If you would teach me, I would teach them, and we would make a brickworks."

Kai grinned. "Sergeant Makur served an apprenticeship as a brickmaker. Lend me three of your smartest young men, and I'll have Makur teach them."

"Thank you," Aidan said sincerely, then brightened. "How is Babatunde?"

"Full of riddles as always."

"Are you solving them?"

"All things in time," said Kai. "They still hurt my head, though."

The two friends laughed as they reminisced, catching up on all that had happened in the intervening months. Together they toured Aidan's crannog, wrought in an attempt to bring his people safety and stability.

After Kai had much admired the efforts, they found a quiet corner, and Aidan pressed his old friend for answers.

"Kai . . . it is wonderful to see you," he confessed. "And your timing is . . . well, almost miraculous. But I can't believe that you rode all the way out here, bearing gifts, just to teach us how to make bricks or to dance with my wife."

"Lovely though she is."

"Lovely though she is. I know you better than that. What do you need of me?"

"So," Kai said, more heavily now. "Are pleasantries concluded?"

Sophia had joined her husband. "I hope not."

"Let us go somewhere more private. I have . . . something to tell you."

CHAPTER THIRTY

AIDAN'S HOME WAS twice as large as his old Ghost Town dwelling, but of much the same rectangular design. Kai and his hosts sat by the fire, enjoying the warmth of smoldering logs and companionship. As Sophia kept Mahon quiet and occupied, Kai finally began to speak his mind.

"This all concerns the Caliph's household," he said, after he had explained the nearness of war, and the risks for southern Bilalistan. "According to spies, the Caliph has a deciphering device used for secret messages with Egypt."

"What?" said Aidan. "Please, *shwei-shwei.* Slow down."

"Ciphering is like putting a message into another language. A cipher *machine* speaks that language."

"A talking machine?" Sophia asked.

"Yes. If you write in Arabic, it speaks in some tongue none of us can understand. This one speaks hieroglyphs."

"What?"

"Old Egyptian, but scrambled so that not even a scholar can read it. Information suggests it is almost certainly kept in the Caliph's office, in his home, which is closely guarded. If we had it, it might be possible to read his messages and learn their plans. The question is: how to get to it?"

"Yes," Sophia said. Although she seemed not to have been listening, her voice was decidedly suspicious. "How?"

"We believe that there is one weakness in the Caliph's security," said Kai.

"And that is?" asked Aidan.

"He enjoys his gambling. And his favorite game is the Arena. Fighting slaves."

"I have heard of this," Sophia said. "There were such arenas in Rome, I believe. The Egyptians enjoyed watching Romans break each other's bones."

"Such contests are rarely to the death," said Kai. "But savage nonetheless. He hosts local tournaments, then feasts and whores the winners."

Kai paused, and there was a world of significance in the hollow moment. "On his *estate.*"

Aidan's face flattened. "I see."

Kai continued rapidly. "My sources say that champions have considerable freedom of motion within the estate's walls."

"Considerable freedom." Aidan seemed to bite at the words. He stood and began to pace. "And you think that such a person might well find and steal this . . . Egyptian talking machine?"

"Yes," Kai said.

Sophia looked from her husband to Kai and down at her child before tilting her face back up again. "And what precisely has this to do with us?"

Instead of answering, Kai opened a leather pouch and withdrew a stiff, glossy sheet of paper. Likenesses of men and women glistened on the sheet, dressed in finery from a dozen nations and peoples. Aidan shook his head. "What manner of image is this?"

"It is called a light-painting, and it is the coming thing. Sunlight paints chemical images on the paper, using a focusing lens. I do not completely understand."

Aidan shook his head in amazement. "This is incredible. So lifelike . . ." He scanned the faces. "But what has this . . . to do . . . with . . ."

And then he stopped dead, his eyes gone wide.

Kai could hear shouts and laughter from outside his old friend's home, and was gladdened that his men had found welcome here, where it might have been entirely reasonable to encounter hostility. After all, what had these people to love about Africans?

He found the silence as Aidan stared actually soothing, like placid water between crashing waves.

Sophia broke the silence. "Aidan . . . ?"

"Good Christ," he whispered. "Where did you get this?"

"I was in a meeting in Radama, the capital. All the attendants had such images rendered. I found this one of interest, and arranged for the artist to make me a copy."

Aidan's fingers traced the face of a light-haired white woman who stood next to a black man in military uniform. The Irishman seemed lost. "So like my mother . . . ," he muttered.

"Aidan?" Sophia asked, growing alarmed.

"Hair?" Aidan said, ignoring Sophia's prompt.

"Blonde, like yours. But redder."

"Like strawberries," he whispered. "When was this made?"

"A few weeks ago."

Aidan pointed at the man beside her. "Who is he?"

"Admiral Amon bin Jeffar, one of the most powerful nobles in New Alexandria. A brilliant, wealthy man of good family." Another pause. "I was told her name was Habiba. It means 'sweetheart.' "

Aidan closed his eyes, fingers gripping at the wooden table. To his left, the fire crackled. "What else?"

"She has borne no children. They say she is Irish."

"What else?" Aidan's eyes were closed tightly, as if muscular contraction could protect him from emotional pain.

"It is said she came to his household about ten years ago, possibly from Eire. A 'wild ghost' they call her, meaning she was not born here. Since the death of his wife, Habiba has traveled extensively with the Admiral. Once, they say, even so far as the court of the Pharaoh."

Sophia winced as Aidan gripped her hand.

"What else." It was no longer a question.

"That is all I know at present. To inquire further would have been fool-hardy."

Aidan opened his eyes. They looked dry. "I see. I know you, Kai. But I'm still not sure what you want from me. There's only one possibility I can think of—and that is insane. I'm no pit fighter."

Kai leaned forward urgently, fingers locked together tight. "I've seen the Caliph's champion fight," he said. "He's strong. Fast. Brutal. Hard to hurt—"

Aidan groaned. "This just gets better all the time."

"But *deeply flawed*," Kai said, speech quickening. "I could train you to beat him. I could. Aidan, you're a natural. Merely watching Malik teach me, you learned more than some of his students."

Aidan threw his hands up in frustration. "Kai, I'm a fisherman!"

Kai bore in mercilessly. "No, Aidan. That's not all you are. We were together at the mosque. I saw your courage and strength. You were one of the first to volunteer. You were one of the first into battle—"

"It was the only way to save Sophia!"

Kai stood. "Did I say you were a mercenary? Or a soldier? No! You are a *warrior*." He said the word as if it was a holy thing, and to Kai it was. "I would wager my life that you descend from a line of such men. And if for a few years your people softened enough to allow the Northmen to take you, still that blood runs in your veins."

Aidan clenched his fists at the side of his head, trying not to hear. Even worse might be to believe. The fact that Kai's words mirrored thoughts

that he and Donough had but recently expressed made it all the more uncanny.

"I'm not going to lie and say I have no personal interests. I want to hold
this country together. I want it to be free of Egypt—"

"*Free.*" Sophia said, breaking in. "An interesting choice of words, Kai.
What does that word mean to you?"

"Yes," he said, grasping her intent. "Bilalistan is the land where you and
yours were enslaved. But a country is not mere grass and rock and hill. It
is also the hearts of its people, its dreams of the future. Do you think that
there will always be slaves, Aidan? And what kind of men do you think
will be able to lead the way to that new destiny? Men like you."

"And you, Kai? What of you?" Sophia asked. "Have you freed your
slaves?"

"No," he said. "It isn't that simple."

"Of course not," she said bitterly.

"Sophia," Kai pled. "Don't judge me merely by my station in life. Judge
also by how far I have come. I am only one man. I need allies, agents, warriors, teachers."

For once, Sophia was pitiless. "How could you come here and use
Aidan's sister against him? If you were his friend, you would buy Nessa,
and set her free. Isn't that what a *friend* would do?"

Kai nodded. "I made an inquiry. The admiral had already turned down
a princely sum for her. If I bid on her, and failed, and then Aidan was able
to rescue her, where first would bin Jeffar look? He would seek among my
lands and associates, and the fugitive slave laws would strengthen his suit.
He would find her again."

"So convenient."

"No," Kai said. "Not convenient at all."

"You're not risking your own blood."

Kai rose and stood facing the fire, his back to his friends, as if unwilling to let them see the pain in his eyes. "Yes. I am. The Pharaoh has
Elenya. If my efforts in behalf of the south, of the Empress, are known, she
will suffer."

Sophia's anger drained away. "Elenya? Oh, Kai, I'm sorry."

Now Aidan spoke. "Kai . . . I have heard talk. All words of emancipation come from the north. The south wishes to keep its slaves."

"Tell me my husband is wrong," Sophia asked.

Kai turned back to them. "I will not lie," he said. "He is correct. Aidan,
you know me, and you know what is in my heart. I can promise only that

I am still your friend, and that I have not forgotten the lessons learned at the mosque.

"But I am also my father's son, and bound to protect our seat in the Senate. That means that there are things I cannot say publicly. I cannot threaten the very men I need to bind the south into a single sword. Half Djibouti and Wichita's wealth is in slave property. To lose it all outright would beggar us. It can never happen until the financial burden is lighter."

He leaned forward. "But I can do everything in my power to undermine the institution, to see it ended, and secure justice for every soul on this continent. I don't know what that future society would manifest, but I know my peers would consider me a traitor for even considering this discussion. Beyond that, I can promise nothing."

He paused. "So, then. I give you this picture, Nessa's new name, and the name of her owner. If you have another way of reaching her, then do it, and Allah give you wings. But if you have not, if you will trust me this one final time, I swear that if you can complete this mission for me, I will move heaven and earth to bring you both safely out. I swear further that I will be in your debt, and you may be certain that when you call that marker, I will answer with all my heart."

Kai exhaled sharply. "As for the rest, it is in Allah's gracious hands. Make the choice that rings most true to you. I await your answer."

Without another word, Kai bowed and left their home.

Aidan held Kai's sketch of Nessa, staring at it. "Look at this," he whispered. "Realer than any drawing, any painting. These blacks are so clever, so damnably clever. What chance did we ever . . ." His hand began to tremble, and a single tear rolled down his cheek.

He stood, stalking back and forth across the room, his face a tortured meld of joy and horror.

"My husband . . . ?"

"All these years," Aidan said. "If I've found her after all these years . . ."

It remained the single most painful memory of his life. In the clay-tiled expanse of New Djibouti's slave market, Nessa was pulled away from Aidan and his mother Deirdre. "Aidan! Oh, Aidan, help me!"

"Nessa!" he cried, desperate to find some words that might, impossibly, lessen the pain. "Listen to me. I'll find you, I swear!"

"Do you swear?" She was desperate, very near the point of breaking emotionally. He could feel it, knew that he had to give her something to hold onto, or they would both lose their minds.

"On our father's life I swear," he said, looking into the eyes that were his eyes, the face that was his face.

And Nessa was hauled away, disappearing into the uncaring crowd. Where once his sister had stood now trod only passersby, on their way to and from whatever unknowable tasks completed and enriched their alien lives, never knowing of the tragedy that had occurred among them.

And even had they known, they wouldn't have cared at all.

Shaking like a dog awakening from a dream, Aidan began to emerge from his trance.

"What is it?" asked Sophia.

"I made a promise. All those years ago I made a promise to my sister."

"Yes." Sophia nodded.

"We were in our mother's womb together. She was born half an hour before me, so that I was her 'little brother.' She always teased me about that."

Sophia knew her man better than to interrupt him.

"Everything was taken from me . . . everything except my promise. I never lost my dream of finding her. Freeing her. I thought that when I was free I might earn money, could begin the search. But every day that passed made that entire world mistier. I barely remember my father's smile. My mother's voice. But I cannot forget Nessa's face, because it is my own. I cannot forget my promise, because it is the only thing that keeps my parents alive. I *swore.*"

Sophia glanced at their child, but it was a brief glance. "Yes, I understand. So. You will do this thing?"

"No," he said.

She shook her head, and stared at him. "No?"

"No. I cannot." He seemed utterly miserable. "Sophia, I was but a child when that promise was made. We have been apart almost as long as we were ever together. I know not what accommodations Nessa has made with her life, but I know what mine has become."

"What?" she asked.

"You," he said. He drew her to him and laid his head against the swelling of her belly. His second child grew in that darkness. Soon it would yowl its way into the light, ready to challenge life. He swore that when it did, he would have done everything in his power to make the new and strange world as welcoming as he could.

"You, and our children. You need me. In this time, more than ever."

"Aidan . . . ," she said, voice soft with wonder. "I couldn't ask . . ."

"You haven't," he said. "You would never ask me to stay. And that is why I do."

He held her, and shook softly.

What a world, Sophia thought, *to force men to make choices such as this.* And cradling the man that she loved, even as she would one day cradle his child now sleeping within her, clarified and sharpened her mind.

"Aidan," she said. "We have a son and he will soon have a brother or sister. What would you have them be to each other?"

"All goodly things."

"And when they marry, what then will they be?"

"Clan and family, still."

"Yes. This place is to be our home, built one precious stone at a time. We cannot build it on the bones of those we love." She turned his face, and forced him to gaze up at her. "You built this place with your own hands. Your walls, Aidan. And you drew these people together. Your people, Aidan. To protect all of us. And now, you are going to have to trust them."

He blinked. "What are you saying?"

"You have given me your whole heart, but half of your soul remains in bondage. I want our son to know that his father did what was right, not what was expected. If we have a daughter I want her to know her brother would come for her, come what may, and that he would select as a mate a woman who would demand no less of him. Family comes first," she said. "*First.*"

"You are my family," he protested, beginning to weaken. Or was it strengthen?

"And so is every man and woman in this crannog," she said fiercely. "Don't you understand that? They wouldn't give you up when it might have cost them their lives. Do you think they will not do all in their power to protect your woman?"

"But—"

"No!" she said, and placed her hand on the swelling beneath her breasts. "Go, or don't go. But by the sweet Lord I love, don't you dare lay responsibility for it on me, or Mahon, or our unborn child. We both need a man who will do what is right, no matter how hard that thing is. This is the man I married. You tell me if he stands before me now."

He stared at her, shaking his head side to side almost unconsciously, and then sighed. "I don't know. If I do this thing, if I can try this task that has lived in my heart for ten years—"

"You can only do your best."

"What if I fail?"

"No," she said. "Don't look to me for those answers. You tell me: what happens if you fail?"

He paused, thinking hard. "If I try, truly try, then whether or not I succeed, I can be complete with my past. I can be here with you, and live my life, and raise my children, and make my peace."

"Can you?" she asked.

"Yes." He sighed deeply. "And all I have to do is embrace that thing I hate most in all the world."

"Slavery?"

He nodded. "Slavery. Yes."

"You trust Kai very much, don't you?" she asked.

He glanced at her sharply. "You think I shouldn't?"

"No," she said. "I think he is the most honorable man I have ever known. I said hurtful things because I love you, and I do not wish to risk what we have."

"Nor do I."

She continued. "There's no helping it, is there? The man I love would keep his promise, no matter the cost. That man would find his sister, and bring her home."

"Am I that man?"

She turned his face, kissed each of his closed eyes gently, tasting his tears, and then his trembling mouth.

"I'm so afraid," he said.

"Yes."

Aidan stood, and wiped his face on his sleeve. "After Kai and his men depart," he said, "we must hold council."

CHAPTER THIRTY-ONE

11 Shawwal A.H. 1294
(Friday, October 19, 1877)

WHEN DAWN'S SUN CLIMBED ABOVE the pines, Kai and his men began their southern trek. Despite the fact that he had freely offered all his information about Nessa, his heart was heavy with self-loathing. Whatever Aidan decided, it would be without undue coercion.

Still, he had opened a door for his oldest friend. Both redemption and death lay behind that portal. But had he really brought all his resources to bear on the question of freeing Nessa? If Aidan's help had not been required, were there not things he might have done?

The answer wasn't clear. Every action carried risks for all. If Nessa had been Elenya, he would have moved heaven and earth to free her. But what were his obligations here?

In truth, he had no answer to that. But if anything happened to Aidan . . .

He knew that not a day would pass, for the rest of his life, that he would not ask himself the terrible question:

Could I have done more?

Kai's black Arabian mare Randa shifted restlessly beneath him, as if eager to be on her way home. "Kebwe has spoken with Constable Oba," he said. "Oba had already relieved his assistant of duty even before we arrived. One of the vigilantes died, but it seems there was no love lost between him and his wives. He had no children to feud for him, and as it was an illegal party, there is no law to plague you. The townsfolk remain a problem. I recommend that you take your trade west to one of the Nations' outposts for the next year. An extra half-day's journey, but it will give the tension time to diminish." Randa shifted impatiently. "Oba is a good man, but will need support in the Territorial Senate to maintain power. He will get that support," Kai promised.

"Thank you," Aidan said.

Kai shook his head. "I did little of nothing. You saved yourselves. Look to each other, and be proud. You have made a strong beginning here, Aidan. If my proposal interests you, perhaps together we can take your beginning to the next level."

"We will see," Aidan said quietly.

Kai paused, looking out into the woods. The wind gently riffled the tree-tops. Kai sighed. "Whatever your decision, you are my friend. Make the choice that is true to you, Aidan. Send word to me." He handed Aidan a leather pouch. "Here is gold to pay the heliograph operators, and a letter carrying my seal. No one will molest you on the road, or deny you services while you are about my business."

"If I answer within the month?" Aidan asked.

"That will suffice. Blessings unto you and yours." His eyes met Sophia's. "You are a wealthy man, Aidan."

Then he wheeled the magnificent Randa about. "Homeward!"

The torches burned over the earthen-floored longhouse as the conclave of elders began its session.

Three gray-haired women sat at the head table, along with Sophia and some of the older men. Not all of them were Irish: two were Germans, and one was Greek, but by agreement of all they conducted this meeting in the way of Aidan's people.

Aidan stood before them and spoke. "Because this matter affects this entire community, I have decided that it should be a matter for council. Grandmothers, may your wisdom lead us to the light."

"So mote it be," they chanted.

The second toothless old woman leaned forward. "What be the matter at hand?" She and several of the other elders had won their freedom after long decades of service, after their health and useful years were gone. Then they had the choice of being supported by the other slaves and tilling a little patch of ground for vegetables—or taking their chances with one of the freedman settlements springing up around Bilalistan.

Aidan cleared his throat. "I've been offered a chance to rescue my sister from bondage."

This revelation triggered a collective intake of breath. "Blessed be . . ."

"Hold!" said Sophia. "It is not so simple."

"Life rarely is." The other crones nodded toothlessly.

"In order to do it," said Aidan, "I must perform a boon for our friend, Kai."

The grandmother spat on the packed earth floor. "No shadow's a friend o' mine."

Another agreed. "Bore five bairn for sech as he. Dusky issue gone fore'er, with barely a dream of me teat to warm 'em. No good can come of this, sez I. I sez he's lyin' to ye."

"I saw a light-painting," Aidan replied. "The face was my sister's. No one could tell me different."

"Kai may be many things," Sophia said in a cool, flat voice. "But he is no liar."

"They's all liars. Every one—"

The second grandmother spoke sharply. "Hush, an' let the boy speak his mind."

Aidan sighed. "I would have to fight the Caliph's champion."

That caught their attention. "What sez ye?" the older woman said, incredulous. "I seen these pit fighters, and they'd tear the pretty right oot yer face. It's madness ye speak."

"Not madness," he replied. "Kai is a dazzling fighter, from a great warrior house. He knows that world. If he says he can train me to beat this man, he speaks truth."

She snorted. "Does he promise to return ye with all yer dangles in order? Ye be a married man, with fleshly obligations."

"And I am his wife," said Sophia, "and I tell you that I abstain from this vote. Whatever the council decides will have my blessings."

"How long would ye be gone, Aidan?" said the grandmother.

"I don't know. Months. Perhaps a year."

The grandmothers grumbled amongst themselves. "This is the sister separated from ye when ye first landed on this accursed soil?"

"Yes."

Now one of the graybeards spoke. "Ye don't know her anymore, Aidan. She might not remember ye."

Aidan shook his head. "That's not possible. We are twins, and I swore her a promise."

There was nodding and agreement in the room. Then quiet. Then the old man spoke again. "I know what I said sounded like coward's talk. But Aidan . . . ye would become a slave again, to save her?"

"Aye. That, and more," Aidan replied.

His eyes met Sophia's. He was risking more than his life and freedom. He risked their future. Although terribly frightened for him, Sophia nodded proudly. That was his woman, and the sudden understanding of her strength made him long to be a better man.

"I knew a man once," said the oldster. "Ran away from New Alexandria to Wichita. Made a living selling himself to rich sinners."

"I've heard of that. They have an agreement that they will free him, and gain smiles from the Prophet or something."

The graybeard nodded. "Aye. These Africans have a rat's nest of crazy customs. Anyway, he made a mistake, and sold himself to a rice farmer, brother to the local judge. Judge said that the agreement paper they'd signed meant nothin'. By selling himself, he became a real slave again."

The old man leaned forward. "You know what happened?"

Aidan could feel what was coming. "What?"

"Went crazy. Fockin' crazy. He'd been born a slave, and then was free, and when he became a slave again something cracked inside him." He slapped his palms together in emphasis. "Like that. He just foamed and chewed the grass."

There was a long pause. Everyone waited, wondering if there was more. There was no more. That was the story, and it implied everything that it was intended to.

"That won't happen to me."

"What if ye can't get back to us?" the old man asked.

"I'll get back."

"What if ye can't?" the graybeard bored in.

Aidan met his eyes squarely. "If I don't come back to cradle my children, to love my wife, to work and hunt and fish with you . . . then you'll know I'm dead."

They muttered to each other, but Aidan spoke first. "If there is any chance at all of finding me sister, I have to try. It isn't just for me. How can we forget what happened just a single day ago? That could have been the end of everything. We need more power, more leverage, or next time, we might not be so damned lucky."

He leaned forward. "Kai came here to use me, but I tell you that I can use *him*, and get the better of the deal." His eyes gleamed. "He has power—power that can make our children safe, protect our lands and homes, our wives. . . ." He lowered his voice until it was very nearly a growl. "Power to grow strong, until we can give the blacks reason to regret they ever nurtured us. If I can do him this service it will tighten the bond between us, place the Wakil of New Djibouti in my debt."

Again a pause, filled with whispers.

"Do you realize what that means?" Aidan pressed on. "To us? To our children? Kai has already assisted us with the Salaman constabulary. If I can find the right leverage with the Wakil, our crannog would be safe. No one would dare interfere with us. There would be one place on this continent where white men would be safe to raise their families and work their fields and love their women. One single blessed place."

The eldest woman nodded. "One can grow to two. To three, and more. It could be a beginning."

There were nods now, assurances, eager whispers.

"Do you see?" Aidan said. "Do you see why I have to do it?"

"Yes, we see," the old woman answered. "But what I don' understand is why ye brought this to council. Boyo, yer mind's made up already."

Aidan smiled wanly. "Because I want your blessings. I'm afraid. Afraid I'll fail, that this is my last chance, and I'll fail Nessa. Sophia. Mahon. Our new baby. All of you. I can't do this alone. But if I go with all of you in my heart, then maybe . . . just maybe, I can do it."

The old women whispered amongst themselves; then the eldest stood and shuffled over to Aidan. She spat on her thumb and made a cross on his forehead with the moisture. Oddly, instead of the expected coolness, he felt only a warmth that seemed to spread up through his scalp and then down the back of his spine until his tailbone tingled.

"*Coire Sois*," she said. "The Cauldron of Knowing. May it be alive within you, and guide your every thought and deed." She lifted his shirt and made another cross on his chest, over his heart. "*Coire Ernmae*," she said. "The Cauldron of Vocation. Ye have many skills, Aidan. May your heart embrace this new one, that you return to us safe and sound." And finally she drew a third cross at his navel. "*Coire Goiriath*, the Cauldron of Warming. The source of your power and vitality. May it blossom beyond your dreams, that your quest be fulfilled."

"So mote it be," said they all, young and old, together.

CHAPTER THIRTY-TWO

20 *Shawwal* A.H. 1294
(Sunday, October 28, 1877)

TWO DAYS AFTER KAI AND HIS MEN returned to Dar Kush, Cetshwayo's negotiator Mpondo Khozi arrived. Khozi was an aged, battle-scarred Zulu lawyer accompanied by an honor guard of eight sons. Servants escorted them to their guest rooms on the third floor, drew baths that they might refresh themselves, and provided a hearty meal. Then Kai met with them in Dar Kush's central atrium. "The ceremony must respect our people," began Mpondo after initial pleasantries were concluded.

"My father had every intention that this be true," answered Kai.

Beside him, Babatunde spoke. "Wakil. May I?"

"Please."

"One of the fissures we must bridge is that of the spirit."

"Excuse me?" Mpondo asked in his graveled voice. Thus far, despite the Zulu's well-known disdain for those of mixed blood, he had been coolly polite to the Sufi scholar.

"The matter of religion," said the Sufi.

Mpondo continued. "It is understood that Nandi's children will be raised in Islam. However, the princess's soul is her concern, and hers alone."

"Agreed," said Babatunde. "We have no interest in depriving the princess of whatever comfort she finds in the presence of her ancestors. We understand and respect the beliefs of the great Zulu people. This is not the Old World. We desire a land in which each may regard and approach the Creator in his own way."

These words elicited a smile from Mpondo. "This is meet, and good."

"We ask only," said Babatunde, "that since any children will inherit the estate and the power and authority that that implies, that they be raised in the traditions of the Wakil's family. That they not have two hearts, the mother must not attempt to teach the Zulu way of spirit until they have reached the age of reason. Then she may share with them what she will."

"It will be," said Mpondo. "If the marriage begins with mutual respect, it may endure in the same manner."

"There is one other thing," the Zulu lawyer continued. "This one came directly from the lady herself. She craves a boon of the Wakil."

"What boon?"

"She said that it is to be specified later, and that if you love her, you will trust her enough to grant this."

Kai looked at Babatunde and laughed, and nodded.

During breaks in the negotiations, Kai showed his guests the extent of his holdings. Maps detailed the salt plantations and Aztecan silver mines, while more personal inspections were possible of the ships, the counting-house, the herds, the fields, the armories, and the slaves.

It was impossible to tell if they were impressed: for all their reaction he might have been a merchant welcoming them into his leather shop's single room, ignorantly proud of goods his guests would not have inflicted upon their meanest servant.

Later, after the day's interactions had ceased, Kai took refuge in spiritual study. As in the negotiations, his Yoruban tutor led the way here as well. It was this night, after the third day of wrangling with Mpondo and sons, that Kai found he could no longer conceal his thoughts and fears.

"Babatunde, I must tell you something," he said.

"Yes?"

"Something that occurred at the Mosque of the Fathers. At the shrine." Kai fidgeted. He did not want this discussion, but saw no means of avoidance.

"During the battle?"

"Yes. During the battle." He paused. "Shaka went insane."

Babatunde snorted. "A brief journey."

Kai shook his head. "He was brilliant, unpredictable, savage—the most frightening human being I have ever met."

"More so than Malik?"

Interesting. So Babatunde had been frightened of Malik, after all! Until this moment, Kai had never been certain. "Yes. Malik's darkness was balanced by love for his wife, and also my father. Shaka had a half dozen wives, none of whom had any real power at all—he was a rogue, more fully in the shadow than the light."

Babatunde nodded. "My assessment as well."

"But during the battle, he used his own troops to lure the Aztecs into the tall brush. Then he set fire to it. He planned to burn them all."

At this, the Yoruba's eyes sharpened. "Everyone?"

"Yes," said Kai.

"Do you mean the mamluks?"

"No. *Everyone.* There were black troops as well."

"I see," said Babatunde. "Bilalians? Or Zulus also?"

That question stopped Kai for a moment. He thought back: most of the sacrificed men would have been Bilalians: Abyssinians, Egyptians, Yorubans, a dozen other people. And of course whites. But there had been some Zulus as well. Sacrificed so that . . . so that . . .

So that his Bilalian allies would not suspect that they had been set out like lambs in a lion trap. Probably some of his least-useful men, a "trouble brigade" established for just such a purpose. Which implied that his troops, many of them, would approve of such tactics, even when they might prove homicidal toward his own men. Why? Because a warrior who marched with Shaka marched to victory. In any war men died: that truth was inescapable. What matter if Shaka consciously and deliberately expended some of these? Even if that were true, a soldier had been more likely to survive a campaign under Shaka than almost any other leader.

"Kai?"

Babatunde's voice seemed to reach from some outer darkness, and Kai suddenly realized how far afield he had allowed his mind to wander. "I'm sorry. What were you saying?"

Babatunde gazed at him curiously, and then shrugged. "All right. What happened when you realized Shaka was killing his own men?"

"Ali tried to stop him. Shaka stabbed him."

"And then you killed Shaka." It was not a question.

That startled Kai out of his trance. "Yes. How did you know?"

Babatunde smiled grimly. "I know you. It makes sense of your behavior these last years. Did you hide his body?"

"No," said Kai. "I think his own people did. Hid, or buried it. Perhaps to keep it from being desecrated, or to conceal the fact of his death, or . . . Allah, I do not know!"

Babatunde mused. "Some say that he did not die, that he returned to Africa on some kind of spiritual quest. Men say many things, think many things when they cannot accept a paler reality."

"In death," said Kai, "Shaka looms larger than ever he did in life."

"And the one person who could refute the stories dares not speak. A pretty problem, indeed. And now Nandi comes."

"Yes."

"Do you think she knows?" asked the Sufi. "That her father knows?"

"The Zulus abandoned us at the mosque. They knew. Or suspected."

"But how? There were no witnesses!"

"They saw Shaka's wounds, and Ali's wounds. Our feet and bodies marked the earth. The Zulus are the finest trackers in Bilalistan. They can read sign. *They knew.* And that means Cetshwayo knows whatever they knew."

Now, at last, Babatunde seemed alarmed. "Then you must call this wedding off! Shaka's niece is your Hashassin."

"But . . . ," said Kai. "But I could be wrong. Fodjour said it best: why not just shoot me at a distance?"

"Kai—if she marries you, *her children will be heir to Dar Kush.* They will kill you *after* the ceremony or perhaps after she bears a son, when a single stroke serves two purposes—vengeance and power."

"But if they do *not* know, I would be responsible for damaging the alliance. Djibouti needs the Zulus."

"They need their Wakil as well."

Kai smiled weakly. "And I . . . want her."

Babatunde smote his forehead with his palm. "Allah preserve us. The fate of our entire empire rests on your loins. Let us hope they are . . . firm enough for the task."

"Firmer all the time."

Babatunde sighed. "Kai, Kai . . . is there nothing I can say to dissuade you from placing your neck upon the block?"

"I wish I knew," Kai said. "But I see no way to deal with this save direct address. Babatunde, if ever I needed my father's wisdom, it is now. Absent that, thank Allah that you stand beside me."

"Never have I felt so inadequate," the little Sufi said. He sighed deeply. "Kai," he said after careful thought. "Have you ever heard the expression 'Zulu Heart'?"

"No," he said, then paused. "Perhaps."

"It is a quality that men strive for: the ability to forget the past, forget the future, live wholly in the moment. It produces both monsters and saints." He paused. "I think that it is sometimes used as an insult, suggesting that Zulus have no values, no honor, nothing save expediency. To the degree that that is true, Nandi is completely unknowable. She may or may not know of Shaka. She may or may not love you. She may or may not have been given specific instructions. But Kai . . ." Babatunde leaned close. "Once she leaves her father's home, *she is a different woman.* All that happened before that moment was another life. She will do whatever suits her, whatever feeds her hungers. I wish I could tell you what that means, but I cannot. That is the question of her soul. In truth, she may intend to kill everyone in your household. Or she may intend to be a good and faithful wife."

"How will I know?" Kai asked, miserable.

"You won't. And then, one day, you will." Babatunde sighed. "Well. So. A wedding it is. And if it is to be as memorable an occasion as I fear, I suppose we had best make it festive. Allah, even more than His creations, loves a good jest."

CHAPTER THIRTY-THREE

EVENING HAD CREPT STEALTHILY across the crannog, and although fiddle music and laughter wafted gently through the darkness, in Aidan and Sophia O'Dere's home, only quiet talk and warm companionship filled the night.

They had shared dinner with the Borus: Donough; his wife, Mary; and four-year-old young Donough.

As the boys played their drowsy games the adults spoke of simple things, personal things, never mentioning the brambled path ahead. It was a time of simple joys and sharing, one that Aidan embraced with his whole heart, opening his senses that he might carry this with him, no matter what might come to pass.

As Donough and Mary left, Aidan's bearlike friend turned and hugged him, and looked down into his eyes. "No matter what happens," Donough said, "your lady is me sister. I'd die for her; ye know that."

"Live for us all," Aidan said, his eyes stinging. "What a long, strange road we've walked, Donough. It just got stranger still, but this ain't the end of it. That, I know." He dropped his voice to a husky whisper. "We're just beginnin'."

Donough nodded, a big grin covering his pain and fear, and then they left.

Aidan walked back over to the fireside and sat there. His son, Mahon, crawled up into his lap and laid his head against his father's chest. When he'd first told the boy of his intentions, there had been tears, and the small, strong hands had gripped at him as if they could hold Aidan safe from a treacherous world.

But there were no more tears now. Every man in the crannog was Mahon's father. Every woman his mother. Wasn't this what had happened in the slave ship, long long ago? What was it that . . . what was his name? *Niad.* God, it all came flooding back to him. Niad of Cumhail, a man disgraced, ashamed to be alive when so many of his fellows had died resisting the Northmen. *"So long as there is a man of Eire living, you have a father. . . ."*

In a land so torn and fearful, it was the only philosophy that gave them any hope at all. Too many fathers were gone, too many mothers torn from their children's sides. Sophia was right: the only safety for any was safety for all.

Safety. A village where every man, woman, and child was family. Where no soul was abandoned. Where no man had to bow to another because of the color of his skin. A place where they might not have to expel the fugitive slave, and could look the black men in the eye and not plead, not beg, but *demand* respect.

Yes. He ran his hands through Mahon's hair. The boy was sleepy. It had been a long day. Aidan had spent it fishing and playing with his son, stretching it out as long as he could, and now it was ending. He would leave in the morning, before his boy awakened. Sophia agreed that that would be easiest.

And even *that* was killing him.

Mahon looked up at him, blue eyes bright and cool in the firelight. For a terrible moment Aidan feared the boy would beg him not to go, make some last-minute tug on his heartstrings. Instead, Mahon reached a stubby hand into his pocket and pulled out a little wooden figure. "Here, Da," he said, and pressed it into Aidan's palm.

He looked at it carefully. Carved from some soft wood, it was the image of a little man: two arms, two legs, a head, clumsily, lovingly crafted.

"Is this me?" Aidan asked.

"It's *me*," Mahon said, pouting fiercely. "Unca Donough helped me. Keep me with you?"

Sophia was watching them both, and he saw, actually saw the moment when the firelight began to glisten in twin tracks upon her face. He prayed that the thickness in his own voice would not betray him. "Always," he said, and kissed his boy's cheek. "And you know? If it's the two of us, that makes it twice as easy. Those bad men better watch out!"

Mahon gave a sleepy giggle and burrowed his head more closely into his father's chest. "Da?" he asked, on the very edge of sleep.

"Yes?"

"Bring it back to me."

Aidan looked up at Sophia, who nodded her head.

"I will, sweet boy," he whispered. "Be damned if I won't."

Sophia put Mahon to bed while Aidan enjoyed a generous pipe of Kai's good hemp. His wife returned to the fireside, took an iron and stirred the ashes, and settled back in her chair, staring into the darkness.

"I hate them sometimes," Aidan said softly. "Every one of them."

"Even Kai?"

"Even Kai," he said in the darkness. "But I love him, too."

"The heart is complicated, my dear."

He looked at her strangely. "You don't hate, do you?"

"Why do you say that?"

"I don't believe you could, and be the woman you are. You seem so . . . above it all."

"Not so far above," she said. "I feel. I remember. But, no . . . I don't hate."

"How?"

"When I was a girl," she said. "I thought that there was no one in the world stronger and more handsome than my father, and I prayed that I would find a man half so fine. Then I was sold away, and used, and taught that I was just a tool for men's pleasure. I prayed that I might find a master who would raise me up and take me to wife. What his character might be, or his heart, hardly mattered, if I could just be free. What I couldn't have known is that the slavers would eventually bring me to you, Aidan." She turned and looked at him. "I don't believe there are two in all the world like you. You fill me."

Aidan tried to speak, and could not.

"I'd have walked the world around to find you," she said. "And if the trials I endured on that path were horrible to the girl I was, the woman I am is glad that there was a path, however hard, that brought us together."

She sighed, and closed her eyes.

"That's the trick of it," she said. "To find joy where you are; and if you do, then you have to make peace with the path that brought you there. If I'm going to love my life, I have to let the hate go."

The dying flames gilded her, as if she were a woman cast from bronze or gold, not the yielding feminine miracle he knew her to be. "So, then. Go, and find Nessa, and come back to me. The crannog will be here. The family will be here. And if I have given birth to your new child by then, then that increase feeds all our hearts. It will be hard . . . but it has been hard to know that half your soul was still in chains. There is only so much a wife or husband can do. Aside from that, we must each set ourselves free."

He reached out, and with the ball of his thumb wiped at the shining place upon her cheek.

She took his hand and kissed her tear. "Go," she said. "And free your heart. Then return to us." She stood, and slipped another log onto the embers. "I will not let this fire die until you return to this house."

He was speechless as he looked up at her, struggling to fathom how she could be so strong after all she had endured. And failing. "And now," she said, "that Mahon is asleep, I have a gift of my own to give you."

She undid the straps on her shoulders, so that her dress slipped to he floor. And she stood naked before his eyes, the gentle swelling of her belly reminding him that life continued. Whatever might lie ahead, life and love went on.

He took her in his arms, and they led each other to their bed. And there, in a ritual as old as human life, they forged meaning from chaos, and strength from sorrow. Then, holding each other, they slipped away from a world of hard choices.

And, together, they spent the night in their separate, hopeful dreams.

CHAPTER THIRTY-FOUR

BLOSSOMS EXUDED SCENTS beyond numbering as the noon sun warmed their petals. Nandi knelt in her garden, trimming thorns, clipping weeds, and aerating the soil. IziLomo, whose name meant "Favored Courtier," crouched contentedly at her side, occasionally sniffing at flying insects. The garden was a place of tiered irrigation networks of her own design, cultivating a hundred varieties of blossoms.

At the moment she was working with one of her favorites, a Persian chrysanthemum. To an uneducated eye it resembled a daisy with large white, pink, and red flowers. Its leaves were fernlike, and exuded an insecticidal substance she hoped to extract and utilize elsewhere in the garden.

For a time IziLomo worried at a bee, but then ceased such dalliance and came to alert, wheeling about with a welcoming bark. Nandi turned, knowing even before she did who the newcomer had to be.

"Chalo!" she said sharply.

The young warrior grinned. "Princess." IziLomo sniffed Chalo's hand, and then licked it. Nandi had to repress a smile: Chalo was the only male who had ever triggered such a response in the hound, and she had sometimes wondered if that had been a deliberate aspect of IziLomo's early training.

"You should not be here." She looked rapidly to either side and saw that they were alone but for the watchful Ridgeback. She felt both flustered and pleased.

"I came in over the east wall," Chalo said. "The guards will not see me."

"I have but to raise my voice—"

"—and my life is forfeit," he concluded. A bold rogue indeed!

"So," she said, meeting his eyes squarely. "What is it you desire?" She almost winced at the use of that word, knowing that she had chosen it with absolute precision.

"Nandi," he said. "I know that your father wants you to leave."

"Yes."

"Is this what you wish?" He drew closer to her. Chalo was all steel sinew and high, well-etched cheekbones.

"There is more at stake here than you can know," said she. "I have known you for many years—"

"And I have always loved you. I knew your father had promised you to this fop, and held my tongue."

Despite her affection for Chalo, Nandi felt herself bristle. IziLomo cocked his head, observing with renewed interest. "Kai may be many things, but he is no fop."

"Feh," he sneered. "Say the word, and I wind his intestines on my spear. None would expect you to marry a corpse."

She shook her head numbly. There was no way Chalo could understand, and she dared not speak.

"Tell me, Nandi," he said. "Let me hear it from your own lips. Tell me true. Do you love him?"

Her eyes flickered, and then held his again. "This is impertinence."

"Impertinence," said Chalo, "is the least of my sins. Do you feel for him what you felt for me?"

"We were children," she said, and lowered her gaze. "We should not have played, even as we did. It was wrong. I am sorry if you thought it meant more than was intended."

She attempted to maintain a haughty expression, but beneath his burning gaze it wilted. By the ancestors, he was magnificent!

He drew closer. "Then tell me it meant nothing to you."

She lowered her eyes. "I cannot."

"Say that *I* mean nothing to you," Chalo said.

She could feel his heat, smell him, dared not close her eyes for fear she would envision their intertwined bodies. "You must put me from your mind," she said, declining to answer him. "No good can come of this. My heart is not my own—I must be who I am. We have our obligations, Chalo. If you care for me, help me have the strength to obey mine."

He took her by the shoulders, arms extended. "Very well. But if he hurts you in any way, I will *open* him. Know this to be true."

Her voice went husky. "I know."

Chalo nodded, apparently satisfied. For a moment she thought he was going to kiss her, and in spite of her best intentions her eyes fluttered closed. There was a small gust of air . . .

She opened her eyes . . .

Chalo was gone. IziLomo made a low, whining sound and pressed his massive head against her hand. She scratched him behind one thick dark ear, comforted by his heat and strength, thanking her ancestors that both would be hers in the trying days ahead.

CHAPTER THIRTY-FIVE

24 *Shawwal* A.H. 1294
(Thursday, November 1, 1877)

BATTING FLIES OUT OF THE AIR and counting the minutes until evening brought his lustmate to his straw bed once again, Olaf One-Ear waited by the main gate's great bell, and was startled to see a figure walking down the road, leading a gray horse. He squinted, not quite believing his eyes.

"Sweet Allah's angels," he said. "It's a vision."

"Very real, and slightly parched," Aidan said. "Hello, Olaf."

The former slave brightened. "Aidan! Never thought to see you again!" Olaf embraced Aidan, slapping clouds of road dust from his shirt.

"How's your old mother?"

The freedman managed a smile. "Oh, she's got the miseries, but I swear she'll dance a jig when she sees you!"

And shuffling his own feet to an imaginary rhythm, Olaf began to ring the gate's great iron bell.

Kai reclined in a great overstuffed chair in his study, reading a scroll by reflected daylight. He heard the bell tolling and rose, walking to the window and looking out toward the gate. A slow smile broke on his face.

"Ar-Razzaq be praised," he murmured.

And the rest of the estate slowly awakened, and wandered out toward the gate to see Aidan O'Dere walking in from the road, and the master of the house of Kush walking out from the manse, their figures so distant and indistinct that when they hugged, it was difficult to tell where one ended and the other began.

Seated in a canopied gazebo on Dar Kush's front lawn, Kai and Aidan spoke. As they did the years dropped away like bubbles floating into the depths of a well.

"Here I am," said Aidan. "Back where it all began."

"Different this time, Aidan," said Kai. "This time, you can set terms for your labor."

Aidan nodded, smiling. "Tell me what you have planned," he said. "What marital insanity have I agreed to?"

"Painful but rewarding insanity," Kai said. "First we will work your body as you have never been worked before. When your strength, wind, and flexibility are better developed, you will learn technique and a bit of philosophy. And after your conscious mind has absorbed this, when you are ready, there will be a special ceremony." Kai smiled. "A sort of marriage ceremony. When complete, you will move and think differently than you do today. And we will be ready."

"How long?"

"That," Kai said, "depends on you. I will not lie; you will have little rest, and many pains. But when you are done you will have knowledge never before given to a white." He paused. "There would be those who would consider me mad even for trying this."

"Well then . . . I suppose we're just a pair of lunatics. There are those in my crannog who consider me daft for trusting you."

"Come, let us sit like friends and negotiate," Kai said. One would have thought they were planning a garden party, not speaking of espionage and mortal combat. Kai poured Aidan a cup of coffee.

Aidan sipped, and groaned in pleasure. "I would be lying if I said I did not miss this. And you."

"And I you," said Kai. "I do not know whether this world is cruel or merciful for we two to have found each other under such circumstances."

"Perhaps it is what we make of it," Aidan said.

Kai laughed. "You sound like Babatunde."

"High praise."

"Not necessarily."

They drank, peering out across the estate, at the distant teff fields, where slaves worked steadily, chopping and hoeing. Other servants passed between barn and Ghost Town, casting surprised and sometimes suspicious eyes at Aidan. Finally, the Irishman spoke. "Here are my terms," he said. "I want your official protection of my village. I want your word as Wakil, and as my friend, that to the extent of your power and influence the rule of law will apply, regardless of race."

"Agreed," Kai said, and Aidan nodded.

"And that is true regardless of the outcome of my efforts."

Kai raised an eyebrow. "Regardless?"

"All I am asking for is justice, and a chance for my family to grow as it should. If I enter into this, I must go with no attachments or regrets, or I will die."

"Well spoken," Kai nodded. "Agreed."

"You don't know what you're asking me to do," Aidan said uneasily.

"Help me understand."

Aidan paused, seeming to gather his strength. Then he leaned forward and, one quiet word at a time, began to speak. "There's a small, pale place in my head where I put all of the anger and pain and fear from my years in bondage. I think every slave builds a place like that, so that in the few moments he has for himself, he can be a man." His hand trembled, and he set the cup down.

"When I won my freedom," he continued, "I closed that door as tightly as I could. If I could live in a world where I never saw another black face for the rest of my life, I would. I can't."

He paused. "Sometimes in a black town, I can go five whole seconds without remembering that these people used to be able to buy or sell me. Or my wife. Or my son. And might again, if the law took my freedom away on a pretext—any pretext." He leaned back and took another sip.

Aidan leaned forward, a warm late-afternoon's wind ruffling his golden hair. "I swore I'd never go back, Kai. No matter what happened. I'd die first. There is only one thing in all the world that could motivate me."

"Your promise," Kai said.

"Yes. My promise and the love for my sister bound into it. And damn you for knowing that. And bless you for finding her." He paused. "I don't think I much like the Wakil of New Djibouti."

Kai laughed uncomfortably. "It is possible our opinions of him are quite similar."

The friends shared laughter for a time, then settled back down. "So. If I do this, if I really do it, you can get us out of New Alexandria?"

"Yes," Kai said. "But despite my personal feelings, I cannot ask my . . . contacts to expose themselves for anything less than the machine. You understand that?"

Aidan finished his glass. "Yes. Well, then, Kai—it appears that we have a deal."

They clasped hands and shook.

For the first time in three years, Aidan walked past Ghost Town's wooden gates. Olaf One-Ear now occupied the house Aidan had once shared with his mother, and then with Sophia. Without coercion, the older man was bundling his possessions, that Aidan might have his accustomed bed once again.

Waiting and wandering the streets, Aidan found himself among old and painful memories, and did his best to dispel them.

A slave approached him, a garrulous graybeard named . . . T'Challa. "Aidan! I swear, I never thought to see ye again! What happened?"

"Gambling debts?" asked a second man, lean and perhaps eighteen summers. What was his name? Corrin! Yes. Corrin had been a boy when Aidan left Dar Kush. "I hear that they'll clap a 'belly in chains in a heartbeat, he owes money," Corrin said.

"Did ye steal?" asked T'Challa. "Or talk sass to a royal? What happened?"

"None," said Aidan. "I'm here of my own will. I had a sister once."

Corrin scratched his head. "Name of . . . Nessa! Many's the time ye spoke of her."

Aidan smiled wanly. "Yes, Nessa. In a few months, your master will take me north. If I can learn to fight like a lion, I might be able to win her free."

Corrin gawped. "Free?"

"I swore," said Aidan.

"Free," T'Challa mused. "What's life like outside?"

A half dozen of Dar Kush's Irish had gathered, were staring at him, touching his clothes with wonder. Mean as his short robe and pants were, they were still better than any they had seen a white man wear, save for livery worn driving carriages and attending at parties.

"Hard," he said. "A man works, same as here. But we can't be bought and sold."

"The Wakil," said a black-haired, wide-hipped woman named . . . Fanya. Yes, Fanya. "He don't sell us, nor allow messin' with our women. We always got food. Yer pantry always full?"

"No," he admitted. "There have been hungry nights."

Fanya sniffed, and brushed a blousy thread of black hair from her face. "Don't sound like freedom's so much."

Aidan searched his memory. "Were you born a slave?"

"Three generations, right here on Dar Kush!" she said proudly. "Belongs to me as much as the fockin' Wakil."

"No." Aidan shook his head. How could he convey the essence of what he had learned and experienced? Several of those most eager for freedom had died during the rebellion years before, the one that had cost Olaf his ear. Others had been sold farther south, to harsher berths, in punishment for their participation. It seemed to Aidan that those who remained more closely resembled sheep than men. "You don't understand. I don't know if I can *make* you understand, but I'll try." He collected his thoughts. "I wake up in the morning, and the day is mine. No man tells me where to go or what to do. I fish; I work in the fields. I trade in the town."

"And they treat ye like an African?"

"No. But they treat me like a man. They are afraid of me, of what I might want, what I might do. They strike out at me . . . and I have the right to strike back."

At this, his audience gasped. He had exaggerated, but men needed inspiration more than facts.

"I remember," Corrin said, "the day ye thrashed the master. Right here on these streets, and ye lived."

Aidan nodded. "Because our . . . *your* master is an honorable man, who kept his word. He is better than most men, black or white. I have been in the world and seen. Life on Dar Kush is about as good as it gets for a slave. You have no way of understanding this, but you could have been in a thousand other households, where you might be starved, beaten, and raped. Your brothers and sisters are not so fortunate."

The slaves looked at each other, and back at Aidan, murmuring.

"And perhaps one day, you'll have the chance to go out in the world and see for yourselves."

"Perhaps you will lead us," T'Challa murmured.

"Not me. Not me, no. . . ."

"Then who?"

And for that, Aidan had no answer.

And then a quiet voice within him: *Are you sure?*

Aidan walked the streets that he had known as a boy, surprised that so little had changed, that everything came back to him so quickly.

A whine behind him made him turn, and he grinned in pleasure to see Fithr, the *tuath's* old hound, snuffling up to him. The dog had been old when he left, and he was shocked to see that the animal was still alive.

The gray muzzle whined and wagged its patchy tail, and licked at his hand.

"You be Aidan?" a voice said.

He turned to look. There was a child standing there that he had never seen before.

"Yes," he said. "And who are you?"

"Tata," she said. She was standing half behind the corner of one of the houses. She was a ragged little thing. Clean, and dressed in castoffs, but there was something about her, some native energy or intelligence, that instantly appealed to him.

"You the master's friend? I heard about ye."

"That's me," Aidan said. "And you? You're new here, aren't you?"

She nodded. "They say ye come for a bit, and then ye go away again." She cocked her head sideways. "Where will ye go?"

"I have a . . . a home," he said, trying to explain.

"You free?" she asked. He nodded.

She came to him, knelt down next to Fithr, and scratched the dog behind his ears. "He stays with me and the old lady," she said.

"Old lady?"

She nodded. "Widow Llywellyn."

He remembered. "Ah. Angus's widow."

"She say the other slaves kill her husband." The little girl's eyes were hot and deep, and he found himself uncomfortable looking into them. They searched for truth.

"Yes," he said. "That's true."

She nodded, and scratched Fithr behind the ear. "Never had a dog," she said. "Don't take him?"

He shook his head. Without another word the little girl stood and walked away, into a crowd of other children. She didn't say anything to them, either.

He wasn't certain that he had ever, in his entire life, seen such a lonely child.

The prayer grove was at the edge of the great swamp at the northeast edge of Lake A'zam. Once upon a time the grove had been their place of worship. Three years after Aidan's departure it remained burned and blasted, a domain of spirits. A sprinkling of young vegetation sprouted, the beginning of new growth. Around the edges, a dozen or so young trees had been planted. Another beginning.

Aidan knelt at his mother's grave. Deirdre, her name had been. Once upon a lifetime ago, she had promised to work herself to death, if only she were not separated from her family. She had kept her word, even if their masters had not.

"Well, Mother," he whispered. "I'm back. I made it away, but I'm back. There's something to do; and I know you can see my heart, and know what it is, but I just wanted to say aloud that if I have your heart, and Father's strength, I will not fail."

At the sound of footsteps behind him, Aidan's head jerked up and around. "Kai!"

"This place was beautiful," Kai said. "It will be once again."

"I was hoping you would say that by the time it regrew, it would not be needed. That slavery would be at an end."

Kai sighed. "It will. But I cannot say when. And even if it does, many of the workers will probably stay on. How would they make a living?"

"Free men make their way in the world," Aidan said.

"Yes," Kai agreed, "but many freed slaves choose to stay on as sharelanders, overseers . . . simple, honest work."

Aidan grimaced. "You suggest that that is all they are capable of?"

"Aidan," Kai said. No need for impatience. Much of what Aidan had experienced, Kai could only imagine. "I swear, slavery will end. Industrialization makes it obsolete, allowing men to make judgments with their hearts instead of their wallets."

Kai slapped his back. "Then let us get to work. Treat this as your home. Rest well from your journey. Tomorrow we begin."

CHAPTER THIRTY-SIX

BABATUNDE TURNED HAPPILY as Kai entered the labyrinth of scrolls and beakers he called his study. "Kai!" he said. "What brings you here?"

"Truth," said his student.

"And what truth is that?"

"That for some years now, you have aided slaves in their escape from Djibouti."

Babatunde sputtered. "What? I never—"

Kai was laughing. "Oh, come now. I know, Babatunde. I know, and my father knew, although he could never speak of it outright. Your network is clever, but might have fallen. My father needed to be able to state honestly that he had no direct knowledge of such a thing."

Babatunde sputtered some more, and then sat down, confused. "Well," he said finally, too nonplussed to dissemble further. "So. What does this mean?"

"It means that I get to enjoy the confusion on your face. I don't often see it."

Babatunde growled at him. "Insolent pup."

Kai bowed. "Indeed. And now to cases." He sat at Babatunde's side. "There is not time for children's tales. I need plain talk from my old friend."

"Very well," the Sufi grumbled.

"Your route runs south to north, yes?"

"Yes."

"Occasionally west?"

"We have the ability," he admitted, "The northern, unincorporated territories are less hospitable than those to the west."

"Why?"

"The Northmen have a taste for slavery, you might recall. Ironically though, the northern route is more secure."

"Ah. Tell me, Babatunde: do you believe that Allah's purpose would be better served by the Caliph's victory?"

Babatunde paused, thinking hard. "I do not know. I believe that freedom is good, and the north would free the slaves sooner than the south."

"I agree."

"On the other hand, the north would have us stand with Egypt against Abyssinia, and that Lady I am sworn to serve."

"But that is a personal obligation," Kai said. "Not a holy one."

"Yes. But if we side with Egypt, Bilalistan remains an Alexandrian protectorate. Our children will fight in their wars of conquest, and the Pharaoh has plans. He casts his eye to India, to China. Perhaps even Persia, although currently the Shah is his ally. He will need soldiers, and sailors, and materiel. He wishes to own the seas. Abyssinia has stronger mercantile ties to the Eastern kingdoms; therefore peace suits the Empress more than war."

"Yes."

Babatunde closed his eyes briefly. "What does that mean for the future of this land, the land that Bilal said would host the rebirth of Islam? It means that we will be controlled by the same greedy, political machinations that have turned Africa into a nest of warring states, and Europe into a colonial wasteland. I believe that we must be free to determine our own future, and that here, in this new land, something extraordinary can grow." He sighed.

"And so?"

"So . . . I must trust the boy I have loved for so long. I do not think that wealth or power can melt the steel within your heart."

"It is strange how similar your words are to Aidan's."

"Not strange at all," his teacher said. "We both trust and love you."

Kai lowered his eyes.

Babatunde shook himself from his trance. "So, young Wakil, I will do as you wish. Not for the gain in months to come, but for that which may require decades and lifetimes. You are taking a step—deciding to risk, to move into that larger circle you rejected with your uncle's death. It is right what you do, and I will stand with you." He paused. "What exactly do you require?"

"It is hugely important that your associates safely and clandestinely transport two Caucasians."

"North? Or west?"

"South," said Kai.

PART III

Joinings

"You teach," said the student, "that there are three great forces in the universe: affirming, denying, and reconciling."

"You have studied well," said his teacher.

"But the most fundamental expression of human emotion is duality: friend and friend, male and female. How can you reconcile that?"

The teacher smiled. "In a marriage, there is male, who affirms that all existence must bow to his might."

The student regarded his own small arms, and blushed.

"And female, who through a thousand daily miracles, challenges this omnipotence, opening the way to a deeper understanding of existence."

"And would it be their child that reconciles?"

"Children, when they come, come from love, which Allah makes possible to all unions. It is love itself that is the third part of the marriage: in the form of children, home, or Allah Himself. It is love that reconciles all."

CHAPTER THIRTY-SEVEN

10 Dhu'l-Qa'dah A.H. 1294
(Friday, November 16, 1877)

ACCOMPANIED BY MUCH RINGING of cymbals and prancing of horses, Nandi kaSenzangakhona arrived with her entourage. Her coach was of hand-carved ebony inlaid with gold and ivory. When passersby glimpsed the princess, her mood was indecipherable: a wedding mask of golden mesh concealed her face. At her side crouched the great hound IziLomo, a creature larger and stronger than many human warriors, whose dedication to his mistress was legendary.

The master of the manor did not go forth to meet his intended. Rather, he preferred to keep watch from the house as his representatives welcomed her. Babatunde found Kai in his room, and chided him. "It is not required that you stay here. You are the Wakil, and could welcome her in that capacity."

"I am uneasy," Kai said.

"It is natural to feel a bit of nervousness, even at the taking of a second wife."

"Oh?"

"Of course. It is never possible to know everything. She will change your life. What do you remember of her?"

Kai inhaled deeply. "Her beauty, her pride. Her courage."

Babatunde smiled. "And more, of course."

Kai donned an absurdly pious expression. "It would be unseemly to speak of it. What occupies your days?"

"Working with Doctor Kokossa on his plans. A brilliant man, Kai. You will not regret supporting him."

Kai's mind seemed elsewhere. "I have had two real relationships in my life: Sophia and Lamiya."

"How would you hold their difference?"

"Sex with Sophia was . . . exquisite. Artistic. Every motion and breath choreographed."

Babatunde's face changed not at all, except for the fractional raising of his left eyebrow. "Your father chose your birthday present well."

"Indeed . . . but it was . . . let's say biological and psychological. I don't believe I ever saw her true heart."

Babatunde smiled. "It would have been foolish to offer what you could not return."

"But Aidan could return it."

"Yes."

"With Lamiya . . ." He sighed, and closed his eyes. "I think that I have loved her all my life." When he opened them again, his smile was as soft as a boy's. "She pledged her troth to me, and it is all she has in this world. She has offered me all that a woman can, and it is all that I require."

"And?"

Kai's voice was contemplative. "I am a happy man. Her love, and the child she has borne, healed me, Babatunde."

"So?"

"Yes," Kai said. "In the days following our marriage, I struggled with a great depression. I had the woman I wanted, and power beyond my dreams, but the price I had paid for it all was unspeakable." He shook his head. "I was broken beneath its weight. To the degree that I could, I shielded everyone from that knowledge."

"I remember," Babatunde said. "It seemed as if you were passing through a long, dark tunnel, a journey I could not walk with you."

Kai looked at his old teacher curiously. "Perhaps we should have discussed all of this long ago."

"Perhaps. Perhaps not. It was not time."

"Did you believe I would emerge?"

Babatunde smiled. "You wish the truth?"

"Always."

"Then yes, I knew you would emerge. You were striking what, in the study of the *Naqsh Kabir*, would be called a 'shock point,' a point at which irreparable damage has been done to your sense of self, and you have no choice but to leap forward in faith, or spiral down into destruction."

"And you thought I would make this passage successfully?"

"Allah assured me that it was so." There seemed a curious weight to the little man, a gravity about his voice and posture that made Kai wish to dig deeper.

"There is something else, isn't there?"

"Yes," Babatunde said. "I have known you all your life, and the patterns of your life have been consistent with my dreams. You have yet to grasp your destiny, but the road is not smooth, or straight. You are still afraid of who you really are . . . as are most men. You have direction, but lack clarity. Still, the weight is pressing upon you. You will reach another shock point, another tunnel, this one leading to a place of even greater darkness. And if you make the right choice, you will finally be the man you were intended to be."

"How can you know such things?" Kai asked, mystified. "Can you see the future?"

"Only in that it resembles the past. You were born for greatness, Kai, and great men are created by great challenges. It is both curse and blessing. Your father and uncle are at war within you, contesting for your soul, Kai. Your heart is the battlefield."

"Must one lose?"

"That is for you to decide."

Kai stood quietly, thinking on these things for a time. Then quietly, he asked, "And who will I be after the battle is done?"

"Who you are now, with fewer illusions. To see clearly that which is, is what men call enlightenment. It is a simple and profound thing. Be prepared, Kai. Once begun, there is no turning back from this path. Not for such as you."

Kai considered. "Will I still love Lamiya? And Aliyah?"

Babatunde laughed uproariously. "You imagine that the light of heaven banishes love from your heart? You are still the silly boy I taught to fish. Kai: all the world is love. We are never more than children striving to more closely approach that Father who gave us life. The meanest man, the most corrupt woman, does nothing that is not, in his or her way, an attempt to approach Allah."

Kai shook his head as if it were a basket filled with bees.

"Of course you are confused. Your mind is filled with twenty years of lessons. I could only give you a piece at a time: your eyes and ears are too small to force a complete idea into your head! Soon, you will construct your own map of reality, and when it aligns with Allah you will stand in the center, and understand what I have never been able to teach . . . and be as frustrated as I that there are no words to convey it."

"Never? What a gift we could give our children."

"No. It is they who give the gift to us. They are more recently from heaven, closer to the divine. They know, even if they cannot say. And that is one of the reasons we love them so. We touch them, smell them . . . and it awakens something in us that slides to sleep as we read our books and talk of gold and land and pretty politics with our neighbors. Kai, the *true* light will but bring you and Lamiya even closer together."

"That . . . would be wondrous."

"Even though there is already much love between you?"

"Yes. I built a wall to keep others from knowing the depth of my pain." He shot his teacher an irritated glance. "Obviously, I should have built my walls a bit thicker."

Babatunde merely smiled.

"Lamiya and I are satisfied to collide with each other's walls, which neither of us seems fully inclined to disassemble."

"Real love takes time," said Babatunde. Only artificial intimacy flowers on demand."

"Like Sophia."

Babatunde said nothing.

"Sophia's artifice, her sexuality, was her tool—her weapon. Her only weapon, I suppose."

Babatunde folded his hands. "In the war between slave and master, one is far more likely to lose than the other. She sought to lose most gently."

Kai nodded. "Aidan had the right of that, long ago. There was no avenue for that love, no soil for it to sprout in, nor sun to nurture its growth."

"And Lamiya?"

"She is gentility. Even in her heat, there is a reserve. Even when she loses control and grips at me, she is cautious not to use her nails."

His tutor sighed. "Strange, the things that devil men."

"Nandi, though . . . ," Kai mused. "Nandi is something else altogether."

Babatunde's face grew stern. "You have not transgressed?"

"No, no!" Kai paused. "Well . . . not quite."

Babatunde put his hands over his ears. "Do I want to hear this?"

Kai grinned. "That depends, man of the spirit, on whether you are more spirit than man."

A swift glance at the door, then Babatunde cleared his throat. "Speak on."

Kai leaned forward conspiratorially. "She had a way of clasping me between her thighs which, while not risking pregnancy, was more carnal than any tavern maid."

"Ah! *Ukulobonga.* I have heard of this."

"But never tried?"

He shook his head sadly. "No, once upon a time I promised myself that I would . . . in the name of science only."

"Of course."

Babatunde stretched and yawned. "But the years roll past and I am now an old man."

"Maidens beware."

"You wound me. But continue."

"No, no . . . ," Kai protested halfheartedly. "I wouldn't want to offend your ears."

"It is my other parts that seem most affected."

"An answer, then, to my earlier query. Nandi is . . . something very different, from either Lamiya or Sophia. I think she may frighten me a bit."

"Then, my son, you have found a woman indeed."

"She makes love the way she rides a horse. She commits all, holding nothing in reserve."

"If that is true, you have nothing to fear. There is little room for dissembling in such a woman."

"But I cannot tell her my true mind. . . ."

"Thereby creating the room for her own dishonesty." Babatunde sighed, but managed a comforting smile as well. "You have dug yourself a deep hole, young Wakil. I pray you will not have to sleep in it."

CHAPTER THIRTY-EIGHT

THE SHORES OF LAKE A'ZAM had begun to resemble a Bedouin camp. The Dahomy were lodged southwest of the great house, and Nandi, her mother, Munji, and her retinue were welcomed into great billowing tents southeast near the public gardens. There they would remain until the wedding, at which time the Zulu princess would move into her new rooms.

After she had refreshed herself, attendants escorted Nandi to Dar Kush's main door, where Lamiya met her with arms outstretched.

"Welcome to my home," Lamiya said. "Soon to be yours. I ask that you accept me as a sister."

"It is my heart's wish," Nandi said from behind her golden mask. She stepped forward. IziLomo's ears perked up, but at a subtle, fluttering hand command, the hound remained seated, although he watched the humans carefully, as if searching for signs of treachery.

Nandi and Lamiya hugged, the Zulu girl taller by three or four digits.

Munji smiled with obvious pleasure. "It will be my pleasure to bring you into the company of my daughters. I know they would welcome you."

Lamiya motioned to her servants. "I know you have sufficient retinue to manage your affairs. We have made room in the house and also an encampment by the lake. It is quite comfortable."

Lamiya escorted Nandi to her new quarters. Although most of the human servants and attendants were shown to their temporary dwellings, Nandi's mother and canine companion went with her. IziLomo padded quietly behind them as they walked up the central staircase to the second floor. Lamiya's room had once been Abu Ali's, in the northeast corner of the house, as Kai's was at the northwest. Nandi's room had been brother Ali's, in the southeast corner of the second floor. It was spacious but rather barren, currently occupied by only a bed, empty dressers, and a bureau drawer. Of course, all of its appointments would be modified, added to, or replaced at Nandi's whim.

"You may keep as many of your belongings here as you wish," Lamiya said.

"Thank you," Nandi replied. "But until the wedding, I will remain in the tent city with my mother and guardians." She scratched IziLomo behind the ear as she said this. The dog pressed his head against her thigh in response, and panted. And watched.

"I understand," said Lamiya. "But you may wish to begin your decoration or restructuring."

"You are very kind." She turned to Lamiya. "We two must come to terms, must be able to communicate directly. It is best you know quickly that I speak my mind, and have little patience for protocol over honesty."

"It is not necessary for these two things to be in conflict," said Lamiya. "However, if ever they are, please know that I would prefer honesty over false courtesies of any kind."

"Well said. Then I will take you at your word and speak plainly: men have been known to play wives against each other. We both know that we are here to knit empires and nations together."

Lamiya inclined her head. "Although a *feqer näfs*, I know that among the gentry, marriages are more often matters of the head than the heart."

"How, then," asked Nandi, "can we be sisters?" She reached up and undid the golden mesh concealing her face. "How then, can I remove my mask?"

Lamiya faced her prospective co-wife squarely, evaluating with great care. "It is my understanding that the Zulus desire nothing contrary to the wishes and needs of the Empress. Is that your understanding?"

"Indeed. We seek a homeland. My marriage to the Wakil is seen as a step in that direction."

"Then there is no conflict between us."

"To the degree that we can trust each other's words, no," Nandi agreed. "None."

"Then all that remains is time. In time, we will find common ground, and learn to trust, if that is what we both desire."

"Yes. I am certain that is true. *If* it is what we both desire."

They exchanged a wary smile—perhaps the first genuine one since Nandi's arrival.

"I will leave you now," said Lamiya, then bowed and retreated with Bitta.

When they had walked far enough down the hall to be out of earshot, Lamiya asked, "What do you think?"

Bitta made a brief, sharp series of motions. *She will speak honestly, in her way,* she signed. *If she seeks to displace you as First, it will be by winning Kai's heart.*

She will not risk the Empress's wrath—unless she believes that the Immortal One will pay no heed to your destruction.

Lamiya chuckled. "If her sense of honor is as yours, I need not fear. I do not know the Zulu well. I sense that in coming weeks, that gap in my education will be filled."

Nandi closed the door to her room and spent the next few minutes examining the room's furnishings. She was a long way from home, and despite the presence of IziLomo, her mother, and the accompanying entourage, she had never felt so alone in her entire life.

CHAPTER THIRTY-NINE

12 Dhu'l-Qa'dah A.H. 1294
(Sunday, November 18, 1877)

NANDI HAD WAITED A DECADE for her marriage, but in some ways the final thirty-six hours at Dar Kush were the hardest to bear. Despite her fear that time itself might die, the time of joining did indeed finally arrive.

Despite its delayed beginnings it promised to be a memorable affair, attracting celebrants from hundreds of miles around.

Some of them noted the pomp and were impressed. Others considered such an affair ostentatious. After all, they reasoned, no such elaborate ceremony had attended the Wakil's *first* wedding.

Indeed, the Empress had never formally acknowledged the marriage, sending no representative, or present, or anything at all save a terse note wishing her niece health and happiness. The Wakil, mindful of Lamiya's feelings, had attempted to mount a suitable wedding, but expenditure is not the same as enthusiasm: the nuptials had been imposing, but not impressive.

This Zulu affair, on the other hand, was another matter altogether. The guests were vetted by a combination of Kai's personal guard, his regiment, and the Dahomy women, all in full regalia. Musicians culled from the finest in New Djibouti played in a half dozen locations around the grounds, and servants circulated constantly with plates of confections and bite-sized morsels of lamb and buffalo.

By complex negotiation, it had been agreed that there would be two ceremonies, one bonding in the manner prescribed by the Prophet, and the other conforming to the way of the Zulu.

During the *nikah*, the Muslim wedding ceremony, the guests crowded into Dar Kush's main indoor garden as Kai and Nandi took their place before Babatunde. There were witnesses from Djibouti Harbor and Radama, but most were local friends, or members of Djibouti Pride. There were also a few pale faces, Aidan's among them, standing with a clutch of servants honored to witness the proceedings.

Nandi's face was obscured by the golden mask. Gazing upon it, Kai realized he had not seen his new wife's face in more than three years. Babatunde began the ceremony. "Do you, Nandi kaSenzangakhona, wish to be married to this man, to assume the responsibilities of his household, to be his friend and companion, and to uphold his honor?"

"Yes," she said, voice clear despite the golden mesh. "I so desire."

The Yoruba turned to his student. "And do you, Kai ibn Jallaleddin ibn Rashid al Kushi, wish to be married to this woman, to take her into your household with all the responsibilities and privileges that entails, to be her friend and companion, and to protect her honor with your life?"

"Yes, I so wish."

"Then may the two of you live your days in peace and contentment under the sky, upon the earth, and in the eyes of Allah. You are now man and wife."

He turned to the guests and pronounced, "I marry this man and woman." Babatunde turned to the left side of the garden. "I marry this man and woman," he repeated, and then turned right. "I marry this man and woman," he said for the third and final time, and in that manner, Allah came to smile upon their union.

In every way, the Zulu ceremony was more complex and challenging.

It began almost an hour after the Islamic ritual, and during those sixty minutes, the roads leading to Dar Kush streamed with arriving guests.

"It is hard to believe that no formal invitations were ever sent," Kai said to his teacher.

"Word of mouth, Kai—and the command of Cetshwayo. In a Zulu community, everyone wants to be involved in an *indwendwe*."

"*Indwendwe?*"

"Wedding." Babatunde clucked. "Best learn your new bride's language."

Swarms of Zulus, as well as locals temporarily adopting their customs, crowded the gate, dancing and singing joyously.

Everywhere he looked, Zulus indulged in ancient dances, swirling and capering. Whenever two drew close together, they seemed to automatically coordinate as if they had practiced for weeks. Then they separated and found other partners or pairings, and the exact same phenomenon reoccurred.

He felt their call, knew again for the first time why the Zulus were so loved and feared: they were not Bilalian, but were in some ways the very

spirit of Bilalistan. They refused to abandon their dream of a separate empire, yet were in war and science the very finest of citizens. They were in-
fidels who had been the first to march to the defense of the mosque.

They were still a mystery to him, and Kai felt he was about to embark
on the journey of his life.

In glittering rows, Zulu warriors twirled sticks and spears, chanting as
they danced their way in. They dressed representing clans and families
rather than towns or cities. They wore kilts, sandals, short jackets fes-
tooned with cow or lion tails. Some carried rifles and spears in a sort of
honor guard, all metal finishes gleaming.

The unmarried Dahomy women evaluated the fine young Zulu warriors
with interest. Kai's men watched, growing increasingly uncomfortable.

"How many of them are there?" asked Kebwe.

"More than us," Fodjour replied. "We'd best be glad this is a wedding,
not a fight."

The Zulu warriors made aggressive combative motions, that often
seemed on the very edge of insult to Kai's men.

"What are they doing, Sufi?" Kebwe asked Babatunde.

"Fighting *giya*, battles with imaginary enemies," Babatunde replied.

"As if they hadn't enough real ones."

There was a pause, like a lull before the storm, filled with joyous
singing and ululating, ancient dances and mock fighting by lone warriors
as they slaughtered *giya* by the score.

Single girls with bright colored *ibaye* wraps covering their shoulders
danced onto Dar Kush. Married women in *indloko* headdresses, beaded
necklaces, and soft leather aprons swayed behind them.

The young maidens danced gentle steps together, as one, again moving
in that odd, unplanned coordination. Kai was swept away by the images.
"If I close my eyes, I feel as if I can see their ancestors, rank upon rank of
them, stretching back into eternity, all dancing the same movements."

"That's all well and good," said Fodjour. "But leave your eyes open.
Please."

"Allah gave you a heart devoid of romance."

"Not a drop, I'm proud to say. Eyes open, please."

Cetshwayo and Munji had joined Kai by this time, and seemed both relaxed and focused: the waiting was over; the day of their daughter's marriage had arrived. They would remain with Kai until the ceremony was
complete.

Powerful men bearing sticks and shields appeared as regiment after regiment arrived. All the while, respective family groups sang over the existing sounds of celebration and song. An ordered mass of humanity swayed back and forth, performing different steps to the same beat, as old women ululated and waved branches of green leaves, staggering tiredly back and forth ahead of the girls and young men.

Where had they all come from? He imagined endless streams of wagons and horses, boatloads of Zulus and steam-dragon compartments by the score crammed with celebrants, eager to attend the party of their lives.

"Is this really a celebration of a marriage," Kai asked, "or a show of force?"

"Both, I think," Fodjour replied. "It is their way."

"Again," Kai said softly. "I wonder what they know. And what they *think* they know."

Fodjour checked to be certain Cetshwayo was occupied elsewhere, and then whispered, "You must also ask yourself what your reaction would be were it not colored so with guilt."

At that truth, Kai flinched.

Throughout the day, a friendly banter of insults was exchanged as each party tried to outdo the other to show that they had a superior status.

"Who is that one?" Kai said, pointing out a tall, leanly handsome warrior who had first dazzled and then disarmed his hapless opponent, one of Kai's territorial guards.

"He is Chalo, my finest houndsman," said Cetshwayo.

"He is skilled," noted Kai. Strangely for a Bilalian, Chalo wielded the spear with his left side forward. That would create a momentary hesitation in his opponent, a lack of tactical alignment that an experienced fighter could exploit. Dangerous.

With almost contemptuous ease, Chalo disarmed another of Kai's men. He reversed his grip on his spear and knocked the wind out of the hapless loser with the butt, laughing heartily the entire time.

Kai found the jollity unsettling. "It is unseemly to laugh at another man's pain," he said.

"The laughter is not mockery," said Cetshwayo. "Rather, it is a celebration of existence. From birth, we train our sons to thrive in the crucible of death. Every victory means another day of life. And so we laugh, but there is no cruelty there." He paused, perhaps weighing his words. "At least, no more than exists in nature herself."

Then there was the lone, powerful call from a single voice—fast, staccato. A unified response burst from the men, sitting up expectantly, calling. Then another solitary call.

Suddenly, hands were being clapped as if to the beat of a drum, a blood-stirring chant, powerful voices rising. All in unity.

A lone warrior appeared, flaying sticks and a shield about him in an almost mystical battle with imaginary enemies. A great *giya* had been won, a great warrior defeated. Kai glimpsed another truth about the Zulus that seemed difficult to grasp consciously. Their contrasts were intoxicating. They scaled the heights in the fields of military, biological, and legal sciences (Shaka himself, for instance, had never attended Bilalian military academy. He had been skilled in martial science by his own people, and sent by his family to study Bilalian law. Kai knew that Shaka had in fact been his class laureate, said to be lethal in debate. Kai guessed that that was an understatement.) Yet these people exalted in a pure sensual celebration of life.

Ululating women rushed around the triumphant warrior, careful to remain clear of the whistling sticks. They encouraged, teased, and challenged, but he strutted off, unconcerned, as if he were alone and nothing had happened. The women remained, dancing.

Then, a rush of wind, as the *amaqhikazi*, the young engaged girls, ran forward from one side. They were brash, bold, beautiful, and powerful in their quasi-martial movements. With pebbles in cans tied to their ankles, they performed a strange mixture of jumps and offbeat steps.

"They are neither unattached virgins, nor married women," Cetshwayo said.

"What are they, then?" asked Kai.

"We call them 'in-betweens.' They unite today to mark the passage of the bride from her first family to her second."

Now, finally, came the bridal party, the dignified matron's dances contrasting with that of the *amaqhikazi*. Some of them also wore thinner, lighter veils—some of gold, but others of silver or even copper. They mimed cutting at the veils with their knives, which in turn symbolized a severing of the past.

Nandi, face still invisible behind her golden veil, approached with Munji at her side.

This was, perhaps, the most important part of the ritual for the bride's family, as it meant the loss of a valuable family member and was the very basis of the tradition of *Lobola*, brideprice.

This was very much in alignment with the Islamic practice, and therefore had been one of the easier points of contention during the earlier negotiations. There were ways in which this ceremony and the events leading up to it were a subtle conversation between people who could not speak their true minds. The implications of every action, every game of spear and staff, every shrill ululation created tension aplenty.

Lobola placed a physical value on the girl's contribution to her family and the subsequent loss they experienced once she was married.

Therefore Kai felt some trepidation as Nandi's father turned to him in a confrontational posture.

Cetshwayo stood two digits taller than Kai, and loomed over him in a manner calculated to intimidate. "You have stabbed me," he glowered.

There was a moment in which all was still, and dust seemed to hang suspended in the air. Cetshwayo leaned forward. "Something must be done to soften the blow."

It was all that Kai could do to keep from retreating. Almost, he could feel Cetshwayo's blade sliding into his guts. But he knew that this was another ritual, one for which he was thankfully prepared.

"Your men asked for five hundred head of cattle," said Kai. "I thought this an insult."

There was a great intake of breath. Cetshwayo's eyes narrowed. "So . . . ?"

"Your daughter is of such beauty, such intelligence, such fire that no man could offer less than a thousand head for her hand."

Cetswayo's eyes widened, and Kai was gratified to see his mouth open slightly in surprise. He offered the Zulu prince a scroll.

Nandi's father relaxed visibly. "Ah."

"Title to the herd in the western pasture," said Kai. "Twelve hundred head of the finest Kikuyu cattle, for your daughter's hand. Other gifts are mentioned, of gold and silver and land. But I know that your people hold the living wealth of cattle most dear."

"You speak truth," said Cetshwayo, nodding in satisfaction.

"And so this is the lion's share of my payment to you. I pray that it meets your approval."

Cetshwayo smiled expansively, white teeth gleaming against black skin. "It does. You have my blessing. May our families be one, from now until the end of time."

Her father extracted a knife from his belt. After a brief pause, he handed it to Nandi.

Nandi accepted the blade as if she had slept with one in her cradle, flipping it this way and that with dexterous twists of her wrist, a juggler's trick adapted to steel and ceremony. Then with a flick she cut the strap to the mask, and handed it to her father.

Of all her splendors, to Kai, Nandi's eyes were her most striking trait.

They were so direct and piercing that it was almost like facing a male adversary. So different from Muslim women! She gazed upon him as if in judgmental evaluation. Her full lips, which once had kissed his with shameless passion, her skin, so finely grained that she seemed to have no pores at all . . .

All of it combined to overwhelming effect, and Kai's heart raced.

The Zulu princess left her father's group and went to stand with Kai among his warriors.

She still, he noticed, carried the knife. Even now, Nandi's hand might be tightening upon the blade . . .

But instead of a lethal thrust or slash, with another fluid flourish, she reversed the knife in her hand. She sheathed it and extended the sheathed blade, hilt-first, to Kai, her eyes lowered respectfully.

And he understood the message: *I am a woman of the Zulu,* she said. *I conceal or reveal what I wish. No man can touch me without my permission. And I hand this, my only weapon, to you. I am yours now—but yours to protect and love. Misuse me, and I take my blade back again. Misuse me sorely, and I may give this blade another, warmer sheath.*

He accepted it, and bowed. This was as close to a formal ceremony as existed among the Zulu—the cutting of the veil, and the handing of the knife to Kai. It was in this fashion that Nandi's Zulu ancestors came to smile upon their union.

CHAPTER FORTY

THE ZULUS SEEMED TIRELESS in their celebration of a royal wedding, providing one elaborate display after another. There were more *giya* as warrior after warrior showed his prowess, strength, and masculinity. More dance, more song, and the arrival of yet more dignitaries and common celebrants.

Kai, Fodjour, and Mada joined with the other drummers in a spontaneous concert.

As the sun sank low on the western horizon, the gathering began to quiet. Older men sat in the shade, drinking traditional beer from clay *izinkhamba*. Married women, noble and dignified, laughed and joked together. The atmosphere built until another song and dance burst from the assembled.

Toward the end of the celebrations, young warriors and girls gradually drifted off in pairs.

Kai smiled. "It seems to be a night for romance among your people."

"The celebration is far from ended, my husband," said Nandi.

On a clearing north of the platform where the wedding had taken place, another gathering was under way. To the uninitiated, what one saw here appeared to be rampant violence as men yelled and charged, as sticks and shields whirled. In reality, it was yet merely another entertainment.

At first, great lines of warriors formed and began sparring against one another. It was extremely disciplined, ordered, and controlled by the great charisma and exceptional leadership of the battle-scarred warrior captains. Zulus were often squared off with Kai's men, an ostensibly friendly contest that all understood to have more serious undertones.

It was at this point that the real challenges started, with young warriors attempting to move up the ranks. A sudden hush, a circle of men, and two young gladiators become framed by the blurring of whistling sticks.

"*Nayi inkunzi!*" a young warrior cried.

"What does that mean?" Kai asked.

" 'Here is the bull!' " said Nandi, smiling in pride. "They will challenge each other now, like young bulls challenging the leader of the herd."

Nandi's mother grinned at Kai's apparent unease. "Should one man fall or falter, ordinarily the warrior captains immediately stop the fight. But since this is a friendly match between our two families, perhaps you should allow the men themselves to decide the point of yielding."

This inevitably meant bruises and perhaps even broken bones, but Kai could only nod, and wonder in his heart exactly what the game might be. "Yes," he said. "Perhaps we should."

Cetshwayo spanked his hands together. "Excellent!"

The night rang with shouts and crashes as Cetshwayo's men dueled with Kai's guard. It was customary, once the tension had subsided after the brawl, for the victor to bathe and bind his opponent's wounds, openly demonstrating that he held no malice.

However, every fight was a fight, and the outcome would be remembered in the victor's praise poem. Each fight, through its very greatness, would increase the *isithunzi,* the status, of these men.

And despite the general celebratory air, Kai was feeling a bit prickly. Contributing to his irritation was the unavoidable fact that his warriors weren't doing well. Bluntly put, the Zulus were thrashing them. Kebwe himself challenged a Zulu and actually won a match, only to be driven to his knees by the man called Chalo. Despite their lumps and limps, Kai's men, especially noble Kebwe, wanted to fight on, but Kai saw no point in it.

"Hold!" cried Kai. "Our great guests are indeed the matchless warriors of repute. I implore you to spare further injury to the good and faithful men in my service."

Cetshwayo seemed satisfied with the plea. "Hold indeed. And you need have no shame—this is our game, not yours. Had we not taken the measure of your battlefield skills and courage, there would have been no alliance twixt Shaka and your father."

Kai paused, trying to read the meaning behind *those* words. When it came to interpreting Zulu communication, he felt as if he were eternally playing catch-up. No wonder they made such barristers! "Well spoken," he said finally.

It was this entire complicated ritual of celebration that comprised the Zulu wedding ceremony. At no point had vows, in the Abyssinian sense, been exchanged.

And yet he wasn't fooled. All of the critical points had been negotiated twice, first by Kai and Cetshwayo, and then by Babatunde and the lawyers sent to represent the family interests. Once those contracts were fully in operation, the rest was mere formality.

"Keep my daughter well," said Cetshwayo formally. "Return her if she causes any trouble, or if you tire of her."

"I have never tired of the dawn," Kai replied with equal formality. "Nor shall her spirit ever fail to enchant me."

To Kai's surprise, Cetshwayo's eyes softened. For a moment, he could see a touch of confusion in the older man's eyes, as if he was uncertain of his next action.

"Good luck to you," the prince said finally. Was that a catch in his voice? "Both."

CHAPTER FORTY-ONE

As THE AIR COOLED and the guests began to drift away, Kai and his bride returned to the house. Demurely, Nandi excused herself and went to her chambers, while Kai retreated to his own rooms, there to groom and prepare himself for the evening.

Aidan joined him there. His former servant had remained on the outskirts of the ceremony, watching from Ghost Town, or in the company of the servants, in respect to the Zulu attitudes toward whites. Nonetheless, he was in a high mood. "You have waited three years for this night. Your loins must burn."

"In truth," Kai said frankly, "never in all my life have I desired a woman as I crave Nandi."

"May she surpass your dreams."

"Insh'allah," Kai said automatically; then the two friends laughed, holding each other's shoulders.

"I don't know how you Muslims do it," Aidan said. "One to one, our women are more than enough to handle. I'm not sure if Allah made your men stronger, or your women weaker."

Kai smiled. "The former, old friend. Wish me luck."

Aidan nodded. "Luck, Kai."

And Kai left.

"Luck of the Irish," Aidan murmured.

As Kai stalked the hallways, the servants deferred to him, bowing, lowering their eyes. Nandi's room was on the second floor, as was Lamiya's, but discretion suggested he take a separate hallway to her door.

He knocked, and heard nothing from within. Another knock, and Munji finally opened the door.

"I wish to see my wife," he said.

"Nandi requests the boon you promised her," her mother said.

"Of course. And that is?"

So fleet as to be barely glimpsed, a triumphant smile flashed across the

Zulu woman's face. "That you wait one-hundredth as long for her as she waited for you. Ten days."

Kai felt his knees weaken. "But . . . I . . ."

"You promised, Sidi," she said.

"Very well," he snarled, angrier with himself, and his childish reaction, than he was with his new wife. "Ask your daughter if she would do her husband the honor of accompanying him on a ride in the morning." He paused, and could not stop himself from adding, "If that would not be too much."

"I will indeed, Wakil. And anything else?" Munji's tone was so utterly polite and formal, that it was almost possible to overlook the mockery beneath the words. Almost.

"Yes." Kai ground his teeth until he feared they might splinter. "Bid her a very pleasant evening." Then, pivoting toe-heel, he stalked away.

In her bedroom, Nandi heard the terse words as well as the heavy tread of retreating feet.

She lay in her bed, lazily scratching IziLomo's ear as the ridgeback lay curled on the floor at her side. "And what did he say?" Her eyes were alight with mischief.

"I believe that you heard it, Daughter."

Nandi twinkled. "And is that all?"

"No," said Munji. "Not all. He asked if you would ride with him on the morrow."

"I'll give him my answer . . . in the morning."

"A woman cannot exert her power directly before she has entrapped her husband's heart."

"Oh," said Nandi. "Have no fear. I will do you proud, Mother."

The older woman beamed. "I know you will. And now, my daughter, I return to my tent. This is your house now, not mine. I must not remain beneath your roof until you have truly become this man's wife."

A glimmer of sadness crossed Nandi's face. "But when I am truly his wife, you will return home, leaving me here."

"You are a woman," said Munji, "and cannot build your home while I am here, telling you to do this and that thing. You must find your own way, but your attendants will take good care of you."

"Will you always love me, Mother?"

Munji enfolded Nandi in her vast and beautiful arms. "Before your father gave me his seed, I loved you. After the earth has embraced my bones, I will love you. Do you not know these things to be true?"

Nandi gazed into the face of the first human being she had seen in this world, and nodded slowly. "Good night, Mother."

After Munji left, Nandi pushed back luxuriantly into her pillows, yawning, a lazy, satisfied smile on her face.

Her right hand slipped beneath the covers, beginning the slow, circular massage that would shortly send alternating chills of heat and cold through her body.

Soon, Kai.

Not now. Not yet.

But soon.

The erotic chill was balanced by fear. Soon, a barrier would be crossed. On the other side of it, no matter how much she thought she knew herself, a different woman lived. What would she be like? What would her life be?

Nandi smiled, that smile melting into a grimace of pleasure as waves of fire and ice wracked her body, and she screamed her joy into the pillow that smelled of cedar, and wool, and home.

CHAPTER FORTY-TWO

IN THE MORNING KAI DRAGGED HIMSELF from his restless, lonely bed, threw water on his face, and performed his prayers and meditations, the hour of breathing, flexion, and visualization with which he invariably began the day. Then washing, he dressed and without breakfasting headed for the barn.

He pulled on his riding boots, pausing to scent at the leather. *What is that smell?* It was faint, but distinctive. Urine? Kai beetled his brow. Where . . . ?

He quelled the speculation, wiped his boots clean, and equipped both horses. He sat astride his own when Nandi appeared, fresh and beautiful in her riding togs, IziLomo trotting at her side. "Good morning, my husband."

"Good morning, Wife," he said, as casually as possible, keeping a keen eye on the hound. He could not read dog emotions. But if he could, he would have sworn the hound was smirking.

"What a fine day it is!"

Kai's smile stretched a bit tight. "One might have expected the night to have been more incandescent than the dawn, but yes, it is a great day."

Unexpectedly, her face softened, and she reached out a warm hand to touch his arm. "My husband. All good things to those who wait."

He glared at her. "I believe that it is time I met your champion."

She scratched the dog's thick neck. "IziLomo," she said, "please give courtesy to the master of the house, my husband Kai."

The dog looked at his mistress, and then at Kai, and walked forward. Kai tightened.

"Hold still and he will not tear your hand off," she said.

"Hah hah," he replied. Kai had seen dogs before, of course, and occasionally even interacted with them. Dogs were not common pets among the upper class, although the slaves in Ghost Town had several such animals, and some of the poorer blacks kept them as well. This was reportedly not the case in Alexandria, though. There, it was said, dogs were quite popular.

Nonetheless, Kai kept quiet and still, extending his hand. IziLomo sniffed at it, and then backed away, eyeing his putative new master warily. "Well trained," Kai said, hoping that his slight unease would not weaken his voice.

The dog returned to his mistress and sat, awaiting her next command with infinite patience. With huge, dark eyes it watched Kai.

"I have energy to burn off," Kai said impatiently.

Nandi clucked. "My poor husband."

"I seem to remember that you can ride. Come with me!"

As lightly as any boy Nandi seated herself, and the two of them dashed off, IziLomo loping along behind them.

Nandi, now one of the ladies of the household, explored her new holdings with Kai. In a strange way, she was more reserved than the girl who had offered him her honor those years ago. Because of Shaka? Or because she felt spurned? Or was it the fact that she was away from her home territory, and therefore treading cautiously?

Perhaps because mother and sisters were watching them, wondering how long it would take for her husband to prove himself a man.

For every conceivable reason, Kai was eager to bid them good-bye.

He was motivated to try to crack Nandi's reserve, and realized that her temporary power over his libido was simultaneously frustrating and inflaming. The situation was both repulsive and attractive. This was loss of control. Loss of control meant danger . . . and to the part of Kai's mind that belonged to his uncle Malik, danger was an intoxicant.

Lake A'zam's waters were warm and calm, sparkling in the afternoon sun as Kai showed Nandi his father's boat-building facility. He had taken the opportunity of their coerced celibacy to familiarize his Zulu wife with Dar Kush in all of its aspects. After all, she and Lamiya would be responsible for running the household, the servants, and conducting much of its business.

As interested as she was in these details, she was even more fascinated by the social differences between Bilalians and Zulus.

"I have my own room, yes," he said in answer to her query.

"Strange to me," replied Nandi.

"In what way?"

"Among my people, the *umnumzana*, the head of the household, has no home. His women's home is his home."

She paused, looking into the boat dock. "And what is this?"

"My father's fortune was made in shipping, and he retained an interest in it throughout his life. He enjoyed the water, and actually worked with Kokossa to design a few vessels."

"He was a great man," she said. "I am saddened that he did not live to see us wed."

That statement, and the moment containing it, seemed to Kai unusually frank. *I wish this as well. In such a case, my brother might still live.*

"Come," Kai said.

They dismounted, and entered the facility where Kai's pleasure dhow Sea Horse had been constructed. Within rested the bones and hide of another, half-finished ship.

"Incomplete," Nandi said.

"Yes. It was my father's, commissioned but uncompleted after his death."

"Will we sail?" she asked.

"Wherever you like."

"I have never been on a ship," she said.

That took Kai by surprise. "Never?"

"What is it like?"

"Do you swim?"

"Yes." She paused, then added, "A little."

"I will teach you," Kai said.

"You will?"

He nodded. "We have a whole life, a whole world together. If you have patience, you can learn."

The day seemed to have quieted just for them, just for this moment. "If you have patience, *you* will learn as well."

Her eyes burned, and her lips parted slightly. The tip of her pink tongue traced her upper teeth. He leaned forward and kissed her. Their shared breath was spicy and sweet.

She returned the kiss, but after a moment, backed away. "My husband," she said huskily.

"My wife."

They grinned, and at that moment, Kai realized that despite, or perhaps due to his frustration, he was enjoying this game very much indeed.

Holding hands, Kai and Nandi entered the main house. IziLomo trotted just behind them, attentive but not intrusive.

Lamiya sat in the parlor, a servant cleaning and buffing her nails. "Did you have a good ride?"

"Excellent," Nandi said, and then brightened as a new thought occurred to her. "Would you like a gallop this afternoon?"

"Perhaps," Lamiya said. "Yes." She smiled, pleased by the invitation. She looked at IziLomo. "Will your friend accompany us?"

Nandi smiled. "Would you wish it?"

"I have never really known a dog, and your companion intrigues me."

"Then let it be."

"Oh . . . Kai? I'm expecting the Guptas for tea tomorrow. I wanted to use a hairstyle more like those of their own homeland, and that last girl isn't working out. Can't take direction. Do you think you could find me another? One used to working with hair?"

"I will see to it," Kai said. "There is a girl, Tata, who I purchased in Radama. She knows something about adornment. I think that she will suffice, if you would have her."

Lamiya cocked her head slightly. "This is the girl from the . . . ?"

"Yes."

She smiled. "I would be glad to try her. If she can learn, it might be the best for both of us."

Kai spoke to one of the slaves, and they summoned Tata from the kitchen, where she had spent the morning scraping grease from the ovens. She appeared almost at once, smudged and perhaps weary, but eager to please.

"Tata," he said.

"Yes, Sidi?"

"I would like you to begin to work with my wife's attendants. I hear from the kitchen that you have clever fingers. Is this true?"

She lowered her gaze. "I do me best."

Lamiya gently cupped her chin, raising Tata's face until their eyes met. "I never ask for more than your best, Tata. And am never satisfied with less, either. If you are a lazy child, it might be to your advantage to find a position less likely to bring your insufficiencies to my notice. What do you think?"

Tata blinked, as if trying to calculate the advantages and disadvantages of obscurity. Then she glanced at Kai, then back to Lamiya and nodded. "Ma'am, I be happy to learn anyt'ing you want teach."

"Good," Lamiya said, and then turned to her husband again. "I think she will do just fine."

*　　*　　*

Lamiya appeared perfectly turned out from coiffure to pedicure, and Nandi, for once in her life, felt just a bit overmatched. She herself had many skills and talents, whereas it seemed that Lamiya had been born and bred to one task alone: to be the most exquisite gift one monarch might offer another. Among her own, there was no one to rival Cetshwayo's daughter. But what standards did Kai hold most closely to his heart? And by those deepest, unspoken standards of beauty and grace, how might Nandi fare?

The question deviled but did not daunt. There was more than one way to catch a man's heart. . . .

While Kai and Lamiya spoke the girl working Lamiya's nails continued at her clipping, shards falling to the floor. With her toe, Nandi nudged the scraps into a tiny pile, and then pushed them under the chair for later retrieval.

Kai continued on. "And by the way—thank you for taking over the Gupta lunch. It might well have slipped my mind."

To Nandi, Lamiya said, "You will find, Nandi, that your new husband has his uses. Hosting is not one of them. Do you enjoy entertaining?"

Would the servant notice that the clippings were gone? It was all she could do to keep her guilt from shining in her face. "Supervising the kitchen is a joy—but I don't know your cuisine. If you would guide me a bit, I think I could make myself useful."

Lamiya smiled. "Kai, I think you brought home a gem. Come with me, my sister. We'll show these Indians how Africa feeds both belly and soul!"

Nandi waited until Kai, Lamiya, and the body servant had turned their backs, and then scooped up the clippings.

Despite her stealth, Nandi was observed. The spying eyes were small, and brown, and new to the household.

Tata had had trepidations about her journey to Dar Kush. Surely the Wakil had lied, and despite all of his words, would want her for his bed. What else did men ever want? But no, to her surprise, that had not been the end result of her travels.

Dar Kush was a place of wonder, of unknown sights and scents and sensations, glorious sunrises and blissful sunsets. She wanted desperately to fit in, to make herself useful. The Wakil himself was the most fearsome and powerful man she had ever known. When he had stormed into the brothel and forced the cowardly Kaleb to cease his harsh, clumsy thrusting, she had thought him an avenging angel, come to kill them both, that her misery might cease and justice be served.

She now knew the Wakil to be a man, but what a man! And if she could only find a way to make him think well of her, well, it would be a right blessing.

This new woman, his second wife, the proud and haughty Zulu girl, was up to something. Tata didn't know what it was, or what it might mean, or even what she should do about her suspicions. But she would keep them to herself, and wait, and gather.

And one day, perhaps when it mattered most, she would have what she needed, and then the Wakil would be so proud of her that . . .

That he might . . .

She was flushing, suddenly aware that her emotions exceeded what a poor slave girl should feel for her owner. Shamed, confused, but not forgetting for a moment what she had seen, Tata retreated.

CHAPTER FORTY-THREE

THE SECOND TIME that Kai discovered dried urine puddled on his riding boots, he decided it was time to do something about it.

The fact that he was also stressed, that he felt as if he were an engine on the verge of tearing itself apart, increased his need to correct an increasingly intolerable situation.

IziLomo had watched the two of them all week, sneaking about, being the very picture of canine obedience when Nandi was near, and then growling throatily as soon as her back was turned. Twice he had tried to speak to Nandi about it, and the situation had become intolerable. He assumed that Nandi always took IziLomo back to his kennel, or up to her room, but obviously she had allowed him to run free long enough to get into mischief.

And yet, what to do?

Like most south Bilalians, he had never owned a dog, and didn't know them well enough to make a judgment, or devise a strategy. Did one treat dogs like horses? Should he take the monster hunting, or play with it, give it bits of meat? A bath?

The questions raced around and around in his mind.

On the other hand, an accident for the beast might be arranged as well. Dogs were, he believed, known to simply wander away. . . .

No. He would not start his marriage with a lie. He owed Nandi, owed himself, more than that sort of disastrous action.

A thought occurred to him: there had always been dogs in Ghost Town. There had been a dog at the Ouachita crannog. So there was one person he trusted who might have an answer to his puzzle, and it was in search of that person he went.

Aidan was currently torturing muscles and sinews in the workout area. Today's exercise in controlled agony involved running and hefting a set of clubs one and a half cubits long and two sep in weight. Tapering to a narrow handle, they were probably the single most widely-used exercise device in the world, known from China to India to Persia to Ghana. Kai was pleased with the way the lines of Aidan's body had grown more angular and sinewy. He forced the Irishman to do sets of twenty club swings, then run a lap around the pasture, and then perform the swings again, over and over again. The combination of steady-state exertion and a brief spike of intensity created a powerful training effect: the ability to work almost endlessly, a capacity for labor that would shame an ox, combined with the speed and dynamism of a race horse.

At the moment, he doubted if Aidan appreciated the subtle physical science that he and Babatunde had culled to create the program.

On the other hand, Aidan was perfectly happy to see Kai approach, chiefly because such an approach signaled time for a rest. He came running around a curve, approaching him, and stopped, ribs creaking as he gulped for air.

"Ho, the warrior," Kai said.

"Ho, the lazy noble," Aidan gasped between retches. This method of increasing wind and power had a tendency to clench the stomach like a fist.

"I have a question for you," Kai said.

"Great. Just wait . . . until . . . I stop puking." He made a few more heaving sounds, and then looked up at Kai, a purely evil expression on his face. "God . . . I hope you've stopped training, Kai. After the shyte you're putting me through, I would purely love to kick your arse."

"Alas"—Kai smiled—"Allah gives us but one life to live, and insufficient years remain in yours to approach such a level."

"We'll see about that."

"At your convenience," Kai said merrily. "But I really do have a request."

And while Aidan waited for his heart to cease galloping, Kai explained his dilemma. Aidan listened, asked questions, and then laughed. "So you know everything about everything, but don't understand dogs?"

"They are unclean animals," he said. "They eat their own feces."

"And yours too, given an opportunity. I hope I'm there the next time IziLomo tries to lick your face. Or your wife's face, which you hope soon to kiss."

"You are a dreadful man," Kai said.

"Thank you. I do my best." Aidan leaned back against the fence, and gazed up at the sky. "Well," he said finally. "Like wolves, dogs are pack animals. And the pack always has a leader. He is testing you to see if you are strong enough to lead. If not, *he* will be the leader."

"How do I change that?"

Aidan smiled. "Not as a man, with sticks and swords and guns. You need to deal with him in the language he understands."

"What does that mean?"

"Since he can't communicate to you in your language, it's up to you to communicate to him in his."

They spoke a while longer, and when it was done, Kai walked away, shaking his head, but at the same time his eyes glowed, as if the promise of a challenge were invigorating.

Aidan watched him, his formerly helpful smile transforming into something a bit more mischievous as Kai retreated. "Well, boyo," he said. "Not exactly a lie, was it? Just a little somethin' to keep life more interesting. . . ."

The very next day, Kai decided to implement his plan.

As always, he and Nandi took a morning ride, and IziLomo accompanied them, running alongside their horses, rarely falling far behind unless Kai truly allowed his mount to gallop. Nandi seemed overjoyed with the chance to let herself blend with her mount and simply surrender to the rhythm of the ride.

When they were concluded, Kai trotted the horses back to the house, and Nandi dismounted, looking up at him with her lips curved in the slightest of smiles. "What now, Husband?"

"I thought IziLomo and I would put the horses away." He turned to the dog, smacking his hands together. "Here, boy."

She raised one eyebrow. IziLomo remained where he was, but looked back and forth between the two. Finally she nodded, and said a few words in Zulu, pointing at her husband. IziLomo licked her hand. "Good," she said. "The two of you need to get to know each other."

Kai nodded. "Yes," he said. "It is time."

She bent and scratched the dog's head. IziLomo looked from his mistress to Kai, perhaps a bit confused. "Go on," she said. "Go with Kai."

"Come, IziLomo," Kai said again as Nandi headed to the house. Then he turned his horse and led them both toward the barn. He looked back and saw the ridgeback walking slowly behind them, watching him carefully.

At the barn door Kai dismounted. Once they were alone, he never looked directly at the dog, merely going about his business of removing saddle and preparing the horses for grooming.

Olaf One-Ear, in the barn sweeping up dung and straw, looked up with a start. "Master!" he cried, then corrected himself. "Sidi. Is there something you require?"

"No. Not at all. In fact, I would appreciate it if you would find duties elsewhere, allow me to take care of this."

"Are you certain?" he looked from Kai to the horses to the dog, perhaps sensing that something was amiss.

"Absolutely," Kai said. He kept IziLomo within his peripheral vision, but still had not looked at the dog directly. The servant left, and he saw that the ridgeback stretched its legs and stepped a half cubit to the side, allowing Olaf to pass.

Kai closed the barn door.

Light filtered down from a window above the hayloft, and as Kai walked back to the horses, he could feel the dog's attention on him, a fierce focus not quite like anything he had ever felt before. He had hunted, of course: deer and bear and mountain lion. But once he had *been* hunted, and that sensation was similar to what he felt now.

Kai hung the saddles and led the horses to their stalls, locking them in.

Now the wide aisle between the rows of stalls was empty, straw-strewn, ready.

He turned and faced IziLomo. The dog crouched near the door, watching him carefully.

"I know what you've wondered," Kai said, and unbuttoned his shirt. "You wondered if, without my sword, my gun, my knife, I could survive you. You wonder if it would be worthwhile to wait and find a time when I am without these things, and then to determine the answer to that question your heart holds dear."

He slipped his shirt off. The ride had warmed his body and loosened his muscles. A thin sheen of sweat gleamed along his torso's graceful lines and curves.

"I say these things knowing that you cannot comprehend my words, but may well understand the emotions behind them." He unbuckled his pants and let them drop, stepping free from them so that he stood before IziLomo clad only in his undergarments.

"I say these things knowing that you love the woman I love. That you want only what is good for her. That being so, you need to know me better. And what I say to you, one male to another, is: why wait?"

He stood with his legs spread apart, arms spread, in a posture of openness and perhaps even vulnerability. He bent his knees, bringing himself down closer to IziLomo's level.

"Come," Kai said. "Let us learn what is true."

His heart beat faster than he liked, but he felt good, loose. He met IziLomo's eyes directly, and the dog shook itself and rose. It seemed to Kai that at that moment the air took on a deeper chill.

This, he knew, was madness. The intelligent thing to do was probably to net the beast and simply beat it into submission.

And yet . . . something about what Aidan had told him of dogs rang true, seemed the same for both beasts and men. And as he had explained to Nandi only days before, he had energy to burn off.

His complete focus was on the hound as it approached him, head down, tail up, eyes locked on his own. Kai could feel it, could sense that IziLomo had recognized and accepted the challenge.

The muscles and tendons in IziLomo's back and shoulders bunched and released. Perhaps because he had been so irritated with Nandi, Kai hadn't really noticed how majestic her companion truly was, and for an instant felt inadequate. Then Kai remembered himself and watched IziLomo's jaws. *His teeth.* Those were the dog's only real weapon. If he could neutralize them, he might just emerge from this encounter unscathed.

If not, well, Shaka was probably watching this even now, and hell's corridors would peal with Zulu mirth.

IziLomo's approach had been measured and slow. At a distance twice the length of Kai's leg he ceased his advance and began to circle. A very slow padding, almost as if he were trying to get *behind* Kai, and that sense chilled him. For just an instant Kai allowed his mind to stray, thinking of the first time he had seen Nandi and the hound together—

As if IziLomo could somehow detect his distraction, the dog lunged for his leg from a position just to his right rear.

Low. Stay low. Stay on the hound's level. Make it personal. Motion timed with a sharp puff of exhalation, Kai pivoted back. IziLomo's jaws snapped on air, and as they did, Kai braced himself, and clubbed the dog in the neck with his balled fist.

The blow would have broken a human femur. IziLomo didn't even react, merely backed and lunged again. This time, he adjusted to Kai's speed of retreat, the teeth gnashing shut only a digit away from his skin. Kai pivoted, stepped back, and then even more swiftly slid in again, striking with the ball of his foot in the dog's heavily padded ribs. The kick was perfectly timed and distanced, and the heavy *thwack* made him wince sympathetically. That blow would have sent a man writhing to the ground clutching broken ribs.

Again, no apparent effect at all.

A furrow of self-doubt wrinkled his brow, swiftly banished by discipline. He felt his breathing shift, realized that it indicated a surge of fear, and deliberately calmed and centered himself, reintegrating body, mind, and emotion as he did. *Breath. Posture. Motion.* This Yoruban triumvirate, and the Sufic breathing techniques that united them, were the gift Babatunde had given him, the Cricket's way of continuing the training that Malik had begun. *Any distraction, any fear, any anger, any tension will begin the disintegration of your structure. It will manifest physically before it occurs mentally or spiritually. Learn to recognize its first signs. Use those first signs to trigger the reintegrative response. Breathe, as in the zikr breath, saying "Allah," never ceasing the flow. Control your abdominal muscles—they control your breathing. Hold your head as if you are suspended by a string from above. Thighs tight. Hips loose.*

Breathe.

IziLomo growled, deep and low in his canine throat. His brown eyes were hooded and murderous. He paused, and then charged Kai, snapping. This time Kai hit him a crushing blow directly on the nose, meeting the charge head-on with hairline precision.

This time, IziLomo felt it. He backed up, shaking his head as if trying to dry himself, and then came in again.

But now Kai knew his adversary. The dog was fast, powerful, fearless— but his tactics had been chosen by nature, and ingrained by a thousand generations of breeding. IziLomo could not change them, no matter how strange an adversary he faced.

Kai stood still, eyes closed. IziLomo padded in a circle, flanking him, moving to the rear, perhaps surprised that Kai let him do so.

He knew that such dogs were trained to operate in packs, with each animal fulfilling a very specific role in the attack. IziLomo had tried front and side: perhaps he would have more luck from the rear.

Focus. Eyes closed, he had nothing but hearing, but his ears were acute. And more than hearing: stripping off his clothes, confronting the animal as one naked beast to another, had done something, taken away some civilized barrier, forced him to rely more on instinct.

Here it comes. Kai sidestepped a charge, and as IziLomo came in he pivoted, striking into the same spot on IziLomo's neck he had first attacked. This time he put more hip into it, so that the dog was driven sideways and backward, skidding a bit, paws scrabbling on the straw for purchase.

This time it looked at him with something different in its eyes. Not respect. Not fear . . . but awareness. The dog coughed, and when it took a step, its front leg quivered . . . just a bit, but Kai saw it. He crouched. Time to end this before one of them was hurt. Hopefully, he had made his point.

Kai snarled, showing his teeth. He spread his arms wide, exposing his belly.

IziLomo lunged, faster this time, and the teeth actually tore Kai's shin before snapping on air. Kai pivoted, snaking his right arm around the dog's neck, falling to the ground and using his weight as a weapon to pin it.

IziLomo thrashed madly, foaming and snapping and howling. Kai struck it in the ribs with hammer blows: once, twice, three times before feeling the slight *give* that told him that tendons had surrendered, muscle traumatized, bone bruised.

End this. He felt his own carefully maintained structure begin to disintegrate as his bloodlust began to surge. The moment was upon him, and he felt his breathing spiral out of control, his vision tinge with crimson.

Now, now, before it is too late. He wrestled IziLomo onto his back, his hand gripping the dog's muzzle. Its claws scratched at him, raking skin from his legs and side, but he clamped the cold hand of control onto his emotions, refusing either to retreat or kill.

He pulled IziLomo's muzzle back, and clamped his teeth on the dog's throat. IziLomo went rigid, eyes wide and staring. Kai could taste the hound's pulse.

For a long moment they remained in that posture; then Kai opened his mouth, finding the taste of dog not at all to his liking. He rolled back, releasing IziLomo's muzzle and taking a safe measure.

The dog rolled over onto its feet, and Kai noticed that one of its legs was a little loose. Those same blows would have stopped a man's heart, but evidently the ridgeback was crafted of sterner stuff.

Still, IziLomo whined as he stood, listing, and now he had a problem meeting Kai's eyes. It was clear that IziLomo wanted nothing better but to limp off and lick his wounds.

"Look at me!" Kai commanded. IziLomo turned his head slightly to the side, but Kai knew he was watching. "*I* am the master of this house," he said. "Your mistress is my mate." Kai rubbed his hand along his side, and it came away red.

"You wanted my blood?" he asked. "Here it is." He held his hand out toward the dog. IziLomo whined again.

And then the ridgeback crawled across the ground, belly brushing the straw, toward Kai. At first Kai was surprised, thought that it was some kind of trick, but IziLomo put his head on Kai's naked foot and closed his eyes.

Kai stood, breathing heavily, feeling the rush of adrenaline as he finally allowed himself to feel his fear. What an animal! Never had he seen its like. And without thinking Kai knelt, touching its head, looking into its eyes.

Kai felt a rush of unexpected emotions: shame, pride, hope. There was something in IziLomo's expression. . . . Perhaps it was just the urge to project human emotions on a lesser beast, but Kai didn't think so. It was something else.

Kai scratched IziLomo behind the ear, and the dog whined, head still down, but now its eyes were open and watching him. Kai ran his hands over its body, feeling the strength, marveling at the speed that had almost undone him, and feeling something else—an emotion for which he had no certain label.

IziLomo had just accepted Kai as the leader of his pack. But what had Kai accepted in turn? "Easy, boy," he asked, feeling the places where his blows and kicks had landed. IziLomo winced when the wounds were touched, but did not pull away. Kai examined him as he might have a horse. Bruises, but he thought nothing was broken.

Then he stood. IziLomo trembled as Kai dressed, watching him without moving. Kai went to the barn door. The dog remained crouched in the straw.

"IziLomo," Kai said, and the dog's ears perked up. He stood, and trotted over to Kai, and lowered his head. In spite of himself, Kai smiled.

"Allah preserve me," Kai murmured. "I think I have a dog."

Two minutes after they left, there was a rustle in the straw of the loft. Aidan rolled out and sat on the edge, feet dangling, shaking his head.

Perhaps he shouldn't have done that, convinced Kai that the only way to earn IziLomo's respect was to meet him as one animal to another. It had been damned risky—the dog might have savaged his old friend.

Well, that was another *might* that hadn't come to pass. Life was full of *mights*. And Aidan had to admit that it was fascinating to witness his old friend in action. Watching Kai was like watching a shadow passing over water—never there, never within reach, but always in striking distance. His speed and power were incredible. Not since the duel with Malik had Aidan seen its like . . . and perhaps not even then. Incredibly, his friend was faster, somehow *cleaner*. Babatunde, while no martial artist, had tapped some deeper well in Kai, and Aidan was now quite happy that Kai had not accepted his implicit challenge.

Well, so what if Kai had a few scratches he hadn't awakened with? Served him right for listening to a mere pigbelly.

And humming to himself, Aidan found his way out of the barn and wandered back to the training dome for another dose of measured masochism.

CHAPTER FORTY-FOUR

20 *Dhu'l-Qa'dah* A.H. 1294
(Monday, November 26, 1877)

AS THE SUN KISSED THE WESTERN HORIZON, the air was finally beginning to cool. Aidan, who had spent another agonizing day battering his body, gave a silent gasp of thanks as the breeze dried the sweat on his back. He bent, lifted a cast iron cannonbell, and heaved it as four of Kai's orphans cheered him on. Not "cannonball"—no battlefield implements were these. Although the cannonbells were of cast iron and about the right size and shape as those deadly projectiles, they also had thick looping iron handles jutting from their sides. The one that currently deviled him weighed about five sep, and he was utilizing it in a curious ritual: throwing it as far as he could, then immediately sprinting to the spot where it landed, picking it up with a bend and dip, then heaving it again to begin the pattern anew.

Kai rode by. "Ho there, the warrior," he called.

"Ho there, the lazy noble," Aidan panted in ritual response. Kai's charges had been alarmed by Aidan's familiarity at first, but taking their cue from the lord of the house, had swiftly learned to giggle instead of wince.

Kai climbed down off the horse. "Not so lazy," he said.

"Oh. No? Well, your orphans have me heaving these great bloody chunks of iron. Have you ever lifted one of these damned things?"

Kai cocked an eye at the iron ball. "Upon occasion."

"Favor us," said Aidan. "I have ten deben on you, so I don't expect you to hit my mark, but still—it would do my soul good to watch you flail about."

Kai grinned. "Guests first."

Aidan selected a heavier ball from the selection afforded him: this one, a nine-sep monstrosity, seemed appropriate to the task at hand. He bent, levered it to his shoulder, then torqued his hips and heaved the cannon-bell about five cubits. His orphan audience applauded. "Beat that?"

"Doubtful," Kai said. "Very—" He bent his knees and swayed gracefully, almost like a woman dancing. The bell floated back, and then he snapped his hips and it sailed a dozen cubits, thudding into the earth. Aidan gawked.

"Very doubtful indeed."

Aidan glared at him. "Well. I'd heard that sexual frustration increases power."

"Is that why you heaved your stone so heroically? Or should I inform Sophia that you've found a softer bed in Ghost Town among your old friends?"

"Ouch," Aidan said, and then sidled closer. "Honestly, Kai . . . how long will Nandi make you wait?"

Kai shrugged. "Tonight is the ninth night. Tomorrow the tenth."

"Ah . . . and then the gates of heaven open?"

"It would be indiscreet—"

"Yes, yes, yes," Aidan agreed. Then he whispered, "But you will tell me about it?"

"Of course," Kai whispered in return, and they both laughed uproariously.

Aidan wiped his hands on his pants. "The bells await."

"They are a jealous mistress," said Kai.

Both turned as the sound of racing feet grew louder. They turned to see a boy, perhaps twelve years old dashing out from the main house. His name was Conair and his father had died raiding the Aztec encampment. "Master Kai? The mistress asks ye to come."

"Lamiya?"

"The new mistress. Missus Nandi."

"Tell her I'll be right there," he said. Then to Aidan: "Enjoy your torture."

Kai freshened himself before walking the long hall to his wife's room. By the time he reached it, the evening shadows had grown long. The door was open a digit, and he pushed it until he could see her. "You called me?"

Nandi lay in her bed, and by the modifications she and her ladies had wrought, a gauzy, incense-misted wonder it was. All about her, beeswax candles burned as if she were a goddess of creation surrounded by newborn nebulae. "Yes, my husband."

He scanned the room. "IziLomo has abandoned you?"

"He is with my mother this evening." She paused, watching him carefully. "She is good with dogs, and IziLomo seems somehow to have acquired a limp."

"Yes," Kai said. "I noticed. I trust it will heal soon." He came closer. "Is something amiss?"

"Yes, I think so," she said, as if half asleep. She stirred lazily in bed, body moving as if possessed of a sensual will of its own. "I am having trouble remembering."

"Remembering?"

"The day of the week. Of the month."

Kai closed the door behind him and slid a cautious step closer. "And this troubles you, my love?"

"Yes," she said. "Because I *think* that tomorrow it will be ten days since we wed, but I *feel* that tonight may be the significant night. Tell me, husband: which is correct, my head, or my heart?"

He touched her shoulder. Her nightgown, a sheerest breath of silk, slid off at his caress. "What does your body say?"

"It says that I am yours, and have been for three years."

There was something different in her face, something just a little frightened . . . but simultaneously proud.

"Yes," Kai said.

"Tell me. Now," Nandi whispered. "Did you miss me?"

"With my whole heart," he said, knowing that he meant every word.

"Do you want me?"

"I feel . . . that my father was a wiser man than ever I knew. That if what . . . happened to my family had not happened, that you would have made me the happiest man in the world."

"And now?"

"Now . . . I am certain no mortal man has ever been more fortunate than I." He bent, brushing her naked belly with his lips. "That no earthly flower," he murmured, "has ever rendered so exquisite a perfume."

Kai slid the covers back, and nosed his way up her body, stopping to blow a puff of warm air every few digits.

Nandi smiled mischievously, with just a hint of nervousness. "And . . . will you pluck me?"

"No," he said. "I will help your roots grow deep, brush the clouds away that you might grow drunk with sunlight. Water and nurture you, and urge you to give seed, that your beauty and power might increase."

"And you will take . . . ?"

"Everything that is mine."

"And nothing more?"

"Nothing that is not offered."

She embraced him, and they sank together into the bed. A sudden gust of wind blew out a candle, and the first night of their marriage began.

With his hands, he read her, like a blind man reading his lover's face. With his tongue and lips he traced her body's contours, textures, and tastes.

And when he found that place where her perfume was most exquisite, the uppermost spot where her folds drew together, he there traced his tongue in tiny circles and patterns, working his way through the alphabet, as another man's wife had once taught him.

At every instant he noted her body's response. When she heaved, when she turned, when the textures and heat changed, he remembered the letter that had caused it, each representing a different pattern and pressure. And when he strung those letters together into a word, in writing that word again and again with tongue-tip he brought her to heat, and then to flame, again and again so that she begged for him.

And the word was *seneddu. Ready.*

And so she was.

And later, after the night had deepened, she cried out in the darkness, and clung to him with strength that might have shamed a warrior. The tears that coursed her cheeks moistened his, so that in that timeless moment, it would have been most difficult to tell where one of them ended and the other began.

And in the greater scheme of things, that mattered not at all. . . .

Kai drifted toward awareness only to find Nandi already awake, lying on her side, smiling at him. "Good morning, Wife."

"And to you, Husband."

He yawned himself more awake. "What are you smiling about?"

"The splendid sight before me, and my memories of the night." She stretched luxuriantly.

"Was it dream, or fact?"

"I am not certain," she said. "I may require additional evidence." She reached below the covers, grasping him firmly. He started a bit.

"Ah . . ."

"So . . . ," she purred. "One part of my dream has proven real. What other aspects may as well?"

Her eyes locked with his, face so close that her exhalations were his inhalations, and vice versa. "Last night," she whispered, "you carried me to womanhood. This morning, in thanks, I would take you to the clouds."

She licked her hand, and again grasped him, running her thumb and fingers slowly, luxuriantly, up and down his shaft, so that he arched his back and groaned with pleasure. Whenever he opened his eyes, hers were locked on him, as her palm and fingers continued to caress. Again and again she massaged him until he nearly lost control, and then would stop, purring, playing, until his breathing once more steadied itself. She seemed to sense his response almost as if every nerve in his body was linked to hers: his breathing, heartbeat, perhaps even the dilation of his eyes telling her all she needed to know to slowly, steadily move him to a place where his mind seemed not to operate at all, where every warm, slick motion of her hand educed another groan, and he produced fluid of his own, such that when she paused to lick her hand again, he knew that she could taste him.

At last she took him over that crest, caused him to shudder and cry out, his muscle locking and mind cleared of all thought save a long, long exclamation of delight; when at last he calmed again she wiped him carefully clean with the sheet and then nestled against him, kissing and stroking for delicious minutes until he was ready once again.

She rolled atop him, adjusted him, and then settled down with a slow, deep exhalation.

"Indeed . . . ," gasped Kai, "You are the horsewoman I remembered."

"Last night was a canter," she said. "I favor a gallop this morning."

"I am at your command."

Her eyes were half-lidded. Lazy. Dangerous. "Be careful what appetites you awaken, Husband."

"You'll find my pantry full."

She dropped lower, closer, gazed into his eyes. "Feed me," she said.

And he did, until the sun stood at its zenith. Then, limbs entwined, both fell into a drowse as deep as a bottomless well, the sweet smiles of satiation curling lips that touched even as they slept.

When Nandi awakened again, Kai was gone. She allowed all of the memories and sensations to flood back through her, selecting among them, shuddering when a memory grew too visceral. Then taking a deep breath she pulled the covers back to reveal an Alexander-sized dampness on the sheets. There blood and semen mingled, the fluids of their bodies joined in a single glistening patch. She scraped at it with a knife, and then wiped the fluid off into a little glass jar, and sealed it.

She smiled, that twist of her lips cool and remote. "And now, Lamiya Mesgana," she said, "we will see who is dearest in our husband's affections."

Later that day, after sober inspection of the bloodied sheets, Munji smiled sadly. "It is time I went home."

"When will I see you again, Mother?" Nandi asked, doing everything in her power to stand straight and tall. It was vital that she show strength now, despite the fact that her knees felt weak, and she wanted to cry.

The older woman kissed Nandi's forehead, smiling fondly. "You have a new home, my daughter," Munji said. "And now I give you my last piece of advice: Never forget your past, your people. But keep your eyes on your future. This is a good man you have married. I believe he actually loves you, which is more than your father did when we were wed."

"But he loves you now."

"Yes, and that was my gift to him. My gift to you is this: be your own woman, Nandi. You will always be my daughter. Now it is time to be a wife. The future is yours." She held her daughter at arm's length. "You have never disappointed me. Always, you were my favorite."

"You say that to all your daughters."

"Yes," her mother replied. "And mean it with every one." And with those words Munji left her. By nightfall their tents were packed and stowed, and Munji's retinue began their journey home, leaving Nandi with IziLomo, her old nurse Baleka, and four retainers, the massive Zulu women who had pledged their lives to her safety. Officially they were but chambermaids, but in actuality they were of stock comparable to Bitta's, as capable of violence as any man—and every one of them considered Nandi to be their only child. To say that they would die for her would be a dangerous understatement.

Far more importantly, they would kill for her.

CHAPTER FORTY-FIVE

FROM THE BEGINNING, Kai had enlisted his orphans to help cheer Aidan on, running with him, fetching and carrying for him, and sometimes driving him on by their youthfully energetic example. Although he was white, they accepted the Wakil's friend as an admirable oddity: a veteran of the war that had claimed their fathers. He had slain Aztecs and could, at night, regale them with tales of battle and honor, and for that they admired him.

At the moment, they had been pushing Aidan in relays, giving him just enough time to rest before forcing him to run or lift or tumble or strike again . . . and again.

When meal break came, they brought him only a little fruit, and a bit of meat. He looked at the paltry victuals in his bowl, and glared at Kai. "If I'm going to work as hard as you say, I need more food than this!"

"No," said Kai. "You don't. Today we deepen your discipline. What I ask you to do is not comfortable, but it is natural, and your ancestors understood it."

Aidan clutched his growling belly. "Help my stomach understand. Please."

Kai laughed. "You will eat as warriors eat, when on the march. In the old days, they would march and fight all day, and feast at night."

"I'll die."

"Hardly," Kai chuckled, "although you may well think you will. But at night, you will eat all you wish."

Aidan rolled on his back, staring at the ceiling. "Why are you doing this to me?"

"A hungry man is an uncivilized man." Kai considered. "Well, not that an excess of civilization was ever your problem."

"Fock ye."

"Such language. We need to tap into something below all of your conditioning, all language and manner. We must find the wolf within you."

That, finally, caught Aidan's attention. "The wolf?"

Kai nodded. "Any man captured as a slave is a sheep. The wolves all die. Any few wolves that sneak through are killed. It is one reason most of my people have no respect for you—they know that they would never be slaves."

Aidan eyelids slid half way down. "I hope you never learn how wrong you are."

Kai shrugged. "Whatever difference of opinion we may have about this, you can see how your men have been turned into something less than warriors."

"How could you let them be otherwise and control them?" Aidan countered.

"How could they be otherwise and be controlled?"

Aidan bit back his thoughts. Love Kai he might, but there were some subjects on which they would never agree. "So eating in this way awakens this thing, this wolf within me?"

Kai nodded. "It is one of the things we will do. Some of these things I will tell you about. Others will happen but won't be well explained to you. Conscious understanding can be a liability."

Kai stood, and faced Aidan. The floor beneath them was thickly matted. The children sat in a circle around them, watching eagerly. Aidan looked at their black, shining faces, and some small part of him was transported back to an earlier, simpler day, when he and Kai had played together without lives and families and empires in the balance.

Kai seemed to be reading his mind. "Now," he said, "as we used to in the old days: attack me."

"Now, Kai—I've learned a thing or two—" In midsentence, Aidan lunged at Kai with a right punch. Although the attack was swift enough to ensnare a bird in flight, Kai leaned easily out of the way. With an eye-baffling motion, he spun his back into Aidan, hips low, throwing him without using hands or arms at all.

Aidan tumbled across Kai's back and fell like a sack of meal, facefirst onto the mat. "Woof!" The children laughed, but Aidan felt no embarrassment, only a deep gratitude for the thickness of woven straw.

"And there we will begin," said Kai. "With falling."

"What? What about fighting?"

"Throwing blows and opponents is only half of the circle," Kai said, speaking as much to the children as to his old friend. "There is more—you must learn to receive without injury. Throw me."

Aidan grabbed Kai around the waist, bent his knees, and heaved him through the air. Kai seemed boneless as an old rag, collapsing, rolling, and bounding back up again. "Loose. Loose," said Kai. "Come."

Their youthful audience watched in awe as the two friends practiced. Again and again Aidan hurled Kai over ankle, hip, and shoulder. For his part, Kai flowed effortlessly from fall to fall. When he stood, Aidan was blowing hard, and Kai was still fresh.

"I can run for hours," Aidan complained. "Why is this so damned hard?"

"Because you have never done it. And never having done it, your body fears it. Fear creates tension, and tension constricts your breathing, disintegrates your body's harmony. Lacking air, your fire dies. Come. Let us try this."

Kai swept his leg back along an imaginary line, miming a foot sweep.

"Can I see that again?" Aidan asked.

"Oh, yes." Kai seized Aidan and let him see that throw from *extremely* close range. Aidan fell just as clumsily as he had the first time.

"Oof!"

"Up!" said Kai. "And now you do it to me."

"With pleasure," Aidan growled.

He heaved Kai from the ground. Kai bounced up, seized Aidan, and threw him. This time, Aidan managed to land with a hair more grace. He rose and tossed Kai in return, and so it went back and forth, the two exchanging throws in like manner from one end of the room to the other, the children scrambling out of the way with delighted cries.

By the time they'd traversed the room four times, Aidan's shirt was dripping with sweat, and he gasped for breath like a beached sailor. Kai, on the other hand, had only dark half-moons of perspiration beneath his arms to show for his efforts.

Aidan growled something thoroughly obscene and climbed back up to wage mock battle once again.

Often at night Aidan was so sore and tired that he stopped wanting to walk the three hundred steps to his room in Ghost Town. Instead, he curled onto a mat in a corner of the exercise room, bruised and dappled with sweat. His rest was more akin to passing out than falling asleep.

The next days passed in a blur. They began just before sunrise, and every one of them was remarkably, monotonously, the same. The orphan Conair arrived to awaken him, bringing a pitcher of water and a bowl of fruit. Aidan ate some of the fruit, allowing its sweet juice to awaken his senses and wash some of the sour sleep taste from his mouth. Then he performed basic ablutions, and a series of whirling and stretching exercises prescribed by Babatunde. Then he ate the rest of his fruit, and guzzled water until he thought he would burst.

Then, exercise. Running, lifting, throwing, tumbling, until exhaustion. Then a nap, followed by another few pieces of fruit, and perhaps a palm-sized chunk of chicken, lamb, or beef. In the afternoons Kai might teach him holds and blows.

The evening meal was more extensive, and here Kai had spoken truly: after a day of near-fasting, Aidan was allowed to eat until all hunger was sated. He bolted great heaps of salad greens in sour wine dressing, then feasted on beef or fish, and finished with rice or teff-meal cakes. Despite his rumbling stomach's daily fears, Aidan never went to bed hungry.

In the evening, there was quiet time with Kai, or Babatunde would teach him to still his mind, to synchronize body and will with the thread of breath.

"Three things you must control for mind and body to unify," Babatunde said. "Those three are breath, motion, and posture. Lung, muscle, and spine."

"Why breath? I know how to breathe."

"So you believe." Babatunde smiled. "Breath is the only physical process that is both automatic and conscious. It is the doorway to the deep mind. Have you ever noticed that, unlike my masochistic student, I never exercise formally, and yet my body is firm, my energy as a child's?"

"Yes . . . ," said Aidan. It was true. Most men Babatunde's age were beginning to slow down, to complain of aches and pains. But the little Sufi enjoyed nothing better than a twenty-mile walk or a morning cutting wood. "How do you do that?"

"In my youth, of course, I was taught the basic Yoruban martial sciences. But it was among the Sufis that I learned that every breath, every step, every motion or activity can be a prayer, if one understands the true nature of mind and body."

"Which is?"

"The body exists within the mind. The ignorant merely exercise their bodies. The wise strengthen the *connection* between mind and body. After every prayer, I spend two minutes practicing my breathing. Then when sitting, or walking, or chopping wood, I remember my breathing, integrating it with the task at hand. After a time, my body learned to exercise itself. Motion becomes prayer, prayer motion. Every activity is a different form of the same discipline: the appointment of the appropriate attention to each of life's tasks. All is all." He paused, and smiled at Aidan's confusion. "I will teach you some of this, now."

And they breathed together. Aidan learned to tightly tense his stomach muscles on every exhalation, squeezing the air from his body with a hiss or a shout, curling his tailbone under. Then on inhalation he would relax his shoulders backward, and allow his belly to distend. And whether he practiced sitting, standing, walking, or running, always he monitored the integration of these three aspects.

Breath. Motion. Alignment. Any time you are fearful, or fatigued, or depressed, the unity of these three are broken. Merely begin to breathe properly again and the reintegration process commences.

Now: breathe.

Somehow, those conversations and sessions of controlled breathing sealed the day in his heart, so that although his mind could never remember all that it had been taught and shown, every morning found him answering the call with not only renewed vigor, but improved skill and focus.

Although he seemed to be sore all the time, Aidan's flexibility increased radically, in directions and arcs previously unimagined.

Aidan learned to lift the cannonbells above his head, using swinging motions to induce deep fatigue, and odd twist-and-balance postures to develop strength at bizarre and unexpected angles. Much to his surprise, he learned that the secret was less in the body than the mind: learning how to relax *this* muscle and tighten *that* one, to create both stability in his belly and side muscles, and liquid motion. And it was during this time that he began to grasp how Kai could be smaller than he, and yet stronger. His life seemed to consist of one revelation after another, until he wondered if he had never known his mind and body at all.

At least twice a day Kai dropped in on his exertions, explaining, demonstrating, answering questions. "The body follows the mind," he said. Then to demonstrate he removed his shirt. His body was smooth-muscled, not so corded as Aidan's. Yet when he slid his feet from his sandals and gripped the ground with his toes, a startling transformation occurred. Over every digit of his torso, muscular ridges leapt into relief, swelling and cording until his arms and legs resembled vine-wrapped tree limbs.

In one corner of the room was an iron bar transfixing two massive square concrete blocks. Aidan reckoned it had to weigh almost fifty sep, and his best guess was that it was some sort of decoration, an impossible goal toward which one might strive. It would have broken Donough's back.

To his surprise, Kai approached it confidently. Aidan's friend inhaled, tightening every muscle in his body. He crouched, looking straight ahead, and wrapped his fingers around the bar. Then exhaling in a long, hissing stream . . .

He straightened his legs slowly, almost as if he were some kind of machine, and not a man at all. One digit at a time, the massive weight levitated from the floor. Kai stood erect for a moment, arms locked straight, eyes rolled up. Then he lowered the weight again. Kai shook himself like a wet dog, inhaled deeply, relaxed, and then grinned.

"Shyte," Aidan whispered. "How the hell . . . ?"

"I cannot tell you," said Kai. "But you can, and will, learn."

Occasionally, at the end of the day Kai would play drums for Aidan and make him dance with the children, urging him to mimic their steps. The rhythms were African and Arabic patterns even more complex than the Irish music he loved so dearly. The dancing was no more exuberant than that of the crannog, but . . . different. The sense of connectedness with the earth was the same, but the children were looser in the hips, moved in a way he had only seen his own people dance when drunken.

One day at a time, he learned.

Twice, Fodjour and Mada joined him. The boy Mada was a demon on the drums, but Fodjour was better. Moving to Fodjour's rhythms was like discovering a body he'd never known he had. But twice when Fodjour had entranced him, Kai's neighbor took the lead in the drumming, increasing the tempo, varying it so that Aidan was caught in the rhythm, turning this way and that with a ferocity that was almost painful.

And Aidan looked at the drummers, and while Kai and Mada were lost in the percussion, off in their own worlds, Fodjour was staring at him. And there was an expression on his face that was strained and focused and almost hateful. Then in the next moment the expression vanished, and Aidan was convinced that he had imagined it.

Except . . . that Fodjour never came back to the training sessions, and when Aidan encountered him in Kai's company, the Irishman had that same sensation, and was never quite able to convince himself he was mistaken.

Days were endless rounds of exertion and fatigue, the nights deep wells of rest in which he gratefully submerged his aching body.

During sleep, Aidan's dreams were filled with fighting and dancing. *He was back in the Ouachita crannog. Again and again, each and every night, the dragon ships emerged from the fog and disgorged Northmen.*

Alone, Aidan fought them, vanquishing all with rifle and knife and empty hand. He broke limbs and cleft skulls, roaring triumph as he protected Sophia and Mahon, who watched him with shining, admiring eyes.

*　　*　　*

Babatunde observed as Aidan twitched in sleep. The Irishman's arms and legs traced anxious arcs beneath his thin blanket. He heard a footfall behind him, and turned, unsurprised. Kai's orphans were curious and intelligent, and it seemed impossible to discourage them from following him about whenever possible. In truth, he did not care to try.

What did surprise him was the identity of the child: Tata. To Babatunde's pleasure, she had swiftly proven herself an excellent acquisition, working twice as hard as any other slave, always looking for ways to make herself useful, not hiding after her appointed work was done, as was the habit of most other servants. He suspected that, despite all they had said and promised, she imagined that if her new owners were displeased with the quantity or quality of her work, she would find herself returned to a Radaman whorehouse. Or worse.

"What's he dreamin'?" she asked in her little-girl's voice.

"Of fighting," said Babatunde.

"Why does he smile?" asked Tata, uncomprehending.

"He has found a way to enjoy it."

The little Yoruba felt both satisfied and saddened at the observation, and wondered why as he left.

As the sun first rose above the eastern horizon, Aidan performed his morning cleansing. Behind him, Kai entered the exercise room, already impeccably dressed and appointed. "Allah has given us another precious day."

"I am sore everywhere," Aidan moaned.

"Good. You will grow strong."

Aidan finished his ablutions and turned to glare. "I dreamed about combat again last night. When I walk, I feel like I'm sliding. When I look at people, I'm automatically measuring their reach and weight, guessing at their speed, reckoning whether they're trained or untrained." He paused. "You're changing my head, aren't you?"

"A great ugly rogue like you should be glad of that."

Aidan tapped his temple. "Hah. Hah-hah. No, I mean that you are changing my *mind*. Opening doors in here."

"And what do you feel?"

"That you are showing me a world I never dreamed of. Is this what Malik taught you?"

"No. It is what Babatunde taught me." Kai paused. "He has little martial skill, but he knows things about the body and mind that few men could dream of. He helps me to better use what I already have, and to free my mind to flow beyond Malik's teaching."

Aidan ground his fists against his temples. "I thought that fighting was being strong, fast. Skilled."

"Yes," Kai said. "And more. If you are righteous, you fight only for love of Allah. Then there is peace within you, no matter how violent the action. You are like the hub of a wheel. The rim can speed, but the hub stays still. A warrior must find this within himself."

Aidan remembered occasions when he had seriously tested Kai's abilities. Twice they had fought: once for love of Sophia, in which Aidan had claimed victory. The second occasion had been only a year later, when Aidan had begged permission to fight in the Aztec Wars. In that latter conflict, he had been vanquished with ease. "So . . . ," he said slowly. "This stillness you speak of is the difference between the two times we fought?"

"That . . . and the fact that the first time I fought for ego. The second, for love."

"Love?"

Kai smiled. "I did not wish you to die at the mosque."

The *Naqsh Kabir* was a sacred symbol, also called *Al Naqsh Al Wajid Allah*: "The sign of the presence of God." It comprised a circle inscribed with an equilateral triangle as well as six other linking lines. The *Naqsh Kabir* was plotted out on the ground, its circle cubits in diameter. Kai instructed Aidan to move along the lines, crouched low enough to make his legs burn. "Move," he chanted, his voice become a hateful thing that pushed and challenged and never accepted less than a total effort. "Down, up!"

Aidan performed a corkscrew motion that Kai had taught him, called a *selo*, going from standing position, turning from the hips without moving the position of his feet, going all the way down until he was in a cross-legged sitting position, then reversing the motion so that he returned to standing, and then screwed back down in the opposite direction.

Grueling.

After a repetition, he stepped to the next position on the *Naqsh Kabir* and performed the movement again. He carried a cannonbell at his shoulder, elbow tucked tightly to his side to prevent undue pressure on the joint. Every breath was torture as his chest fought to expand against resistance. "Kai!" he gasped. "Kai. I am dying! What worse can this German do to me?"

"None. Which is the point. The more I hurt you here, the less he can hurt you in New Alexandria."

Aidan snarled at him. Kai laughed and spanked his palms together.

"More?" Aidan gasped.

"I think that that is all for now," Kai averred.

"Thank goodness," Aidan said, flopping onto his back.

"And now, massage."

Aidan sat up and grinned. "Ah," said Aidan. "I have seen the masseuses you enjoy. Things are finally starting to look up."

Bitta entered the room, her bare arms like ebony timbers. She smiled without mirth.

"I leave you in the most capable hands I know," said Kai.

Bitta knelt at Aidan's side. She began gently enough, but within two minutes was torquing and twisting his arms until he thought she would wrench them from their sockets. "Kai? I . . . uh . . . ow!"

Kai smiled as he left. Behind him, Aidan howled into the mat.

As the days passed, Kai, Babatunde, and the other students used the *Naqsh Kabir* symbol to help Aidan visualize what they called "lines of engagement." They drilled him without mercy on a few very simple motions, corkscrewing up and down from the floor. When he screamed for mercy they asked him to reexamine the structural triumvirate, to reintegrate breathing, motion, and posture.

And to his surprise and grudging delight, whenever he paused to balance them, his acid emotional surge decreased, and he tapped reservoirs of endurance and coordination he would never have imagined.

Breath. Motion. Posture.

Aidan came to understand that he was undergoing a simplified, condensed version of the program Kai and Babatunde had devised after Malik's death, a program which had been designed to use pain, exhaustion, and stress to implant lessons deeply in Kai's brain. It would teach him to relax and maintain what they called *wasîr hurûm*, "soft eyes," even in the midst of a killing frenzy.

The Irishman thought that the terrifying Malik would have been proud.

The cannonbells with their ungodly thick handles were used sometimes at the beginnings of sessions to force him to labor in a condition of fatigue, and sometimes at the end to drain the very last strength from his unresisting body.

Then, limp as a dead fish, Aidan was massaged, fed, and rested. He had no obligations but to exercise, train, eat, and sleep.

And for that, he thanked the God he no longer believed in.

CHAPTER FORTY-SIX

IN THE PRIVACY OF HER SUITE, Nandi touched her forehead to that of her old nurse, the sixty-year-old Baleka. In addition to her other skills, Baleka also possessed extensive knowledge of traditional Zulu medicines.

"I know," Nandi said to her, "that your knowledge of herbs and *umuthi* is complete."

"*Uphethwe yini?*"

"No, no . . . I am well. There is another need I must ask you to fill."

"I have a few skills, ma'am," said Baleka. "Time to time, I make up a little something. A poultice, or an *umuthi*."

Nandi nodded. "I am certain. I need a favor of you, one that requires that you follow my orders explicitly, and tell no one."

Baleka retreated a step, tilting her head a bit sideways. "Especially . . . ?"

"The masters of the house."

Baleka smiled. Happily, at no time had Baleka seemed intimidated by their new home. At the moment, that attitude worked to the princess's advantage.

"Good. I want you to find me these things." Nandi extended a slip of paper. Baleka scanned it, and then as Nandi had expected, nodded in the affirmative.

Kai and Aidan sat comfortably cross-legged on the floor in Babatunde's study, awaiting instruction.

Three nights a week, Babatunde taught lessons to Aidan, but his duties hardly stopped there. He was intimately involved with the orphanage and its operation, still gave *zikr* to his flock in the tiny mosque the Wakil Abu Ali had once constructed for him, and was tasked as well with continuing Kai's education.

Ordinarily he might have taken a free evening and spent the night in Djibouti Harbor working with his friend Kokossa, but he had chosen instead to delve more deeply into the Irishman's mind and heart. He was not trying to create another Kai: for that, Babatunde had neither the skills nor the time. This was not a long-term program, but a shortened path to the ability to conquer one specific foe. Still, whatever tools they gave Aidan would have to function under the most severe stress imaginable. To do that, he had to anchor those skills where fear and despair could not reach. And to do that, he had to understand Aidan's previous spiritual teachings. How much simpler this might have been if Aidan were a believer! Still, Babatunde believed that the Irishman's quest was honorable, one pleasing in the eyes of the One God, by whatever name He might be called. "Where were we yesterday?" He asked.

Kai spoke first. "Aidan was telling us of his people's beliefs."

"What I can remember," Aidan said. "I am not a student of these things."

"Posh. Yesterday you mentioned a blessing your wise women placed upon you. Tell us again. This may work well for us, Aidan. As there is but one God, the creator of the universe, worshipped by all men under many names, there are phenomena of mind and body that men all the world over have seen, truth that goes far beyond culture and even race. What are the names of the 'three cauldrons'?"

Aidan furrowed his brow. "The *Coire Sofs*," he said. "The Cauldron of Knowing."

"And its location in the body?"

"The forehead, I think. *Coire Ernmae*, the Cauldron of Vocation." He thumped himself over the chest. "*Coire Goiriath*, the Cauldron of Warming." And here he touched his navel. "I think that's it."

"Those who have achieved vision, be they of whatever culture or people, see the same inner truth. What the Irish call the *Coire Ernmae* is called *Anahata* by the Indians and *Kheper* by Egyptians. My own people consider this space sacred to the god Ogun. It is generally known as the 'heart center.' It corresponds to emotion, and also forward motion."

Kai cocked his head slightly to the side. "Malik alluded to this, although he rarely spoke directly."

Babatunde sighed. "Malik lived in the material world, and was afraid to open his eyes to the ocean of energy birthed by Allah. Although his body was attuned to it—explaining his mastery—his mind could see nothing greater than himself. To such a man, old age and death are the greatest horrors imaginable." He looked on the verge of saying more, but appeared to change mental paths. "Tell me, Kai, what you remember of his teaching."

"He said that the !Kung people of the Kalahari say there are three major centers in the body: head center, heart center, and belly brain."

Babatunde nodded. "There are similar divisions among the natives of this continent, I believe. Continue."

Kai closed his eyes, urging memory. "Through these centers flows the Life Force." He shook his head. "I cannot remember the word."

"I cannot help there. My own people, the Yoruba, call this force *Ashé*. The Egyptians call it *Ra-Buto*. The Indians *Prana*. The Chinese *Chi*. The Greeks, who learned the concept from Egypt, called it *Pneuma*." He leaned close to them. "Listen to me," he said. "Whenever you find similar concepts in dissimilar cultures, there is a good chance that wisdom lies beneath the façade."

Kai closed his eyes and recited. "What Malik said is that to the warrior, the importance of the three centers is thus:

"One: the head center controls motion left and right.

"Two: the heart center controls motion forward and back.

"Three: the belly brain controls motion up and down. It is also the seat of instinctive motion, and is the most important center for the fighter to master." Kai blinked and then opened his eyes. "That is what I chiefly remember."

Babatunde smiled. "Yes. But he left something out. The other centers are essential if the fighter would *be* a master. The lower centers are 'animal,' dealing with survival. *Anahata*, or the domain of Ogun, marks the beginning of wisdom. Until wisdom is attained, one cannot truly 'move forward' on the road of life."

"Do the Sufi have a word for this same center?" Aidan asked.

"Of course. The heart is the place of the 'moving soul.' Its business is with the knowledge of the spiritual path. Its work deals with the first four of the Beautiful Names of the Essence of Allah."

"What are they?" Kai asked.

"As with the rest of the twelve Names of the Essence, these four Names have neither sound nor letters. They cannot be pronounced.

"The twelve Divine Names are within the origin of the Confession of Unity, *La ilaha illa Llah*, 'There is no god but the One God.'"

"What is this 'moving soul?'" Kai urged.

"The place of the 'moving soul' is within the life of the heart. It can see Paradise, its inhabitants, its light, and all the angels." Babatunde's voice became contemplative and far-off. "The speech of the 'moving soul' is the speech of the inner world, without words, without sound.

"It is the heart of the heart. Its business is divine wisdom. The Prophet, Peace Be Upon Him, said, 'Knowledge is in two sections. One is in man's tongue, which is the confirmation of Allah's existence. The other is in man's heart. It is in this secret heart that He deposited His secret, *sirr*, for safekeeping. "Man is My secret, and I am the secret of man." '"

"I don't understand," Aidan said. "My head hurts. What does all of this have to do with fighting?"

"Your head hurts because it is too small to contain Allah's creation. But that same creation is contained within your heart. Every beast of the field knows naturally how to fight for its survival, and the survival of its family. Only man must be taught to open his heart, because only man is divine. And yet priests and Imams, being human, seek to insert themselves between man and Allah, telling us that the secret to salvation lies outside ourselves. Why would Allah create a creature that he loves without giving that creature means to seek counsel directly? To whom must a baby plead to have access to his mother's breast?"

At this odd thought, both Aidan and Kai chuckled.

"That would be thought heresy in many places," Kai said.

"Sufism has almost always been regarded as heresy. We believe that the universe and God are one. Since humans are part of creation, a human being can, through true journeying along the inner path, become one with Allah."

Babatunde stood and paced. "Each of you will understand my words in a different way. Although you are the same age, your life experiences have differed greatly. But the heart-space connection between you could not be stronger if you were twins."

Kai and Aidan glanced at each other, and after a moment, gave embarrassed smiles. "It does no good to argue with him," Kai said. "He'll just wear you down with another hour's lecture."

"The heart, my students. Aidan: listen to the Cauldron of Vocation. It beats within your breast. Sit quietly, and listen to what it has to tell you about your path. Then put your feet on that path, regardless of the cost, and you will approach your truth.

"And Kai," he said, facing the Wakil. "Follow the path of *Kheper*, the home of the moving soul. You are surrounded by serpents, who will challenge you in manners you cannot now comprehend. To either side of you will be knives. But as Setepenamen was said to have cut the Phrygian Knot, your heart will see you through the complexity, and the dark night ahead."

He paused. "Aidan, you think that Kai saved you that terrible day in Malik's courtyard. Yes. He saved your life, and family. But your heart connection, his love for you, saved his soul, and his uncle's as well."

At that they were both stunned into silence. "To do what is right as opposed to what is legal, or expected, or customary, is the action of the righteous man. But to follow your heart when mind as well as body urge you toward disaster—that is the door to enlightenment."

"I don't understand," Kai said.

"Not yet," Babatunde said. "But I see the clouds forming. One day, and not a day far away, you *will* understand."

Kai closed his eyes. "It is strange," he said. "I feel fear, and am not certain why."

"Because to truly move from one level to another is like awakening as a surgeon is sewing up your abdomen. Do you imagine that a child in the womb feels no trepidation when his mother brings him into the world? We would avoid this at all costs, but cannot. We can but lose ourselves in the pleasures of the world—sex, drink, power—to distract us from death."

"Death?"

"Death. Of the body, or the ego. 'Die before you die,' remember those words?"

They had originally been uttered by the Prophet. On becoming a sufi, Kai had been asked to compare that statement with another, found in the holy *Hadith Qutsi:* 'My servant hates to die, and I hate to disappoint him.' Both statements related to the dissolution of what is transitory in man: ego and will. With the "death" of these, true wisdom might flower. "Never could I forget them."

"Remember them," Babatunde said gravely, "in the days ahead. Whatever man has done to lift one of you, and lower the other, know why you were brought together."

"And why is that?" Aidan asked.

"I think you have one heart. You are brothers, born in different worlds, who now share a common path," Babatunde said. "The world will not embrace what you are," he said. But now he smiled. "So perhaps, you must change the world."

"*Mashallah.*" Kai answered. *Whatever Allah wants, happens.*

"Just this once," Aidan said, "I'd rather it be what *I* want."

"Why not? You believe in God in your way, your Christ. . . ."

"My mother believed in Jesus," said Aidan. "I tried to."

"Please," said Babatunde. "Go on."

"No offense, Kai—I can understand how you can believe in God. After all, His light shines upon you, and all your people as well. But fate has brought me little save misery. My mother believed, and her days brought her only pain, shame, and death."

"We are not meant to understand the mystery of His ways," said Babatunde.

"Again," said Aidan, "easy for you to say. I can't believe. I'm sorry."

There was a pause; then Babatunde sighed. "We can proceed with your willingness to open your mind. Do you trust us?"

"With my life."

"For now, that will suffice."

Kai shook his head. "I feel sorrow that your tribulations has driven you to question the existence of He who created us all."

"And chose that you, and those like you, could buy and sell me, and those like me. I am afraid that if I believed in God . . . I would hate him."

Babatunde gave one hard, flat chuckle. "Then unbelief is a better place to begin, my young friend."

With a piece of yellow chalk, Babatunde traced the *Naqsh Kabir* upon the wall.

"Oh, damn," Aidan said. "*This* thing again?"

Kai nodded. "We have to structure your mind, give you a way to hold and associate all that we're teaching you. You will dream this symbol, the *Naqsh Kabir*."

"Nightmares, more likely," said Aidan.

"Shall we begin?"

Aidan agreed, and Babatunde moved closer. "Close your eyes. Visualize a circle. Can you do that?"

"Yes."

"And now the triangle within the circle. Then two parallel lines . . ."

Later, while Aidan sat cross-legged and attempted to meditate, Kai and Babatunde talked outside the room.

"I did not know," Kai said.

"And you blame yourself?"

"How can I not? If my friend dies without the light of Allah, his soul perishes."

Babatunde gazed up into his student's eyes. "It is our task, our privilege, to bring lost sheep to the fold. He thinks that his people's bondage is a sign that there is no God. What do you say?"

"I say that I know there is a God, and that slavery is an institution of men."

"It is not the creation of Allah?"

"No."

"So Allah exists, and is good?"

"Yes!"

"Would you be so certain, were you Aidan?"

Kai opened his mouth and then closed it again, then furrowed his brows as Babatunde walked away.

Day by day Aidan flowered, his mental and physical efforts awakening a hunger to *know*, to find some truth beyond the pain and pleasure of his senses. God there might not be, but still he sensed a world that seemed to expand as he explored it, revealing one layer after another, a richness surpassing expectation.

Often there were new games: Babatunde delighted in waiting until Aidan was completely exhausted, and then forcing him to recall some complex piece of information. After one particularly punishing session, just as the Irishman was ready to collapse into the grass, Babatunde appeared and asked Aidan to trace the lines of the *Naqsh Kabir*. Although his legs trembled with exhaustion, Aidan clinched his teeth, visualized the circle and triangle, and moved from point to point and along the internal lines perfectly, with strong balance and surprising grace. Then he collapsed, lay on his side, and panted up at Babatunde. "Is that . . . all right?"

"You have an incredibly fine mind," the Yoruba replied. "I doubt you have ever really acknowledged it, tried to better yourself."

"I suppose you're going to tell me that I am so damned unusual, not like the rest of my people. . . ."

Babatunde's face was unreadable. "Aidan. Is that what you feel?"

"That's what Kai says. That's what I see in the eyes that watch me."

"Even mine?"

"I don't know. We've never spoken of it."

"What does your heart say?"

"In my heart, I don't know how a man, a good man like you, can believe in an Allah who would place one group of men so far above another."

"Allah is merciful," said Babatunde, "and deserving of love."

"And if he did create such separations between men?"

"Muhammad said: 'There is no superiority of a white over a black or of a black over a white. All of you are the children of Adam, and Adam was made from dust.' "

"He said that?"

"Yes."

"Well, that's all well in theory," Aidan said. "But it does not reflect the world as we know it. I ask again: what if he *did* create such separations between men?"

Babatunde paused, and then said quietly, "I would not love him. Aidan, one day the world will change. It is changing even now. Indeed, you may be one of the reasons it does." He paused, then leaned forward, his eyes piercing. "Aidan—you cannot do what has been asked of you."

That startled the Irishman from his musings. "What?"

"You cannot do it . . . for yourself."

Aidan wagged his head as if it was beginning to hurt. "Then how can I?"

"You must do it for your children, and your children's children. You must place yourself on the righteous path in the mind of God."

Aidan sat, reflecting for almost a full minute. "I feel . . . different. As if my actions have a different meaning."

"Yes," said Babatunde.

"But I'm the same man."

"Yes, but you are not the man you thought you were, and your prior actions were based on illusion," Babatunde said. "None of us are what our minds think. To accomplish what you set out to do, you must live in the mystery."

"What is this path?"

"It is the way of the holy warrior, one who lives for the light of God." Although the little Yoruba said the words softly, they seemed to echo in Aidan's mind.

"But I am not Muslim," the Irishman said.

"So you think. Aidan, what is a Muslim?"

Aidan shrugged. "You know—someone who follows Muhammad, bows to Mecca every other minute. Thinks he's the lord of creation . . . you know the type."

Babatunde chuckled. "Admission of ignorance is the first step toward wisdom. It is long since time you take your first step."

"All right then. Let's say I don't know."

"It means, 'one who has submitted to the will of God.' "

"Even a Christian?"

"Christ, Abraham, Moses, and Muhammad were all prophets. The people you call Muslims consider Muhammad to be the last and greatest of these. But Aidan, your path does not need to be as mine. Or as Kai's. In fact, it *cannot* be. But still, it can be a true path."

"I don't believe in God," he said numbly.

Babatunde smiled. "Once, you did. Today you do not. Tomorrow you may again. Our minds are like water, the surface ever changing. You must slide beneath that surface, to something that does *not* change. That part has the answer to your questions."

Aidan gazed at his friend's tutor as if searching for a crack in a china plate. "You seem so certain."

"When you are ready, the answer will present itself. As for now . . . heh. It is once again time for pain."

And as always, it seemed, Babatunde was correct.

CHAPTER FORTY-SEVEN

AFTER ENDLESS HOURS OF HARD WORK and agony, the time came again for dreams.

Aidan tossed on his sweat-soaked mattress, his mind swooping over distant, long-lost O'Dere Crannog. The man-made island appeared exactly as it had the day of his forced departure.

Gliding out of the fog, oars sculling their dreadful rhythm, dragon ships drew up to the dock.

The gangplank clattered down. Aidan stepped out, onto the weathered boards he had trod in childhood.

Children lay asleep upon the dock. He looked down at them. One of them was a younger Aidan. The other, his sister, Nessa. Without attempting to waken them, he entered the town.

The people drifted by without speaking to him.

"Hey!" Aidan called. "Dreigner! Don't you know me?"

The villager walked past Aidan without any sign of recognition, carrying a load of hay upon his back. A woman passed, her plaid shawl fluttering in a nonexistent wind. Distantly, Aidan heard a fiddle's fierce but oddly distorted wail.

"Hey!" he cried to another villager. "Sorcha! Don't you know me? I swore I'd come back!"

Sorcha glanced at Aidan without curiosity and continued on her way. Aidan continued through the village. The mist seemed to have followed him from the dragon ship, lapping about his feet like milk tea. He turned and saw, through the mists about the dock, more dragon ships gliding in. Belatedly, his nerves burned with alarm.

"Wait—wake up!" he screamed. "Wake up!"

He ran now, seeking his own house. He broke in through the door—and saw his mother's face. She was abed, one of two bundled figures moving steadily beneath a woolen blanket. Confused, he turned away, then turned back, and walked closer—

And saw that it was a Northman abed with her. Aidan looked behind himself and saw his father, standing with a slit throat, watching. Aidan's mother grinned up at him over the Northman's shoulder. She was inhumanly beautiful, with her strawberry hair and red, laughing mouth. And then in the next moment the hair whitened and fell from her head, her lips withered, and she became a haggard crone. And in the next the flesh melted away, leaving naught but bones.

Screaming, Aidan ran from the house into deserted streets.

He ran to the dock. The mist had risen. Behind him, the village churned with flame. Dead all, the inhabitants were trudged up the dragon ship's gangplank in a funereal lockstep. With ravaged arms they beckoned to him. He ran toward it as the children who had been at the dock arose and walked toward the ship. The children bore no wounds. They were alive, but all else were dead.

He saw himself treading up the gangplank. He screamed out, "Aidan! Nessa! No!"

They looked toward him with sad, wise eyes. He tried to run, but suddenly the fire closed in around him . . . the ground beneath him burned, and he could find no traction. His out-stretched hands caught fire. His burning flesh sloughed away until he could see the bones.

Young Aidan, stepping into the ship, turned to him and waved. . . .

Aidan lurched upright, sweating, gasping for breath. He looked around himself, at the empty gymnasium dome, at the armor and weapons filling the room, and panted, running a hand over his sweat-slicked face, and then lay back down again. . . .

One of Kai's slaves came into the room, rubbing his eyes. *Conair,* Aidan recalled. *His name is Conair. I remember watching his father stabbed at the Mosque.*

"Are you all right?"

"What?" Aidan's head was still full of sleep.

Conair was too thin, straw-haired and freckled, with eyes wide as saucers and jug ears. He was evidently on some manner of early-morning duty: preparing the day's bread, perhaps. "I heard you scream."

"I thought . . . that I could work hard enough to stop the nightmares."

"Of what do you dream?" asked the child.

"My mother," said Aidan. "My father."

"They are with Allah?" asked Conair.

Aidan paused, trying to put his thoughts into words. "Yes," he said finally. "With Allah."

The student nodded. "Then they are at peace. So you should be, too. Sleep. Tomorrow will come." He paused. "My own mother and father are in Paradise. At night, I speak to them. Perhaps they could give your mother a message. Would you like that?"

Aidan sighed. "No. But give your parents one."

"What is that?"

"Tell them Conair is a good boy."

Conair rubbed his eyes sleepily, grinned, and nodded, padding out of the room.

And somehow, Aidan's sleep for the rest of the night came more easily than it had in weeks.

CHAPTER FORTY-EIGHT

DJIBOUTI HARBOR LAY SIX HOURS by carriage or four hours by brisk horse-back ride south of Dar Kush. Unless in the mood for a serious day's exercise, a round trip usually entailed an overnight stay. When Kai grew satisfied that Aidan's training was progressing in a satisfactory fashion, he bade Fodjour to clear his schedule. The two friends left Lake A'zam shortly after dawn, alternately trotted, raced, and walked, and saw the blue crescent of the Bay of Azteca before noon.

Maputo Kokossa's workshop occupied a medium-sized warehouse in the dock district. This might have proved hazardous to most men, but Kokossa's reputation had been such that the dockworkers and even many of the petty thieves who made the harbor their home considered it a matter of pride that Kokossa chose to live among them. According to widely circulated legend, once upon a time a thief had broken into the workshop, stealing a thousand feet of gold wire used in electrical experiments. That was fine, as such things went, but the thief's first mistake was to fracture the famed inventor's jaw in the process. His second error was to fence the gold in Djibouti Harbor. The wire had been recovered, as was the thief's body, found floating facedown next to a *dhow* in the morning tide.

Kai had spent long hours there with Babatunde and now Fodjour. The workshop was a marvel, crammed wall to wall to ceiling with scale models of ships and dirigibles; jars and tubs of chemical compounds; spools of gold, silver, and copper wire; distillation equipment from India and China as well as Egyptian and Abyssinian design; electrical experiments that often crackled, hummed or glowed with a secret life of their own.

He had thoroughly enjoyed his morning there, examining new contraptions, and speaking of new ideas. He spoke to Sallah Mubutu, the little toolmaker who had once knelt before him at court, and now gladly worked twelve-hour days crafting marvels in copper, steel, and wood. Seldom had Kai seen a man who seemed more deeply satisfied with his lot in life. Mubutu's hands seemed to have their own intelligence, such that he could speak and laugh with employer, face turned away from lathe or drill-press, and yet never err by a fraction of a digit.

Today after holding forth on the subject of iron ships, mines, and submersibles, Kokossa had wandered off to conduct an electrical experiment, leaving them with Chifi, who had immediately turned the conversation to her favorite subject, the evolution of science in Africa.

Central in their discussions was the story of Kyanfuma, a celebrated African scientist who had dressed as a man to gain respect. She was Chifi Kokossa's hero, and Chifi often seemed startled when men knew her story.

"Kyanfuma?" said Kai. "Dogon woman, wasn't she? Invented the telescope and microscope."

"More than that," said Chifi. "She made massive discoveries in the fields of medicine and astronomy, as well as optics."

"I'm sure I had heard that," said Kai. They had actually had this very discussion four years earlier, but he pretended not to remember.

"Oh, yes," Chifi said, a sarcastic twist to her voice. "A standard part of Bilalian education is the scientific contributions of women."

"My tutor is in no way 'standard.'" Kai said, a bit defensively. "It is my understanding that Kyanfuma was a genius at discovering principles in one arena and then applying them to another."

Chifi was not mollified. "A genius that eventually led to her stoning as a witch."

"An unquestioned tragedy," Fodjour said.

"We'll never know how much we lost," Chifi said, such pain in her voice one would think she had witnessed the execution personally.

Kyanfuma had been born too soon . . . or too late.

Fatimite Islam, the faith preached by the Prophet's daughter, had deeply influenced Abyssinia and sub-Saharan Africa. Matriarchal cultures embraced it more swiftly than the male-dominated regimes who often preferred to ally themselves with Alexandria.

The Prophet's teachings on matters of gender had been extraordinarily progressive for the time and culture in which they first took root. Women were ensured the right of property, of divorce and choice of husband, of increased status under the law. During the Prophet's lifetime, it was possible that women in Islam were the freest in the civilized world. But with Muhammad's death, Arab patriarchal attitudes overwhelmed social innovation, and there matters had remained mired for much of the proceeding thousand years.

"Too many of those who follow Islam seem to think it a license to repress women," Chifi said passionately.

"I wasn't aware you wore chains," Kai said.

"Luxury is its own chain." She sniffed. "It fetters the mind."

Fodjour raised a placating hand. "Why discuss gender politics when we can discuss the luncheon menu at Abdul's? I understand they have a peanut sauce kabob worthy of an armistice."

Chifi's eyes glittered, as if wondering if he was attempting to distract her from a favorite subject; then she realized that it didn't matter at all. She was hungry. "Well, all right," she said. "But only for the kabob."

"For the kabob," Kai agreed.

CHAPTER FORTY-NINE

THE DAY HAD BEGUN like any other, but as Aidan was preparing his evening meal, Conair and Tata appeared at his front step.

"Yes?" Aidan had expected one of Kai's orphans perhaps, so roughneck Conair and the lovely but dour Tata caught him by surprise. The two made an odd pair: Conair all elbows and knobby knees and fierce energy, and Tata with her shy, coltish grace. Conair seemed to have adopted her, or she him, and it was common to see them together.

"The Wakil asked us to bring you to the prayer grove," Tata said. And now Aidan understood. In all of Dar Kush, only Ghost Town and the prayer grove were more commonly habituated by whites than blacks. Kai had all but warned his overseers and orphans away from the grove, in respect for the worship services conducted there weekly.

Aidan walked between the two children, Conair uncommonly quiet, as if sensing the night's import. Kai met Aidan where the path widened into a clearing, and clasped his hands. "I respect your people's need for privacy," he said, "but your elders have given their blessing for us to borrow your place of worship for the next few hours. Yours is a holy quest, Aidan."

Crickets began to chirp in the bushes, and the air's temperature seemed to plummet. "What's going to happen?" Aidan asked.

"There are no words," Kai said, then thanked the children and led Aidan to Babatunde, who handed him a bowl filled with sweet, chewy mush. "Eat."

"What is this?"

"You will dream, awake," said Babatunde.

"This will teach me what Kai knows?"

"No drug can do that," Babatunde said. "What you see in Kai is a combination of rare potential, years of grueling work, and grace."

"Grace?"

"The light of Allah, shining on our mortal efforts."

"Allah again," Aidan groused. "What will this do, then?"

"You must make *Rabitah* with Kai, in order to absorb what he wishes to teach you. *Rabitah* is a deep connection of the heart. Students do this with their teachers, aspirants make *Rabitah* with their shaykh. Kai makes with me when he comes to a spiritual wall, and wishes my help to circumvent it."

Aidan started to speak, then paused and thought. "I don't understand."

"This will help Aidan go away for a while. What remains will be the one we can teach."

"You're talking in riddles," Aidan said.

"Yes," Babatunde agreed. "Now, eat."

And he did.

Within minutes, Aidan felt himself growing woozy.

A stubby black student appeared. "This is what you must learn." The student performed a series of motions, tight punches, an elbow strike . . . all performed from a stable, unmoving lower body in low posture.

He performed one of the corkscrew *selo* movements, and came up facing the other direction. Then he repeated the movements in mirror-image on the left side. "Now you," the boy said.

After three hours of working and then collapsing in pain and fatigue, his legs consumed by flaming cramps, Kai reappeared. Had he been gone? Aidan wasn't certain.

Aidan lay on his side, panting. "What are you doing to me?" he gasped.

"It is called 'marrying the *djuru*.' "

"*Djuru?* What is this?"

"It is a word from Djava and other islands to the east of India. There are fearsome fighting arts there, brought back by Abyssinian sailors who melded them with our own techniques. We must go beyond your conscious mind. If we have only your mind, when fear comes, as it must, all your skill will flee."

His words were a blur to Aidan. The woods, the stars, the grass itself seemed surrounded with flickering flares of light, glowing, dancing, wavering.

"Come," said Kai. The air around him flamed. "Dance with me."

Kai and his students played with Aidan in relays, so that there was always someone there keeping Aidan moving, moving, through sunrise through the heat of the day, and then when night fell once again.

With movement and potions, they kept Aidan awake for grueling hours of martial motions and ceaseless, pitiless combat drills. Exhaustion became an ocean of pain on which he floated, bobbing and eddying in that acid tide.

When the stars shone above them Kai came to him once more. In slow motion and then with increasing speed the two danced, blocking and kicking, tripping and throwing at accelerating speed and intensity, until it was impossible to tell who was initiating, and who was receiving. Until even Aidan did not know whether he was attacker or defender. And in that place beyond exhaustion, when it felt as if his body would die but the drugs kept him upright and awake, something at the core of Aidan O'Dere began to change.

There were no longer punches and kicks. Yes, there was motion, but at the core of it was stillness. Strange. His body moved, but it almost seemed that he stood still and the rest of the world fluxed around him. And the deeper the stillness, the more slowly the outer world seemed to move.

He felt himself at the center of the universe.

Aidan O'Dere released a sigh that was almost a sob. All of the grief and pain and fear flew out of him and he stopped, reeling, gazing up at the sky. *So many stars, and he was at the center.*

Then he looked down. Kai sat on the ground, staring up at him, an expression of astonished pleasure on his face.

Aidan blinked. "What did I just do?"

"Put me on my ass," Kai said. "And I was coming at you hard."

Kai reached out his hand, and Aidan caught it. "Come on," Kai grinned. "Let us begin again."

As the sun rose that second time, Babatunde gave him another potion, and all of the fatigue that had been repressed for the past thirty-six hours hit Aidan O'Dere like an avalanche. There, in the middle of the clearing, they made a bed for him, and there he slept.

For twenty-four hours he slept, dreaming of star clusters and vast spaces. When Aidan awoke, he was alone.

Aidan found Kai sitting by the stream. His entire body seeming one huge mass of sore, intractable muscles, he crouched down and shared the silence.

From time to time they threw stones. Water rippled where the stones splashed, then quieted again. The ripples seemed to expand to include him. Was that just the herbs, or something else? He wasn't certain. In ripples now, Aidan felt flashes of that space, and something so calm fell over him that he was speechless.

Aidan felt himself on the brink of some deeper knowledge. He thought that he could sit there for an hour, or a day, or a lifetime.

"You are done here, we are ready for New Alexandria," Kai said. "You have seen."

"Yes." He pitched a rock underhanded, watched it skim across the surface of the stream. "Is that . . . what you see?"

"That truth is there," said Kai. "But we must also live in the world. It is that place you found that anchors my family arts."

"So much violence from such peace?"

"Violence exists in perception. There is motion. Action happens. The body defends itself. It is not separate from the way of peace, if the cause is just."

"You used the herbs?"

"No," said Kai. "Hallucinogens are the short route. It is hard, and fast, but does not endure. The route prepared for me was longer. More solitary in some ways."

"The route Malik taught you?"

"And Babatunde. And my father. This was my path, Aidan. Prepared for me before ever I was born. I needed only give my whole heart to it."

Aidan watched the ripples, considering. "And I will lose what I now feel?"

"What is it you feel?" asked Kai.

He paused, considering, and then spoke. "That I am in the center of a great wheel, and all the spokes connect to me. To *me*. My father and father's father . . . It seemed that . . . that . . ." He couldn't bring himself to say it. Kai was silent. Finally, Aidan was able to finish.

"It was as if everything that has happened, happened for a reason. That it was all good. That . . ."

"That what?"

Aidan had to whisper the next. "That I should forgive God." He shook his head. "I cannot. And yet . . . I sense that all this is connected."

Kai's smile was gentle. "And what is wrong with that?"

"What do I do with my anger?"

"Anger with me? With my people?"

Aidan nodded.

"If you wish your anger, I'm sure you can find it again." Kai paused, and then after considering, continued. "You are familiar with the indigenous peoples Bilalians have pushed steadily westward."

"Of course. Like the Ouachita?"

"Yes. This story comes from natives called the Missouri. A Missouri grandfather was talking to his grandson about how he felt. He said, 'I feel as if I have two wolves fighting in my heart. One wolf is the vengeful, angry, violent one. The other wolf is the loving, compassionate one.'

"The grandson asked him, 'Which wolf will win the fight in your heart?' The grandfather answered, 'The one I feed.' "

"I don't understand," said Aidan.

"You don't need to understand," said Kai.

"Do you?" Aidan asked. "Understand?"

"Better still," Kai said. "I know."

Aidan nodded, astounded that on some deep level he understood what the hell Kai meant.

"Aidan," said Kai, "this path was carved for me by my family. Few walk it. Fewer in my life have opened themselves to it as you have. Once again, you amaze me."

"This was just the first step, wasn't it?"

"Yes."

"I . . . Kai . . ." Again, words came hard. "I am not a Muslim. And do not wish to be. But I feel something. It is as if I disappeared for a time. Just a short time, but I felt it. And something else was there—something I'd never experienced. Its name was not Aidan . . . but I felt that it was more truly me than anything I have known." He took a deep breath, and leapt. "I want more, Kai. And I don't know how."

"Islam means to submit to the will of Allah. I am sure that your own ancestors had some means of walking the same path. It must be open to all of true heart. . . ."

"Or I would not have been able to take even the initial step."

Kai smiled shiningly, like a father pleased with a child's first spoken word. "I had feared to lose both my brothers. I see that one has come home."

"My home is the crannog."

"Yes. As mine is Dar Kush. And yet, I think we have another home as well."

"Are you above me there, as well?"

"In the eyes of Allah, no man is truly above another. I have no need to be above you, Aidan. I have duties in the world, else I might renounce my wealth and lead a life simpler than your own. Since I cannot do that, I would lift you up instead."

The wind blew.

"You're lonely, aren't you?"

"At times," said Kai. "Not now." He paused. "I want to caution you—you won't be able to hold onto this experience."

"Why not?" Aidan inhaled deeply, as if drawing the essence of the woods into his heart. "How could I ever forget this?"

"Not forget." Kai groped for words. "But right now, your spirit walks the road. That clarity will fade. The herbs do not take you there. They are a way to glimpse a reality: it will take years of work to hold it."

"Can you hold it, Kai?"

Kai nodded shallowly, just a silent whisper of affirmation. "But not always. It is as if the one who can remain in that space is a different man than the one known to my friends and family. I cannot summon it at will, but have touched it often enough to know it is real."

"What can I do?"

"It would take years of work," Kai said.

"I have years."

Kai pitched a rock out into the water, and smiled. "There are ways that I envy you, the ease with which the doors of your perception have opened. But in other ways . . . it can be a trap. Men have spent the rest of their lives seeking another glimpse."

"And they cannot?"

Kai nodded. "Because they try. Your danger will be despair, or addiction as you waste your life in a vain attempt to bathe in the same waters again." Kai threw a rock into the rushing waters. "But if you survive your challenge, I think that you have some serious questions to ask. I was born to the sword, and had no choice. You seem to be choosing that path. Some would say that if I loved you, I would dissuade you."

"And?"

"I tried that once."

"It didn't work out, did it?"

"No. Throwing you through a horse stall helped not a bit."

Aidan laughed. "More heart than head, I'd say."

"Well, my friend," Kai said, stretching his arms. "If you return from your mission, I fear there are decisions to be made."

CHAPTER FIFTY

IN THE SILENCE OF NIGHT, long after the majority of the household had embraced their dreams, Nandi rose from her solitary bed and crossed quietly to her dresser.

Turning up her lamplight until its soft flickering glow lifted the darkness, the princess ground and mixed the substances Baleka had provided her. As she did she chanted to herself, songs that she had learned in childhood, rhymes that had seemed humorous at the time, but now were only a thin, frail wall shielding the force of her will from blind fear.

If she was discovered . . .

If Kai suspected . . .

If Babatunde, with his razor wit, detected anything amiss . . .

Then all was lost, indeed.

In the kitchen the next day, Nandi very surreptitiously sprinkled two different powders: one in Lamiya's food, and one in Kai's.

Her actions, careful though they were, were observed by one of the house servants, who remained silent and backed out of the kitchen without being seen, speaking of what she had seen to no one until that night, in Ghost Town, where she laid her burden on Maeve's strong old shoulders.

From there it went to the crannog's council, and the fierceness of their debate raged until midnight without reaching a clear consensus.

As time passed, it became increasingly common for Lamiya and Nandi to spend quiet time together. Although neither had dropped all formality, the conversations ranged widely, from politics to economics to news of scientific developments in Africa. Lamiya had fully explained the system of ledgers and files holding the business of Dar Kush. She, not Kai, was the expert here: Kai had never been trained for it, while Lamiya had spent over a decade in preparation to be the wife and partner of the Wakil. To Lamiya's pleasure, Nandi proved a quick study.

Hardwood filing cabinets were built into the walls of the Wakil's office on the ground floor, and a backlog of letters and forms had built up over the last months. It was a pleasure to have Nandi helping to sort and process them, and as they worked, they spoke of Abyssinia, of Indian fashions, of nutritional allotments for the servants, of astrology, of local politics, cattle breeding, child-rearing, and a dozen other subjects.

While they worked on ledgers for teff and corn sales, Lamiya coaxed Nandi into speaking about Zulu legends and history. "When did your people originate?" she asked.

"Eight hundred years ago. We trace our ancestry to the Qwabe clan. Their chief, Malandela, had two sons named Qwabe and Zulu."

"And what exactly does that name mean?"

"Zulu?"

"Yes, please." Lamiya signed off on a requisition slip and slid it into a scroll.

" 'Zulu' means 'the heavens' or 'the sky above,' " Nandi said. "Each brother struck off on his own to establish his own following, who became known after their founding father. Zulu's people called themselves *amaZulu:* 'Zulu's people.' Or *abakwaZulu:* 'they of Zulu's place.' "

"Ah!" said Lamiya. Nandi seemed genuinely eager to talk about her people, and the Empress's niece considered this a happy sign.

"Each clan had its dominant lineage, its royal family, and it was from the male line of this family that the hereditary chiefs were drawn. . . ."

As Nandi spoke, and Lamiya compiled a barter list, Kai's First mused that she knew much of the rest of the tale: the expansion of the Zulus into an empire rivaled only by Abyssinia and Egypt, ruled by an absolute King as Abyssinia had its Immortal Empress and Egypt its Pharaoh. Only seventy years ago, a similar split had happened again. A prince had been born, too young to have any real hope of the crown. He took his fortune and followers and traveled to the New World, buying vast tracts of land, chiefly in the region now called Azania.

His sons had been named Shaka and Cetshwayo. And Nandi, as Cetshwayo's daughter, was therefore heir to a lineage almost as long and proud as Lamiya's. Perhaps fiercer. Still attempting to consolidate its power, the Zulu empire might prove less stable, more aggressive in its goals.

She watched the Zulu woman as she sorted scrolls and papers and spoke of her ancestors. Even if she was as she seemed, their goals needn't be absolutely congruent. Nandi might well have secrets. It would behoove the Empress's niece to remember that they were co-wives, and perhaps even sisters, but not yet friends.

Not yet.

Later, lounging in Lamiya's room, Kai sought to convey his thoughts about Nandi. Despite his joy in his Zulu wife, or even their shared passion, he could not escape the sense that she still remained essentially unknown to him. Was she just waiting for the right opportunity? Even if not his murderess, could she be a spy?

"I have concerns," he said.

"Of what, my husband?"

"Nandi. I was promised to her, and she to me. But much changed between those promises and our wedding."

She nodded. The fireplace crackled and the room brightened for a moment, creating highlights in her hair. Kai brushed her coiffure with his fingertips, and she caught them with her own. "Something changed, yes. But you have never spoken of it with me."

"I regret that I have secrets from you of all people. But in this case I have little choice. It is a burden I would never ask you to suffer."

"Very well. But to help you, I must at least know what you fear."

"I fear that Cetshwayo has designs beyond my comprehension. That he might send his own daughter to speed those ends."

"I wish I could say it was not possible, but the business of marriages is hardly confined to matters of the heart," Lamiya said.

"You came here to marry my brother. You stayed to be my wife."

"Yes."

"I know that you did it in part to gain Dar Kush's wealth and resources for your aunt."

Lamiya refused to so much as blink before her husband's gaze.

"Do you deny it?"

"Of course not. And when war comes, if Bilalistan can ally herself with my aunt, and I have been instrumental in that, she will forgive me for marrying you. My guess is that she will announce she had a sacred dream."

"Will her people believe it?"

She shrugged. "She walks a tightrope. The Muslims never believed it in the first place. But I think that most will understand. Love, real love, is not so unique that it can only be experienced between two exact people. Most would never meet a partner. Allah would not be so cruel. Between good and honest folk there is always something to love. If there is kindness, and hope, there can be love."

"Have I been kind?"

"More than kind," he said.

"Given you hope?"

"I feared that I would go home, and into sequestration. You gave me the hope that I could have a family, and a life, and also honor obligations to my aunt. Yes, you have given me hope."

Kai approached her more closely. "And have you, in truth, been able to find a way to love me?"

"Yes, my husband."

"Do you think that Nandi might love me?"

"She would have married you whether there was love or not. But once in your home, she is bound by her honor, and her oaths."

"And oaths to her father?"

"Is she a woman or a child? Whatever promises she made as a child, ultimately she will make her own choice. A woman like Nandi has nothing save her reputation. She will navigate the shoals of conflict with absolute care. If she stumbles, there will be no one to catch her."

"No?"

"No. Who would marry her if she betrays you? And her own men would not take her as first wife if her virginity is gone." When Kai did not answer, Lamiya's smile grew saucy. "And might I assume that to be the case?"

"For the sake of argument."

A pause, and then both of them laughed. Kai took her in his arms.

"We are leaving tomorrow. Aidan is done here. Lamiya—do you feel comfortable with the Dahomy?"

"Why do you ask?"

"Because if you are, I intend to send my personal guard to the territorial militia."

"Leading by example?"

He nodded.

"I suppose. They are competent, and seem loyal." She held his hand softly, a wistful smile curling his lips. "It is not the guard I will miss."

"I have neglected you of late. This is wrong, and I will make amends."

"It will take time," Lamiya said. "After you return, we will speak of it."

"I'd like to begin that conversation tonight," Kai said, and leaned to extinguish the candle. Then there was only flickering firelight to guide the eye; murmurs to guide the ear; shifting bodies, softness, and firmness to guide the touch; salt and perfume to guide taste and smell as the night stretched its leisurely way toward an unwelcome dawn.

Walking the halls of Dar Kush on the way to one of her myriad errands, Tata encountered Nandi. She bowed deferentially as the Zulu princess brushed past her, waited until her new mistress was out of sight, and then hurried down the hall.

The thoughts brewing in the girl's mind had grown to obsession. What was happening in her new home? Murder? Betrayal? Or simple cookery and minor mischief? How could a simple Greek girl understand the rituals and goings-on of wealthy, powerful blacks?

But she knew she had to have advice. Who should she speak to? If she made a mistake, it could prove disastrous. She could not speak to the Empress's niece: giving First wife a weapon against the Second could prove poisonous and actually evil, especially if her fears were groundless. The husband? She could not speak to the Wakil. He was unapproachable, terrifying. Then to the slave council? No. They debated endlessly and were afraid to do anything.

What she needed was to pass her information on to someone who was wise. Who was impartial. And most importantly, who would remember that a girl named Tata had attempted to do the correct thing.

Who then? There was only one person whom everyone in the household seemed to trust, who was considered a man of spirit and wisdom.

If the little shaykh could not be trusted, then Tata feared she would be back in a whorehouse, trapped beneath nameless, grunting men, earning her bread with her soul. Dar Kush might have been prison, but at least it was not hell itself.

She thought for another ten minutes before tiptoeing to Babatunde's study. She balled her little fist and rapped upon the door.

"Yes?"

"Sayyid, may I enter?"

"Certainly," said Babatunde without correction. "What can I do for you?"

Nervously at first and then with growing assurance, the child began to speak.

CHAPTER FIFTY-ONE

26 Safar A.H. 1295
(Friday, March 1, 1878)

A FEW SCRAGGLY CHICKENS ran in the spaces between houses in Ghost Town. The old village dog chased one of them, void of malice or harmful intent, merely for the sport.

Aidan listened to their cries as he lay in his old bed; the first rays of dawn brushed his cheeks. He groaned, rolled over, and his eyes opened wide. For a long moment he blinked and stared at the ceiling, waiting for his vision to clear. For an instant he wondered if everything he had experienced in the last three years had been a dream. Had he ever left Ghost Town at all?

Then he sat up.

In a weary blur, he washed his face, dressed, packed. All of this was in a muzzy-headed fog, slowly lifting as action cleared the sleep from his mind.

Finally he stood in the center of his old home.

Had he ever left Dar Kush? Did Sophia exist? Was there any evidence at all that his mother Deirdre had ever lived? And if he didn't return from this insane adventure, what would that prove he, Aidan, had ever lived at all?

Aidan took his knife and carved the following on the wooden door: *On this day Friday 26 Safar 1295, Aidan O'Dere left Ghost Town for New Alexandria, on a mission of mercy.* He paused, wondering what else he should write. What else mattered? Nothing came to mind. He slipped his knife back into his belt and stepped out of his door—

And was shocked speechless at the sight of Ghost Town's entire population standing just outside, waiting to bid him farewell.

"We know where yer goin' and why ye do it, Aidan," said Maeve.

"We just wanted to wish ye luck." Olaf said "Come back whole, with yer sister."

His mouth opened and then closed, any possible words drowned in the tide of emotions swelling within him. "I'll do my damnedest."

He picked up Conair. "Thanks for the help, lad," he said. To his surprise, the boy wrapped his arms around Aidan's neck.

"You coming back?" Conair said.

"I come back. Then I'll leave again, for home."

"Take me with you?"

Conair said it, and then grinned as if it were a joke. All a joke. Then he couldn't meet Aidan's eyes. Turning without another word, he ran away toward the chicken coops.

With the villagers singing Aidan on his way, he emerged from Ghost Town. Kai awaited him just beyond the gates, holding two sets of reins. "Quite a send-off."

"I need another favor," Aidan said.

"That being?"

"There is a boy. Named Conair. About twelve. The same age I was when I came here. His mother died of the fever. His father died at the mosque. He has no one—"

"He has now. He will join my orphans."

"And when my work for you is done, I will take him home to the crannog."

"Of course."

Aidan grinned at him. He opened his mouth to speak, and then could not.

They were greeted by Lamiya, Babatunde, and Bitta, whose fingers fluttered fluidly.

"What is she saying?" asked Aidan.

Kai pursed his lips and seemed to study her movements carefully. "Something about another massage. . . ."

Aidan managed a sickly smile.

"No. I jest. She says she will watch over my family while I am gone."

"So will we all, Kai," said Babatunde.

Aidan heard the horseman before he saw him. He turned to see a familiar figure galloping through the main gate. Fodjour. He had never shown Aidan either affection or regard, and the past weeks the Irishman had seen a greater deterioration of what little relationship there might ever have been.

If Aidan had thought deeply about Fodjour's attitude toward him, the word *jealousy* might have come swiftly to mind, but been just as swiftly dismissed.

Fodjour rode up. "Aidan," he said. "I hear you have suffered well."

"I hadn't thought of it in those terms."

Fodjour laughed mirthlessly, and turned to Kai.

"Old friend," Kai said. "Watch over my family while I am gone."

Fodjour smiled. "As if they, and all you possess, were my own."

Kai and Fodjour exchanged smiles. Aidan watched them both, wondering if Kai had noticed that Fodjour's smile was just a bit too hard and bright.

By the steam-screw *Kabîr Haram* from Djibouti Harbor, Kai and Aidan began their journey to New Alexandria.

Aidan leaned against the rail, watching the water churning beneath him. "The last time I took a boat . . . I left my homeland forever." The boat's chimneys belched smoke, and occasionally steam. He watched them for a bit, shaking his head in amazement. "I have never understood how these things move."

"Water expands when it is heated," Kai said, reciting an ancient lesson. "You can use this expansion to turn an engine, the force transferred to the water with the screws."

"And this makes the ship move?"

"Yes. When you push against an object, it pushes back as well."

"It is wonderful," said Aidan. "Who discovered such magic?"

"We all know it. If you apply a paddle to water, doesn't the water push you forward?"

"I suppose. I had just never thought of it."

"The trick is in taking things that we have all understood, and turning them into laws and principles which help define Allah's universe." He paused, then added idly, "It was a woman who first wrote many of these things down."

"A woman?"

"Yes. Her name was Kyanfuma."

"A woman. Black?"

Kai chuckled. "Of course."

Aidan gritted his teeth. "Just asking."

As the sun reached the western horizon the steam-screw passed the mouth of the Brown Nile. As it did, it skirted a flotilla of warships anchored loosely in the bay. Most were the ubiquitous steam-screws, but triple-masters with triangular, billowing sails and cannon ports along the sides also graced the waters, simultaneously beautiful and menacing.

Kai squinted against the glare. "Hovering," he said.

"Warships, bound for Azteca?"

Kai shook his head. "Even now New Alexandria forces the Aztecs to a treaty. I suppose these could be reserves, but I don't know. . . ."

As their first night fell more fully upon them, Kai retreated to his cabin for the evening prayers, and then settled in for the night in his luxurious bed. Aidan had made a place for himself on a straw mat on the floor. Kai gazed down on his friend. "I trust you'll be comfortable?"

"Better than sleeping in the hold, I'll wager. Still, I'd rather have a bed."

Kai handed Aidan one of his blankets. "You'll be warmer with this, I think. I would provide you with more, but the cabin stewards would talk."

Aidan chuckled. "A likely story."

They settled down, and Kai dimmed the lantern.

"Kai?" Aidan said.

"Yes?"

"Thank you for the blanket."

Just as Aidan was nestling his head on his arm, Kai threw down his pillow as well.

PART IV

New Alexandria

"Today a strange thing happened," said the student. "While running to the market, it felt as if I stood still, while the world revolved around me."

"Ah," said the teacher. "You experienced a moment of sayalin."

"What is this?" the student asked. "What is sayalin?"

"It is infinite abundance, the gift of Allah. You move, but your inner world does not. Men search for such moments, struggle for them. Sayalin allow us to travel without leaving home. To enter new worlds, and yet not be a stranger."

"How do I find this sayalin again?" the student asked.

"As with all true things," said the teacher, "when the time is right, it will find you."

CHAPTER FIFTY-TWO

New Alexandria

2 Rabi al-Awwal A.H. 1295
(Wednesday, March 6, 1878)

THEIR STEAM-SCREW ROUNDED THE HORN and headed north along the eastern coast. On the morning of the sixth day, the *Kabîr Haram* pulled into Alexandria Bay. The shadow of the Alexandrian odalisque lighthouse shrouded the entrance.

Kai drank in the sights and sounds. He had never been this far north before. He had been warned that New Alexandria was Egyptian in temperament, but never having been to the Continent, his exposure to such things was limited to newsprints, textbooks, and paintings. He knew that the people were a bit lighter-skinned than Abyssinians, with more Arab and Greek blood flowing in their veins. He knew also that, incredibly, Alexandrians considered that their mixture of bloodlines gave them an advantage over either pure black or ignoble white.

This was a vista of pyramids, odalisques, titanic statuary, and vast Babylonian-style gardens. To Kai's eyes it was a world of marvels. He half expected to see teams of men using huge kites to drag blocks of stone for pyramid construction, as he had once seen in a yellow-sheet novel.

Although such a sight escaped him, he saw other marvels almost as daunting: the wheeled machines that moved along parallel tracks, a variety of landlocked steam-screw. Contraptions with two and three wheels powered by human legs and lungs. Wires strung from poles and buildings, said to carry messages as did the heliograph towers of the south. Everywhere were the signs of an exploding new age. He knew that an ancient Pharaoh's dictates had kept Egyptian technology frozen for half a thousand years, but it seemed to him that Bilalistan's capital was making up for lost time with a vengeance, speeding toward its future at breakneck pace.

As they descended the gangplank an Arab was waving well-dressed passengers toward a platform where a light-painting apparatus made images of their families, with steam-screws and sail-ships floating in the background.

Stripped to the waist, sun-bronzed slaves carted goods down the ramps and onto horse-drawn carts. The horses pulled the groaning cars to a platform erected beside a set of iron rails, supporting a wheezing iron monstrosity that belched smoke and steam.

"What in hell is *that?*" asked Aidan.

"That is what they call a steam dragon," Kai replied. "They are said to be the coming thing. There are more than a thousand miles of track here in the north—we have only several hundred in the south, but more every month."

"Steam . . . like the ship?"

"Yes."

"Water moving wood across the water . . . I can almost understand that. But water moving iron across the land? It makes my head hurt."

Kai laughed, and then whispered, "Mine too."

The streets were laid out with mathematical precision, like roads in a Dahomy farm commune. Major streets were labeled with the names of ancient cities in the Egyptian world. He noted thoroughfares named Giza, Cairo, Saqqara, Abydos, Denderah, Luxor, Edfu, Kom Ombo, Aswan, and Abu Simbel: the names of ancient cities arrayed along the Nile.

The streets bustled with folk in strange headdresses, perhaps modeled on the attire of ancient royalty. He saw braiding integrated into clothing in a manner than suggested an almost military stratification, as if these people adhered to a far more rigid caste system than the south. Some of the women wore false beards, perhaps as badges of Alexandrian office or position.

Kai hated himself for it, but couldn't stop gawking, simply staring at the height of the buildings and the complexity of the culture.

There had been talk of war, and it was impossible to avoid one conclusion: the forces of social organization were more powerful in the north, and that promised trouble. Where there was organization, there were also larger surpluses of capital and resources. That implied the ability to afford a larger standing army, which could be dangerous for New Djibouti and her allies.

Army, yes . . . but what of her navy? More numerous than that of the south, but less experienced, more used to navigating coastal than deep waters, he thought. Egypt's naval forces had never been the equal of her armies, and Kai hoped that that weakness might have traveled to the New World.

"Have you ever been here before?" Aidan's words wrenched Kai out of his reverie.

"No," he answered. "I must admit that it is somewhat daunting. So many more machines and factories. How can we defeat them?"

"I didn't know you were so intimidated by appearances. We have conquered impossible goals more than once."

Kai seemed to snap out of it, and slapped Aidan's shoulder affectionately. "So we have."

New Alexandria's slave markets were vast affairs, covering five or six city blocks. Slavery in the north was said to be different than in the south. Less harsh, perhaps. The slaves were used more for domestic work than crops. It was therefore said to be easier for a slave to buy his way out of bondage here. But there still existed a vast market of menial factory jobs, as well as billets on the docks and in shipping or fishery.

One way or the other, New Alexandria's luxurious lifestyle rested largely on the labor of bondsmen.

"The slaves here seem better dressed," Aidan said. "Perhaps even better fed. Why is that?"

"First, this is what we are seeing right now, in our first moments off the ship. Later you will see other servants. Second—you may be right. But that may be because the average northern slave is more skilled, and therefore accorded better conditions."

Aidan bristled. "What do you mean?"

"When slaves are captured, literate ones are given the chance to demonstrate their ability. Those of capacity are sent to better berths."

"More of us have 'capacity' than you think."

"I'll grant you that," Kai said. "I speak of custom only."

In Aidan's memory, he was again in the Andalusian slave market. Aidan, Nessa, and Deirdre stood in a line of miserable captives who were being separated and ranked according to literacy.

"Sign!" barked the trader, holding a piece of paper out. Tentatively, nervously, Deirdre signed her name.

"Yes. I remember," Aidan said. "My mother signed her name."

"Yet still you came to Djibouti?"

"I couldn't write my name. Neither could Nessa. We would have been separated. I think they would have sent my mother to Egypt."

"Or elsewhere along the Egyptian Sea. There are many places where educated slaves are prized."

"My mother wouldn't do it. Wouldn't leave us."

He remembered Deirdre falling to her knees, pleading before a giant, grotesquely corpulent black man.

"She begged them to let us stay together. Swore that she'd work herself to death if they did."

Kai's reply was quietly respectful. "And she kept her word."

"Even though they didn't keep theirs."

"We will find Nessa," Kai said, and gripped Aidan's hand once, hard. Aidan said nothing, but finally nodded.

There were greyhounds and a few other highly trained dogs trotting on their leashes, and several varieties of domesticated apes: small reddish ones sitting on shoulders, long-limbed black ones scampering at the ends of chains. Nowhere, thank goodness, did he see anything resembling the dreaded thoths. There was something obscene about their resemblance to humanity, as if their captivity mirrored his own.

Kai noticed that the streets swarmed with cats: gray, black, spotted. Never in his life had he seen so many strays. He doubted New Alexandria had much of a rat problem.

Kai felt uncomfortable: so many monuments, so many images of the Caliph and Calipha, so many signs of respect for those things the old Egyptians had worshipped. Replicas of the Colossi of Memnon; statues of Sobek, the crocodile-headed god; a painted, raised belief of the demon-god Bes. . . .

Egyptians would claim them merely art, but Kai had to wonder. Did all of this not balance on the thin edge of idolatry? And if so, what of the Prophet's other teachings might the northerners discount? Those were his thoughts, but what he said was, "Why build them so tall?"

"When I first saw buildings like this," Aidan said, staring up, "it was in Andalus. When the northerners herded us off the ship, I thought gods must live there."

"Everywhere I look, I see the works of men. I wonder if it is not easy to forget the hand of Allah in all of this. To believe that men have made the world."

"You fear they are worshipping their own works."

A dirigible glided between two of the gleaming towers above them. Steam-powered engines hauled their goods. This was a different world than the one Kai knew. It behooved him to be careful. This world could seduce a righteous man into complacency, and that could be fatal.

It required only a few inquiries for Kai to make contact with a fight booker, a small, bearded man named Mem. "I have a wager!" said Kai.

"Yes, Sidi?"

"My man can survive your battle royale," said Kai. "I want him entered!"

Mem looked Aidan up and down. Perhaps because Aidan massed about twenty sep, he was unimpressed. "It is a dicey business, sir. Are you certain?"

"Quite."

"Very well." Mem sighed. "Sign here—but remember, I promise nothing for his personal safety."

"His safety is not my concern," Kai said in his haughtiest voice. "My profits are. Move along, boy," Kai said, signing Mem's contract.

Aidan glared back at Kai, but moved. "Master . . . ," Aidan said in suddenly broken Arabic. "When I see ye again?"

"After the fight. Now make me proud, and you will be rewarded."

Aidan nodded, his shoulders hunched, his head slightly bowed. "Thank ye, thank ye sir . . ."

Kai glared at Aidan a bit for his ghosting about. But before he could say anything, his friend was seized by two huge, muscular guards, and hustled away.

Aidan was escorted to a plank-floored holding pen. Two barred windows admitted dusty streams of light, and the floor was matted with straw. There were about twenty men in that room, some sitting, some standing or leaning against the stained wooden walls. Aidan was smooth-skinned in comparison to many of the other slaves. They seemed a brutal, brutalized, scarred, dangerously quiet lot, who glared at him without a word. After a few minutes armed guards appeared and began leading the men away. Aidan was twelfth to be taken, led down a dark corridor to a cell just large enough for one man. The air smelled of vinegar and urine.

Mem appeared in the doorway before it could close. "There's a mat, and a blanket. Rest. Do you want a woman?"

"No."

"Hemp? Beer?"

"No."

"A boy?"

"No!"

The booker rubbed his scraggly beard. "You may die tomorrow."

Aidan ignored him and settled back against his mattress. Hard it might be, but he had slept on worse, and less.

"You are an odd one," said Mem. "I will watch you."

"Do that," Aidan said, and closed his eyes.

It was three hours later that he was called for the first meal, taken to an open area filled with hard, quiet, dangerous pale men.

He glanced over them idly, shocked when he recognized a familiar face. Aidan hunkered down close to a man who huddled in a corner, arms wrapped around his knees. "So, Simon," he said. "You do not recognize me?"

The other man looked at him incuriously. "Who are you?"

"Months ago, on the frontier. You came to my village, seeking shelter."

Now Simon's eyes widened. "Oh, yes. And you turn me down, din' you? High and mighty then, weren't you. Look at you now, coal-licker."

"What happened to you?"

"What the hell you think?" Rage seemed to expand Simon like a bellows. "Got caught before I could get halfway to the Nations. Wouldn't tell them who my master was, and he hadn't branded me, so I went on the block. Here I am. They'll use me up, throw me away when I'm broke." He gave a bitter, broken smile. "Same as you."

Aidan felt terrible, but swallowed his urge to apologize. This was no place or time for softness. Nevertheless, he said, "I'm sorry we couldn't help you."

Simon grunted. "You'll be sorrier tomorrow. Now get the hell away from me."

Aidan retreated, joining the line where men were served steaming piles of bland, hot cooked grain with chunks of fish folded in. It wasn't good. It wasn't bad. It was just food, and in memory of weeks of semistarvation, Aidan ate every scrap of it he could get.

CHAPTER FIFTY-THREE

5 Rabi al-Awwal A.H. 1295
(Saturday March 9, 1878)

AZINZA'S BIRTHDAY PARTY expanded across Dar Kush's house and grounds like a sprawling, blind but happy living thing. Servants prepared food, readied games on Lake A'Zam, sent troupes of jugglers in, and organized slaves for singing and dancing.

Near the lake, troupes of wrestlers competed as their exertions were accompanied by growl-throated *lambe* and hypnotically rhythmic Gambian *mbung-mbung* drummers.

The grounds were thronged and decorated for the pleasure of four-year old Azinza and two-year-old Aliyah. A thousand concerns crowded for Lamiya's attention, and she was delighted to encounter Babatunde walking serenely through the crowds of delighted children, thriving on the joy and sheer aliveness they radiated. "Babatunde!"

"Yes, my dear?"

"Would you be a blessing and check that the supervision is adequate at the lake?"

"I thought the Dahomy were seeing to that."

"Yes, but . . . check on them, would you?"

Babatunde nodded. "Of course."

Babatunde walked from the house out toward the lake's crystal waters.

A slave driving a cart filled with kids called to him. "Master, give ye a ride?"

Babatunde's dark round face wrinkled; then he sighed and accepted. He hoisted himself up on the wagon, surrounded by squealing black and brown children.

He turned to one of them. "You . . . actually enjoy this?"

"Fun!" the child squealed.

"Yes, fun." He scowled. "So is running and walking. You should use your legs while you're . . . Oh, never mind."

Babatunde passed a troupe of Middle Eastern jugglers entrancing the children with almost magical feats of coordination and skill.

They reached the lake, and Babatunde gratefully disembarked. The lake was filled with children swimming and boating . . . under the watchful eyes of Kokossa and his daughter Chifi, and of the warrior-women. The children could not have been safer in their own beds: the Dahomy took their responsibility to the Wakil and his family seriously. Kai knew that, but the Empress's niece was a worrier.

"Maputo," said Babatunde.

"My friend. How wonderful to be young, eh?"

"Or too old to be involved in such things. Ah!" He moved nimbly to the side as a group of shrieking, wet children ran past.

"Once we were so young."

"Never so young as that. I swear that I was born with stiff joints . . . Ganne!"

He turned in time to see the leader of the Dahomy women approach. Her expression was businesslike, but there was a bit of sway in her walk.

"Babatunde," she said. "I had hoped to see you."

"Oh. Is there a concern?"

"Only that I have not seen you in some days, and I miss you."

Kokossa and Chifi shared a little grin at this, and moved away, much to Babatunde's discomfort.

"Ah, well, duties, you know."

She watched the playing children, standing very close to him. "Have you never wished children?"

"I have hundreds of children."

"Spiritual children. Did not the Prophet—"

"Peace Be Upon Him," Babatunde murmured.

"Yes. Peace Be Upon Him. Didn't the Prophet encourage his followers to marry and have children?"

"Yes. Well . . . I have been married to my books and scrolls and duties these many years. . . ."

She was very close now. "And now that some of those duties have slackened? Have you never thought of taking a wife?"

"I was married once."

"Oh," she said. "Your wife is . . . ?"

"Gone now," he said, and seemed to drift away for a moment.

"I am sorry," Ganne said.

He smiled again. "But that was long ago. Life is to celebrate. But strange you should ask me! You are beautiful and . . . ahem . . . your own life path has prevented you from taking a husband."

"Many of my warriors have husbands. I have not met a partner who could walk with me."

"And that is the way of the world. I might say much the same thing."

Ganne's voice dropped into a husky whisper. Although she was a head taller than the Cricket, she somehow managed to seem frailer and shorter than her actual size. "What is the teaching on modesty and submission?"

Babatunde cleared his throat. "Ah . . . yes. 'Men are responsible for women because God has given the one more than the other.'"

"'Virtuous women are therefore obedient, guarding in their husbands' absence that which God has guarded,'" she finished.

Babatunde swallowed. "That is accurate, yes."

"And aside from obedience and faithfulness, what other characteristic would such a woman require?"

"There are . . . a number of characteristics. Ahem . . .'"

Suddenly, and somewhat to his surprise, Babatunde felt a bit muzzy-headed, as he had once in his youth after ascending Kilimanjaro.

Babatunde heard a horse, and turned to see Fodjour walking his mount up behind them. He wondered how long Kai's friend had been listening. Fodjour made a few hand gestures, and then grinning, rode off.

"I don't recognize those hand signs," Babatunde said.

"You wouldn't," said Ganne. "We've been teaching him our battlefield signals."

"What did he say?"

"I may tell you," she said, eyeing him speculatively. "Some night."

Fodjour rode hell-for-leather back to the house, around the other side.

Along the way he saw a juggler entertaining a knot of children. By his relatively pale skin, he knew the man to be Persian. The juggler made eye contact with him, and nodded.

Fodjour rode on. So much noise, so much chaos. It should have been a happy chaos, and was that for so many of the guests, but . . .

His eye was drawn to the back porch of Dar Kush, where a red-haired slave woman was whispering to Olaf One-Ear. They glanced about, thought no one was watching, and Olaf stole a kiss, then swatted her behind and sent her packing. Fodjour recognized the wench—she was a slave purchased from Kai after indicating a willingness to marry one of Djidade Berhar's boss men, Olalye. Olalye had been a sturdy worker once, but the slut had corrupted him. Olalye had been stealing to provide luxuries for his slave bride. Fodjour knew it, and had intended to horsewhip the fool and sell him south. But Allahbas had had a better idea.

As he had suspected, as his *mother* had suspected, the woman Morgan was a whore, using the relaxed rules of festival to establish an assignation. Ordinarily such a discovery would mean less than finding two squirrels rutting in the woods.

But in their current situation, this might prove useful.

Yes, it might. He rode up next to the house, and called out to her. "Morgan!" he called. After a few moments she appeared, flour covering her hands.

"Yes, sah?"

"What are you doing on this side of the lake?"

She blinked several times, and he knew she was busy combining lies and truth. "Miz Allahbas loaned me to the Wakil for the party."

And you jumped at the chance to see your lover, didn't you? "Have you seen Ola-lye, your husband?"

"Not since mornin'. He in trouble?"

"No. I want him to travel to the harbor with me tonight. We may be gone overnight, so pack him a bag and have him meet me at the barn."

"Now, suh?" Her cheeks had flushed. Even this slow-minded slut could see the possibilities.

"No. After supper. Go along now," he said, and turned his horse away.

Nandi was completely immersed in entertaining a group of children, including the tiny Azinza.

"—and our ancestors live in the ground, far below us," she was saying. The children had asked her why Zulus didn't pray five times a day, and her explanation had expanded to include her people's beliefs. "But they watch us, and shelter us, and love us."

"Can they hear us when we pray?"

Nandi nodded. "Yes, of course they can. And if we listen closely, we can hear their answers."

So occupied was Nandi in her explanations that she never heard Lamiya's approach. The Empress's niece was accompanied by guests; Lamiya's Indian friends the Guptas and the pious N'Guy clan from Mali.

"Lamiya," said Lady N'Guy, "you must introduce me to your co-wife."

"Of course. Lady Tinia N'Guy, please meet the former Nandi kaSenzangakhona, new to our house."

Nandi stood, unfolding from her kneeling position with effortless grace. "So glad that you could share this day with us."

"And you know the Guptas," Lamiya said.

"Of course," said Nandi. "You were kind enough to attend our wedding."

"I was not able to attend, I'm afraid," said Lady N'Guy. "Pressing business."

"I understand," Nandi said, and indeed she did: she understood N'Guy's tone as a suggestion that had there *not* been pressing business, she would have manufactured some other pretext for avoiding the nuptials.

But Lady N'Guy had more on her mind than mere one-upmanship. "I overheard your comments to the child." Her trace of a smile was withering. "Certainly you don't believe such fantasies."

Nandi was very quiet. "It is my people's faith."

"I thought that you would be converting to the True Faith. Lamiya," she said, turning to the Empress's niece, "wasn't that a requirement of the marriage contract?"

Nandi squared her shoulders. Taller than N'Guy, but far more compact, she suddenly seemed to dominate their common space. "You need not ask Lamiya. I stand before you and can speak myself."

N'guy's smile was silkily conciliatory. "Surely, I meant no offense." She oozed condescension. "But you are not in Azania now. This is the civilized world, and such provincial beliefs do not become the wife of a Wakil."

Voiced between men, such a rebuke might well have triggered a duel. Nandi's eyes narrowed, and her head tilted slightly downward, so that the white crescent below her pupils expanded. Her breath grew shallower, and her hands knotted.

Sensing disaster, Lamiya stepped between them. "I do not think, I *know* that Nandi brings her whole heart to the union. Whatever beliefs that heart may embrace, I am certain it is for the good of all."

"Of course." N'guy smiled.

Nandi calmed herself, and retreated from the precipice. "Excuse me," she said, and left them.

N'guy clucked. "Goodness. Are all Zulus so sensitive? One would hardly credit it from their carriage and reputation."

Gupta *bamam's* eyebrows arched. "She has a certain . . . vitality, of course, but . . . well, politics certainly makes odd housemates."

Lamiya held her tongue. The Guptas she genuinely enjoyed, but N'Guy's pretensions irritated her more than was ideal for a wise and judicious hostess. She might have taken greater offense had N'Guy's words not mirrored her own thoughts, almost as if her guest had taken it upon herself to say what Lamiya herself could not. Nandi had retreated from confrontation, but Lamiya knew better than to think that she would do so in every instance—or even the next. The young woman was trying to fit into the household, but a point would come when she might well express herself more . . . forcefully.

And if she was anything like other Zulus Lamiya had known, there could be hell to pay.

Trembling with suppressed rage, Nandi wandered the grounds. She felt lonely and ill at ease.

A flash of unexpected light blinded her for an instant, and she shaded her face with one hand. What was that? She searched in the direction of the barn, and watched as a bright flare of light blossomed once, twice . . . a pause, and then it repeated.

This was a message for her. The light shone directly into her eyes, flashing on and off, and she finally recognized the pattern. Once, long ago, she and a friend had used such signals to pass messages and summon one another.

Her heart raced with an overwhelming amalgam of emotions: anxiety, anger, excitement, the anticipation of a forbidden encounter. Since arrival at Dar Kush she had felt almost manacled, only the intensity and depth of her connection with Kai making life tolerable. And Kai was absent. Lamiya herself was a gracious, lovely woman: time would tell if the Empress's niece was genuine. But Lamiya's insufferable guests simply begged for a knife-dance. But since that more satisfyingly visceral route was closed to her, she had to present a public face that satisfied the household and their guests until she had time to root more deeply in this alien place.

To be unchaparoned in Chalo's presence was wrong, yes. But sometimes, small wrongs could forestall the larger. She would see Chalo. Chasten him, yes. But also luxuriate in the knowledge that his love and lust for her had motivated him to risk death for the mere hope of seeing her smile.

And that cast the entire day in a new and warmer light.

"What are you doing here?" she demanded. Nandi's hands were perched on her hips, her head thrown back in a deliberately theatrical gesture. She had entered the barn with trepidation, but as the door closed behind her she felt a mixture of excitement and irritation. So far, the irritation was winning, but . . .

So still stood Chalo that he all but disappeared into the shadow. His gaze was like molten iron. "You know why I came."

She flushed with the intensity of this young warrior's ardor. Her posturing wilted before his simple, honest intensity. "Chalo, Chalo," she said, shaking her head. "You don't know what you are doing."

He reached out for her. "The things we said—"

She took a step back, mistrusting the merest of contacts. "Those things I said to you as a girl. I am a married woman, with obligations." By sun and sky—what was she doing? "I should not even speak to you," she said. Chalo was not the man for her; she knew that now . . . in fact had always known it. But now she saw the folly she had wrought by trifling with his heart.

Chalo's tongue moistened his lips. He spread his hands in a beseeching posture. "What kind of people are these who would take you away from your family, not even allow you to speak to your . . . friend." He paused, suddenly seeming far more youthful than his summers. "Isn't that what I am, your friend?"

"What kind of people are they?" she said, answering him before he could ask the question. "They are people who trust me to uphold the honor of their household—"

Despite seclusion and lowered voices, their conversation was not private. From just outside the barn, Conair watched, fascinated as the two Zulus conversed sharply in their native tongue.

Conair was bright enough to know that what he had seen was dangerous. The Empress's niece was kind, and small smart funny Babatunde even more so.

If anything, he should talk to the little shaykh. If anyone would know what this might mean, it was he.

"Nandi," said Chalo. Her words had leached some of the heat and urgency from him, but still the steel remained. He knew the call of duty, had pledged his life on the field of honor as all Zulu men must do, and knew that the strictures guiding their women were no less severe. If this was the life the ancestors had crafted for them, then so be it. But he would rather have died in the Aztec Wars than utter the words that his lips formed next. "I need to know that you are well," he said. "That you are happy. If you tell me that you are, then I will leave, and never bother you again. Can you tell me that?"

After a pause, Nandi said, "I am happy."

Chalo gazed into her face, seeing both the lies and the truth there, knowing that he had to accept both. "I love you," he said finally, knowing that these were the last and truest words he would ever say to his childhood love. "And in a better world, you would have been my woman. We would have built a life together, and raised more cattle than there are blades of grass in a meadow. Instead, you belong to this . . . man. The Wakil." He finally broke off his gaze, but it seemed that the effort was as painful as splintering one of his own bones. "I pray that you tell me truly. And that you know that if your feelings ever change, mine will stay true."

"Chalo . . . ," she said, and brushed his scarred cheek with the back of her hand.

His own rough hand covered hers, and then he stepped back. "So," he said, his aspect changing from suitor to young warrior. "You are married, and have given this man your promise. I must respect that, if I respect you. But I remain your servant, now and always." His eyes no longer met hers: he was looking slightly above her brows, at her hairline. His chest heaved, the effort to restrain himself as taxing as any battle. Then, without another word, he slipped back into the shadows, and was gone.

Although Chalo took every precaution, and mingled with the crowd as if he were just another parent searching for his scampering children, the Persian jugglers saw him. Even as they tossed clubs, knives, and balls back and forth to the delight of the children, they whispered amongst themselves, and smiled in secret satisfaction.

After the last of the guests began their journey home, Lamiya and Babatunde sat in the downstairs study before a mild and peaceful fire, sharing mulled cider and speaking privately. "I think the day went well," the Sufi said.

"Do you think so?"

"Yes. Don't you?"

"I'm not certain," she said. "There was a bit of trouble with Nandi. Babatunde?"

"Yes?"

"Have I made her welcome? To feel that this is her home?"

He smiled. "You have done what you could."

She watched the fire for a bit. Flames seemed so like living things to her: they ate, they breathed, they reproduced, and they died. It was easy to see how fire and earth and wind and rain might be considered living things, treated with respect and love and awe by any peoples—perhaps by all peoples before more anthropomorphized deities were adopted, let alone monotheism embraced. Fire took, and it gave in return. A living thing. Why was it so important for men to control what others believed in their hearts? Why wasn't it enough to judge others by their actions? "You have always been my dearest friend," she said.

"It gladdens my heart to know you feel it so."

"And I would ask a boon of you . . . ," she said. "Please, strive to be a friend to Nandi as well."

"She has friends," he said. "Attendants."

"Not one such as you," she said. "I want her to feel as a sister. I can think of no greater gift I can give her than the friendship of the man who has guided me since childhood."

Babatunde's face was radiant. "You make your tutor proud." He paused. "So," he said. "If matters come to my attention concerning Nandi, you would prefer that I handle them as her friend than as your companion, or Kai's teacher."

"When possible," she said. "If your judgment cannot be trusted, no one's can."

CHAPTER FIFTY-FOUR

Across the lake from Dar Kush stood the Berhar estate, second largest in all New Djibouti. Two-thirds the size of Dar Kush, it too was a three-storied collection of Moorish towers, vaulted archways, and endless internested corridors. It had fewer windows than Dar Kush, but they were larger, silvered to admit light but maintain privacy, and tended to be rounded or oval rather than rectangular.

While Dar Kush had been disassembled and shipped from afar, Dar Berhar had been constructed forty years ago by Djidade's father from his own plans. It was here that Kai and Fodjour had spent endless hours chasing and mischief-making in the hallways. It was here that Fodjour and his parents met after the children's party had dispersed.

For almost two years now, Djidade Berhar had been quite ill. In childhood he had been stocky to the verge of plumpness, in young manhood a massive, muscular warrior, strongest in the province. But the inheritance of his estate brought ease and wealth. He had, as the saying went, grown into his seat.

His once formidable obesity was a thing of the past. Long illness had withered Berhar to a fraction of his former size. These days, he could barely move from his bed.

Allahbas Berhar, Fodjour's mother and Berhar's only surviving wife, was a woman of impeccable Masai and Persian breeding and gnawing ambitions. For some twenty months she had nursed her husband through his decline. She had been Berhar's Second until the death of his original First in a boating accident on Lake A'Zam, a tragedy that had claimed both stepmother and Fodjour's elder half brother. It was unclear what had happened: the boat should have been completely safe. Allahbas herself had used it only the previous day.

"How went the party?" wheezed Berhar.

"It was fine, Father."

"And the children. They enjoyed the games?"

"As they always do."

"So true," his mother said. "I remember when you and Kai were boys. You fought and argued, but were always the best of friends."

"Yes." Fodjour shifted his weight uncomfortably from foot to foot. He disliked it when his mother cast her eye back to his childhood. In some way that it was difficult to explain, that very focus seemed to strip him of hard-won years.

"And what was it that happened? How did that friendship sour?"

Fodjour furrowed his brow. "You know."

"Yes," she said, and leaned forward, eyes sparkling. "His love, love that should have been yours, was stripped from you because of his affection for that *binzr-batn*."

Fodjour tensed, the muscles in his face drawn taut. It was almost as if there were another man beneath the smiling mask. He muttered something in a voice so low that neither parent could hear it.

"What?" asked his mother. "Louder, please."

"Why couldn't he love me?" Fodjour was unable to meet their eyes.

The father wheezed. "You were his friend."

"Our families could have ruled New Djibouti," said Allahbas. "And now he is off to New Alexandria with his dog-haired bundling-boy."

"Damn!" Fodjour slammed his hand into a table. He did not wish to reveal his emotions thus to his mother. She would only use them against him in a time and manner of her own choosing. "I was there, at his side, at the mosque," he whispered. "He put all our lives in jeopardy for his love of the whites."

"Yes," said his father, breathing as if the sounds issued from a ruptured bellows. "Do not forget this."

"His father died for them. His brother as well."

"Yes," agreed Allahbas. "It is obscene."

"And he killed Malik, his own flesh and blood, over them."

His mother leaned close, eyes gleaming in the firelight. "He is not fit to rule."

Fodjour felt as if thunderclouds were expanding behind his eyes, their pressure splitting his head in two. "I would have been like a brother to him. Our children would have played together. My son might have married his daughter. And now . . . and now that Zulu whore is mistress of his house. Our fate is not in our hands."

Allahbas stretched her head up haughtily. "If Kai is Wakil, either Cetshwayo or the Empress will control our land, depending on which woman gives Kai an heir."

"It must not be."

Djidade Berhar leaned forward. He was almost incandescent with eagerness, the spirit momentarily animating the flesh. "It need not be. You need only be strong now. You *will* be strong, my son."

Fodjour ground his fists against his temples. He hated hearing these things, even as he knew that plans had gone too far for a reversal. His path was chosen . . . had been chosen for him. If Kai would not accept his love, then Fodjour would make a gift of other, paler emotions. To contain all within his breast was torture beyond withstanding.

Allahbas Berhar watched her son, nodding her slow and poisonous approval. She placed a fist-sized glass globe on the table. "This is a gift of our allies. *Agâz ziwân.*"

Anger weed.

Fodjour lifted the globe and stared at the brownish-gold tangle of plants within, feeling something akin to awe. "So," he said. "It is no myth. And it is ours."

"All we need do is test it."

"As I told you, I have placed events in motion," he said, and explained himself.

Djidade Berhar's face wrinkled distastefully. "Is this necessary?"

Allahbas's laughter was not a pleasant sound. "You wish our fates to ride on an untested drug? No. My son's plan is excellent." She kissed Fodjour's forehead. "There are things you must know about our allies," she said. "You have seen them?"

"Persians, yes."

"They observe," she said. "They watch and wait. But one day, on their own time, they will act. Perhaps for their purposes, perhaps for ours. But if one is captured, we must act swiftly, and this is what you will have to do. . . ."

CHAPTER FIFTY-FIVE

"YES SIR?" Olalye said, holding his hat in his hand. The old man had met him in the barn, as ordered. Only a pitiful need to please radiated from him. Fodjour almost felt sorry for the fool.

"Harness my horses," Fodjour said, but then smiled. "I know you've been working all day."

"Yes, sir."

"Some of us were able to enjoy the party. It doesn't seem fair. Not all the guests were Muslim, and the Wakil is a good host, above all else. I brought you this."

He threw a wineskin, and with deceptively nimble hands, Olalye caught it in midair. His eyes widened. "Really, sir?"

"Really," he said. "Go ahead. Drink, and then prepare our coach."

By the time they were on the road it was dark, and Olalye was thoroughly drunk, laughing and singing, egged on by Fodjour, who was actually enjoying himself.

They traveled three miles down the road, and then Fodjour slapped his head. "Ah, Olalye," he said. "I've forgotten myself. Master Vishna said he would be back *tomorrow*, not today. I'm sorry. Turn this around, would you?"

"Yes, sir."

"Do you like that wine, Olalye? "

"Yes, sir," the old white man said, rubbing at his temples. "Got a little headache coming on, but aside from that, it's fine, sir, just fine."

"It . . . tastes good?"

"A little sweet, sir, that's all. But oh, the whole world's sweet right now."

Fodjour smiled. That was *Agâz ziwân*'s reputation. Little taste, and little reaction . . . unless one experienced a violent emotional surge. And then . . .

By the time they returned to the Berhar estate, the night was quiet. The distant lights of the slave quarters beckoned the old man. He stepped down from the cart, eyes glazed.

"Olalye?" Fodjour said quietly.

The slave looked up at Fodjour, a certain quality of confusion in his eyes. His pupils were huge. "Yes, sir?"

"Why not give your wife a big surprise. Creep in and give her a big kiss."

Olalye nodded, and almost as if sleepwalking, headed in the direction of the slave quarters.

For just a moment Fodjour Berhar felt guilt, then shook his head. No. The drug must be tested. Think of what's at stake. And besides, only if the slut is guilty . . .

Despite that thought, he couldn't escape a leaden feeling in his belly as he walked the cart back to the barn.

CHAPTER FIFTY-SIX

AT THE SUFI'S REQUEST, the next day Nandi met Babatunde in the gardens. He greeted her warmly, and led her to a more secluded section, where they could talk.

"Is there something you wished to discuss with me?" she asked. "Your note contained a hint of urgency."

"Oh, no . . . I apologize for that," he said. "But I would be gratified if you would help me understand a few things."

"Such as . . . ?"

"If I could understand your traditions more fully, it might help prevent misunderstandings."

The word hung there in the air for a minute, and Nandi waited for him to continue. When he did not, she asked, "Where do I begin?"

"Let us compare religions," he said. "We believe that there is but one almighty God. This God made the earth and the heavens, and men and animals to inhabit them. What do you believe?"

She nodded slowly, connecting this conversation and the previous day's unpleasantness with Madame N'guy. "I believe," said Nandi, "that the earth and heavens are alive and divine, that there are many gods and spirits that animate the wind, the rain, the animals we hunt and that hunt us. This would be very different from your ways."

"That is possible, but not inevitable. Tell me: what created the universe?"

Nandi answered without hesitation. "There was a First Cause that set all things in motion."

"Ah," said her teacher. "The difficulty is often found in labels rather than concepts. What if I was to say that this 'First Cause' was Allah? If I was to use that word, would you take exception?"

"No," she said carefully. "I think not."

"In our own tradition, we say that Allah has many aspects, and we name them. Ninety-nine names to be exact. These are not separate gods, but rather separate names for the same divine reality."

"That is what the Muslim in you says. But what of the Yoruba? Have you forgotten that side entirely?"

"Not at all," he said patiently. "The two live as one within me. The single God is known among the Yoruba as Oludumare. The other gods could be considered his aspects, rather than separate entities. The Hindus play a similar game."

"Is that the only difference?" she asked.

"No. As do the Zulu, the Yoruba consider the world to consist of processes rather than things. Dynamics rather than objects, energy more than substance. The Greeks and Arabs tend to think the opposite."

"And you?"

"Me? Like Kokossa, I believe that these two worldviews will ultimately resolve, as in the Chinese image of the Dao. Energy and matter as one flux, divine and eternal."

She cocked her head to the side. "I see. You believe that all of these cultures are seeing the same reality, as a mountain may present many faces, but still be the same mountain."

Babatunde beamed. What a student she would have made! "Yes."

"But it is a considerable distance from that agreement and *Llah illa bah illa Llah,* 'There is no God but God.' And farther still to *Muhammadu razul Allah,* 'and Muhammad was His only prophet.'" She dimpled. "I, too, have studied."

"Excellent, but incorrect. We do not say he was the only prophet. We say that he was the *last,* the one who brought the most complete Word to mankind. Moses was a prophet. Jesus was a prophet as well."

"It still seems so far."

"It need not. There are many, many instances where the two traditions live side by side, neither dominating the other. It is in Kai's heart to respect you, and your traditions, in every way. Your character is paramount. Rejecting love for the *form* of your worship would be like Fata sending his wife away because of her hump."

Nandi laughed. "Excuse me?"

"Apologies. An old parable. Once upon a time in Ghana, there was a great King of the Mandinka people named Son Djata."

"Of course I have heard of him," said Nandi.

"Then you may not know that his father Fata was Muslim. The mother was not. In fact, she was a hunchbacked animist."

Nandi glanced back over her own shoulder, as if checking for a hump.

Babatunde chuckled. "While not exactly a beauty mark, in that time deformities were often considered magical. Now, at this time, Berbers had come raiding south, and were destroying Fata's kingdom a bit at a time. Fata was old, and unable to lead his people in battle. Fata's advisors told him that if he married this humpbacked woman, she would bear a great King. So he married her."

"Ah."

"Even though the Berbers were ravaging them, Fata's prophecy gave the Mandinka hope. His wife was allowed to keep her beliefs; the child was raised in a home respectful of both ways. And in time, Son Djata became a great King who freed his people and repulsed the Berbers."

Nandi was quiet for a few seconds, and then said, "You are a man of Islam. Your people believe in one God. My people believe in many forms of God. How can we reconcile?"

"I live in the real world," Babatunde said. "Would I rather all men saw the same light I see? Yes. Would I make widows and orphans to create such a world? No."

"And if I see the divine in trees and clouds," asked Nandi, "in the rushing of waters and the play of fishes? What if I hear my ancestors murmuring from the earth?"

"Allah made the world, and all it contains. To gain true union with that world is to approach union with the divine. The fruits will be your *actions*. I cannot, will not judge your heart without them."

They walked a while longer, then Babatunde said, "There is love in your heart for Kai?"

She looked up at Babatunde, and her face, while strong as a young boy's, was also yearning. "I was not married for love," she said. "You know this. I am not a child. And yet . . . both my father and Abu Ali chose their children's partners carefully, with the thought that love can blossom between those who are suited one to another."

Wisely, Babatunde declined to speak.

"I am profoundly grateful that Kai was chosen for me." She paused, fully aware that she had yet to answer the Sufi's question. "Tell me. You were Lamiya's tutor when she was promised to Kai's brother. Did she love Ali?"

"In truth?"

"Please."

"No," he said. "She admired and respected him."

Nandi shook her head. "That is not enough for me. All I have is my honor, my body, my heart. I could not give those things to a man I did not love. I could not lay in his bed, give him children, share his burdens, know that the one earthly life I have been given is shared for power, and not love. I was raised to accept this, but I cannot."

She exhaled harshly. "So. Finally, your question. Yes. I love Kai. I have since we were children. Since first he chased me into a stream and we were both spanked when we ran home with dripping clothes."

Babatunde chuckled. "I remember that, and counseled Abu Ali to halve his proposed strokes, but double the time you had to wait to receive them."

She shook her head. "The longest hours of my life." She gave a long, sincere sigh. "I love Kai, Babatunde, and know that I should have been first wife. It should have been *me*." As she said this something broke in her voice, and for a moment Babatunde could see through the carefully cultivated emotional reserve. And just as swiftly, the shell formed once again, and the window was gone. "And something happened. I know not what. And he withdrew from me."

She looked at Babatunde as if hoping that he had answers for her. "No," she said finally. "I didn't expect anything. My only thought is that he did not return my feelings. And I made my peace with that. I did."

"And opened your heart to another?"

"No!"

"You spoke your heart to another?"

She nodded her head.

"The young man in the barn?"

She seemed startled, but nodded her head again.

"He should not have come here." And now, at last, his voice grew stern. "For the new wife of a Wakil to meet with a man of past acquaintance, alone and unchaperoned, is by itself grounds for divorce."

Nandi froze. "No. Say that you jest."

"You did not know?" He watched her carefully.

"I . . ." Her lips pressed together tightly, and she closed her eyes. "I made a terrible mistake. I will not again. From the time my father decided that the wedding with Kai would go forward, Chalo has been forbidden to see me. He wished only to know that I was happy, and to say goodbye."

"And that is all?"

"That is all." She stopped, suddenly startled by a thought. "How did you know Chalo came?"

His only answer was a smile.

"Will you tell Kai?"

"I do not know." It was the honest truth.

"I understand," she said. "But Babatunde . . . if you choose not to do so, I will never give you reason to wish you had. I swear this."

Babatunde's lips turned upward at the corners. "By the one God?"

"By that force that created the universe and all of its beauty, that force that watches over the hall of my ancestors."

"Do we see the same mountain?"

"Yes," she said. "And not, I think, from very different paths."

"Let me think on these things," he said.

CHAPTER FIFTY-SEVEN

DOWN A DARK HIGHWAY RODE CHALO, bound for Wichita, and Cetshwayo's manor. He crooned a low, mournful Zulu song. In addition to being a blooded warrior of his people, in addition to his duties as houndsman, Chalo was a soloist in one of the most distinguished Zulu choral groups, famous as far as the courts of Gupta. His voice, like his heart, was powerful. But unlike his voice, his heart was breaking. The song helped him to find the strength to ride on, to accept that which he could not change.

He loved Nandi for who she was: the niece of the greatest warrior who had ever lived, daughter of their tribal leader, and the most beautiful woman in the world. It was madness to think that one such as she could ever have belonged to him.

But the moon was out of reach that men might be inspired to dream, and dream he would. And sing he would. And between dreams and song, there would be a way to live his life without Nandi, and he would find it.

So enmeshed in thought was Chalo that he was slower than usual to notice the approaching horsemen. Still, they were a spear's-cast away when he broke from thoughts of love and gave full attention to their presence. There was nothing apparent to give alarm, but Chalo's blood began to quicken. Although they hunched in their saddles, their horses were superb, and they rode with perfect balance. They were feigning fatigue or boredom. These men were not what they seemed.

Chalo's nerves burned, but he welcomed the sensation: a chance to vent his frustration on would-be assailants would be wonderful. If cutpurses they were, truly they had chosen the wrong man and the wrong night!

"Who goes there?" he called, hand drifting closer to his *umkhonto*.

"Fear not," said one. "We are merely wayfarers."

"Hold to your side of the road, then."

There were two of them, cloaked in robes dark enough to blend their outlines with the night. Of course, he could be wrong. . . . They might merely be travelers on a lonely road, approaching an armed stranger. Perhaps what he assumed to be dissemblance was merely anxiety.

The smaller of the two passed him first. "Good journey, friend."

"Good journey to you."

As the second man approached he gestured expansively, smiling, hands open and empty.

A third man, hidden until now, stepped out onto the road behind the Zulu, whirling a leather strap above his head.

Chalo's keen senses alerted him an instant too late. He wheeled around in his saddle, but the stone had already been released, and struck him squarely on the side of the head. The young Zulu tumbled from his horse, but a lifetime of training did not fail him: despite his pain-muddied thoughts he rolled to one knee and began drawing his spear. No time. The smaller man had goosed his horse up and unfurled a whip, casting it with snake-swiftness to curl around Chalo's neck.

Choking, the young Zulu's fingers dug for the coils, struggling to loosen them, but his brain was too dazed from the stone-strike. He crashed onto his side.

Chalo fought for breath that would not come, and struggled against unconsciousness as if it were death. Although not that great darkness, it was as inevitable as the end of life itself.

"He was very alert," said Omar Pavlavi after Chalo's struggles had ceased. "Bind his arms and legs."

CHAPTER FIFTY-EIGHT

STUMBLING ALONG WITH THE OTHERS, Aidan was herded through a mile of twisting corridors into another group holding pen. The cells were matted with stinking straw and were poorly ventilated through tiny barred windows. He felt tumbled back into the past, into a world he barely allowed himself to remember. His skin crawled with the sense of sheer confinement, uncertainty, the feeling that his fate was completely out of his hands.

No. I control my destiny, he thought, attempting to stave off panic. The sights and sounds and smells of this were worse than anything he had experienced in ten years, since the first slave pens in Djibouti Harbor.

"Get the hell in there, pigbelly!"

Aidan breathed a silent prayer that this would be a very temporary lodging. The men were pushed in until there was no more room to sit or lie, until they were shoulder to shoulder and belly to back. The stench of fear and rage was almost overwhelming. Inevitably, tensions began to rise, jostling and shoving and cursing growing more intense by the minute. These men were more than ready to hurt each other for the pleasure of strangers. Some of them actually seemed eager.

They elbowed each other, fighting for room, for air. Just when Aidan feared that the shoving would lead to blows the guards returned, and their cell door opened. The guards might have lacked humanity, but their discipline and caution were admirable. The prisoners never had a moment's opportunity to revolt, to turn on their captors, to convert bondage into a desperate scramble for freedom. The door swung back and locked into place, opening a dark passageway. If Kai was correct, it would lead to an arena only a few cubits to the side—small enough for the milling, thrashing, panicked slaves to find each other.

"Go on! Get out!" the guard said. Two men behind him held cheap pistols that they kept pointed directly at the prisoners. Cheap those weapons might have been, but Aidan had seen flimsier blow men straight to hell.

The slaves were silent, knotted up with tension. In the corridor they were fitted with leather hoods. Aidan's stank of sweat and old dried blood.

It blotted out vision, but he could breathe through nose and mouth slits. Then he was told to place his hand on the shoulder of the man in front of him, and march.

From Aidan's perspective, the darkness was absolute, and absolutely claustrophobic as they were marched in.

He could *hear* the crowd but not *see* them. And hear the voice of the announcer as it rang over the roar of a thousand greedy throats. The crowd had come for blood, and blood they would have.

"Peace be unto you, gentlemen!" cried the announcer. "The Pharaoh's court welcomes you to the evening's entertainment, a battle royale, with the last man standing to receive his weight in pig fat!"

That feeble witticism triggered a general roar of appreciation.

Aidan's breathing constricted. If he peered down toward the nose slit, he could catch a sliver of light, but nothing really useful.

"Let the battle begin!"

At the instant that he heard that cry, Aidan dropped onto his back, knees up to his belly, elbows clinched at his sides, chin tucked against his chest. He heard cheers and groans and the sounds of blows and harsh breathing. He heard curses and shuffling feet, and the dull patter of coins tossed onto the sand by an appreciative audience.

When a foot struck his side he grabbed for the leg, rolled over it to force the man down, struck a sledgehammer blow to the groin. This sensitivity Kai had taught him: to touch one part of a man's body was to know where all the rest of it had to be.

The air clotted with strangled grunts and screams as, one after another, the blindfolded combatants went down. Bones crunched. Aidan had come back into a low position, crouching this time. A man stumbled against him, went down, and Aidan finished him with a vicious series of elbows to the head. When the man went limp, Aidan hunched back down again.

At first the crowd had booed his actions, but as some of the observers began to understand his tactics, there were shouts of encouragement for *al zalil*, "the sneaky one."

The sand beneath his feet became tacky with what he could only imagine was blood. His ears rang with desperate struggles, choking sounds, the splintering of a bone.

At last most of them were down, and moaning. He heard the attendants haul them away. How many opponents remained? One? Two?

Two, he thought. He remained very, very still, allowing the others to move first. *There*: his ears picked up one, to the left, moving toward him. It was all Aidan could do to control his breathing, to prevent himself from gulping for air. That would give him away, and begin the disintegration of his own structure. It was quite possible that the other two thought they were the only ones. The crowd could give him away, of course, but their agitated rumble suggested that they were amused by the situation, and approving of his strategy.

The other two men circled each other, each locating his adversary by sound. They crept closer and closer together, and then collided. Fists hammered skin, men gasped, and one went down hard enough to raise a cloud of sand. Aidan took a chance and came out of his crouch, took two leaping steps, and flung himself, low. Something whistled past his cheek, grazing and bruising skin. Then he had his hands on one of the men, wrapped his arms around the man's knees, and rolled him down. There was a brief, terrific struggle. Aidan smashed a sledgehammer fist into an already wet and sticky face, and the man went limp. Aidan rolled up, away from the second man, and froze again.

He could hear his own heartbeat, and above it, the second man's desperate wheezing. Sand crunched, followed by another pause. Whispery sliding sounds as the man pivoted *this* way and then *that.*

The Irishman weaved backward just in time to avoid a thrashing kick that cost his single remaining adversary his balance. The man's supporting foot slid, and he fell and then lurched up, blowing blood or mucus from his nose with a slobbering exhalation. *There.* Aidan knew where the man was as clearly as if his eyes had been open. He kicked with the side of his foot, as Kai had taught him, his heel spearing into ribs and gut. Something cracked, and the man went down cursing.

The crowd cheered, and the horn blew.

Aidan was the last man standing.

In the audience, Kai watched, and was well pleased. He had held his breath during the last few moments, uncertain of Aidan's tactic. The kick had been risky, requiring too much commitment, but ultimately a man must make his own decisions about such things. If Aidan had gone against his advice, well, his old friend had still done just fine.

Just as important to his plan, he watched the tall, thin man that the arena manager had pointed out to him. This was Muata, agent for Fazil Dosa, industrialist and third of the New Alexandrian "Triumvirate"—with the Caliph and Admiral bin Jeffar—the three men suspected to be leading the way to war.

Muata was said to attend all the fights, looking for talent. And Muata had observed Aidan's display with great pleasure.

Now, of course, the game truly began.

CHAPTER FIFTY-NINE

11 Rabi al-Anwal A.H. 1295
(Friday, March 15, 1878)

STILL USING HIS FALSE NAME, Kai arranged a meeting with Muata. "So . . . I watched your man. Like you say . . . he is very good. Very unusual."

"I believe he can beat the German."

"Heh," chuckled Muata. "That would be a day."

"Yes."

"So why don't you match them?"

"I must return home to Azania," Kai lied. "I haven't the time or the patience to train my man for that fight. You do. I would sell him to you at an excellent price. You will wager for me, and we will share the proceeds. You train him, feed him, house him."

Dosa's agent stroked his chin. "If a price can be reached . . . come! Let us have refreshment, and speak of business."

"A man after my own heart." Kai grinned.

"And your wallet! Watch out for your Alexanders."

Kai rubbed his hands with relish. "A bargaining man, then! Let the game begin."

So they sat and drank coffee, and talked business. The blend was unusually smooth and flavorful, and Kai was of a mind to ask that a few pounds of the beans be thrown in to sweeten the deal. "What grind is this?" he asked.

"*Kopi Luwak!*" said his host. "You approve?"

"Very much."

"Well, it comes from the island of Djava. It is quite a delicacy here in Alexandria." Muata's eyes sparkled. "Would you care to hear more?"

"Of course," Kai said and sipped again. Delicious!

"Well, first the beans are fed to a small furry animal called a *fungo* cat."

"Umm?"

"Then, some time later, the droppings are harvested—"

Kai stopped, staring.

"Oh, the beans are well cleaned, but the cat's digestive juices have tempered the beans, providing the exquisite bouquet you enjoy."

Kai stared at his cup. It was rude not to at least *pretend* to enjoy the food and drink served by a host, but he couldn't get the image out of his mind. *Kopi Luwak* indeed. Was there no end to New Alexandrian decadence?

He pretended to sip at his cup, continuing to smile and talk, but that image continued to recur.

But stirring in and around his wave of revulsion was a bit of genuine curiosity . . . and mischief. Kai wondered again if a deben of *Kopi Luwak* beans might be obtained. He would enjoy providing a new, and unique experience for his old friend Babatunde . . .

And perhaps having the pleasure of watching the Yoruba's face as his morning brew's origins were described in loving detail.

And at that thought, he smiled and raised his cup in salute.

Later that day, Kai went to Aidan's solitary cell. He wished he could have hugged his old friend in congratulation, but was forced to assume that their words and actions could be somehow witnessed. All he could afford was a brusque "well done."

Kai maintained his emotional and physical distance until he heard the patter of feet approaching down the corridor. They had only a few moments together before Muata's men arrived. Caution warred with affection.

What if this goes terribly wrong? What if you never see him again?

Affection won, and Kai hugged Aidan hard. "Even now," he whispered, "if you change your mind, it is not too late."

"Do you have doubts?"

"How could I not? Still, you have learned well, and it is your choice to make."

"Did you like the fight?" Aidan's eyes shifted away. "I mean, did I do well?"

Kai smiled broadly, remembering the sight. "Quite well indeed." He searched his own emotions. Had he himself done right? Made sufficient effort to talk his friend out of this perilous course? "You are certain you wish to go through with this?"

"I've come this far. . . ."

Kai rested his forehead against Aidan's. "I am with you. Always. May Allah give wings to your quest."

"Fock the wings. Just give me a hand out when I'm done."

"Aidan, Aidan." Kai shook his head. "You'll always be my favorite infidel."

The door opened, and Muata's men appeared. Without a word, they shackled and chained Aidan's feet.

"You take care of him," Kai said. "He's good, as his kind go."

"We know how to deal with thin-lips," one of the guards said. "The boss paid a fistful for him, and we like to protect his investments."

Aidan went with them, with only one backward glance at Kai, then was gone. Gone.

No more way around it now, for Aidan. The only way out was through.

Aidan suffered a jouncing half-an-hour's cart ride, bringing him to Dosa's fighter compound, a courtyard walled with white brick and stone. Guards swung a broad wire gate open, and then locked it behind them. Aidan gazed back at it longingly, tasting a jolt of fear as the latches engaged.

The men behind the fence were a coarse bunch who ceased their rolling, grunting, and sweating on raked sand to get a better look at the newcomer. They seemed a forest of scar tissue and knotted muscle. His relatively smooth limbs made him stand out like a polished stone in a gravel pit.

Dosa himself greeted Aidan on that first day. The industrialist was a black man of average height and build who wore far more jewelry and golden cloth than any man of the south. "This is your new home," said Dosa. "And these are your brothers. They are a rough lot, but I think you'll get along. This is your trainer, Rhino."

"Rhino" was a huge, blunt Italian with deceptively intelligent eyes, and eyebrows so pale they were almost invisible. Now that Aidan noticed, all of Rhino's hair was extremely fine, almost downy. He inspected Aidan emotionlessly, and then without warning of any kind, swung a thick gnarled arm and buffeted him across the face. Aidan had time to roll with it just a hair, but the blow threw him halfway across the compound, to land in a dazed sprawl against the wall.

"Well?"

Rhino shrugged his mountainous shoulders. "His reflexes are fast enough."

They watched as Aidan pulled himself back to his feet.

"And he's tough enough." Rhino grunted in approval. "He'll do."

"Good. Aidan—you follow Rhino's instructions to the letter, and you just may avoid crippling."

Aidan rubbed his face. "By the German, or by your man?"

"Flesh doesn't care who bruises it," Dosa said. "Work hard. This is your home now. Sleep. It is most of what you will do here. Sleep, and eat, and train."

"And fight?"

"Yes. And fight."

Rhino arched his nearly invisible eyebrows. "You are eager?"

"If I win for you, earn gold for you, I can earn my freedom, and rejoin my wife. I am eager for this. Fighting is just the doorway."

Dosa looked at him strangely, as if just seeing him for the first time. "I heard about your fight. You may have promise. We will speak again."

Rhino led him through the courtyard and to a lantern-lit corridor on the far side, and from there to a series of small rooms. The fifth one was bare-walled, and Rhino shoved him in. "Be back later wit' your t'ings. Rest." The door closed, but Aidan noted that there was no telltale click of a lock. So, then, he had some small freedom of motion. That was reassuring, in a way. He curled himself into a ball on the straw-strewn floor, and tried to sleep.

Before he could even begin to drift off the door opened, and three men stood there, each of them larger than Aidan.

"Look at the mouse," said the first. "So peaceful."

"Should we let 'im sleep," asked the second, "or mebbe break 'is 'ead a little?"

Aidan rolled over on his side, peering up at them. "There'll be time enough for head-breaking tomorrow, don't you think? More fun in breaking the head of a rested mouse, I'd think."

The first fighter laughed. "Yer right aboot that. Sleep tight, smooth-skin. Tomorrow we'll see the color of yer blood."

"And maybe a bit of yours," he said.

"Ooh. Ye talk so swell." They laughed and left him. Aidan's smile wavered. He was far more frightened than he was willing to let on.

Once the door shut, he stood and walked to his cell's barred window. From there he could look out on New Alexandria, and up into a starry sky. The moon was terribly bright, the same moon that illuminated the sky over the crannog. Somewhat to his surprise, he heard himself begin to pray. "I don't believe in You," he whispered. "But if You're there, and You give a damn, please help me. I've never felt so alone in all my life."

He paused. "And if You won't," he added, "then fock Ye."

And shaking, he crawled into a dusty corner of the cell, and fell asleep.

CHAPTER SIXTY

THE DIRT-COVERED ARENA was filled with white men performing body-weight exercises: the spiderish push-ups called *dhands*; rolling forward, backward, and sideways; gymnastics to develop balance and spring. All these, he knew, were merely preliminaries.

For most of an hour Aidan was right in the middle of the group, suffering and sweating along with the rest of them. Then they were paired up.

"This is the training ground," Rhino said. "Each of you was bought at a price: some for good prices, others on the cheap. No matter. You belong to Master Dosa now, and this ain't the place to cripple each other up before you've had a chance to earn the money back. So rein it in. No biting, pulling of dangly bits, or eye gouging. You get a lock, and I want the partner to submit. Say it, or slap the ground, or slap your body or your partner's body, then break and begin again. Understood?" His diction was precise and intelligent if untutored.

All replied, "Yes, Sidi."

Aidan was the last to answer. "Yes, Sidi!"

"New man," Rhino said. "Your name?"

"Aidan."

"Irish name. Your master didn't love you enough to give you a proper name?"

"I guess not, Sidi."

"We can do better. We'll call ye . . . Aden."

"I don't understand," Aidan said.

Rhino grinned his broken-toothed grin. "It's a piece of water next to Djibouti. You got a problem with that?"

"No, Sidi."

"Then get to work."

Later that afternoon the men in the training arena yelled derison or encouragement as the practice fighting began. Aidan was matched with one of the big men who had entered his cell the night before.

"Ready for a bone-breaking?" his prospective tormentor said.

Aidan shifted his balance, sand crunching under his bare feet. "Make your move, pig-face."

"Name's Hotep," he spat. "I'll carve it on your stomach."

"Either there, or on a tombstone. Your move." Aidan was so calm and centered about his response that for a moment the bigger man hesitated. He was also, Aidan noted, entirely too close. The Irishman stepped in and smashed a forearm to his face, following up with a knee to the gut. Hotep went down like a felled tree. The entire group stopped, silent, as he tried to get up. The fighting slaves looked at each other, and then at the bigger man, and then at Aidan with newfound respect.

Rhino walked over to them. He looked at Hotep, who still gasped for air as he tried to rise.

"Good move," said Rhino. "Show it to me?"

"Won't work on ye," Aidan said, deliberately coarsening his speech.

The huge man's little eyes shifted behind the gristle. "And why not?"

" 'Cause ye know it's comin', and 'cause yer Rhino."

After a long pause, Rhino nodded his head. "You've got a brain, all right. Let's see you again. Quat!"

As he called out, a second man rose, this one looking a bit unnerved. "Sidi!" said Quat.

"Give him a workout."

Aidan managed to swallow his fear, muttering, "Remember what Kai said. Remember what Kai said."

"What?" asked Rhino.

" 'Always go for the head,' " Aidan said.

Rhino grunted. "Not always true, but we'll see. Begin!"

Quat balled his fists and came after Aidan. Aidan ducked, went low, and rammed his shoulder into Quat's belly, uprooting him. Quat clipped Aidan with a wild, swinging blow, but Aidan was able to roll with it. He stayed close, close, hammering with both hands, and Quat went to one knee.

"Halt!" screamed Rhino. "His knee is touching the ground, boy. That's all we need here. You're not to hurt the merchandise."

He approached and circled Aidan, studying him with care. Then he said, "Hold still," and began to probe and knead Aidan's dense and hard-won physique. "You're a sound one," he finally said. "Where'd you learn to fight?"

"Here," he said. "There. If you wanted a woman or a good meal, you'd better know how to take a man down."

Rhino nodded. "Good. I notice you didn't go for his head."

"I took your advice."

Rhino furrowed his brow. "Don't be too smart. All right—exercises for you, no more fists for a bit. Get to it!"

Strenuous hours later, the men finally completed the day's workouts. They lined up for a huge, coarse, but nourishing meal, and lastly, were massaged.

Hotep grunted, rubbing the side of his head. "Ye caught me good, boyo. Not been clocked like that for quite a time."

The masseuse's fingers dug deep. "Ooooh!" Aidan moaned. "That feels good."

"The life here's not bad, if you have a taste for it. You like the girl?"

Aidan glanced at her. She was pretty in a sharp-nosed, pale-skinned way.

"Ye can have her for the night," Hotep said.

"She's delicious."

The girl blushed. Her hands kneaded his muscles more vigorously. "My name Vida," she said.

"But I have a wife," Aidan protested. "And a child."

"They not here," she said, leaning over closer to his ear. "Vida here."

"Yes."

"Vida make you happy?"

He took her hands and gazed into her eyes. "You are beautiful. But I love my wife."

Vida smiled shyly and lowered her eyes.

"She lucky. You . . . buy her freedom?"

He paused. "Yes. Freedom and safety."

She gazed at him, all seductiveness gone. What remained was a vulnerable, frightened girl. "You good man."

Then Vida turned and fled the room.

Hotep scoffed at him. "Now why you go and do that? You married? So what? Ye here now, man. Have fun. Have fun." He began to grope his own swarthy masseuse. She reached beneath his towel to stroke him. As they chuckled and fondled each other, Aidan retreated from the room.

CHAPTER SIXTY-ONE

THE LAIR WAS NOT A MOUNTAIN CAVE, or far redoubt. It was the disheveled castle of a northern New Djibouti noble who had squandered his inheritance and was more than willing to accept gold for a month's lease, and absolute discretion.

There within the shadowed walls gathered the Hashassin.

In the basement beneath the castle, Chalo pulled against the chains binding his wrists, attaching him to the dank wall, screaming his rage and fear. The chains had soft leather wraps inside. He pulled against them, but despite his best efforts, made not the slightest impact on the thick iron links.

"Who are you?" he called. "What do you want?" He had screamed this intermittently for the last two hours, with no answer.

Somewhat to his surprise this time the door opened, and a man wearing a black cloak and a black leather mask entered. He set a bowl of beef on the ground, out of Chalo's reach, and then pushed it farther toward him with a stick.

"You say you are Cetshwayo's dog trainer," said the masked man in Arabic.

Chalo looked at the meat, and his stomach rumbled. He sniffed the bowl suspiciously, but did not touch it. "Yes. It is true," he answered in the same language.

"He values you?"

Chalo raised his head proudly. "Above any of his servants."

"Good. He will pay for your release?"

Chalo seemed to swell. "Gold!"

"Good." The man seemed satisfied. "Eat. Negotiations may take some time."

Chalo seemed satisfied with the answer, but still did not eat. The masked man reached down, and with the point of a knife dug a chunk of meat from the center of the bowl, lifting his mask to pop it into his mouth.

Chalo nodded. Slowly at first, then with growing eagerness, he devoured the food before him. The Hashassin left, locking the door behind him. Once outside, he doffed his mask, and a second Hashassin addressed him.

"He believes he will survive?"

"Of course. All men wish to believe in miracles."

"Good. It would be ill if he mutilated himself trying to escape."

"Watch him carefully."

The second bowed. "On my life."

CHAPTER SIXTY-TWO

21 Rabi al-Awwal A.H. 1295
(Monday, March 25, 1878)

As Kai rode the last few miles to Dar Kush, all memories and speculations blurred together. So much depended upon Aidan, and he feared that all they had taught the Irishman would be insufficient. His dearest friend might be killed, or crippled. He might fail to find the code scroll, or be captured and tortured. He might simply be unable to escape once his assignment was complete. . . .

So many mights, so many possible catastrophes.

The closer he got to Dar Kush, the more Kai found himself looking for broken fence wire, or fire smoke, or sign of a runaway . . . anything to justify his increasingly urgent sense that something was amiss.

"Master's home!" cried Festus.

"Good afternoon, Festus. Things well while I'm away?"

"Oh, not so good, Sidi," he said.

"Was Azinza's party a success?"

"Oh, birthday party came off fine, like I knew it would."

"Good, good. What then?" He had noticed a broken strand of wire in the north pasture. "Problems with the herd?"

Festus scratched his graying hair. "Missin' a few cattle. Them Kikuyu been lively."

"Well, think not to change the leopard's spots," Kai said. "We understand each other. It's a game, and an unnegotiated part of their wages."

Nandi and Lamiya emerged from the great house. They each took an arm, and Lamiya squeezed hers tightly.

"What's wrong?" he asked. "I couldn't get old Festus to say."

Lamiya dropped her voice. "It's horrible, Kai," she said. "Olaf and Morgan are both dead."

Kai stopped. "Morgan? The girl we sold to Djidade last year?"

"Yes."

Nandi also lowered her voice to a whisper. "They say her husband caught them in bed together. Used an axe."

"Horrible!" Kai said. "I would never have thought it. Old Olalye always seemed as mild as cream." He scratched his head, sighing. "Trouble there. Old Olaf One-Ear. He could be a mischief-maker and a slacker, but I never thought anything like this. His mother is still alive, I think. See that she's taken care of, would you?"

Lamiya nodded.

"And what of Olalye?" Kai said.

"There was nothing to be done. Fodjour slew him that same day."

Rough justice. That must have been dreadful for all, but order had to be maintained. Still . . .

"Are you all right?" He studied each of them in turn. "Both of you?"

"Fine," Nandi said. "It happens. Slaves drink and fight, and sometimes . . ." She shrugged. "Our servants are a little scared, but fine."

"I'll have a talk with our boss boys, but later. A dust-covered wayfarer like myself would like nothing more than a hot bath, a meal, and a quiet evening with his ladies."

They managed to smile at him.

"Why do I have the feeling that such simple pleasures are not on the menu?"

"Oh, Kai," Lamiya said, squeezing his arm. "The hot bath can certainly be accommodated."

"And the meal as well," said Nandi. "But the quiet evening . . ."

"Have I forgotten something?"

"The dinner party?" asked Lamiya. "Fodjour and Chifi? A chance for them to get to know each other better? In truth, I thought you would return too late."

Kai smacked his forehead with the palm of his hand. "Allah burn me for a matchmaker. Ah, well . . . fine. Let us make the most of the quiet time we have until then. . . ."

"Husband," said Nandi, "already, three supplicants rest in the parlor, seeking audience."

"Ayye. Their business?"

"The choral house and the bank."

"Al-Wali preserve me. Now I know why father's hair was gray before its time. Very well, give me not even time for a quiet rack of lamb," he said. "Lead me instead to the slaughter."

*   *   *

Kai had long noted the warmth and ease of conversation between Chifi and Fodjour, and had decided to play Oshun and lend romance a hand. With this in mind, he had approved the dinner party.

It was lush but small, held in the eastern formal dining room. Just a few families, with Kai making very subtle moves to link Fodjour and Chifi closer together. Throughout the meal, a group of servants sang and played their simple musical instruments, providing atmosphere. The guests talked, and listened, and offered appreciative murmurs. They dined on *kitfo*, with freshly minced, lean and tender chopped beef seasoned with *nitter kebbesh* butter, served *lebleb*-style, very rare indeed.

"Chifi," said Fodjour, "do you think you might one day travel to the homeland to complete your education?"

She shrugged her broad shoulders dismissively. "Oh, no . . . I learn more from Father just puttering around the shop."

Her father patted her hand. "Still, dear, you might want to think of it. There are many things about the world beyond the reach of my mind and heart. These things I cannot teach."

Chifi smiled indulgently. "Perhaps I don't wish to learn them, *Abbabba*. Perhaps I am content just as things are."

Kai wanted a few minutes to speak to Fodjour. He had been forced to do a hard, terrible thing, and Kai wanted to be certain his old friend was dealing with it well.

A group of slaves hovered about, catering to their every culinary whim. Allahbas Berhar occupied Djidade Berhar's usual chair, representing her ailing husband. Although she attempted to sound merry, Kai noted a certain forced calm straining both voice and carriage. Doubtless that ugly business with her servants. It was enough to put anyone ill at ease.

"Kai," she ventured, "as both officer and Wakil, what is your opinion of the military levies?"

Kai considered. "New taxes? In most cases I would oppose such a measure, but as you know, I believe that war is coming, and that it is best we maintain our troops in high alertness."

"Still." Her voice was carefully modulated. "You actually lent the majority of your own personal force to the territorial guard."

"It is best to lead by example." He saw Fodjour on the other side of the room, and wished for an excuse to cut his conversation with Allahbas short.

"But," Fodjour's mother continued, "doesn't that leave you a bit . . . unprotected?"

Kai bowed. "Allah protects the righteous, my lady."

The slaves concluded their concert, and the guests applauded. "Well done," Kai called. "Your reward is waiting for you in the kitchen."

Nandi stood. "And now we have a special treat," she said. "Our Dahoman visitors have consented to entertain us with their traditional music."

Yala and Ganne emerged from the central foyer, followed by twenty of their warriors, streaming into two arcing rows. For a few seconds they paused as if girding themselves, faces composed in concentration.

Then the eldest sister began to strum a miniature *lelit samäy*, not much larger than a Ugandan *lamellaphone*, but capable of far more complex melodics. The rhythms were supple and engaging. Then they began to hum, and they blended the sounds together into a single tapestry, until it seemed that they were human instruments. As they wove their harmony they swayed, so that even the most muscular and aggressive of them were graceful and appealing. Kai found it enchanting, and his guests did as well, weaving in time and applauding their efforts roundly.

Allahbas Berhar leaned toward Kai. "They are really quite . . . feminine. I had heard so many fierce tales that I was uncertain what to expect."

Maputo Kokossa agreed. "They are gentle indeed. It is a shame that their men do not see after them better, ease them to their proper place in the world."

Kai repressed a chuckle at this, both contemplating the sort of man who could dominate such women, and noting that Kokossa himself had hardly prepared his only daughter for an entirely womanly existence.

The songs continued through the entire second course, and then with an elaborate flourish, the Dahomy concluded their recital and filed from the room heading west toward the kitchen, where they would be feasted.

Feeling vastly content, Kai leaned back into his chair, and belched loudly. The guests thumped the table in approval. A matching series of eructations ensued, followed by much good-natured laughter. He grinned in satisfaction and leaned toward Kokossa. "Would you care to retire to the patio? We have a fine bit of Turkish in the hookah."

Kokossa nodded and stretched. "Just the thing after a good meal. A shame you don't partake, Babatunde."

"I have enough bad habits of my own without adding yours," the little Yoruba said.

"Ah . . . for instance?"

"A fondness for the company of the opinionated."

They adjourned to a covered room set at the eastern edge of the house. Its roof was of glass, but the northern wall was open so that they could watch the night sky or gaze north or east. A roaring fireplace provided heat and a measure of light. The women sat in a separate section of the patio, so that the tobacco smoke drifted away west of them. Nandi disappeared for a few minutes, doubtless to the kennel, because on reappearance the great IziLomo trotted obediently behind her, and sat placidly at her chair-side. The hound looked up at Kai, made a low whining sound, and then backed away to the safety of his mistress.

Kai repressed a chuckle: dogs, it seemed to him, could be more honest in their relationships than humans.

He unbuckled his sword and placed it at his side, then took a hose from the hookah and inhaled with deep satisfaction.

And there they talked, puffing and enjoying a leisurely evening.

Kokossa turned to Babatunde. "My friend—" he began. He flinched, and then his expression froze in a puzzled frown. The inventor fell forward and slumped out of his chair.

He began to convulse, shivering and thrashing so that for a moment they were uncertain of what had happened, or what to do. Kai sensed the truth before he saw any actual proof of his suspicions. For a long moment he felt suspended in time, like an insect frozen in amber. Then he screamed, "Down!"

Lamiya and Nandi exchanged a glance, then Kai's First bolted from the adults' to the children's table. Despite starting a second later, Nandi's long legs and speed served her well: she arrived a step before the Empress's niece. The two women swept the screaming children to the floor, shielding the helpless youngsters with their own bodies.

IziLomo stood between them and the door, head down, ears back, teeth bared, snarling warning out into the night.

Kai raised his head, and was driven back down by a volley of rifle shots.

"Damn!" said Kebwe. "Snipers."

"Yes," Kai snarled. "Covering retreat." He glanced at the fireplace. He seized a bucket of water and hurled it into the fire. The room clouded with steam and smoke.

Kebwe screamed and leapt. "Haii!"

"Out!" screamed Kai.

Shots pinged among them, but they managed to get the guests back into the house, to safety. Kai strapped on his *shamshir,* its forty digits of steel a comforting weight in his hand.

"In pursuit, they get to choose the ground," said Kebwe. "They will be waiting for us. We need men."

"Well thought," said Kai. "I know just the thing."

Ducking whenever he passed a window, Kai raced across Dar Kush's first floor through the main dining room, through the foyer and to the west wing and the kitchen, where the Dahomy had gone for their meal. The women were crowded in the nook and at the back porch, holding bountifully heaped plates of food. Not one of them touched the steaming victuals: all fixed their gazes on Kai as he exploded through the door.

And at this sight, he was well pleased. They had heard shots and screams, and were ready. Calm. Prepared and alert were the Dahomy, but not one had taken arms without summons. Practiced warriors indeed, they knew that precipitous action often interfered with a calculated defense. *Good*, thought Kai. He could make use of spirits as cool and firm as these.

His fist crashed against the oak counter rimming the kitchen. "Any woman who would be a warrior in my house this night, mount and follow me!"

"Sisters!" Ganne cried. "We ride!"

"Fodjour!" Kai screamed. "Take the Dahomy, get horses and meet us. Then return to protect my family."

"Aye!"

Fodjour ran past his mother, who sat on the floor glaring up at him with narrowed eyes. Swiftly, he glanced to either side, determined that no one watched. "Why, Mother?" he whispered. "Kokossa was harmless!"

"Fool!" she whispered, managing to convey both contempt and fear simultaneously. "I knew they would act, but not how or when. Stand fast! Prepare for whatever may be required."

"Bah!" he said, and headed toward the barn.

The two Hashassin in the rear glanced back over their shoulder, evaluating pursuit.

"He has no men," said the first gleefully, his red kerchief masking his face. "They are women only, the same breed who guarded the barn!"

"He must be mad."

Omar had agreed with his cousin Allahbas that murdering Kai of Dar Kush might be less desirable than simply crippling his ability to lead. Martyrs could be incredibly powerful rallying points. But Kokossa had been afforded no such protection: the death of an inventor would stir outrage, but not wide action.

On the other hand, an agreement not to simply *murder* the Wakil did not absolutely protect him. If Omar had the opportunity to capture Kai, or even slay him in single combat, such an end would not raise the same ire as a bullet from the shadows. *First the test, then the trap.* "Engage!" cried their leader. Without question or hesitation, like machines in human form, they wheeled their horses about.

"Hai!"

They charged to confront Kai and the Dahomy.

With a clang that sent sparks spiraling into the night, Kai deflected a sword-blow without riposting, riding onward, trusting in the riders behind him to kill his foe. He heard, but did not see the death stroke, a song of steel on flesh.

Beautiful.

The second man swung at Kai's head: Kai ducked, and took him in the midsection with his left fist. The colliding forces transformed the blow into a rib-cracker. The Hashassin tumbled from his horse, and struck the ground with a groan, leaving Kai's sight.

"Take him alive!" he called back, realizing that never before had he placed his safety in a woman's hands, but also realizing that he felt bless-edly secure in doing so.

Two Dahomy warriors leapt down, bracketing the Hashassin.

Temporarily disarmed, the killer pulled two knives from his belt. His arms snaked back and forth, weaving a deadly web. Ganne whipped her scarf from around her neck, snapping it like a whip. The seams had been invisibly weighted with lead, and the Hashassin ducked down only to dis-cover the first snap was a feint. The second caught him squarely on the temple. He dropped to his knees, knife tumbling from his right hand. Within moments he lay on his side, bound and helpless.

Kai had lost sight of the masked Hashassin leader, but knew this road, knew that there was no turn-off until a mile after an old wooden bridge up ahead. Surely that would give him enough time to—

He and his men thundered around the bend, and as they did, were alarmed by a glowing light. *The left side of the bridge was ablaze.*

Instantly, Kai grasped the Hashassin stratagem: on their way to Dar Kush, the killers had left some men behind, who had slathered the left side of the bridge in oil, and now set it aflame. Fleeing, the murderers spurred their horses through the narrow gap, clearly intending to seal it after the last fled to safety.

The man in the red kerchief was the last. Kai assumed him to be the leader, a man who would take the greatest danger for himself. Grudging admiration merely stoked his resolve.

The gap was narrow enough for Kai's horse to rear back in fear. No mind. Randa was a fine beast from a noble line, but not yet war-trained. But the Hashassin leader had dismounted, stood in the middle of the bridge with sword in hand even as the flames chewed away the left railings, his posture unmistakably one of challenge. Kai raised his pistol, and then lowered it. A chance to capture the leader, get some answers . . .

He dismounted, and strode toward the giant in the red kerchief. "Who are you?" Kai asked.

"Your death," the taller man said, and his sword leapt at Kai's neck in a downward arc.

The Hashassin's onslaught commenced at blinding speed and with ferocious skill. If not for countless hours of preparation at the hands of his beloved uncle, Kai would have perished within the first five breaths. Instead, he met stroke for stroke, bending and twisting to present angles that frustrated his taller opponent. The Hashassin strove to drive Kai toward the flames, but Kai stood his ground or managed to slide away as the fire crackled beside him, tongues licking at his pants until the fabric felt hot enough to ignite.

But his opponent flinched not, and Kai steeled himself and fought on. In defense he was like a reed in the wind, but a tiger on the attack. After the first few seconds the pace of engagement slackened, as he knew it must, and he was able to actually think for the first time since steel had touched steel. In that instant Kai saw a flaw, a possibility to deflect, riposte, and take the Hashassin in the ribs. Whether the wound was lethal or not would depend on his opponent's reactions in the next few seconds. *I have you.*

And with that thought his blood quickened, his own fever beginning to rise. Malik's blood within his veins burned with a heat to match that searing his left leg.

But as he deflected, Kai's sword shivered in his grip, and he felt it crack.

Damn! To his dismay and everlasting disgust, he now remembered that he held his *ceremonial shamshir,* one lighter and less tempered than the Benin man-killer he had carried to war. He had to retreat, or his adversary would simply shatter his sword and gut him.

Aching with humiliation and the effort needed to fight his own battle lust to a standstill, Kai stepped back. As if in response, the flames blossomed around them both. The Hashassin retreated through the fire seemingly without concern for injury, lifting his sword in ironic salute.

*   *   *

Omar brushed ashes from his clothes, gazing after the horsemen who bristled on the river's far side as flame swallowed the entire bridge. His clothing had been impregnated with a fire-retardant chemical, and the red scarf around his face prevented inhalation of flames or vapors. He had not been completely heedless of the danger, but hoped the Wakil had been even more unnerved.

"That was Kai of Dar Kush?" one of his men asked, impressed by the smoke rising from his leader's garments, but too wise in Omar's ways to let it be known.

"None other," the chief Hashassin said. "That was Malik's sword style . . . but something else, as well, something of which I am uncertain."

"But . . . surely he is inferior to you."

Their leader was thoughtful. "Surely," he said.

"Why did he retreat? The flames?"

"Perhaps. No," he said upon reflection. "I believe his sword may have been damaged."

His acolyte raised a heavy eyebrow. "They captured Ahmed."

"Then his journey ends tonight," Omar said. "My cousin will understand what is needed. Fear not. The game is in play."

CHAPTER SIXTY-THREE

THE CAPTURED KILLER was chained in a makeshift cell in Dar Kush's basement. So far he had suffered the expected pain, but remained unwilling to speak even a single word.

"Who sent you, dammit?" Kai demanded. "Speak!"

In reply, Ahmed turned his bruised face away from them, spitting blood onto the floor.

"We know you are Persian," Kai said. "By your actions, I think you Hashassin. Who hired you?" Their captive said nothing. "Very well," said Kai in his coldest voice. "Tomorrow you will be turned over to the territorial marshal. And then you will wish you were still in *civilized* hands. Sleep well." And with those words, Kai left.

Behind him, Ahmed tested and twisted his chains and only ceased when blood ran down his arms, dappling the wooden floor.

Now, alone in the dark, a sound escaped his battered lips, a thin, high wail of mourning, a fearful keening audible only to the walls of his dark and lonely cell.

Midnight approached and retreated. For solitary hours Ahmed had craned his head, listening to Dar Kush's silence, praying for a miracle. He would make pilgrimage. He would give half, no, two-thirds of all he earned for the rest of his life to the poor. He would—

Then the cell door opened. Fodjour Berhar stood in the doorway, a plate of fruit cradled in his hands.

No miracles, then, for either the Zulu boy or poor Ahmed.

"You know who I am?" Fodjour said.

Ahmed shook his head, but the gesture was a lie. Instinct told him that this man, standing in the doorway, was his ending.

"*Some eagles fly at night,*" said Fodjour.

"*But with dawn, the hatchlings die,*" the captive said in a numbed, beaten voice. No words had ever terrified him so fully, but Ahmed had answered as he had sworn to do.

"You have done well," Fodjour said. "You know that your wife and children will be cared for?"

Ahmed nodded, a slight sheen of madness in his eyes.

"Are you ready to fulfill your bargain?"

Another slow nod.

"Good. Good," said Fodjour. "I have brought you a meal. Just some
fruit."

The chained man lifted his hands. "I cannot feed myself," he said. He
hoped his meaning was clear: *The Prophet was explicit. I cannot end my life.*

"I understand," Fodjour said. "Here." Without another word he placed a
chunk of poisoned banana on the man's outstretched tongue.

"Estafghuar Allah." God, forgive me. And with that hopeful whisper upon his
lips, Ahmed began to chew.

CHAPTER SIXTY-FOUR

22 Rabi al-Awwal A.H. 1295
(Tuesday, March 26, 1878)

IN THE MORNING, a string of horsemen and one camel arrived at Dar Kush's gates.

They were greeted by yawning, straw-haired old Festus, who led them past the guard and into the kitchen. "He is in here," he said, escorting them down to the basement.

The door opened, casting a widening wedge of light which, finally, fell upon the sprawled and silent body of a dead man. The servant's eyes stretched with shock.

"Wakil! Wakil!" Festus screamed. "He's dead!"

Within minutes, cries and alarms had roused the entire household. Babatunde knelt by the dead man's side, examining his eyes and fingernails. "Poisoned," he said finally.

Lamiya was stunned. "But how could they get in the house? I thought the bridge was burned!"

"Rivers can be forded, given enough time. The more important question is: what did he know that was worth such risk to kill him?"

The Constable was a heavy, densely bearded man named Kareem T'Kuk who had a reputation for stolid, if uninspired efficiency. T'Kuk knotted his hands into fists, trying unsuccessfully to stop his trembling. "The Hashassin, if that they were, are silent as shadows. May as well try to stop the night."

"The attack last night was hardly silent," Babatunde said. "Precise, yes. Intended to deprive us of a great mind, and also to warn us. The precision is what disturbs me. . . . it implies not only a political motive, but accurate information about the affairs of this house." He gazed at them thoughtfully. "And from where, I wonder, does that information come?"

*   *   *

As Kai entered Lamiya's bedroom, Bitta, sitting on a hassock in the corner, came instantly and alertly to her feet. His First reclined against a
mountain of pillows, reading the Qur'an for the nineteenth time: once a
year, every year, since her eighth birthday. "Husband?" she said anxiously.
"It is you?"

"None other."

Lamiya placed the sacred text on her bed-stand. "You may go," she said
to her companion. Bitta nodded once to the imperial niece, once to the
Wakil, and left the room.

"Ah." Lamiya sighed when the door closed behind Bitta. "I had begun
to wonder if you would keep to your rooms this evening. It is good to see
you."

He shook his head. "I felt the need for your company."

"And I for yours. The events of the last hours frighten me . . . the murder, the suicide, an attack in our own home."

"Yes. Calculated to make us cautious, not so eager to back secession.
And to remove a valuable ally." He shook his head. "Poor Maputo. I trust
that Allah has shared those secrets Master Kokossa sought most keenly."

She extended a slender hand, caressed his cheek. "These waters run
deep, Kai."

"No deeper than your eyes." He leaned toward her, and she pushed him
away.

"No," she said. She held his hands tightly, commandingly, and locked
eyes with him as if she would communicate by force of will alone. "Listen
to me, Husband. You must understand: no matter what you do now, your
enemies will make play of it. If you act, you are rash. If you do not, you
are a coward. If you enlist followers, you are dragging your friends to hell.
If you act alone, you have no trust in your companions."

Kai pressed his palms against his temples. "My head hurts."

"These are the waters your father hoped you would avoid. You should
have been a scholar, perhaps a shaykh. Instead, you are in a world where
nothing is as it seems."

"Are you as you seem?" he asked.

"What do you see?"

Kai gazed into her eyes. "I see a woman raised from birth to a role, told
only that she must obey those who raised her, who took a chance on a
young man who needed her more than he needed food, or water, or air."

"And what kind of woman is that?"

"One easy to underestimate."

"Would such a woman make a mistake?" she asked. "Choose the wrong man?"

"I hope not."

She opened her arms to him, and Kai went to her. They held each other, gently, with warmth but without passion, until fatigue overtook them and they slid to separate sides of the bed to sleep, the soles of their legs still touching, occasionally rising close enough to wakefulness for their legs to intertwine, their lips to murmur sleepy endearments.

But for the greater part, they slept.

CHAPTER SIXTY-FIVE

FOR THE INTERMINABLE WEEK following her father's funeral, Chifi had not strayed from the workshop. Kai and Fodjour rode down to the harbor to visit, to attempt to draw her out. As they entered the workshop, Kai felt saddened, remembering the hours of pleasure he had spent here with Babatunde or his father. All was silence and darkness now, and the world outside his doors seemed a quieter, less joyous place as well.

Sallah Mubutu met them at the door, and welcomed them in. Kai was gladdened to see that the little man had made himself useful in the months since coming to Kokossa's shop. Kai had been paying attention to see that his little experiment worked. Sallah Mubutu's skills as a machinist were even greater than he had represented at court. Swiftly, Sallah had become indispensable.

To Kai's eye, Chifi seemed not to have slept, or bathed. Or perhaps even eaten.

"I am sorry for your loss," Kai said, "and ashamed that I was unable to kill them all."

"Death would not have brought my father back." Chifi's face was an icy mask. "But the sound of their screams might have driven the emptiness from my heart."

To that, or to the cold gleam in her eyes, Kai had no answer at all.

"I understand," said Fodjour. "None of us can feel what you, feel. But Chifi, though he had a single child, you are not alone in mourning. He was a man of singular brilliance. No empire can survive the loss of men such as Kokossa."

Kai nodded. "I hate to think that our enemies—*his* enemies—will profit by his death."

She turned away from him, as though speaking to the wall. "They need not," she said.

"I see no other way. The designs are unfinished."

"They can be finished," she said.

Kai shook his head.

"Allah has not blessed us with two minds such as the one that created these patterns," said Fodjour.

"Perhaps that is true."

"Then . . . ?" said Kai.

"What if that mind still lives?" Chifi whispered.

Fodjour studied her more carefully. "What do you say?"

"Things are not always as they seem," she said carefully. "You have often said, Kai, that the world is not its maps. That one must be careful not to be deceived by appearances."

When Kai spoke next, he chose his words with exquisite care. "Had your father some need to promote a deception?"

"Tell me, Kai. How much money went into his . . . our programs?"

Kai wanted to hold his breath. "Perhaps ten thousand Alexanders."

"Why?" she pressed.

"Because your father was extraordinary."

"Yes," she said. "A man of genius. What if he had not been?"

"A genius?" asked Fodjour.

"No," said Kai, comprehension dawning. "A man."

"What . . . ?"

"What if he had been a woman," said Kai. "A girl?"

"Yes," said Chifi. "Like Kyanfuma. Who gave so much to the world, and was burned for it?"

Suddenly, the air seemed peculiarly hot and heavy. "Allah preserve us."

"You speak nonsense," said Fodjour.

"Tell me, Fodjour," she said in a flat, calm voice, "that the deception was not necessary. Tell me that if my father had gone to the great men who guide our great country and said, 'Honored sirs, my eleven-year-old daughter came to me with a dream, and when I turned that dream into steel it surpassed anything I had ever made for you.' "

"The Tortoise," Kai whispered.

"If he had come to them and said, 'My daughter dreams of a ship of iron, that no ship's cannon can pierce, and has drawn plans worthy of that dream.' " Chifi was slowly working herself into a slow frenzy, barely seeming to remember that she was speaking to them. " 'My daughter, who I bounced upon my knee, has dreamed of a war in which men might tear other men to bloody bits behind the safety of steel, and has made a design to implement these dreams.' Tell me, dear Fodjour, brave Kai, what would they have answered?"

"They would have laughed," said Kai. "And tightened their purses."

There was a pause in which no one spoke. "So there you have it. And here I stand. They killed my father. They should have slain the daughter. It was I who dreamed of war, not he."

She collapsed against her father's oaken desk, eyes red-rimmed now.

"Chifi . . . ," said Kai. "If what you say is true, the Empress's court might be a better place for you."

She looked up at them. Her black eyes were as hot and merciless as flaming gun-sights. In that moment he wondered if Chifi was wholly sane.

"They murdered my father to stop my mind. Would *you* hide, Kai?" Her gaze, her tone was savage. "Fodjour?"

"No," said Kai. "But I—"

"Am a man?" she finished for him.

"Yes."

"Then think of me no longer as a woman. Take my breasts, and unsex me here. I am nothing but mind and will. I will not mourn my father until his slayers are consumed by pigs."

"Chifi . . . ?" said Kai. "What are you saying?"

She took a knife and cut away her braid, the symbol of her gender and maidenhood, unsevered since childhood. It fell to the floor, just a few kites of dead, useless tissue. "Think of me no longer as a woman. Or as a friend. I am your weapon, Kai. Use me."

CHAPTER SIXTY-SIX

EVERY COUNTY IN NEW DJIBOUTI TERRITORY had its own seat, where representatives from the leading families converged to hear discussion and debate of the day's pressing issues, as well as decide what their representatives might say to the Senate in Radama, or ultimately in the Great Senate in New Alexandria.

Its central chambers were nestled in the city of Natchez, a day's ride east of Dar Kush. A steam-dragon spur ran between Djibouti Harbor and Natchez, but Kai and Chifi chose to take a carriage with a regimental honor guard. Although not so impressive as Radama, the county seat was a Moorish-style confection of brick and tinted glass, larger than most office buildings in Djibouti Harbor.

As he had only thrice previously, Kai stood before his Djiboutan peers. "I would like to introduce to this august body the true innovator of the Tortoise design—Chifi Kokossa!" Chifi stood, hands clasped before herself modestly, head respectfully veiled.

"What jest is this?" Councilman N'Guy charged. "Wakil, we come because you say you have important words for us. But in the wake of our great friend's death, what manner of strangeness have you placed before us?"

"Bring your engineers, Councilman," he said. Frankly, Kai found the councilman as great a boor as his wife. "Ask any question you wish of her. You will see the truth in my words."

"This is intolerable. We need no outside advisor to share our embarrassment." N'Guy turned to Chifi. "Girl, who has put you up to this?"

"No one has put me up to anything," she said. "I have my own mind."

"Do you indeed?" There was a bit of rumbling.

"Councilman Rouman? Would you care to resolve this?"

A rotund, sharp-eyed man stood. "Young lady," he said. "You contend that the ironclad was your invention?"

"Mine, yes," she replied.

"Then when I spoke to your father of my concerns about the pressure seals, he was merely parroting back answers you had supplied him?"

She pressed her lips together. "I find that disrespectful. My honored father needed parrot nothing. He had a mind of his own. Sirs, if I see potentials that others do not, my father still was the one who taught me the
physics and dynamics of the world."

He harrumphed, politely covering his smile with a hand. "I apologize.
Well. There are answers that your father gave me that you might repeat
by rote. I then propose a simple test."

"I stand prepared," she said.

"Do you indeed? Well. A concern for the construction of an ironclad,
raised since my last conversation with your father, has to do with the com-
position of seals protecting the propeller shaft."

After a pause, Chifi began to answer. "The difficulty had to do with the
acquisition of materials capable of retaining flexibility during innumerable
cycles of heat and cooling. The answer was discovered in a variety of Indian rubber."

"This substance had the desired durability?"

"Not in its natural form, no."

"So how was it to be strengthened?" asked N'Guy.

"A simple process devised almost a century ago, involving the addition
of sulfur to the heated rubber. Frankly, I am disappointed that your question is so elementary."

The room rumbled with whispers.

"But—"

Chifi's back seemed to stiffen. "Any who wish to question me further
need only take horse or dragon to the machine shop. There you can see
and question anything you wish. But if you are not willing to take this trip,
no verbal answer can convince you."

Councilman Rouman gestured expansively. "No. That will not be necessary. I think we can agree that Kokossa's daughter was, at the least, integrally involved in the creation of his latest devices."

Another rumble.

"Then you will—" Chifi began excitedly.

"—which explains the somewhat bizarre nature of these supposed in-
ventions. A submersible? A ship made more of iron than wood? These were
thought the delusions of a declining intellect. I now see that they were the
result of an indulgent parent risking his own reputation as well as—"

"But sir—" Chifi raised her hands imploringly, but the damage was already done; their prejudice and her haughtiness had turned the momentum against her.

"As well as the safety of his country—"

"And the gold of his patrons!" said another.

"—on a spinster's fantasies. This must be brought to an end, and now!"

She looked up at the men, chewing at her lip. "They killed my father," she said, her voice barely a whisper. "I can help."

"That will be all, *sitta-t.*"

"But—"

"That will be *all.*"

Chifi left, tears streaking her cheeks.

How ironic, Kai thought in disgust, *that it is a woman who insists on preparation for war, while the men sue for peace.*

"Well, young Wakil," said Rouman. "I hope you are proud."

"No," said Kai. "In fact I have seldom been more ashamed. Madame Kokossa's father was murdered, and you deny her the right granted any commoner to serve her country and avenge him. She warned me that this would be your response. It is obvious what this concerns."

Kai gripped at the edge of the podium. "Good day, honored sirs. And I hope that in the coming days, you have no cause to regret your shortsightedness."

Kai left the room, ignoring the shouts of "Sidi!" behind him. He caught up with Chifi in the hall outside. Tears streaked her face, and her fists were knotted and trembling. He tried to put his arm around her, but she pushed him away.

"Chifi," Kai said, searching for words that might comfort. None came. "War hovers all around us, and these idiots sit with their heads in the sand as the great flightless birds are said to do."

"I would put my hands around the throats of every one of them. . . ." Her eyes blazed with challenge.

"So. What will you do now?"

"Go home," she said, and lowered her head. "And close my father's lab."

He was saddened, but not wholly surprised to hear her say that.

Then she slowly raised her face and locked eyes with him. "Then, with your permission, I will move it to Dar Kush."

"What?" For a moment his head spun. *What in the world . . . ?*

"Kai," she said, and then amended her thought. "*Wakil.* I came here not for myself, but for you. For you to see the reality I have faced every day of my life. You operate under the illusion that men hold the power for the protection of women. As you probably were raised thinking that slavery was good for the slaves."

Kai flinched.

"Now," she said, "while your eyes are open, I make you a business proposition. My honored father made thousands of Alexanders, and lost them continually reinvesting in his work. But you *know* this ship can work. And that if we can prove it, our countrymen will want more than we can build."

"Chifi—"

"Listen to me!" she said in a fierce, low voice. "I ask no charity. Or for your assistance in revenge. I offer you half the value of my father's patents. The differential gear alone will make you a hundred Alexanders a year. Help me, Wakil. You are the only one who can."

She looked up at him, so small and feral, like some kind of forest creature. She would have him build this device, would have him set himself against his companions, so that she might have her revenge . . .

And continue her father's dream. And protect her country.

And use the precious talents Allah had seen fit to give her. She had not asked for the mind that could dream such dreams. Genius came in its own time and place, and answered to no force save heaven. She was one of Allah's miracles, and she had asked him to see it, acknowledge it.

What would Abu Ali, his father, have done?

What would Babatunde do?

"I know exactly what my father would do," Kai said slowly, and she looked up at him, eyes suddenly fearful.

"I was but a child when your honored father died," she said rapidly. "He never saw—"

He raised a finger, and smiled. "He would back Maputo's work—*your* work—with his own fortune, trusting that when his country saw the worth of it, he would either be repaid, or not." He took her shoulders. "Chifi," he said, "Let us make history together. I will back your device, and when our country comes calling and wishes a thousand Tortoises, *we* are the ones who they must pay. They will own *nothing* of the plans or the processes. We will serve our country, gain our vengeance, and *you* will become wealthy in the process."

Her eyes blazed. Again, he was a bit taken aback by her intensity.

"You would do this for me?"

"And for the memory of your father, whom I loved." He stopped, and then added softly, "And for my daughters, that they might know a woman of your caliber."

She spat in her hand and extended it. He clasped, surprised by the strength in her small hand, but more disturbed by her expression.

On Chifi's face was the palest, most arctic smile he had ever seen.

CHAPTER SIXTY-SEVEN

ADDITIONAL STEAM-SCREWS and sail-ships had arrived in the harbor, and as they crowded the water, it seemed that Djiboutan resolve was deadlocked in argument. Most maintained, at least publicly, that the ships were merely preparing for a strike against the Aztecs. Kai and others believed it was nothing more or less than a naked show of force.

This was a high-stakes game of *satranj*, and Kai wished that Elenya was present to speak to about the positioning of pieces before striking.

Elenya. Just the thought of his sister seemed to stab his heart. Was she well? Terrified? Had the Pharaoh decided he had reason to make her suffer?

Kai stood with Chifi as workers, directed by Sallah Mubutu, began dismantling crucial aspects of the workshop and loading them onto carts. The Tortoise itself was housed in a secure slip a few hundred cubits away, and would follow later. The lab equipment would be taken by road or barge to Lake A'zam, there to be reassembled.

"More ships," said Chifi, peering out at the bay. "They arrive by three and leave by two. And every week there are a few more."

"Here and at the Brown Nile, they amass their forces. Tease and threaten us. Move their ships farther south if we rumble, then slowly mass them again. It is an ugly game."

"What do we do?"

"I know what Elenya would do, were an opponent to try such a tactic."

"What?" Chifi asked.

"Maintain the strength of her position. Continue building her own plans. Refuse to be intimidated . . . and . . ."

"And what?"

"And win."

Fifteen years ago, Kai's father, Abu Ali, had built a mosque for Babatunde, but the Sufi services were conducted quietly, and with great regard for the sensibilities of some of the area's more conservative Muslims.

With Kai's accession to the office of Wakil, local prejudices had been driven even farther underground, and as long as he held that office, Sufis congregated more openly.

As a result, Babatunde found his days filled with teaching, counseling, and conducting the *zikr* ceremony. When not so engaged, the Yoruban shaykh passed time studying scrolls in his room. It was there that Kai approached him, sorely needing his old friend and tutor's guidance.

"I don't know what to do," Kai said, dropping into a chair. "Or if I have done the right thing. Elenya is in danger; I may lose my influence in the Senate; war is imminent. And . . ."

"And?" said Babatunde.

"And I fear that you spoke truly: our enemies know too much about our household. They slid past my guards and murdered a man under my own roof. There is a serpent in my house."

"Who do you suspect?" Babatunde asked. "Your new bride?"

Kai looked up quickly. "No. Perhaps." He cursed. "She was quicksilver itself during the attack, swift to protect children who were not her own."

"A powerful plea for trust."

Kai nodded. "But *someone* killed the Hashassin. Someone I trust. Damnation!" Kai stood and paced. He looked up at Babatunde. "Two wolves fight in my mind, Babatunde. One has my father's aspect, the other my uncle's. One speaks of love, and the other, betrayal."

Babatunde was very quiet.

"My *uncle* thinks only of attack and defense. My uncle thinks that any woman not under his control is a danger, and that I have never faced greater danger than that under my own roof. My uncle bids me send her home now, while still there is time, no matter what the political cost."

"Your uncle," Babatunde said quietly, "is dead."

Kai regarded him balefully. "As Shaka is dead."

"You will not send her away?"

"No," Kai said. "Not yet." He sighed, and dropped to a chair. "And there is more. I do not know how Aidan is faring in his quest, and until I know that, I fear I may have placed my friend in mortal peril for nothing. What am I doing, Cricket?"

"The best you can," Babatunde said. "Unfortunately, you have the burden of learning as you go. Mistakes are inevitable. Success is not. You will have to live with this." A pause, and then he continued. "As your father did."

That caught Kai's attention. "Did my father doubt his ability to rule?"

"Every day of his life."

Kai looked at his old tutor in amazement. "But . . . he always seemed so strong, so certain."

"As a leader must. But he was a man, without the infinite knowledge of He who made us."

"What do I do?"

"Pray," said his teacher. "And love. And work. And live."

Enough other landowners had joined their riches to those of Dar Kush that, although Kai was the largest single shareholder in the Lion's Blood trading company, large disbursements were usually made in the form of loans from an investment fund, rather than outright withdrawals from Kai's private or family account.

Djidade Berhar was the largest shareholder after Kai, and had lent his authority and experience to the board of directors since Abu Ali's death. Since Berhar's illness had accelerated, Kai had taken a more active hand, assisted by Lamiya, his First.

Its marbled halls rang with debate as Kai argued with the board of directors regarding his expenditures. Lamiya sat by his side, head covered modestly, watching and listening.

"Kai," said the vice chairman, "we have done all we can to accommodate your wishes, but we are entrusted with the financial health of this institution . . ."

"My husband's requests have not been exorbitant," Lamiya said. "Nor do they endanger the stability of this institution."

"Not in sheer financial cost, no, although the Wakil has authorized . . . ah . . . three thousand Alexanders to this project."

Kai smiled dismissively. "A month's interest on the island investments, if that."

"That is not the only concern. Any modern financial establishment depends on reciprocal loans and agreements with other institutions. Our northern trading partners would be quite uncomfortable to hear of your expenditures. This 'Tortoise' is a short-range vessel, with no conceivable trade usage. In other words—"

Kai placed his hands flat on the table, and met their gazes squarely. "A ship-killer. Yes."

The directors folded their hands, and regarded each other uncomfortably.

"Kai," said the director. "It was your father's request, and your request, that we consider our primary responsibility the protection of Dar Kush's assets for future generations."

"You are obligated to present a case for fiscal conservatism." Lamiya said. "And so you have done. But my husband also expects you to honor his wishes, and so do I."

The board members exchanged dubious glances, but finally recognized the inevitable. "If you are set on this path . . ."

"And I am," Kai said.

"Then we will do all in our power to make it so."

"Excellent," Kai said. "And that concludes my business for today."

Lamiya took her husband's arm, and together they exited the main chamber, leaving the elderly officers shuffling papers behind them. He managed to reach the outer hall before bursting into laughter. "Did you ever see such a bunch of stiffbacks? I swear they sleep strapped to a board."

Babatunde had waited in the hall outside, speaking with Rashid, the old man who was caretaker and night guard for Lion's Blood. Rashid had been an old man twenty years ago, and oddly, had hardly seemed to age in the intervening decades. "Ah, Sidi, it's not that they don't respect you," he said. "They just remember when your father brought you here, and you'd get into one mischief after another. Men their age have a hard time trusting anyone under fifty, let alone someone they remember peeing his pants."

"Rashid!" Lamiya gasped.

Kai laughed. "It's all right. And it's true, if embarrassing."

"Had to take you and clean you off myself, sir."

Babatunde's eyes were mirthful. "On a drier subject," he said, "how went the talk?"

They bade good-bye to Rashid and walked to the window facing the harbor. The northern ships studding the harbor seemed ever more ominous.

"Strange," said Kai, more serious now. "A sane man would hope only for peace. But if peace there is, I will likely lose my seat in the Senate, and possibly my Wakilship."

"That may be an exaggeration," Lamiya said.

"Oh no." He laughed bitterly. "Even if I maintain my status as Wakil, my enemies will undercut my authority sufficiently to cripple my court. The complex web of titles and contracts, legal and financial, that maintains Dar Kush will begin to unravel. If things go wrong in New Alexandria, and Aidan is traced back to me, I could end up a criminal, my family in disgrace."

"And if war comes?" asked Babatunde.

"I am a hero. And thousands die."

"And so . . . ?"

Kai smiled. "So I pray for peace, of course."

The Yoruba laughed. "Of course. Come. I have two words for the both of you."

"Which are?" Lamiya asked.

"*Doro Wate*. There is a new and wondrous Abyssinian restaurant on the bay. Let me purchase lunch."

"With the money we pay you."

"Of course, my dear."

"Make it an expensive one," Kai said, surrendering. "Lead on."

CHAPTER SIXTY-EIGHT

DESPITE THE GNAWING TENSION, and the storm clouds hovering on the horizon, Nandi had continued to customize her rooms, making them reflect her personality to the extent that when Kai entered them he felt almost as if he were entering another world.

At the moment, they reclined together in a twining that was sensual, but not yet sexual. IziLomo reclined in a corner of the room, but if loveplay truly began, Kai would send him to the kennel. It would be unseemly for the hound to bay in chorus to his mistress's passionate cries.

"You did well during the attack," he said, tracing his finger along her back, which was as well muscled as any boy's.

"You expected less?" Her smile was mischievous.

"You are a woman, and so skilled at womanly things that I forget you are also Shaka's niece, with all the hmmm . . . dynamism? Yes."

"I like that word," she said, and reinforced her opinion with a slow, subtle pulsing of her body against his.

"Stop that," he said, fighting distraction. "All the dynamism that that implies."

"It pleases me to have many skills," she said. "It pleases me more that my husband approves." She stretched like a great cat. "You approve, my husband?"

"Greatly."

She sighed and seemed to relax. "Then it is good. I could be happy here, Kai of Dar Kush. *We* could be."

"I am happy now," Kai said.

"You could be happier still."

He came closer. "Oh? How is that?"

She snuggled tightly against him, as if trying to make their two bodies one. "I could give you a son," she said. "The women in my clan are famous for sons. For five generations, the firstborn of my line have all been sons. This gift I would give to you, my husband. A son to carry your name, a warrior to learn your swordcraft, who will stand proudly at your gate."

Kai enfolded her in his arms. "You need make no promises," he said.

"No?"

"No," said Kai. "Just be my companion. Share my days and nights. Help me."

Her eyes dropped. "You are so strong. You need no help."

Kai blinked. "Is that what you think?"

She brushed her cheek against his.

"Strong, but gentle, also. For a time I did not understand. I wondered. Then, during the attack, I saw you, as perhaps you have not seen yourself. *There* was the man I was born to marry."

"I also am that man."

"Yes," said Nandi. "But only then did I recognize him. How strange, Kai." She rolled away from him, staring up at the ceiling. "How strange and wonderful."

"What? Tell me this strangeness."

She peered into his eyes almost as if she had never seen him before. "You are not as our men, but you are still a man. Lamiya is not as our women, but is still a woman. I think that, perhaps, after all, there is room for Nandi in Dar Kush."

"You doubted?"

"Yes," she said. "Once, long ago, I doubted. But no more."

She nestled back against him, and they talked, and sang songs to each other in low voices, and told jokes, and made plans until Nandi grew drowsy and, closing her eyes she rested her cheek against his chest and slept.

Kai looked down at her, wondering what dreams passed behind her eyes. Nandi no longer doubted . . .

But Kai ibn Jallaleddin ibn Rashid felt little save doubt.

Doubt, and love.

And that was the damnation of it.

Lamiya watched as, one cartload at a time, Kokossa's laboratory was relocated to Lake A'Zam's yacht dock. Kai and his people stood wondering on the shore as the ironclad was towed in.

"Ugly thing," said Fodjour. "Do you really believe it can work?" The Tortoise was constructed of flat black iron, a hundred ten cubits in length, with a draft of eight. Its revolving turret housed two ten-digit cannon, such that in battle only the turret, and not the entire ship, needed turn.

"I believe that Chifi believes in it," said Kai. "She and her father never failed us."

"Yes . . ." There was a reservation in Fodjour's tone, but he seemed reluctant to speak it, and at last shrugged in submission.

The Empress's niece watched as her husband scanned the ship. Kai had tasked the Dahomy to general assistance of Chifi and the maintenance of security around the construction site. With her father's death, almost half of the Tortoise's crew had left her employ. Kai was pleased to note how swiftly the Dahomy learned the various nautical tasks. Using ropes and poles they guided the Tortoise into the empty dock: the Sea Horse had already been moved to a sheltered berth in Djibouti Harbor.

"So much money and time," Kai said. "Well. In days to come, we may be able to salvage something."

"Risky to back this, isn't it?" Nandi said.

"Yes," he agreed. "But riskier still not to. The harbor grows daily more crowded with northern ships."

"You can smell it, can't you?" Nandi said.

"What?"

"Blood," she said. "Blood, carried on the wind." She turned and looked up at him. "Aren't you worried about sabotage here? Your guard still patrols the borderlands."

"The Dahomy patrol our grounds," said Lamiya. "And they will be working with Chifi, now that the sailors have quit."

Fodjour managed a laugh. "Female guards . . . a female crew . . . quite a secret weapon, Kai."

Chifi guided the ironclad into the dock. She turned, and waved to them. She was suffused with a glow of intense joy, uniting her features so that they became not merely attractive, but actually lovely. She gave a special smile to Fodjour, who waved back somewhat less effusively.

"I think she likes you, Fodjour," said Lamiya, too casually by half. "Have you any feelings for her in return?"

Fodjour cleared his throat. "She is a fine woman, but . . . well, no."

"If this venture succeeds," said Kai, "she will have the greatest dowry in the territory."

"Is gold all you think of?" Fodjour asked.

"No, but it certainly seems the center of your fascination."

"True, true." Fodjour's apparent irritation vanished as Kai's words sank in. "Will she really be that wealthy?"

"Most certainly," Kai said.

Fodjour turned and waved warmly back at Chifi.

"You are a scoundrel." Lamiya clucked.

"But a lovable one."

They laughed and turned away from him. But Lamiya's expression hardened when she turned. Fodjour was Kai's friend. And he was a compatriot, and had saved her husband's life.

That didn't mean she had to like him.

CHAPTER SIXTY-NINE

21 Rabi al-Thaani A.H. 1295
(Wednesday, April 24, 1878)

IT WAS WITH SOME SURPRISE that Aidan had been told to dress, don cloak and collar, and accompany Rhino to a party on the Dosa estate. It was not utterly unknown for fighters to attend such affairs, and in fact they were, if suitably restrained, treated much like the leopards and greyhounds brought by some of the other guests: dangerous but controlled, a symbol of Alexandrian power that such creatures could be managed as mere pets.

"This is your chance to watch the German," said Rhino. "Keep your eyes open."

"I'm going to fight him?" *Not tonight, I hope.*

"Dosa will put his best fighter against the champion. Your master sold you for that purpose." Rhino watched him with a certain humorous reserve. "You move strange," the big man said, "but smooth. Makes me want to wager a few coppers on you myself."

"Try to get good odds," Aidan replied, hoping that his sour stomach would not rumble so loudly as to attract the leopards.

The public fighting ring was a dirt-floored arena within Dosa's walled garden, with spectator seats set behind a stone wall.

Aidan watched from a section of the audience reserved for slaves.

At the back of the most exclusive section, a statuesque woman entered, and began seeking her seat. Gray streaked her hair, and there were signs of softening at the corners of her jaw. Still, considering the ease with which hair color might be altered, and the fact that she had eschewed the fashionably high collars that many mature highborn women sported to conceal wattling at the throat, it suggested an astounding level of self-confidence.

She wore the fashionable false beard affected by many other highborn women, but her copper skin was smoothly feminine and magnetic to the eye. Her body, beneath a sheer dress no decent Djiboutan woman would have worn between bedroom and bath, was as firm and flexible as a girl's. Altogether, she one of the most stunning creatures he had ever seen. "Who is she?" he asked Rhino.

"She is Nefriti, the Caliph's wife," said Rhino, and for the first time in Aidan's experience, the walking boulder sounded a bit nervous. "Avert your eyes if you would keep them."

Nefriti was as sleek as the greyhound trotting at the end of her leash. When she scanned the room, he immediately dropped his own eyes. "She's unbelievable."

"Yes. I've heard rumors . . . ," Rhino began, and then let his voice trail away.

"What kind of rumors?"

"Well . . . let's say she has her own reasons to love the fights."

The champion entered, and immediately Aidan's mind returned to business. The German was a brown-bearded giant, almost a full head taller than Aidan, and thick-fisted. His opponent, entering from the other side of the arena, was shorter than Aidan but broader across the shoulders. A squat, powerful wrestler, a Turk by the look of him. This, Aidan thought, would not be pretty. The German looked almost bored.

"The man is an animal," said Aidan.

"We're all animals," said Rhino. "He's just the king of the beasts."

After an announcer sang their merits, the two men began circling each other cautiously, the wrestler remaining just out of reach. As the German studied his smaller opponent, the wrestler charged in, swooping low. The giant hooked a punch up from the ground. The Turk barely got his head out of the way, and that mallet of a fist struck his neck with a thump audible two dozen cubits away.

The crowd groaned sympathetically, and Aidan cringed, unable to keep from wondering what it would feel like to have that lump of gristle break his own bones.

The wrestler backed up, a bright red splotch marring his neck, a trickle of blood running from torn skin. The German's fists were probably toughened with brine or some such agent. The bigger man grinned through his beard, and stalked his prey.

The wrestler took two steps back, then with eye-baffling speed pounced forward, arms wrapping the German's legs. With strength it was difficult to credit, he heaved up, and the German went over his shoulder. The wrestler fell backward with him, so that they struck the ground together, the German just a moment sooner, so that the wrestler landed atop him.

Good move, Aidan thought. *That will show the arrogant bastard that he can't just walk in on his opponent.* Now the German would judge his action more carefully, and reacting to that solid thump, probably even become a better, more dangerous—

But the German never had the four or five seconds that it might have taken him to recover. Lizard-quick, the wrestler crawled over him. The German got in several more punches, including one that would have broken the wrestler's nose if it hadn't already been a lump of gristle. But without his feet under him the German had nothing but arm strength, power insufficient to prevent the Turk from finally attaining an armlock, twisting and pulling with the strength of back and butt and legs until he produced a *crack* that chilled Aidan's spine.

The German screamed in agonized humiliation.

The wrestler rolled away and came to his feet, mopping the blood from his face with little apparent concern as the bigger man thrashed on the ground, holding his shattered arm, howling as the guards came for him.

"Oh, shyte," Aidan whispered, and meant it.

The Caliph promptly turned his back on the wounded ex-champion and strode to the Turk's owner, a skeletally tall Somali.

"I would purchase this man," said the Caliph. "Set your price."

The Somali fawned. "Sayyid, I could not presume—"

"Quickly now, before I change my mind. Your price!"

"Say . . . twenty Alexanders?"

The Caliph spat in his palm. "Done."

Riding in the rear of a horse-cart all the way back to the compound, Aidan's mind was a fog of fear and confusion. He had been prepared for a powerful brawler-boxer, not a wrestler like the Turk. Everything he had practiced, every one of Babatunde's visualizations, every tactic of Kai's was based on the idea of defeating the German. Disastrously, no one had even *considered* that the giant might be beaten before Aidan even had his chance—let alone that he might be beaten by someone with an entirely different approach to combat. This was a complete balls-up, and Aidan had no idea at all what to do.

"What is wrong?" Rhino asked, observing him carefully. "You never seemed afraid before!"

"You don't understand," said Aidan, cradling his head in his hands. "You don't understand."

"What is it?" Rhino seemed genuinely confused and, somewhat to Aidan's surprise, compassionate.

"Leave me. Please." He managed to smile, but the curl of his lips was a fractured, pitiful thing.

Within the hour they arrived back at the compound. Rhino accompanied Aidan to his cell, respecting his need for solitude. He left the Irishman slumped against the wall, knees to chest, forehead sunk against crossed arms.

The door closed behind him. Aidan sat, staring into his callused, shaking hands. "Dear Jesus," said Aidan, a bit surprised that that holy oath had emerged from his lips so easily. "What am I going to do?"

The door opened again. Aidan's face was still locked in his hands.

"I said leave me alone!" he screamed into his hands.

"I'm sorry," a woman said. "I thought you might be someone I knew."

He slowly looked up, an oath frozen on his lips.

Her hair was golden, rouged with strawberry. The jaw was strong for a woman, but the generous mouth and sparkling eyes merely lent a deeper and more subtle sensibility. Around her neck she wore a tiny golden tree on a silver chain. He had not seen her for half a lifetime, and would have known her in an unlamped midnight. Aidan fumbled to his feet. "Nessa . . . ?"

She blinked almost as if he had thrown water in her face. "It has been so long since I've heard that name," she said. "I had almost forgotten its sound."

"Oh, God . . . Nessa!" He rushed to her, and they embraced.

She sighed, and her eyes fluttered closed. "Aidan," she murmured. "I never thought to see you again."

He kissed each cheek, and then her closed eyes. "I swore I'd come for you."

"For . . . me?" His six words seemed to shock her, take her utterly aback.

"For you."

She stared at him, mouth pursed in surprise. Then she managed to say, "But . . . you're a slave!"

He, in turn, managed a smile. "Things are not always as they seem. Trust me. I'll tell you more when I can. But . . . tell me: is your name really Habiba now? And are you really in bin Jeffar's home?"

Her eyes widened. "How do you know so much about me?" Then she raised her hand. "No. There is so little time. I bribed the guard to allow me an hour. This is not unusual—I suppose he thinks I want a fighter's seed." She traced his face with her fingertips. "Life has been hard for you. So little remains of the boy I knew."

"None of that is of any consequence," he said. "I survived. *You* survived. Nessa . . . what happened to you, after we were separated?"

"How shall I tell you of ten years gone?"

"Swiftly," he said. "We shall have more time later. But I need to know . . ."

Nessa closed her eyes, as if searching in that ocular darkness for traces of the girl she had been, a lifetime before.

She remembered being hauled away from her mother and Aidan, on the docks of New Djibouti. "I wept for a week after I was taken from you, and Mother. . . ." She paused. "Mother?"

Aidan shook his head sadly.

Nessa sighed. "She's with Father then, and they dance together among the stars."

She returned to her story. "I was taken to a slave market in New Alexandria, where I was sold again to the household of bin Jeffar. I was told he was an inventor, a diplomat, a warrior—a great, wealthy man, and that I should feel fortunate to be in his house. . . ."

Despite her travails, with the passage of time the child Nessa grew into a healthy young woman who remembered the ways of her people, and found other slaves who also knew tales of King Conchobar, the siege of Druim Damhgaire, or the Ogam writings she had only begun to learn when Northmen tore her away from O'Dere Crannog. They met in secret, but they met, and that thread from her past kept her whole, and sane, and vital. That vitality was a double-edged sword: it protected her from the depression and illness crippling so many of the other slaves, but it also manifested itself in a full-bodied, strong-boned Irish beauty, sufficiently glorious to bring her to the attention of the overseers, one of whom forced himself upon her.

The overseer was a married man, however, and his own jealous wife betrayed him to bin Jeffar. Bin Jeffar had the man whipped and fired, and the other overseers left her alone.

"I'm so sorry," Aidan said, not knowing what else to say.

"It was a long time ago," his sister replied. "And from that time on, I had come to the admiral's attention, and he did what he could to make my life easier."

Aidan looked at her a bit askance, uncomfortable with the obvious admiration and respect she displayed for her owner.

"His wife died of a fever five years ago," she said.

"And he came to you?"

"No, little brother. It's not that simple, and he's not that kind of man. He was alone for two years. I saw the way he looked at me, but he is a gentleman, and would never have forced himself, or even made his desires known. In the end . . . I went to him."

He was incredulous. "You seduced him?"

"We seduced each other."

Aidan clenched his fists and hung his head. He wanted to scream at her, but how could he, after all he had seen and done? He knew the paucity of choices available to a white woman, had seen the things that slaves did to survive. What he himself had done. What his wife, Sophia, had done. He wept for the girl she had been, but could not bring himself to condemn her.

"He is a good man. He never lied to me, or promised what he could not offer." She proffered the golden tree dangling on her neck. "He allows me to wear this, even though he considers it a pagan symbol."

"Does he love you?"

That question seemed to evoke a deeper quiet from her, one from which she was reluctant to emerge. "In his way, I think."

"So he would not say it, even when you are in bed."

He regretted those words, for they stung his sister.

"In his way," she repeated.

"They say that he took you to Egypt."

Immediately, she brightened. "Yes! Oh, Aidan, it was wonderful. If only you could see the marvels of that land."

"Did he present you at court?"

"Of course not. But I accompanied him almost everywhere else, and there was comment made, and he stood by me, Aidan. For a man in his position, that is no small thing."

"Are there slaves there, as well?"

"Yes," she admitted. "But they find it easier to buy their way free. Some of them teach, and many of them live in their own homes, as some do here in New Alexandria. They owe a portion of their work to their masters, but not their lives, nor their children's lives."

"Do you imagine that Jeffar will free you?"

She turned her face away. Aidan took her chin, turned her face until their eyes locked.

"Do you think he'll marry his saucy Irish girl, make little brown babies with her?"

She shook her head. "It would not be legal to marry me." Nessa's shoulders hunched as she cast her eyes down. "Aidan, do not judge me too harshly, I pray you. For years, every night I dreamed that you would come for me. And when at last my dreams began to fade, I made my peace with the world. Is that so terrible?"

A pause, then Aidan said, "No, Nessa. It is not."

When she looked back up at him, her eyes were glazed with tears. It was clear that those five words meant the world to her.

"Nessa," Aidan said. "You survived. I think that I have some idea what it cost you. Everything. It cost you *everything*. But you survived. How could I judge you without judging myself? I did so many things to try to stay alive, to remember Mother and Father. To keep my heart whole."

"How did Mother die?" she asked reluctantly.

"She worked herself to death." His voice was an awed hush. "She lasted little more than a year. Losing you broke her heart, and the only salve that eased the pain was work, until she was exhausted, until her hands bled. Work was her balm."

"She swore to work herself to death if they would only keep us together."

He nodded. "They broke their word to her, but she kept hers to them. Almost as if it were some point of honor to her. They never lashed her. They fed us, and sheltered us. But what they had taken was far, far more than she could give."

Nessa hung her head. "She's gone."

"Not so long as we remember her."

"Yes." She leaned her head against him, sighing deeply. "But I would like to see where she is buried."

"You will."

In that moment, she seemed more than ever like his own image, glimpsed in a mirror. He knew that to be an illusion of the heart—the eternal verities of male and female had changed them far too much for any such resemblance. Still . . .

"How did you find me?" he asked.

"I went with bin Jeffar to an affair at Dosa's estate," she said. "I saw you. I knew you at once, Aidan. For all the change, all the time. I knew you in an instant."

"Thank God," he said, believing her utterly. He would have known her in a crowd of Irish redheads, let alone a sea of black faces with lamb's wool for hair.

"What do we do now?"

"Now?" he asked. "Now I will find some way to finish what I began. You have contacts in the arenas?"

"Yes," she said. "Servants are everywhere, and share knowledge."

"Then wait until I fight the Turk. I will come to you that night. Be ready, Nessa. I will come for you."

He took her by the shoulders, and forced confidence into his voice. "Don't doubt me now, when we're so close."

She leaned her head against him. "Aidan, forgive me. But . . . you cannot do this thing. Where would we go?"

"I have a home, where free whites are building a world together."

"But the fugitive slave laws—"

"You will have papers, and a new name, and we will be together. Have faith. Just a little longer."

Then he sat her in the cell, and told her his plans. Holding his hands tightly, Nessa in return answered every question he had about the city streets, the Caliph's estate, and bin Jeffar's residence. Strangely, although he had come to rescue her, strength seemed to flow from her hands into his, as though she possessed a deeper reservoir of peace than all of Kai and Babatunde's patient teaching had been able to impart.

And as he calmed, his own fear of the Turk transformed into something quiet, and cool . . .

And deadly.

CHAPTER SEVENTY

IN ALL AIDAN'S WORLD nothing existed save pain.

Kai had said it: the deeper you are willing to venture into your pain and fear, the greater the reward.

There was no greater reward than that freedom he sought for Nessa. It impelled the deepest commitment to intimate knowledge of the limits of human flesh. Aidan drilled with one arm at a time tied behind his back, one leg at a time hobbled, hopping until his calves burned and his feet bled, working his balance. Every drill he could remember he performed, over and over again until muscle failed and his legs buckled. Then he stopped and breathed, finding that illusive meld of breath, posture, and motion that had been disrupted by his shock at the German's destruction.

And despite his greatest fears, he was damned if he didn't detect an increase in his calm and awareness, as well as improvement of his skills.

During one of his bouts of exhaustion, the door to his cell opened. "The match is set," said Rhino. "Are you ready?"

"Yes." Aidan's voice was flat, with almost no inflection. He levered himself up from the straw, began to drill again, as if he had dismissed Rhino completely.

The big man watched him, his small, scar-tissue-ringed eyes intelligent and questing. "Why did you come here?" Rhino asked.

"To fight."

Rhino wagged his head. "Sometimes, when I look at you, I see . . ."

"What?"

"Signs you've played hands with a royal. That kind of fighting is not slave fighting."

Damn. Aidan dared not coarsen his movement—that would be too obvious. And besides, he would need every edge he could get. He shrugged. "Maybe I watched 'em sometimes. That's it."

Rhino studied him, and then laughed. "Well, every man has a right to his secrets. Good luck to you and yours, tomorrow."

Rhino left, leaving Aidan alone with his thoughts. When the door closed, Aidan began to practice the moves that Kai and Babatunde had given him. Over and over and over again . . .

On and on, into the longest night of his life.

CHAPTER SEVENTY-ONE

CROWDED ELBOW TO ELBOW on the wooden slat seats of the public arena, the common crowd was already swelling and yelling. Highborn men and women filled the lower, more expensive cushioned seats and boxes. Though they may have had more silver in their purses, their hearts were just as hardened to the suffering of their fellow men.

At the moment two gladiators in a chalked circle wreaked havoc on one another. They swung fists and tripped and threw, and the crowd roared with pleasure every time blood flew or a body smashed into the dirt. Finally, one could not rise anymore, and the victor raised his hand in triumph.

Attendants carried out the defeated man.

The announcer walked out. "Your attention, *mahdûm and bâtûn*. For your entertainment this evening we have the Turk, a monster so formidable that he bested the invincible German in only two minutes! Against him we have the Irish, the newest acquisition of the illustrious Dar Dosa. Fighters to your corners!"

Aidan was led out of a hallway to the gate leading to the arena.

"Make me wealthy, Irish," said Dosa, "and you'll have your freedom in a year."

Aidan nodded and came out, blinking his eyes against the light.

The Turk weighed only two sep more than Aidan, resembling a barrel with arms and legs. The Turk nodded in his direction, smiling as a man might smile at a plate of roast bison. He picked a handful of sand up from the floor and rubbed his hands with it. Then he planted himself, knees bent, feet wide, arms spread in welcome.

The drums rolled, and the action began.

Aidan tried to find the state that he reached during the *djuru* "marrying" ceremony, and managed to, to a degree. It was a dubious approach, but all he had to cling to.

Aidan confronted the new champion, and when he charged, found that he had more time than anticipated, as if reality were slowing down a bit.

As a result, he scored early with an elbow to the head, angled off to throw a knee that just missed the face and glanced off a massive shoulder. Aidan was fast . . . fast enough that his own eyes could barely track the motion. His blows were far more accurate than the German's had been. He slid sideways as he threw, planting weight only at the moment of impact.

When the Turk charged in, Aidan scrambled out of the way, amazed to watch his arms and legs flying out, seemingly of their own accord, smashing into the Turk's head and neck with shocking force. Oddly, it seemed the techniques were created not by his mind, but *by the mere position of his body.*

Indeed, one pivot with a knee strike set the Turk back on his heels with blood streaming from an already-broken nose. Aidan went after him in an instant, punching and elbowing, kicking to the supporting leg, and then sweeping that leg so that the Turk crashed to the ground. The crowd roared. For the first time, Aidan thought: *I can do this!*

Unfortunately, it was the last time, as well.

The Turk never tried to get up. Instead he rolled, grabbed Aidan's foot, and curled his body in some odd way to get a heel into the Irishman's guts, using leverage that Aidan couldn't even understand to uproot him and slam him to the ground. In an instant, pain and confusion drove all thought of technique from his mind. Unlike the German, Aidan actually managed to scramble away from the grasping arms, leaving blood and skin on the sand.

He stood in time to be charged by the Turk once again, who smashed him into the ground so hard that he couldn't breathe.

The crowd's initial pleasure dissolved into jeers and catcalls.

Despite his courage, and all of his training, Aidan's face was ground into the sand. He tasted grit, and felt the Turk twist his arm up behind him. He refused to scream, knew that in another instant he would hear his own bones break, and prepared himself for that.

Then, instead, he felt an arm slip around his neck, and felt the choking pressure.

Light faded. *This is death,* he thought. *Good. I've failed you all. Nessa, I'm so . . .*

"You actually fought well," said Dosa, casting a sympathetic gaze down on Aidan. The Irishman had managed to leave the arena under his own power, making it as far as a holding cell before collapsing onto his straw mat. "And the crowd liked the fact that you stood and bowed to the Turk after you awakened. A nice touch. You'll be a favorite, Aidan. It is possible that you might have beaten the German. It is possible. But this Turk . . ." He shrugged. "Well, I'm not blaming you. Heal, Aidan. And then we'll see."

He left Aidan in the darkness. At first Aidan managed to control his emotions; then he began to sob. Deep, wracking sobs that threatened to tear him apart.

He did not know how long he remained in that state, but emerged from it at once when the door creaked, and then opened. Aidan turned around. A tall, slender, cloaked figure stood in the doorway.

"She does not like the winners," an elegant voice murmured. "Her *husband* likes the winners. My lady like the ones with bruises, without the light of victory in their eyes."

"What?" Aidan said, confused.

The figure came closer. "She likes the ones who can lose without breaking. Are you such a man?"

"What . . . do you want?" Aidan groaned. His pounding head needed no riddles.

She came to him, and placed her hand beneath his jaw.

"Luckily, she is not interested in your mind. Wash and prepare yourself. Nefriti will send for you."

The woman turned and left. Aidan sat in the darkness, his former despair converting to something else.

Could this possibly mean what he thought? He remembered Rhino's words: *she has her own reasons to love the fights. . . .*

There remained the chance, just the chance, that not all was lost after all.

In spite of his aches and bruises, he managed a gruff laugh. "Well, boyo," he said, crannog cadences sneaking back into his speech. "Looks like yer net ain't as empty as ye thought. . . ."

CHAPTER SEVENTY-TWO

By the time the guards came for him, Aidan had washed and cleansed himself as best he could. Locked into their cells, the other fighters jeered as he strode past.

"Ah, Aden!" one cried. "Ye'll have wrestling aplenty tonight!"

"Hope ye didn't leave all yer fight on the sand—save some for the sheets!" yelled another, with more than a trace of envy in his voice.

He nodded to them, but Aidan felt somewhat disconnected, floating. He lacked the grounding that had comforted him for the last weeks. In an odd sense, he seemed not even to be living these moments. He felt that he was watching a play, or reading a triptych, a sense that he was floating above himself, behind himself. This entire situation couldn't be real . . . could it?

Another few steps and he passed the cells where the massage girls were quartered. He paused when his eyes met Vida's. She seemed deeply saddened, older than the masseuse who had ministered to him mere weeks before, whose offer of comfort he had regretfully declined. Was she jealous? Did she understand that he could not reject the Caliph's wife without the direst of consequences? Or did she perhaps think he preferred black skin?

All of that together, and maybe more, mingled in her face, transforming it into a mask of pure pain and hopelessness. Poor girl. Her hero had fallen. He wished that there was something, anything, that he could say to comfort her.

But nothing came to mind, and finally she turned away, and curled on her side against her straw mattress.

A carriage took Aidan through a series of guarded checkpoints to the back gate of the Caliph's estate. He watched the carriage's every twist and turn, absorbed as many of the sights and sounds as possible, seeking to engrave landmarks upon his memory.

The gate opened and then closed behind him. The carriage clattered down a cobblestone drive through a maze of shadowed hedges, the way lined with fruit trees and cultivated gardens. The main house was two-storied, of pale brick, with a less ornate and more stolid design than wealthy southern homes. Surprisingly, the Caliph's residence was somewhat smaller than Dar Kush, but he realized that that was almost inevitable: the Caliph lived in the middle of a city. A house the size of Kai's might have dominated the entire nightscape.

The carriage finally came to a halt before a little cabana behind the main residence.

He stepped down gingerly, not entirely certain how best to behave, or what to do. What, he thought, would be most appropriate and effective, least suspicious? Head down and humble? Shoulders back and proud? Sharing a lecherous leer with the guards? The wrong response might be lethal.

Ultimately, he chose a middle ground: posture both alert and proud, but of neutral facial expression.

He was swiftly greeted by three guards wearing tunics, knee-length kilts, and tightly braided hair. They carried short swords or rifles, and chuckled among themselves, making little effort to disguise their insinuating grins. He was shoved through the cabana's door, which was then shut tightly behind him.

"Do I wait?" he called through the wooden panels.

"Not long," said a voice behind him.

He turned with a start, and saw that a woman was waiting in the deeply shadowed bed. "I'm sorry," he managed to blurt out. "I didn't see you."

"Well," Nefriti said lazily. "You see me now."

He shifted positions. The only light was moonlight, flowing through a small louver over the door. That luminescence fell across the bulk of the bed, obscuring her face, but highlighting the sinuous shape beneath the single cotton sheet. "What am I supposed to do?" The air seemed to have thickened, his strength fled. More strongly than at any moment since his abortive duel with Malik, he knew himself to be in grave danger.

Breathe.

"Are you afraid?"

"Yes."

"Why?" Nefriti asked, a mocking tone behind the single syllable.

Why indeed? There was little to fear, save, death, torture, castration, and dismemberment. Especially castration. And another thing, something that he was only now beginning to admit to himself: the fear that his body might not respond. Never before had such a thought crossed his young mind, but once implanted, it seemed impossible to erase.

"I've never been with a black woman before."

Nefriti smiled. Luckily, she enjoyed his discomfort. "And have you ever seen one . . . like this?"

In the candlelight, she peeled back an edge of the sheet, exposing one perfect breast.

Aidan gasped. "No." He was rapidly losing his composure. He felt light-headed, but an accompanying heaviness in another physical realm resolved any lingering doubts about his ability to perform. The only question now was whether the cartridge might explode before entering the breech.

So to speak.

"You seemed so courageous in the arena," said the Calipha. "Even in defeat. Do not tell me that your courage fails now, when I need it most."

"No, I . . ."

He swallowed hard, but was regaining composure. The Calipha opened the sheet the rest of the way. She was extraordinary, and utterly alien to him. She was taller, leaner than Sophia, but her breasts were full and heavy, the nipples a deep and luscious cocoa. He couldn't take his eyes from them: never had he seen their like. Sophia's had been the darkest he had ever seen, but these . . . !

Fear dissolving before the tide of lust, Aidan whispered a silent plea that Sophia would forgive him for this transgression. After all, she had bade him to do whatever it took to bring Nessa home, and if anyone would have understood the implications of "anything," it was his good lady wife.

Still, he, and this moment, felt incredibly awkward.

If he was honest with himself, Aidan had to admit that he had always fantasized about bedding a black woman—so pristine, so utterly unattainable, so lofty and exotic. He could count the number of times he had *touched* one on his fingers.

He sat on the bed and then lay beside Nefriti, and all concerns of ineptitude vanished as she took control of the encounter, telling him *what* she wanted, and *when*, and *how*. By some measures the Calipha was past a woman's prime years, but she was still as flexible and lithe as a cat. Her entire body seemed to have been trained and nurtured solely for sexual congress, so that every muscular twitch, every deepening scent or wave of heat communicated to something deep and primal within him, so that it became difficult to think, or indeed to remember that there was a world beyond the walls of this room.

The clasp of her sex was like a milking hand. When explosion threatened she sensed it, and reached around with fingers and thumb to squeeze points surrounding his sack that turned the urging flames into embers; then began the steady hip-rocking caress anew.

She toyed with him for the better part of an hour. At times her eyes rolled back into her head as she capered in a secret sensual world. Occasionally they locked upon his, as if seeking to communicate without words or actions.

"You are rough," she said when their initial bout was complete, and he had rolled over onto his back, chest heaving. "But ingratiating, in your way." He was pleased to note that it had taken several minutes for the Calipha to collect herself sufficiently to manage speech. Still, what a woman!

Aidan struggled to normalize his breathing, that he might reply to her without gasping for air.

"So," she said, finger drawing a lazy circle on his chest. "What shall we try next?" she asked.

"What is it about slaves that you find so powerful, that a woman with all the world in her hands would want a man like me?"

Her brown eyes opened in surprise, as if taken aback that he would even ask such a question, as if no other man had ever done aught but rejoice in his good fortune. Then she tilted her head a bit sideways, pondering. "A man like you could lose, and still stand proud," she said finally. "You were a bested lion, but a lion still."

A tiny thread of an idea began to wind its way into Aidan's mind. "And this is unusual?"

"My"—she laughed—"you *are* naive. Most men can handle one or the other. Victory or defeat. Few can manage both." She smiled. "My husband is gracious in victory, but defeat . . . ?"

Nefriti laughed harshly; then her expression became contemplative and private. Then she turned her attention to Aidan again. "A woman loves to find something wild, uncontrollable, and make it desire her."

Yes, Aidan thought. *And you are older than you look. It has been long since men looked at you with simple lust and adoration, wishing to possess you for the sake of your beauty, and not your power. Even your own husband has doubtless turned to younger women who can still blossom with child.*

As a slave, I am safe. You can control me. I'm strong enough to make my admiration of you a thing worth having. Strong enough for you to enjoy the conquest.

When he came back to himself, she was watching him carefully. "You are a strange one," she said. "I have had many men, and always they are either frightened of me, or think that this might mean something it does not."

"I was frightened of you," Aidan said, rolling over onto his back. *Careful, now.* He had successfully flattened his voice, but now he had to find that empty place within himself, that place that Babatunde had taught him to reach. Who could have suspected that that ability would be tested in such a manner?

"For a few moments, perhaps. And then not. No matter what I did." She stroked his face with one dark, elegant finger. "You please me, slave. Perhaps I will call for you again."

"If you wish," he said, careful to keep his voice and face neutral.

Nefriti barked delighted laughter. "See! There it is again. You know that I could free you with a word . . . or have you killed in the same way."

"True."

"And yet you do not plead, or beg, or promise, or cajole. You remain yourself, even under stress. No white I have seen, and few Africans, could carry themselves so well." She peered more closely at his chest. "I see your scars. I know your life has not been easy. How then can this be?"

"What?"

"How can you have such *betep?*"

"What is this?" He controlled each breath with extreme care, tensing his anus and abdominal muscles on each exhalation, as if trying to expel smoke from his belly.

"Peace of spirit. A calm place within you, despite the cares of the world."

"Have you ever been with an Irishman?" he asked, gambling.

"No," she admitted. "Northmen, Germans, Greeks—but no Irish."

"And there you have it. This is a thing of my people." Very carefully, he insinuated a bit of Kai's speech cadence into his own words. Highborn speech would make him seem strange, exotic, perhaps more stimulating and unique.

"Truly?"

"Not all," he said. "It was a thing I was taught. Leaders among my people were given such instruction." *Careful. Mix lies and truth.*

She was fascinated. "Leaders?"

"My father was a king," Aidan said. "And I would have followed him." Her smile widened. *Yes, you vain, pampered bitch. You have royalty in your bed, under your thumb. You like that, don't you?*

"But how did that prepare you to be a slave?"

"A good leader is the slave of his people, as they are his. He leads them in war without concern for his own life. And in times of peace he must rise above politics and petty concerns to find justice."

It was a genuinely hazardous course he now traversed. Never would he have spoken so eloquently to a black not of Dar Kush. But Nefriti was fully engaged now—the hook had been set, and he prayed the line was durable enough to land her.

"It requires strength," he said. "Strength to submit without breaking."

"How does it *feel?*" she whispered urgently.

"What is your own experience?" he said, again taking an enormous risk. He had no idea what her experience might be. But he knew one thing: she was sexually aroused by him, and arousal tended to make logic more . . . flexible. This pampered house-pet craved excitement, and suspected that he might provide her with a series of memorable evenings, after which of course he would be discarded. If she was like other men and women he had known . . .

"Power and pleasure go hand in hand," she said. "Which is why all men seek power."

"True power is not in the external world," Aidan said. "It is within. My people say that the deeper the spirit, the more the body is an instrument of the soul. It cannot control the true spirit, but everything experienced by the body is a vehicle to growth."

She stared as if she had never seen a creature quite like him before.

And in truth, perhaps she hadn't.

"From whence comes true power?" he asked.

"Isis," she whispered.

So much for monotheism, Aidan chuckled to himself, cautious not to let his amusement reach his lips. Kai was right: scratch an Alexandrian, and just below the Muslim surface you were likely to find a pagan. "And to allow the goddess to work through you, what must you do?"

"Surrender myself."

"How can you do this if you are afraid? Only the strong can surrender."

Nefriti pondered for several minutes, her fingers crawling about in Aidan's lap. Then she spoke: "In the beginning, Neter created Nut, the sky, and Geb, the earth. Female and male. Our obelisks represent connection between the two."

You mean those pillars are just big penises? Aidan chuckled internally, but again kept his amusement to himself.

"In sacred sexuality, men and women take up the roles of Geb and Nut. By surrendering to each other, they surrender to the gods, and through doing so, to that Greater God that created everything." She gazed into his eyes. "They say that you whites are closer to nature, closer to the beast. That you are privy to secrets that civilized man forgot when he began to build cities. What say you to this?"

"I say that there are no words to explain what I see and feel. I am sorry. There is only experience."

She shook her head in disbelief. "Are there others like you?"

"Yes. In a place where we practice pleasures none would dare bring to the palace."

She stretched hugely, joints crackling as she twisted and bent. "Show me these pleasures," Nefriti said. Her eyes gleamed with unnamed hungers. "Or I will be displeased."

"I'm not sure. I would have to bind you."

"Bind?" She looked at him more sharply.

"I am sorry," he said. "Please forget my words. To be strong, to own one-self so completely that external fetters have no hold on the *ka* . . ." And here he very deliberately used the Egyptian word for "soul," one learned long ago at Babatunde's feet. "This is what I know, the greatest gift I could offer. It may not be suitable. Perhaps some smaller step would be more ap-propriate."

She stared at him intently. He barely dared breathe. "Tell me more. Do slaves do this to each other?"

"Yes," he said. "It is one of the few secrets we keep from our masters. The master is responsible for the safety, care, and welfare of his servants. Who is master? The servant knows the ultimate freedom of surrender. Who is slave?"

Her own breathing had quickened, her lips slightly parted.

"Think of it," he continued softly. "Every limb still, so that no wriggling or jounce can dispel a kite of the pleasure. It overflows, until the eye is blind and the ear deaf. It makes even the pleasure we just experienced seem like . . . a virgin's dry-lipped kisses." *Mother Mary. Is she buying this shyte?*

Her eyes gleamed in the darkness. *Apparently so.* "Then proceed. But I warn you—this is not my first experience with fetters. Show me things I have not experienced, or I shall be displeased with you."

Aidan reached down to the pants so recently discarded. A braided leather cord threaded the waist loops, courtesy of an amused Rhino.

He began slowly and gently enough, stretching Nefriti's arm back for binding to the bedpost.

"Wait," she began. "There is a better way—"

Before she could say another word or take a breath, Aidan spun Nefriti over on her belly.

"No, I—wait!" she sputtered. "How dare—!"

Using her own discarded clothing Aidan gagged her and tied her, hands and feet, then flipped her onto her back again. Her eyes spat poisoned daggers.

"I'll only ask you this once," he whispered. "Are there guards outside?"

She nodded her head.

"That's too bad. Because that means I have to kill you."

"Mmmph!"

He gripped her throat then loosened the gag just enough to allow her to whisper. "*No,*" she said frantically. "No guards. I have my privacy. But they will check come the dawn."

"Fine. I mean you no harm. Stay quiet, and all will be well."

He slipped the gag back in. "I hate to bruise that mouth. It has done so many wonderful things for me this night."

Her eyes blazed with both hatred and fear. Moved by a sudden impulse to charity, he threw a blanket over her. Whoever discovered her . . . well, there was no reason to increase the Calipha's shame. If his efforts were unsuccessful, such a gesture might make the difference between . . . not life and death, but torture and *extremely* slow torture.

What was done could not be undone. For Aidan, there would be no turning back.

groups of tiny, subservient mortals. The tiny mortals were black or brown. Aidan guessed that this was no reference to slavery; it bespoke the Caliph's attitude toward his subjects.

That brought a grim chuckle to the back of his throat. The Caliph seemed to fancy himself almost divine. *Where's your Muslim piety now?*

Stealthily, Aidan searched the office. He knew *what* he was looking for, *how* it appeared . . . but not *where* it might be found. Where? After half an hour every desk drawer was carefully searched, the bookshelves plundered, rows of carved boxes nestled in the deep rug inspected. Nothing. He reminded himself to keep his breathing steady and calm. He had time, all the time that he needed, but none at all to waste. Where was it?

The first sensation of panic was tugging at him when he glimpsed a deformation in the wall behind the main desk. The human figures stood out from the plaster a bit too starkly. It struck Aidan that that might not have been for artistic effect, but perhaps something more . . . practical.

As an accomplished carpenter he knew well how joints fitted together, tongue and groove securing woodwork without need for nails or screws. His eye was sharp enough to detect a variation in level that would have tested any Egyptian building inspector.

He pressed his face close to the wall, and gazed straight across . . . and saw it. One figure, the Caliph's own, stood out farther from the wall than even the Pharaoh's. Clever. He pushed it carefully, toggled it this way and that until he felt the wall groan, and the entire section slid a bit farther out.

Barely restraining a euphoric shout, he continued to apply pressure, and the section swung back, revealing a hidden cabinet.

And there, amid a stack of scrolls, lay a black leather pouch twenty digits long and as thick as his wrist. With trembling hands he opened it, revealing a cylinder composed of ivory disks, the rim of each engraved with a series of Egyptian symbols. He could only pray that it wasn't a decoy, or that he hadn't made any of a hundred other irreparable errors.

What now? What to do? It occurred to him that his best choice was simply to behave as if everything had gone according to Kai's original plans.

He returned to a tube of fire paste previously discovered in the Caliph's desk. Hands shaking as if fevered, he squeezed out half as much black paste as yellow before mixing. In that proportion, it would take almost five minutes to ignite. He smeared the resultant mixture in several choice locations around the office. Babatunde had said that confusion and chaos would be his allies. He had little choice but to trust that that was true. Trust that *everything* his allies had said was true.

CHAPTER SEVENTY-THREE

THE COOL NIGHT AIR dried the sweat upon Aidan's neck and back so suddenly that he fought the urge to sneeze. Marshaling every physical and emotional resource he possessed, Aidan left the cabana and began his efforts to sneak past the guards.

"Thought I heard a squeak a few minutes past?" the stouter of the two said.

"She must be wringing him dry," laughed the other. "Royals. Who can understand 'em?"

By keeping low to the ground and in the shadows, Aidan was able to remain out of their sight. Testing every step to avoid crunching a dry leaf, he made it all the way to the manse's back door.

Slowly, every digit of motion taking nearly a minute, he tested the door. If it was locked, he could try another route, but any additional complication cost him precious time. The latch opened, and he exhaled relief. Apparently, bars were not required to ensure the Caliph's sleep; armed guards were sufficient. Aidan gradually put his weight against the door, praying that the hinges would not betray him. Fortune remained his ally: it was well oiled as well as unlocked. Aidan slipped inside.

Aidan pulled Kai's map of the interior back to consciousness.

A sound to his left froze his heart: when his eyes adjusted to the dark, he was able to make the shape out. His company was a great gray cat, slipping toward him sinuously with luminous, unblinking golden eyes. It meowed up at him challengingly, as if resenting his intrusion into its domain. For a moment Aidan was afraid that it might begin to yowl, bringing the household down upon him, but instead it turned and glided away.

Aidan knew that there were back stairs leading up to the room the Caliph used as his office. There were no lights upstairs, and he hazarded that his luck was holding.

A minute later he was in the office itself. It was far more luxuriant than Kai's, with overstuffed chairs, deep rug, walls carved in Egyptian glyphs: all huge-eyed men and women of superhuman dimension dominating

Or else all was lost.

Aidan slipped the code machine back into its leather pouch and tucked it into his pants, then crept out the way he had come. The same feline greeted him at the bottom of the stairs. This time it yowled softly, and approached him with surprising boldness, rubbing against his leg and demanding a scratch.

He bent, and scratched the nape of its fuzzy neck. Satisfied, the cat wandered off again.

Clutching his precious burden beneath his cloak, Aidan found his way out into the estate grounds. He had only a few hours at the most to complete his mission, and he wracked his memory for the street plan provided by Kai. He had to find bin Jeffar's mansion, and without delay.

He held his breath and crouched in shadows. By some miracle he managed to avoid the estate's roving patrols until he found a section of hedged fence low enough to offer exit. He timed a pair of soldiers, and as soon as they were out of sight climbed up the bushes and found himself at the top of a wall, shards of broken glass set along the rim. He laid his cloak down to protect his hands, and vaulted over it. Aidan fell two cubits and hit the ground in a crouch. He tugged at the cloak: stuck on the glass. Damn.

Creeping from shadow to shadow, Aidan headed south.

Aswan Street was marked with a golden pyramid, and there he turned to the right. He knew that New Alexandria's streets were laid out like the principal cities of ancient Egypt. The wealthiest homes were all clustered in the same section of town, and that was another blessing. Still, he needed landmarks and found them: a sphinx here, a stone obelisk there.

Alarms blossomed in the night as the Caliphate fire was discovered. There were sleepy cries, and the bark of dogs and baboons. With more people running in the streets it actually became easier for him to walk openly, and then run, yelling "Fire!" until he arrived at bin Jeffar's manor.

Nessa had said she would unlatch the gate at night, and bless her, she had not forgotten.

Which room was hers? Bin Jeffar's mansion was certainly smaller than the Caliph's, but in comparison with its neighbors, still an imposing structure, four stories in height, with a dozen windows per floor.

But a golden handkerchief flagged from the edge of a third-floor window, the very same scarf worn by Nessa when she came to see him. That scarf meant that she was alone, and that she was ready.

He threw a tiny stone at the scarfed window. The first missed, almost struck the pane next to it. The next two tinked against glass with greater accuracy. The third brought a ghostly pale face to the darkness behind the pane. A pair of feminine hands pressed hard against the glass. A hesitant wave, and then she disappeared.

Within two minutes, the back door opened, and Nessa appeared.

"It is done?" she asked.

Aidan looked back over his shoulder. In the very distance, he could hear shouts, and wagon wheels clattering on the street. "We don't have long. Will you come?"

She seemed stunned, perhaps disbelieving that he was actually standing before him, and he sensed that she might have wondered if all he had said to her was some kind of fantasy, a slave's desperate attempt to bend reality to a more palatable form.

"Aidan! I don't know. What you're asking me to do . . ."

He took her hands in his. "Nessa. A lifetime ago, I promised you I'd come. This is the only chance we have. I'm sorry it took so long, but we have no time to think about this, only time to act. You have to make up your mind, and make it up now."

Her face was puffy, her eyes spiderwebbed with red. Had she been awake all night, wondering if the rap against her window would ever come? "Tell me again," she whispered urgently. "Tell me of your home."

He inhaled, knowing what she was really saying. *You ask me to throw this life away, Aidan. It may not be much, but it's all I have. Convince me that I'm not discarding it for nothing. Convince me that if the slavecatchers drag me back in chains, I will at least have sacrificed for a treasure worth the having.*

"It's on a lake, Nessa," he said. "It's a crannog, like O'Dere."

"Like O'Dere," she repeated, a wisp of a smile curling her lips.

"Smaller, but still growing," he amended. "And it's ours. There's fishing and hunting. There are only sixty of us, and life is sometimes hard. But we're building something, and you can be a part of it."

Nessa closed her eyes. "I dreamed about you every night for years. Wondered what I'd say if and when this moment ever came."

"And . . . ?"

"And finally I stopped dreaming, and as I told you, I made my peace with the world."

"I never did," he said.

She reached out, and brushed her fingers across his cheek fondly. "No, you didn't, did you?" she said, words tinged with wonder.

"I think sometimes that hoping to keep my promise one day was the only thing that kept me sane."

She wiped at a tear, this older sister whom he had dreamed of so long, and she shook her head, and he knew that she was going to say no.

But to his surprise, Nessa O'Dere said, "Yes. I will come with you, Aidan."

Nessa carrying a small dark bundle of personal belongings in her arms, the siblings hurried through the streets, where horse-drawn fire carts rattled toward the Caliph's mansion.

Aidan and Nessa kept to the alleys, and after almost an hour of dodging police and firefighters finally reached the section of town marked with a Star of David: the Judean neighborhood. Jews, men and women protected by the Treaty of Khibar, were the freest whites in Bilalistan. They traded freely through all four territories, and even provided an economic pore between Bilalistan and Vineland. But even these privileged Europeans had to present papers at checkpoints, were still but second-class citizens. Still, their special status placed them far above any children of Eire or Germany.

It took him another ten minutes to find the proper address, a brown brick building of Numidian design. He knocked hard, desperate to get in out of the street but praying that no neighbors would hear, realize they were fleeing slaves, and flash for the authorities. After an interminable pause, a panel opened at eye level.

An elderly bearded white man stared at them. "Yes?"

As carefully as he had ever said anything in his life, Aidan recited, " 'But indeed if any do help and defend himself after a wrong done—' "

" '—to him, against such, there is no cause for blame.' " The Jew's eyes sharpened once the passwords had been exchanged. "Do you have it?"

"Yes."

He gave the man a glimpse of the leather pouch. When the man still seemed to hesitate, he opened it, and displayed the ivory disks within.

"Hurry," the Jew said, scratching nervously at his curly sidelocks, eyes scanning the deserted street. "I am Ishmael. Come in, come in!"

Together, they entered.

The old man's house was smaller than any New Alexandrian dwelling Aidan had seen, but very neat, clean, and every digit of space seemed to be well occupied.

A silver nine-branched candle holder sat above his fireplace, next to a silver cup and a horn of some kind, perhaps bison.

Books and scrolls were everywhere: stacked, leaning, on edge, open on the single desk in a corner.

Aidan looked down at a scroll, and couldn't read any of the words. "What is this?" he asked.

"The Torah," Ishmael said. "It is the story of our people, and our God."

"Is it Allah?" Nessa asked. "The same God of the Muslims?"

"There is but one God." The Jew smiled. "And if He spoke to us first, well . . . who am I to question His judgment?"

Aidan peered more carefully at his host, and detected a bit of African blood in the shape of the nose and the curl of the hair. "Are you part black?"

"Abyssinian, yes. Both sides of my family can trace ancestry back to Solomon . . . the Queen of Sheba was his woman, and bore him children. Now, then. Enough pleasantry. It is my obligation to help the little Sufi, but the longer you stay here, the greater the risk for my people. There are blacks who would be eager for an excuse to ignore the Treaty of Khibar. So we must be very careful, we must be very smart . . . and we must get you to your next destination immediately."

He smiled. "But first, we celebrate." He took a crystal decanter from the shelf. "Wine, to clear the head and gladden the heart." He paused. "You are not Muslim?" They shook their heads. "Christian?"

"Once," said Aidan.

"Never," Nessa said, fingering her golden tree pendant.

Ishmael poured three glasses and handed two of them to Aidan and Nessa. "*L'Chaim*," he said.

"This means . . . ?" asked Nessa.

" 'To life.' "

Aidan sipped, and almost fell. Never had he tasted its like. Its warm golden glow ran down his throat like a healing river. It was smoother and sweeter than any beer he had ever tasted. His knees weakened. "May I sit?" he asked.

Ishmael nodded.

Aidan found a chair and sat in it, for a moment imagining that this was his home. His chair, his walls, his books. His wine. That in a moment Sophia would come from the kitchen, followed by their children. Ishmael watched him, wise brown eyes bright in his wrinkled face.

"Yes," the old man said. "This was the way it was supposed to be. This is what God intended. For each of us to bend his own back, make his own work, and prosper by the sweat of his brow."

He pulled a chair out for Nessa, who gratefully accepted it. "Thank you."

Then Ishmael sat on the couch, sipped at his wine, and fixed Aidan with a gaze of such clarity that he was temporarily stunned.

"Once, we too were slaves," said the Jew. "And a leader rose, and with the grace of God, Pharaoh was forced to free us, and we built a world of our own."

"Judeah," Aidan murmured.

"Yes. And when we supported Muhammad at Khibar, we found a way to protect our children, and our children's children . . . and even help the occasional *goyim*."

"This is wonderful," Nessa said. "Never have I tasted its like."

"Please, serve yourself," Ishmael said, and turned back to Aidan.

Aidan's head spun. Ishmael's eyes seemed so deep, he felt almost uncomfortable as they fixed upon him. "Why do you look at me like that?"

"I know a bit about you. Your mission. Your friendship with the Wakil. A promise you made, years ago, that you never forgot."

"I just want to get home," he said, emptying his glass. "I just want this to be over."

"Why," said Ishmael, "do you pretend to be something you are not?"

"What?" When was the last time he had eaten? The wine was going right to his head. He was glad he didn't have to stand.

"When the leaders of the tribe refuse to take their role as leaders," said Ishmael, "the tribe suffers."

"I don't have a tribe."

Ishmael smiled. "It is time to awaken from your dream," he said. Then he slapped Aidan's face gently, and winked. "And now, it is time to risk our lives, and freedom and fortune. A bit more wine before we go?"

CHAPTER SEVENTY-FOUR

SMOKE CLUNG TO THE GROUND and curtained the air, smarting the eyes of the servants and firefighters as they hauled and dashed water, pulled precious heirlooms out to safety, or counted the household staff. After stressful hours the office fire had finally been extinguished.

The Caliph himself had not reentered the house yet, although many of the staff had. He paced back and forth, a stout, bald, shaven man of middle years, his hands knotted behind his back. So far, he had managed to keep his rage under tight control, but it was obvious to all that this could not last. "And the damage?"

"It is hard to say," replied a guard. "Scrolls, documents . . ."

"This is a bad business. And my wife?"

The guard hesitated, reluctant to lift his gaze from the ground. "She is well, all things considered. In her room."

"I see. Well—continue on. Well done," he said, with a tone that implied that the man might be skinned later if the Caliph determined that the guard's negligence had engendered this catastrophe.

The Calipha lay abed, swathed in woolen blankets and nightclothes. Doctors and nurses hovered about. Unlike the cabana's spare environ, the Calipha's own bedroom was a feast for the eyes and spirit: gold inlay in the walls, silken sheets and hangings about the bed, thick exotic carpets lining the floor. A huge mirror etched with silver veins dominated most of one wall, making the room appear twice its actual generous size.

"Doctor Vin," said the Caliph to the attending physician, a bulky man with thin, strong hands. "Your diagnosis?"

Clearly, the staff was uncomfortable with the delicate situation. Vin most of all. "Nerve trauma, some abrasions to the wrist," he replied.

"I see. Leave us, please."

A mighty confusion reigned in the halls outside his wife's door. Servants and guards still dashed and yelled and fumbled, disoriented and frightened by the late-night threat of fire. With a deeply respectful bow, Doctor Vin retired from the room. The Calipha felt deeply humiliated by the evening's adventures, but somehow managed to maintain a regal posture.

"My husband," she said.

"My lady."

Quite solicitously, he sat at the edge of her bed and took her hand.

"It was horrible," she said.

"Yes, Nefriti. I'm certain that it was." He stroked her brow.

"I heard that your office was damaged."

"Yes," said the Caliph. Then almost incidentally he added: "And I find it credible that the damage was intended to conceal intent as well as facilitate escape."

She placed one smooth dark hand against her throat. "What do you mean?"

He stood from the bed, and began to pace. "What do I mean?" With those words, he fixed his gaze upon her, and there was such disdain in his expression that she pulled the sheets up more tightly around her neck. "I mean, my sweet, that in days past I have turned a blind eye to your indiscretions, even when some among our peers think to mock me behind my back."

His aspect began to change, grow more massive, as if sucking light and air from the room around him. "Only there *is* no 'behind my back,' my dear. There is *nothing* that goes on in New Alexandria that does not come to my attention. Nothing. We have had our sons and daughters. There will be no more, so this is the *Yadbut Imbisât*, the Time of Pleasure for you, I know. But what you have done in the past—"

She tried to turn her face away.

"What you have done in the past," he continued mercilessly, "a simple slaking of your animal urges, meant little to me because *you* mean little to me, as I mean to you. Little save our shared yoke of power."

Her lips trembled, as if trying to frame a denial, an attempt swiftly abandoned.

He leaned close. "But now you seem to have rendered my home vulnerable to a man with a purpose."

"A purpose?" she said, her voice and cheeks hollowed by fear. "He . . . he sought to escape. He . . . wanted a distraction."

"Is that what you think? That he acted spontaneously to wrest freedom from the grasp of bondage? That he crept into the house, stole no gold or silver that might have earned his way past a guard or bribed his way onto a ship or a Nation-bound caravan, and damaged nothing save my office?"

He pushed himself more closely into her face.

"What if I told you that the only thing missing was the cipher machine?"

Her eyes widened.

"Yes. Waters run deep here. Deep indeed. But know you—if your addiction to their loathsome pale flesh has jeopardized the alliance I have spent years in building . . ." He whispered the next. *"You will go west, my sweet."*

He stroked her again, even more lovingly, and then left. The Calipha pulled her sheet up almost to the lips an Irish slave had kissed so savagely, and she began to quake.

Soldiers swarmed the streets of New Alexandria. Whites were stopped and frisked, their faces compared to a poor drawing of an Irish fighting slave. The vaguest similarity proved sufficient for detention.

A cart drawn by a pair of horses, flying the Judean star, rolled through the street, creaking beneath a load of barrels.

"Halt!" cried a soldier.

"Yes sir?" said Ishmael, the elderly merchant holding the reins.

"Your papers."

The merchant presented a leather sheaf. The soldier unfolded and read the documents within. Then, grudgingly, he handed them back. "What are you carrying here?"

"Tomatoes, for New Djibouti."

"Open up," the soldier said.

"Open . . . ?" the merchant asked. "But my papers!"

"This is an emergency. Come on."

The merchant looked a bit askance, but complied. The soldier pried open one barrel, and then a second. Tomatoes, a vegetable discovered during the African conquest of the New World. He thrust his sword through the slats of a third. When he withdrew, thin red juice glistened on the blade.

"My vegetables!" cried Ishmael.

The guard, clearly disgusted, waved him on. "If you have a complaint, file it with the Caliph's office. On your way."

"I will! I will file!" he cried back over his shoulder as he trundled off.

The soldier was joined by one of his comrades, who had just finished an inspection on the far side of the street. "Jews. Can't tell 'em from the damned pigbellies."

" 'Bellies? Ask me, they're just pigs who don't eat their own," he said, and at that strange and disturbing image, they shared a nasty chuckle.

*   *   *

The cart trundled toward the dock, and rolled past a second check-point. Hapless male slaves were rounded up as the cart backed up against the loading dock.

"All right!" Ishmael said nervously. "Hurry. We sail on the morning tide."

As the men unloaded the barrels, a second cart arrived, this one carry-ing a variety of boxes. A guard sorted through them quickly, saw that the crates were too small to conceal a human being, and waved it on. It sat next to the first wagon. The merchant knocked three times on his own cart.

The "wooden" floor of the wagon was curiously thick, actually metal with a thin covering of sheet wood. A hatch dropped open. Aidan dropped out of the first, and Nessa thumped to earth from beneath the second.

Men loaded the barrels onto a third cart, and Ishmael quickly waved Aidan and Nessa into place behind it. And thus concealed, they crept up onto the ship's deck, to concealment, and safety.

Once on board, they were ushered below with all deliberate speed. The hold was dank and cold, crammed with boxes and pallets, bundles of cloth and odd machinery. Aidan thought he sensed a flash of motion: a rat? But remembering the three cats he had seen upon the deck, decided that they were probably safe enough.

"I am bin Abraham," said the captain, a tall, bearded man with a cloud-shaped birthmark on his right cheek and bright, intelligent eyes. It struck Aidan that bin Abraham would be about his father Mahon's age . . . if only Mahon had lived. "You will be safe here," the captain said. "So long as we are not discovered, this ship is sovereign Judean soil. Welcome to the *Solomon*."

Tears streamed down Nessa's face again, although she struggled for composure. "Thank you," she said. "Thank you very much."

"I will be back later with mattresses. Food. For now, be very quiet, and if anyone but me calls for you—do not answer." He managed a smile at this last.

"I am in your debt," said Aidan.

"Repay it with silence." The captain chuckled. "You know, you will be the first slaves I've ever smuggled *south*.

And still chuckling to himself, he left. Nessa sagged to a seat.

"Are you all right?" asked Aidan.

Nessa hung her head for a moment, and then smiled.

"Just fear, I think. A little weak and sour-mouthed."

She looked around herself. "Maybe it's just being in the belly of a ship again."

The image that comment conjured was simply too vile for words, and he banished it from his mind. "At least we're together," said Aidan.

"Again. And heading to freedom?"

He nodded. "As close to it as we can get, in this world."

CHAPTER SEVENTY-FIVE

7 Jumada al-Awwal A.H. 1295
(Friday, May 10, 1878)

BY THE TIME THE *SOLOMON* REACHED Djibouti Harbor, a blockade was in full effect. The Judean ship was intercepted by a steam-screw flying Alexandria's colors. It dispatched a boat to meet them.

"Ahoy the ship," called the officer in the prow of the little skiff. "This harbor is closed, by order of the Caliph. I am Captain Otomo Ramses."

"Bin Abraham, at your service. Please inspect my manifest," said the *Solomon's* captain. "I left New Alexandria before the blockade began, and carry goods from the Caliph's own storehouse. If I could but complete my run, I will return nothing but gold for his treasury."

"And that is all?" asked Ramses.

"Yes," said the captain.

Ramses brooded. The words had been correct, but he remained unconvinced. "Hmmm . . ."

"And here," said the captain, opening his purse. "I am sure that the Caliph would want you to share in the proceeds."

He handed the officer a half-Alexander. The man grinned and bit it.

"Last shipment?"

"The last," said the captain. "You'll not see me again until the blockade is lifted."

"Very well," said Ramses. "Sail on! Officer—signal the ships that this vessel has my approval to proceed."

Aidan and Nessa clambered onto deck as the ship approached the harbor. The statue of Bilal loomed up above them as they passed, a Titan guarding his kingdom.

"I remember," said Nessa, "so many years ago, seeing that statue and thinking that it must have been a giant, frozen there by God."

"A giant, yes," said the captain. "But a mortal giant."

"Bilal," said Aidan. "First to call the faithful to prayer."

"Yes. He saved the Prophet's daughter."

"The Prophet. Peace Be Upon Him." Aidan's words were tinged with bitterness.

"Yes," said the captain, in a philosophical tone. "Peace upon him indeed. He made peace with us, and commanded his people to keep that peace."

"And they have?"

"For thirteen hundred years. And because of that promise, you are now free."

Aidan nodded, accepting the captain's subtle rebuke. "Yes. We are in your debt. What do you know of these ships—are they Djiboutan?"

"I think not. Supposedly, they amass here for an expedition to Azteca. But similar massings have occurred at other harbors in Djibouti. You saw the one at the Brown Nile. It is no accident." He spat over the side. "War approaches, I'll wager, but not with the Aztecs."

Bin Abraham looked at Aidan. "Your journey is almost over. You said that you owed me a favor."

"Anything."

"Then answer a question for me. I was reluctant to ask it when first you arrived. Seemed none of my business. I was told to help you because you were on a mission for the Wakil of New Djibouti."

Aidan nodded cautiously.

"Tell me, lad: why do you help those who enslave your people?"

Aidan sighed. Why indeed? "I suppose I believe I have to take sides."

"Why the south? Certainly your interests would be better served in the north. It is the northerners who talk emancipation."

"Yes," admitted Aidan. "They talk. But it is a southerner who found my sister for me. I trust a man, not a government."

Bin Abraham smiled, and laid a warm, gnarled hand on Aidan's shoulder. "A man. Yes. Ultimately, it is ever thus."

A small boat, rowed by a bulky black boatman, was making its way from the dock to the ship.

"For us?" asked Nessa.

"Yes. This is where we go our several ways. Good luck to you, Irish. Madam."

"Good-bye, Captain. You are a good man."

"As men go. Farewell."

They climbed down the ladder to the waiting boat. The boatman oared them about and away.

"What now, Brother?" asked Nessa.

"Now? Now our life begins."

An oar stroke at a time, the boat made its way across the bay's oily waters to the dock. Awaiting them, as he had prayed, stood Babatunde and Kai.

"Is this your friend?" Nessa asked.

"He is."

"Is he mine as well?" Her voice was nervous this time.

"He is."

The boatman tied up his craft. Aidan leapt up onto the dock, then helped his sister to disembark.

"Aidan," Kai said soberly. "Despite my best efforts to kill you, once again you seem to have survived."

They embraced, hard.

"And this can be no one but your sister," said Babatunde, and clasped her hand warmly. "Welcome to New Djibouti."

"Thank you," said Nessa. "And you must be the notorious Babatunde."

The smaller man bowed. "My reputation precedes me."

"The heliographs delivered certain code words. Was their optimism misplaced?" asked Kai, feigning moderate interest.

"You know it was."

Aidan extracted the leather pouch, and handed it to Kai. Kai held his breath as he opened it and peered within. He pressed it tightly closed, and then wrapped the cylinder again, and tucked it into his belt.

Kai looked from one to another of them, excitement and respect and love all melding in his eyes. "Oh, Aidan—you have outdone yourself. Come! A feast awaits you—on one condition."

"And what is that?"

"That you tell me *everything*."

They boarded a coach. Aidan settled back into his seat and sighed vastly. *He had actually done it!* "Everything?" He shook his head. "Kai, I don't know. There was violence, and danger . . . and other, well, *intimate* things not fit for an aristocrat's ears."

"Ahh!" Kai groaned. "I die! A quarter-Alexander for your tales."

"Half."

"Whole!"

"Done. . . ."

CHAPTER SEVENTY-SIX

NESSA WATCHED AIDAN SHAKE HIS HEAD ruefully as he saw the two children manning Dar Kush's main gate. Strange how familiar, and comforting, and irritating their happy faces were, welcoming the master and his guests home. Much like bin Jeffar's country estate, but there were differences, too. Seldom had she seen a white and black man interact as did Aidan and the Wakil. Despite everything she and her brother had shared in their days at sea, she still had not been prepared for the obvious affection and ease between the two.

"Master's home! Ring the bell, idiot!" the boy called from the gate.

"Pox ye!" laughed the freckled, black-haired girl beside him.

Kai leaned over to Aidan. "Tata is smiling," he said with a deep and healing satisfaction. "I wouldn't have believed it."

"I'm ringin', I am," Conair called. "I'm ringin'!"

Nessa leaned out of the coach, eager eyes wide and taking in every blade of grass. "It's beautiful." Even as she said that, she saw the dozen slaves who ran to meet them. She cast an eye at Aidan, and he shook his head shallowly. She sensed his reservation and remained silent.

Summoned by her servants and the bell, Lamiya came out from the main house to greet them. "Welcome back, Husband, Babatunde."

She smiled at the sight of Aidan. "You look a bit more bruised and ugly, Irishman."

"I was determined to return—even if only to haunt your husband."

"Then let us rejoice while breath remains. Come. I believe that Bitta can find you a wine flask."

"Blessed be," said Nessa, and meant it. Ishmael's wine had awakened a hunger in her, and bin Abraham had nourished it aboard the Solomon. There was so much to learn, so much to see . . . and a bit of that dark sweet nectar would definitely ease the way.

*   *   *

"Standard hieroglyphs," said Babatunde, scanning the ivory disks. "No diacritical marks." He glanced up. "The code device is as I posited. Twenty rows across, twenty-three positions on each wheel—"

"Twenty-three?" asked Nessa. "Why twenty-three?"

"One for each of the standard symbols," the Sufi said. "Vulture, foot, placenta, hand, arm, horned viper, jar, flax, reed, snake, basket . . ." He closed his eyes, and his brow furrowed. "Owl, water, mat, hill, mouth, cloth, water pool, bread loaf, tether ring, quail chick, double reed leaves, and door bolt."

Aidan rubbed his knuckles against his temples. "My head hurts."

Kai laid out four sheets of glyph-inscribed paper. "Eight months ago," he said, "a ship was intercepted on the passage between New Alexandria and the Egyptian Sea."

"And what became of it?" Nessa asked.

"It is best you didn't know," Kai said soberly. "Let us just say that before open war erupts, smaller, more controlled, but no less lethal actions abound. The Empress and Pharaoh have each authorized ships to prey upon the other's treasure lanes. Everyone knows it; no one admits it. Any damage is blamed on pirates."

"And how came these documents to your hands?" she pressed.

"Again, best you not ask. It is enough that they were obtained, and I have reason to consider them genuine. We believe that the Pharaoh is so confident of the code that they continued to send messages in the same manner. We managed to obtain one further message, following a summit meeting in New Alexandria, in which the 'Triumvirate' were said to have argued fiercely until the early hours of the morning. The meeting did not conclude until daybreak. They were said to be grim, but determined."

"I think I remember the admiral returning in the early-morning hours, after such a meeting."

That piqued their interest. "Did he say anything to you?"

"He never spoke to me of politics," she said.

Suddenly, Nessa understood. "And you believe that the content of that meeting is in this letter?"

"Yes."

Babatunde jumped in. "And that they had received word of new aggressions between Egypt and Abyssinia. We believe that this message is in response to a request from the Pharaoh that Bilalistan provide men and materiel."

Babatunde turned the coding scroll's wheel. Paused, studied it, and then turned again. He turned to Nessa.

"Are you aware that the admiral himself may have created this device?"

She took it from his hands and examined it carefully. "I never saw it. But I believe he once mentioned a paper written on the subject, and spoke of the military college adapting his theories to such a purpose. But again, he did not speak often of such things."

Babatunde probed Nessa with a few more questions before concluding she had no further information.

"Well?" asked Kai.

He shook his head, discouraged. "I feared as much. With every usage of the machine, they change the order of the code wheels."

"What does this mean?"

"It means," said Babatunde, "that this device is even more diabolical than we thought. To create an unbreakable code is one thing. To create one unbreakable *even if you have the key* is something else entirely." His voice was hushed with something near reverence. "Brilliant."

"Are you saying that you will be unable to read the messages?"

Babatunde gave a pained expression. "I will try, my young Wakil. I will try."

Kai, Aidan, and Nessa moved to a corner of the room. Variously they squatted, sat cross-legged, or leaned against the wall and settled in for a long and taxing evening. Nessa tired after an hour, and Aidan decided to show her to his lodgings.

Nessa flinched as they passed the gates of Ghost Town. Everything seemed so new and strange to her.

Aidan spent a few minutes showing her the places he had known as a child, and introduced her to a few people. Then he showed her to the house he had shared with their mother.

"Please, take the bed," he said. "You look tired. I have to go back."

She hugged him, and he left.

Nessa ran her finger along the windowsill, the bed, the counter where Deirdre had prepared meals for her child. It felt oddly as if she was searching for her mother's spirit here.

Then at last she lay in the bed and closed her eyes. Her mother's bed.

She gripped at it with fingers that had been too weak to keep the slave-masters from tearing her family apart, and cried for the first time since childhood.

And crying, she fell to sleep.

*　　*　　*

By dawn's early light, *El Sursur* struggled to unlock the secret of bin Jeffar's codes. His blackboard was crisscrossed with scribbles. Kai and Aidan slept in a corner of the room. Babatunde, eyes red-rimmed and exhausted, pulled a blanket over each of them, and managed a tired smile.

Several times during the night he had drilled Aidan for every piece of information he could extract: where the scroll had been found, the appearance of the environment, anything that might provide a clue.

So far, nothing had helped.

Then he looked back at the blackboard.

"Allah, inspire me," he said. "I know not the stakes, only that the boy I love as a son relies upon me. He wagered his honor and fortune on this, and threw his dearest friend into the crucible. There must be a way. What one man can make, another can unmake. But I fear I have neither the strength nor the wit. These old bones grow tired."

He drew a bath and soaked for a time, glyphs dancing behind his closed eyes. Emerging, he donned slippers and a bathrobe, then sat at his desk again, rubbing his eyes. The writing still looked like gibberish. "Perhaps a walk," he murmured.

Heavy with fatigue and discouragement, he pulled a cloak over his bathrobe, and left the room.

The house was still dark, save for a few drowsy servants going about their early-morning duties.

The sun had yet to rise above the eastern horizon. Babatunde walked across the grass, watching the morning mist as it rolled across the lawn, enjoying the strong dank smell of the fog off Lake A'zam. He studied the moon, low on the horizon now. The early morning was quite still.

The moon transfixed him, almost as if there were answers written on its pale disk. "What were you trying to say, oh Caliph?" he whispered. "What . . . were you . . . always . . . trying to . . ."

He squinted as he saw a female figure walking across the grass toward him. At first he assumed that it was a servant heading for early-morning kitchen duties, but made out that it was Aidan's sister.

"*Sabíya-t* O'Dere," he said. "Taking an early-morning stroll?"

She smiled as she approached him. "The admiral is a great fan of early rising, and I've caught the habit. I thought I would come and see what the legendary Sufi has done with my brother's efforts."

"Less than I might have hoped." He paused, considering. "Tell me," he asked. "What did the admiral think of the Caliph?"

Nessa ran her fingers through her strawberry hair, and thought. "Amon thought him highly intelligent, that he enjoyed wielding power a bit too much, and . . ." She paused, as if struggling to remember, or perhaps decide if she should speak further.

"Yes?"

"That the Caliph pretended to be more pious than he actually was."

"That is often the way with politicians. They—" He paused, staring off into the fog, mouth open.

"Oh! Oh!" he cried, and rushed back into the house.

Babatunde tore apart his study until he found a sheaf of letters, then thumbed through those until he found the one he sought. Then, humming happily, he ran through the hall until back to his own office. "Where is it?" he said.

Aidan and Kai were beginning to stir, but were far too groggy to respond to his question.

"Where is what?" Kai moaned.

"Thank Allah for the *munafiq.*"

"What?"

"Hypocrites. Impious men." Babatunde touched his fingertips together, entering lecture mode. "The Caliphate is a spiritual lineage, supposedly those who hold power in trust following the death of the Prophet, Peace Be Upon Him. But our Caliph is a *political,* not a spiritual animal, and such creatures mistake the form of the thing for the content."

"Eh?"

Aidan rolled onto his back. He had yet to open his eyes. "It is entirely too early for this."

"A righteous man often begins his letters *Bismillaahir Rahmaanir Rahim,* 'In the name of Allah, Most Gracious, Most Merciful.' But the Caliph does it *compulsively.* There—see?" he pointed. "Every letter he writes carries that inscription. There is the possibility, just the possibility, that he made the mistake of doing the same thing with his coded messages."

Kai and Aidan looked at each other without the slightest comprehension.

Babatunde weaved his fingers together, and cracked his knuckles with excitement. "If so, then by mapping that blessed phrase over the coded transmission, I can arrange these wheels until they produce that meaning."

"And when you do?"

"If I do . . . I'll have it."

"Have you slept?" Kai yawned.

"Who needs sleep?" cried the Sufi. "I have a conundrum!"

Kai and Aidan grinned. "I wager that you need breakfast, though—"

"Oh, fine. Have it brought here if you must. There is work!"

After breakfast, Nessa asked Aidan to show her more of his childhood home. Together they toured the main house and gardens, the stables, and fields, and then circled back to walk the shore of Lake A'zam. A hundred cubits from the yacht dock, the pair was confronted by a pair of Dahony.

"Who goes there?" Yala called.

"Aidan O'Dere, and sister Nessa."

Yala smiled broadly, displaying gleaming white teeth against black skin. "Aidan! You are the Wakil's white friend. Nandi says he trusts you above all others."

Aidan was startled by this. "That's me, I suppose," he said. There was a loud hissing sound behind Yala, and Aidan glimpsed a black metallic wedge moving, one digit at a time, onto the lake from the dock. "What is this?"

"Do you know of Chifi's work? The Tortoise?"

"Yes. I never understood it, but Kai spoke of it. A floating metal ship?"

Chifi climbed out of the ship. "Metal over wood, Aidan."

"*Sabíya-t* Kokossa!" he said politely. "It has been years."

Her lips curled in a smile, but the rest of her face remained still. "Indeed," she said. "I hear you've done well with your freedom. Well done. Freedom belongs to no one, and everyone. And is this your sister?"

"Yes, ma'am."

Nessa curtsied. "Your father's name was spoken with reverence as far as New Alexandria."

Chifi's face tightened, and then relaxed a bit. "Would you care to come aboard? I was planning to take her for a short run, and we could use another hand."

"Absolutely," said Aidan.

Chifi took them down into the warm, dank depths of the Tortoise. She showed them the guns, the armor plate, the hot-air pumping mechanism.

"The engine is powered by the changing volume of air as it heats," she said. "We use such pumps to circulate or remove water. Air in the bottom is warmed, expanding and forcing the piston upward.

"Then the displacer is driven downward to the bottom of the cylinder. Since the displacer is of a smaller diameter than the cylinder, the hot air rushes around the displacer to the cool end of the engine. Once in the top end of the cylinder, the hot air begins to contract, sucking the piston downward. Now the displacer moves upward, forcing all the cool air from the top end of the cylinder into the bottom end. Here the air is heated, and the cycle begins again."

Sallah Mubutu showed them other wonders, answering Aidan's questions. The Tortoise was like no other boat he had ever seen, and was one of the great marvels of his life.

Kai and Lamiya were speaking intimately in the central courtyard when Babatunde raced toward them yelling, "Kai! Kai!"

"Babatunde!" cried Lamiya. "Tie your robe!"

"Oh! I . . . pardon me." He turned, tying his robe, but handed the papers back to Kai as he did.

"And what is this? Hmmm."

There was a long pause, and then Kai murmured, "Ali's beard. You've done it! Babatunde, the size of your . . . intellect never ceases to amaze me."

"Kai, you were right," Babatunde said. "Now they have to listen!"

"You would think so, wouldn't you? But we're all mad, my friend. Let's just hope that our particular insanity is communicable."

CHAPTER SEVENTY-SEVEN

THAT VERY AFTERNOON couriers had ridden to the heliograph towers, and within minutes their messages flashed across the district. By midnight, a secretive meeting convened in Kai's offices: neighbors, a councilman, a wealthy merchant, an influential doctor.

"I have read the decoded scroll," Kai said to his guests. "We have all read its words. Pay them heed. Bilalistan is to remain a protectorate of Egypt. Our sons are to fight along the Nile for Pharoah's glory." His guests grumbled. "The Caliph was at this meeting," he continued, "as was Dosa. As he claimed, bin Jeffar was not a signatory." Kai concluded and spread his hands flat on the table before him.

"This is grave news indeed," said Djidade Berhar. He sat in a wheeled chair of wicker and iron. His ashen face made plausible the rumors that illness was winning its contest with medicine and will. Still, his quavering voice projected above the din. "They would raise our taxes, and press our sons and slaves into military service? No. I say no!"

"Kai," said Councilman Pili, "I say you have done great service. My cousin will hear of this!"

"The Governor comes to the opening of the Choral house this weekend," wheezed Berhar. "I say that that may prove our best opportunity, more appropriate than any flashed or written message could be."

"One of you good men may have to speak for me. The governor is not numbered among my supporters."

"We shall *all* speak for you," said the merchant.

Kai nodded thanks. "And now comes the part most dear to all—you have offered strong words. Now I need deeds. I need your gold and your support in the Senate."

"And you shall have it," said Berhar. "We cannot wait for a senate to mandate action. Something must be done immediately."

As the others babbled congratulation, Berhar's dying eyes burned. He wished power for his son and blood and name, that much was true. He had allowed Allahbas to convince him that Kai should step down as Wakil, that Fodjour might take his place. This was true as well.

But New Alexandria's treachery demanded that he place personal ambition in perspective. Kai, the boy he had once labeled mischief-maker and scamp, had, for all of his apparent naiveté, accomplished much in an arena where more experienced politicians and strategists had failed. What this young man had wrought was vital for New Djibouti's survival, and only a fool—or a madwoman—would deny him proper credit. What did that mean for his own secret goals? Of this he could not be certain. Knowing Allahbas's unbounded ambitions, it might be difficult to convince her to forestall her plans until the current emergency had passed.

Very difficult, and as Berhar's disease progressed, he had less and less strength with which to oppose her.

So then . . . whatever would be, would be. And at this point in his life he merely wondered if he would live long enough to see it through.

CHAPTER SEVENTY-EIGHT

As two making a pilgrimage, with the coming of dawn Aidan led Nessa to the still-blackened remnant of the prayer grove. Burned stumps still scarred the earth, but dozens of transplanted saplings bore a promise of new life and hope.

They were quiet as they entered, displaying that natural awe experienced on entering a holy place, a place of worship or sacrifice, a place where whatever gods there were approached most closely the mortal world.

He led her to a weathered wooden cross thrust upright before a small heap of stones.

"Is this hers?"

He nodded, and ran his fingers over the weathered wood. "I carried every one of these stones myself, as a boy. I added a new stone a year every year until leaving to seek my fortune at the Ouachita crannog."

Nessa sank to her knees before the cross, and pressed her lips to its splintered wood.

"I remember one of our father's tales," she said in a low, reverent voice. "He called it 'The Voyage of Maelduin.'"

Aidan shook his head sharply. "I haven't thought of that poem for ten years."

"I don't remember it all," she said, "but I used to chant it to myself on the boat from Andalus. It told of the journey between life and death. I remember the island of lost women." She closed her eyes, and began to recite in a Gaelic singsong so high and sweet that he was momentarily transported back to their childhood:

"The flowing green waves brought them over the sea to a mountain island.

"Beautiful maids dwelt therein, grooming and bathing each other in a bath of the purest water.

"Their Queen Mother rode on a fleet horse to greet them, the maidens at her side all curl-haired and open-handed. She said:

"None who dwell here will die. Rest unafraid, swathed in gentle garments, sleeping on a woven bed . . ."

Her voice broke, and she began to cry, digging at the grass around the rocks with her fingers. "Mother," she whispered. "You did not fail me. Memory of your love sustained me. The boy you nurtured rescued me. You would be proud. Rest easy, sweet." She rested her forehead against the ground, and there for a time she wept.

She looked up at him. "I had not cried for five years. I swore that I would not, again, and kept that promise to myself until I slept in Mother's bed."

Finally Nessa dried her eyes and turned to her brother. "We have many sorrows, Aidan," she said. "I say we bury them here with Mother. She was strong enough to bear them all, and she would want us to begin afresh."

"Can we do that?" he asked.

"We're the only ones who can," she said, and threw her arms about his neck, pillowed her face against his shoulder, and remained there for a time. Then finally they rose together and walked back to Ghost Town.

Aidan and Nessa had taken up temporary residence in the old *tuath*. "So . . . ," she said. "This is where you spent your youth?" The previous night, she had been too tired and stressed to do much save collapse onto the bed. For the last hours the siblings had dusted and straightened, trying to turn a house into a home. As Nessa tidied she rested her hands here, her eyes there, almost as if in so doing she was making mystic connection with her long-lost mother.

"It was home for many years, yes."

"I had no better," she said. "No, you did well."

"It can't compare to the lodgings you left."

She paused, adjusting her apron strings. "You are here," she said. "And that makes it home."

Conair poked his head in through the door. "Master's here," he said.

"Wish me luck," said Aidan.

She touched his cheek. "And more."

Aidan left. Nessa looked at these simple surroundings, and, safe from even her brother's eyes, began to shake.

"Walk with me?" asked Kai.

"Gladly," Aidan replied. "How have things progressed?"

"Blessedly. And now we come to matters of reward."

"I have what I was promised."

"That was not an answer."

"There was not a question."

"Hah! Implied only. Well then—what do you think is the proper reward for a man who has rendered service such as yours?"

"I have thought of this," said Aidan. "Hoped you would come to me with such a query."

"And have you an answer?"

Aidan collected himself and then spoke. "Tell me, Kai, how often does your military regiment drill?"

"Djibouti Pride? Generally three times a year," he said. "Why?"

"And it is my understanding that some members travel, so that they participate in training even less frequently. Is that correct?"

"Yes, but . . ."

"And that as Wakil you can give commissions to men who have given service to the state or nation?"

Kai's eyes widened. "Aidan!"

The Irishman drew his shoulders back. "I wish to be a member of your regiment, even if the lowliest among them."

"Aidan," said Kai sadly, "that cannot be done."

"Can it not? I hear it is thus in Africa. In Egypt, slaves are soldiers. Officers. Generals. Some have risen high."

"True. But custom here forbids this. Mamluks can win freedom, but that is the end of it."

"Custom is made by men of power," said Aidan. "You are such a man."

"Aidan . . . why do you want this impossible thing?"

"I saw the village I built nearly destroyed because the black citizens of the nearest township knew they could kill us, and we would have little recourse to law. We live in an unincorporated territory."

"I've extended protection to you. . . ."

"And for that I am humbly grateful. But if I was a soldier, a real soldier, not a mamluk, I would have all the rights of a citizen."

"But you've already been guaranteed those rights!"

Aidan laughed bitterly. "It is not your fault, Kai. There is no way you could be expected to understand. The government gave out hundreds of those emancipation documents. But paper does not equal privilege. That mob could have burned my entire village to the ground, buried us in shallow graves, and there would hardly have been an investigation. Freedom means being able to kill a man who harms your family—"

"Aidan, the law—"

"As you would, Kai. As your brother and father *did*. There is only one way to have real freedom: to be strong enough to take it. And there is only one way for me to do that: to be a part of something larger than myself. To earn the right of comradeship with men of strength and honor, until those who would harm me are afraid to act. I could organize my people into a militia, prepared to defend Bilalistan . . . or our own walls. We would have access to weaponry and training. If my service is honorable my son would inherit my billet. It is a path to honor and freedom. *Real freedom.*"

Kai shook his head. "Aidan . . ."

"You, above all, know that real freedom is not given. Nor can it be provided by a protector. It must be purchased at the edge of a sword. Give me the right to wield that sword, in the service of this country. *Make this country my own.* That is the boon I ask." He paused. "If you could do this thing for me, I would serve you faithfully, all my days."

Kai paused, the automatic refusal frozen on his tongue. He more closely examined the man he had known half his life. He had the odd sense that for the first time in years he was really *seeing* Aidan. Had his friend really changed so? Certainly *something* had changed. "It is so important to you?"

"Put yourself in my place, Kai. Tell me you would not want the same. You spoke of the path of a holy warrior. Perhaps I cannot embrace that. But let me be at least a man, capable of defending his family and home. Allow my courage and strength and will to take me where it will, regardless of my color. You will never regret it."

"No," Kai replied. "I don't believe I would. Let me think on this, Aidan. Will you trust me to do what I think best here?"

"I trust you with my life . . . and my family's."

Kai peered more deeply into Aidan's eyes, then clapped his shoulder, sighed, and walked away.

PART V

The Abyss

"Why," said the student at last, "can we not see Allah? Is he so far away?"

"What separates man from God," said the teacher, "is but a thin partition. God is infinitely close to man, but man is very far from God indeed."

"How can this be?" asked the student.

"The entrance to heaven is obscured by a mountain," said the teacher, "which Man must remove with his own hands. He digs and digs, but the mountain remains."

"Then there is no hope?"

"If he digs in the name of Allah, one day the mountain will vanish."

"How can this be?" asked the student.

The teacher smiled. "It was never there at all."

CHAPTER SEVENTY-NINE

THE CHORAL HOUSE ROSE like a crown with a golden dome in the center. This was its opening night, an occasion that had achieved a dominant position on every social calendar in southern New Djibouti.

The luminaries were out in force, dressed to display their wealth and social position. The estate of Dar Kush was no exception: Kai, Babatunde, Lamiya, and Nandi were all in attendance, accompanied by Kebwe, Makur, and Fodjour. The Wakil had also purchased a row up high in the back for twenty of his orphans, who were dressed in sparkling-clean cotton shirts, dresses, and breeches.

Accompanied by a roar of applause from the audience, Governor Pili approached down the aisle, accompanied by his wife Pili *Hamam* and two hulking bodyguards.

"Your Excellency," said Kai.

"Wakil," came the curt return.

The Governor and his wife walked past them without the courtesy of another word.

"Their Excellencies seem in a poor mood this evening," Nandi said.

"And will be in a worse one still once we have had our discussion." Kai clucked. "I hope he enjoys the music—it is likely to be his last real entertainment for quite some time. I fear I have fallen out of favor."

"Like the seasons," Nandi said, "life turns in cycles."

"At some future point Governor Pili will need you," Lamiya said. "Then, all will be forgiven."

"As you trust the Empress will forgive you."

"Yes," she said. "Precisely."

"At times, you have a pessimistic view of human nature," Fodjour said.

"I have associated with Kai and his jolly barbarians for far too long," she replied.

They took their seats in the domed amphitheater. The attendants were tough, wiry, kilted men, with the strong brows and shaven heads typical of the Kikuyu. One of them handed Babatunde a program. He looked at the man's fingers, and frowned.

Those fingers were strong. Square. Callused. And what did that bulge beneath his shirt conceal?

"Babatunde . . . ?" Kai asked, puzzled by his teacher's curious expression.

"Nothing," the Sufi said. "I thought I had seen that man before." He settled back into his seat. "Let us enjoy."

"The program seems promising," said Lamiya.

Babatunde nodded. It was not uncommon for men to carry blades. Pushing aside thoughts of a knife and those strangely tempered hands, he slipped effortlessly into teacher mode. "There are many ways to interpret the Pharaoh's myth," he said. The use of the term *Pharaoh* with a special emphasis was always understood to refer to the Great Pharaoh, not the ambitious toad currently squatting on the Egyptian throne. "So many phases to his legend. This collection of works is unique, allowing a variety of composers to speak to us. As boy, student, young warrior-prince, conqueror, ecstatic, king, philosopher, husband, father, architect of a military empire lasting two thousand years . . . Alexander played so many roles that no one composer could serve them all."

After an introductory piece lasting half an hour and displaying a wide and rousing variety of tempos and melodies, the orchestra retreated. After a brief intermission, the Zulu chorale took the stage, and Nandi's interest increased considerably, virtually radiating pride as the clean-limbed young men and women took the stage.

They numbered three dozen, all younger than sixteen summers, not yet obliged to their mandatory military service, serving their people now by promoting their culture.

Accompanying them were a dozen musicians on a variety of woodwinds, stringed, and membraned instruments. The traditional instruments that formed half of the assembly had been gathered from all over Africa: an *agwara* trumpet, an *enanga* East African zither, a *mizmar* Egyptian folk oboe, even the one-stringed Ugandan *rigurigi* fiddle.

The conductor was a grave, hollow-faced man in his fifties, with triple scars emblazoned upon each cheek. He bowed to the audience, then turned his back to face his pupils, raised his arms, and began.

The songs formed a story, the story part of a triptych detailing the history of the Zulu migration to Bilalistan.

The most moving section told the story of the legendary Fraternal War, a great battle between two sons, each of whom had been promised the

throne by a dying King. This was a story of special significance: it was the tale of Nandi's grandfather.

The sons had loved each other in childhood, and now deeply regretted the death and destruction that might come to their followers if they continued down the path of war.

As was Zulu custom, the two armies stood on opposite sides of a river, the rushing waters symbolizing the tides of fate, and sang to each other of their courage and unmatched skill in battle. They spoke of sexual prowess, and cruelty, and mercy.

As the songs peaked, Kai glanced at Nandi. Tears sparkled on her beautiful cheeks. The singing swelled in intensity as it became clear that there was no way to avert the coming disaster.

The interplay of voices and instruments was a wondrous thing indeed. After another brief intermission the saga continued, but now *al sant*. This agreed with Kai, for in the past hour he had come to prefer the purer strains of the Zulu voice. It called to something in him, something deep and almost frozen by convention and duty: the call of life itself, strong and pure, devoid of politics. There was something in the voices that went far beyond mere bravado or braggadocio. *We fight to prove who is superior. Then one shall follow the other, as it has always been. But we need not kill each other. Our mothers need not weep, our sweethearts mourn. Listen to the tales of our greatness, tremble before us. Lay your weapons, not your lives, down. Then we can be as one people.*

He squeezed Nandi's hand, and together, they watched and listened.

The evening progressed, until finally the Zulus relinquished the stage. The curtain closed, and the gaslights glowed more brightly for ten minutes, during which patrons stood and stretched.

When the lights died back down, the curtains opened, and in the middle of the stage stood a concert-sized *lelit samäy*. A slender woman of indeterminate age took her place at the bench. It was obvious from the very first feathery trills that her skills were complete. The membrane's echoing tones rang from roof and walls and heart until the audience was moving together with the rhythms, smacking their hands against their legs appreciatively.

During one of the great musical swells, a deep bass note reverberated through the walls, shook Kai's bones . . . and then continued to roll on, the chandelier overhead trembling with the echo.

At first Kai thought that this was the most stupendous musicianship he had ever witnessed; then some older, deeper part of himself whispered that this was no musical note. No entertainment. This was *threat*. A second

rumble followed. On the circular stage, the musician ceased her play. The choral house quieted as the patrons grew apprehensive.

The hall went silent. Some stood, panicked. Kai's hand went to his *shamshir*. This was *Ruh Riyâh*, his father's battle sword. The incident on the bridge had made him far too nervous to carry the lighter, inferior ceremonial blade, regardless of the occasion. "What in nine hells was *that*?" he asked, not truly requiring an answer.

"Kai—?" said Lamiya. By now, more of the audience was standing than sitting. Behind her came a clamor of fearful voices, panicked questions, and the cries of children. *Mamma, is this a part of the show?*

"It seems to me," muttered Kai, "that our northern cousins are no longer satisfied with a blockade."

Not two hundred cubits away, a shell exploded against the armory's red walls. Brick and masonry rained into the streets, and sparks leapt up from the wooden frame.

Despite the constant drizzle, a blaze erupted in the ruins. Distantly, the first alarms of the Djiboutan fire company howled into the night.

Amid the wall hangings and sculptures lining the corridors of the choral house, Omar and his Hashassin clustered. Those of appropriately dark skin and African birth were still garbed as guards and ushers. The actual staff had been dealt with hours before, through accomplices infiltrated into the management. Those who cooperated had been allowed to retain life and health, if not freedom. This was neither mercy nor squeamishness: it was good policy for Omar's enemies to know that surrender was not an automatic death sentence.

Despite their intense training and preparation, anxiety chewed at them all as Omar awaited a signal.

"When, Sayyid?"

"Soon," said Omar. "For now, we wait. All things come to those who wait."

He had not long to wait. As if in psychic communication with Omar, only a few dozen cubits away a group of his men were planting a shaped explosive charge against the choral house's western wall.

Miles to the north, at the side of Lake A'zam, Aidan and Nessa shared food with Chifi and the Dahomy. His stew bowl brimmed with *Yemeser-Wote*, swimming with split lentils and onions thickened with teff, hot enough to raise sweat on the brow of a Kalahari native. The air was tangy with its spices: clove and *ber-ber* pepper.

Yala and Ganne peered toward the south, eyes narrowed.

"What is that?" asked Chifi. "Another storm?"

Yala cocked her head. "That? Cannon fire."

"The battle has begun," said Chifi, fear and eagerness warring in her voice.

Several of Chifi's workers came running. "Ma'am! We have to move, and now!"

"How is the Tortoise provisioned?" Chifi asked.

Sallah Mubutu spat on the dock. "The fore and aft guns are ready, and have a full supply. The engines are ready. The only problem is that half of our crew is off duty."

Chifi seemed conflicted. "The ones we do have—can they man their stations?"

"We can launch with a minimal crew—but we need four hands with the water buckets in case of fire, and . . . we need you."

"Me?" Chifi seemed genuinely stunned at the thought.

"Only you know the engine well enough to captain her." Sallah said. "If it isn't you, it's no one."

Clearly, Chifi was torn—both frightened and excited by the possibility.

"I need four people I can trust," she said. "Kai trusts you, Yala, and so do I. Choose two of your women."

She turned to Aidan. "Aidan—everything you have done until now has been in balance. You fought at the Mosque for your wife and child. You went to New Alexandria in exchange for your sister's freedom. Some say you wish to fight for this country, as a free man. This is your chance."

Aidan looked at Nessa, who clung to him. For a moment it seemed he gazed into a mirror. He opened his mouth, then closed it again, searching for words that eluded him. Before he could collect his thoughts, she spoke.

"Aidan," she said. "Bin Jeffar says that in every life there are a handful of moments that define us."

He snorted. "Bin Jeffar again."

"Listen to me," she said, gripping his shoulders with her thin, strong fingers. "It doesn't matter where truth comes from. Only that it's true." He raised his face to look at her. "You told me you feel wasted as a fisherman. That you found yourself at the Mosque. Is that the truth?"

He nodded.

"Then go." Her blue eyes, eyes that had been dry for so many years, were wet once again. "And what a treasure you are," she said, pride and fear mingled. She kissed his cheek, and then hugged him. "Go," she said again. "And then come back."

CHAPTER EIGHTY

OMAR PAVLAVI'S MEN had mixed the fire paste and scurried for cover beneath the shattered wall of offices farther north. There, hidden by shadows and brick, there was barely time for a twenty-count before the street thundered with the force of the detonation.

Inside the opera house, an entire wall burst into flame, smoke, and brick fragments. The reaction within was immediate chaos as smoke gushed into the hall like water through a shattered dike.

"We've been hit!" someone yelled. "Evacuate!"

Kai stood, eyes narrowed. "*That* was no cannon shell," he said.

The attendants hustled to assist with the evacuation, beginning of course with the aristocrats in the lower seats. Several of them clustered around the cordoned-off section holding the Governor and his wife. "This way, sir!"

Governor Pili offered no argument, seemed almost pitifully grateful that someone had come for him. He and his party were hustled out through a side corridor.

Kai watched them leave, then observed several of the wiry attendants following behind. His stomach clenched.

To Nandi and Lamiya, Kai said, "Something is wrong. The attendants are normally young men, or old men. These are young enough to be strong, but old enough to be veterans—I can see it in their eyes, in their body shape, and in their carriage."

"Additional bodyguards?" asked Kebwe. "Governor Pili is not the bravest of men."

"They were here before the Governor arrived," Kai said.

"I believe one carried a concealed knife or pistol," Babatunde said. "And their hands were tempered for combat."

"Not ushers," Kai said. "And they went after the Governor. Babatunde, Makur, Lamiya, Nandi—get the children out of here."

"To where, my husband?" asked Nandi.

"The trading house. They won't fire upon it. You may be captured, but not killed."

"And you, my love?" said his First.

"I'm going after the Governor. Kebwe? Fodjour?"

"Hai!"

"Follow me."

Kebwe saluted, fist to heart. "Our steel is yours."

In private corridors beneath the choral house, attendants hustled the Governor toward supposed safety. Without warning, they sprouted knives, transforming from sheep to wolves in one coordinated instant.

Blades flashed in the tunnels. The thick-chested bodyguards never had a chance to draw their blades. First their sword hands were pinned, then, a dreadful moment later, honed edges slid between ribs or beneath jaws. In seven seconds of lethal bloodshed the Governor and his wife stood alone but for the slayers.

"What is this?" Pili whispered.

"Your death," snarled the Hashassin, "if you do not follow my every command."

Pili glanced from the gashed bodies of the bodyguards to his wife, and then back again. "And if I do?"

"No harm will come to you or your lady," said the false attendant.

Omar and his men were moved to the stream of fleeing Djiboutans. Another shell struck, this one close enough to spill tiles from the adjacent building's roof. The ground beneath them shook so violently that they were thrown from their feet.

"Fools!" said Omar, rising to one knee and dusting off his robes. "In their eagerness to crush Djibouti, they'll kill us all."

They hurried on, eager to make rendezvous with their men.

Kai, Kebwe, and Fodjour worked their way through the panicked crowd, into the tunnel behind the governor. Progress was halted by an iron gate sealed with a massive, rusty bolt.

"Locked!" said Kebwe. He tried tugging at the lock. When that failed, he put his shoulder to the gate. Again, nothing.

Where to go? What to do? Kai was lost and without a plan; then a forgotten memory sparked.

"I know this tunnel," Kai said. "My father funded it, and I played here as a boy. It comes out in the trading house, but there is another door in the storm drain. Hurry!"

A new and even more ferocious detonation shook tiles from the ceiling. The sparkling candelabra above their heads creaked, swayed, spat screws, and then fell, crushing several screaming audience members beneath its jeweled weight.

At the tremor of impact, the orphans dissolved into hysterics. Like shepherds managing a frightened flock, Nandi, Lamiya, and Babatunde used gestures more than words to guide the children. Goggle-eyed with terror, their young charges followed them like pups, skittish, sobbing and shivering, but obedient nonetheless.

In Djibouti Harbor, the outnumbered, outgunned ships fought back against the blockading navy. The southern ships had fewer guns, and smaller guns, but they had courage, and the assistance of the men ashore manning the gun placements. The air churned with smoke, fire, lightning, and the smell of burned blood. Men screamed and dove into alligator-infested waters to escape the burning ships.

If, as some said, Jahannum's lost souls swam in an ocean of burning blood, it must have resembled Djibouti Harbor on that night.

Bilal's noble statue gazed down on all of it, the great man's expression unchanging, his iron thoughts unknowable.

Kai, Kebwe, and Fodjour exited into an ally, only to be forced back by a tide of screaming, desperate people seeking the precious illusion of safety. Kai looked out to the harbor. "We're outnumbered two to one." He swore explosively. "Damn that whoreson of a governor! Paper never stopped steel."

"What of the Tortoise?" asked Kebwe.

Kai looked north, peering as if he might actually see Dar Kush. He knew that, harbored in Lake A'zam, there was a boat, a metal boat that might make a difference on this terrible night.

What would Chifi do? As incredible as it seemed, Kai thought he knew.

At the lake, the men were scrambling aboard even as the Tortoise pulled away from the dock, gathering momentum. To the south, rumblings and flashes lit up the sky.

"Come back to me, Aidan," Nessa said.

He kissed her forehead, wishing that there was more he could do to comfort her. "There's no night dark enough to keep me from finding you."

She stopped, thought, and then took off the tiny golden tree around her neck. "I know that you don't believe," she said. "But please—take this, Aidan. Know that my heart is with you."

"But if something does happen to me, I want you to go to the crannog," he said. "You tell my son how his father died, do you hear me?"

"Aidan—"

"*Shh.* This is just the way of the work, lass. I don't feel much like dying today. This isn't my night." He kissed her fondly.

"Aidan!" called Chifi. The Tortoise steamed south along the dock. It glided slowly at first, gaining momentum as it did. Aidan took a running leap, and landed in a crouching balance on the iron deck. It felt more solid than anything he had ever felt floating on water, but still it rolled with ripples on the lake's surface. Already his body was searching for the elusive connection of balance, that magical, fluid thing that made mariner and boat like one.

A thing that he had learned long ago, at O'Dere Crannog, at his father's side.

The Tortoise rolled beneath his feet, and he rode it, found a balance of hips and thighs that made this feel comforting and familiar.

I'm not a farmer, he thought.

Kai, Kebwe, and Fodjour had walked and crawled through muck for a quarter hour, following Kai's childhood memory of the sewer schematic. The storm drain and sewer were separate systems beneath Djibouti Bay, but still waste of all kinds found its way down here. A greasy thin light filtered its way down into the darkness, casting everything in tones of gray and yellow before the companions lit their torches. Darkness fled before the flames, making their shadows twist and caper on the walls like animated cave paintings.

Kai kept his breathing steady: he didn't want to admit it, but this was becoming oppressive. Ever since the assault on the mosque he had disliked confined spaces. During his escape, a tunnel had collapsed upon him, and if Aidan had not dragged him out, he probably would have died. The memory of those airless moments still brought a cold sweat to his brow. Those seconds had triggered something unthinkingly lethal within him, something that still resisted his efforts to control it.

Before now he had largely been able to avoid such situations, and therefore he never been forced to deal with it, but now it was beginning to sap him, slow him, trigger more internal friction than he was prepared to deal with at this crucial moment.

At last, they reached a metal door set in a concrete rim. It opened to the turn of an iron wheel. "We should be ahead of them here," Kai said, hoping against hope that he was right. *Action will soothe your nerves,* said a familiar voice within him. And with every passing moment Kai found that voice more intoxicating and impossible to resist.

As carefully as they could under the circumstances, the Hashassin hustled the Governor along through the tunnel. The leader paused as he heard a groan up ahead—a heavy, metallic sound, echoing in the dank, wet, narrow corridors.

"Wait. What was that?" the first said.

A shell burst on the street above their heads. The entire tunnel rang with thunder. "Fools! They will kill us all."

"Isn't that your intent?" asked Pili.

The Hashassin grunted. "You are far more valuable alive. Every mon-eyed family in the south is connected to you—by blood, marriage, or gold. You will encourage them to a peaceful solution. The Pharaoh will reward you."

"For betraying his people?" Madame Pili asked scornfully.

"For serving a higher purpose." Only his lips moved. As stolid as a statue, the Hashassin listened. "Come. Let us—"

There was only a brief warning splash. Then a sword flashed in the darkness as Kai and his two friends took the battle to the enemy.

Kai went at the first man with every intent of sparing his life. If it was possible to interrogate one of these rogues, many important questions could be answered.

But capture can be riskier than simple killing. The opportunity to take a lethal thrust might not happen twice. Hesitation can give the merciful warrior a serious disadvantage against a ruthless foe.

To effect a capture there must be a differential in the skill level, such that one or the other has enough of an advantage to merely wound or restrain.

In the first few moments, Kai knew that this wouldn't be possible. Not because he wasn't a more capable swordsman than his opponent. No, the difference was that his opponent would see capture as much less desirable than death.

In his fourth clash Kai sustained a thin gash on his left side. He gave a brief, vicious curse, beat the man's sword to the left, and made a back-handed riposte to the throat.

As his adversary fell gagging into the soupy muck, Kai turned in time to help his companion. Without a moment's compunction he stabbed one Hashassin in the spine, and as the other man turned, attention split, Fodjour beheaded him.

Men grunted and screamed, and slid into the filth trying to stanch gaping wounds with bloody fingers. Then it was over, and only Kai's men and Governor and Madame Pili still stood. They stared at Kai and his panting men first with open horror, and then gratitude.

"Wakil!" said the Governor. "I have never been happier to see you."

"You've never been happy to see me at all."

"Not true! I—"

"Polite lies later, Governor. If you value life and freedom, you must move, and now."

CHAPTER EIGHTY-ONE

FLEEING A WESTERLY WIND, dark, swollen clouds crawled across the sky. They flickered with faint lightnings. Under Captain Kokossa's command, the Tortoise passed into the canal leading from Lake A'Zam and headed south at eight miles an hour. The distant reverberations of cannon echoed like thunder.

Within an hour the wind shifted to the south-southwest and increased to a gale. Aidan was assigned to the lee wheel, and made a good showing there, so that Chifi allowed him to keep his post.

All about them rain and fire vied within the shattered walls. The Alexandrian ships' cannon seemed to pour an endless stream of ball into the city, undeterred by the Djiboutan ships' frantic defensive maneuvering.

For Babatunde, leading a flock of children through rain-swept streets during this hellish night of bombardment tested even his long-cultivated patience. The children cringed and cried, as could only be expected, but had sufficient survival instinct to stay near the Sufi, huddling together like ducklings following their mother.

Although most of the shells were exchanged between the harbor ships, from time to time one of the enemy vessels seemed to take deliberate aim at the city itself, as if delighting in the opportunity to wreak havoc.

Flame wreathed several venerable old buildings, and the men and women of Djibouti Harbor were fighting fires and trying to pull the trapped and injured from damaged structures.

After long minutes of dangerous flight, Makur pounded at the iron door of the Lion's Blood holding company.

"What do you want? It is dangerous! Go home!" said old Rashid, answering their knock.

"My husband, the Wakil, told us to come here," said Lamiya.

"My ears hurt!" an orphan wailed.

"Here, fill them with this," Nandi said, and tore a bit from the edge of her dress.

"It is too dangerous," said the old man. "If they land, soldiers will try to take Lion's Blood."

"Our husband told us to meet him here," said Nandi. "We but follow his instructions, as you will if you acknowledge his authority."

Rashid momentarily seemed as if he would attempt to challenge her command, but the look in her eyes said she was not to be trifled with, and he backed down.

"Of course, of course, but . . ." His white eyebrows furrowed, more with frustration than fear. "Oh, well—hurry."

Not fifty cubits away, an adobe house disintegrated into a cloud of smoke, flame, and shattered masonry. Babatunde ducked a spray of flying fragments, turned, and looked out at the harbor, where the ships were firing with terrifying force and growing accuracy. One triple-master listed in the bay, deck aflame. Despite the drizzling rain, several buildings gouted smoke.

"I pray Allah will protect him," Babatunde said.

"Protect us all," said Makur fervently.

In the tunnels below the harbor, Kai, Kebwe, Fodjour, and Governor Pili and his wife made their way carefully through the muck. The Governor's wife's gown was a muddied disaster, and she seemed balanced on the edge of shock.

Kai took the lead position, holding one of the torches out to provide light. He stopped.

"What is it?" said Kebwe.

"Quiet," he whispered. "There are others who understand ambush."

"What—?" Pili began.

Kai held his finger to his lips. *Silence.* Then he flicked his head to the side as something came zipping past. "Down!" He pulled Fodjour down. Kebwe snapped his head back as if someone had backhanded him. He grunted and slapped the side of his neck.

"Kai . . . ?" Kebwe's eyes rolled up, and he flopped facefirst into the water. Kai was there within a moment, and on his knees. He tried to roll his friend up, and it was at that terrible moment that the attack came.

The battle was faster than conscious thought, and all the more frustrating because of his need to keep his sergeant's face out of the water.

With Kebwe half-conscious, trying to keep himself erect, Kai pushed him back against the wall of the storm drain, using his own weight to keep his friend from drowning.

This limited his ability to move, of course, and made him more of a target.

"Get his face out of the water, damn you!" Kai screamed at Pili, voice echoing in the tunnel. The Governor helped, but he was trembling so badly he could barely manage. His wife emerged from her own torpor first, pillowing Kebwe's head against her stomach, pulling at his waist with both arms, her gaze locked disdainfully upon her husband.

"Help me," she whispered to her husband. Kebwe slid down again, struggling feebly as his nose slid beneath the filthy water.

Kai cursed, spinning to strike the shoulder of a Hashassin, then, hoping that he had bought himself a moment, turning again to help his friend.

At that critical moment, Kai's attention was split, and he felt the slash before he even sensed the swordsman's presence. Pain exploded in his right arm. He switched hands. Still deadly with his left, Kai split his assailant's skull.

Kai and Fodjour managed to win their way free. From the corner of his eye he caught a bit of Fodjour's swordplay, and if there was more energy than inspiration about it, still it was lethal and courageous, and he was glad to have his childhood friend at his back.

"Kai!" Fodjour said, alarmed. "You are wounded."

"Just a touch," he said, pressing fingers against the wound. Damn! Pain erupted like a flash of acid. This would require stitches and salves. If this muck got into the wound, and it was not promptly treated . . . well, he had seen battlefield amputations before. "Unless there is poison on the blade, there is little to fear."

"Let me see—Kebwe!"

Kebwe's head lolled back, pink foam drooling from his lips.

"We must get him to Babatunde," said Kai.

"Where?"

"The holding company. It should be . . . a left turn." He searched desperately for a landmark, peering up through one of the grates at the smoldering city. He recognized a statue of Bilal on horseback at the battle of Medina, sword raised on high as two Arabs attempted to drag him from his saddle. At once, he knew their location. "Here!"

They splashed through the muck, Governor and Madame Pili supporting the wounded man.

*　　*　　*

Nandi watched through the windows of the depository as the ships fired volley after volley, until their barrels threatened to melt. Clearly, the seven Djiboutan fighting ships were outmatched. Several of them sagged smoking in the water.

Just at the edge of her sight the land-based cannon fired until the barrels smoked and one exploded with a murderous roar. She flinched back from the glass as the pane exploded, showering the room with fragments. The children howled in fear and pain.

Trembling, she peered through the windows again, nodding as Lamiya joined her. The two women exchanged a single horrified look before they distantly heard: "Fire, dammit!" and another cannon roared.

The first cannon was a smoking, twisted ruin, its crew strewn about like poisoned ants. Still, the others fought on.

She watched as fire rained down on the crew of one of the Egyptian ships, and clasped her hands over her ears, trying to drown out the sound of screams.

East of their position, another building's brick wall simply exploded, gouting flame out into the street. To her horror, Nandi actually watched as a pair of concert patrons were engulfed in fire and fragments of obliterated brick.

The walls of the Lion's Blood holding company rattled as the neighboring building burst a wall. The children wailed and wept, clinging to each other for dear life. Twenty terrified children, each more certain than the others that death and doom had come for them all.

"Cowards!" cried Nandi. "No Zulu fights children."

"They don't even know we're here," said Lamiya.

The accountant's eyes widened. "What is that?"

There was a creaking sound as a floor grille rose up, revealing a blessedly familiar face.

"Fodjour!" Lamiya screamed.

"Help us! Kebwe is badly wounded."

"Quickly!"

But Nandi was already moving. Kai appeared, groaning as his wounded arm was ground against the side of the trapdoor, and as the building lurched to the shock of yet another explosion.

A bank of cannon roared on the ships, and a horrific moment later a series of shells impacted in the streets of New Djibouti, disintegrating a fleeing merchant in a single hellish instant, and triggering a shock wave that collapsed a corner of the holding company's roof.

"I thought you said they wouldn't attack Lion's Blood," Lamiya said.

"I don't believe they are," Kai replied, grimacing with pain. "Those shots are off-target—"

With a thunderous roar, a neighboring building exploded. The children screamed again, and then began to sob.

"Barricade that hatch," Makur said. "The men who attacked the Governor won't give him up so easily."

"Kebwe is dying, Kai," Babatunde said. "I have no medicine to stop it. Pressure points can ease his pain. . . . I can postpone but not prevent the inevitable."

Kai closed his eyes, pained. He came to Kebwe, and cradled his head.

Kebwe looked up at Kai, his eyes bloodshot. He trembled, and his teeth chattered. "Fire in my veins. Oh, Allah, I did not know . . ."

"What, my friend?"

"I have seen many men die. But I did not know."

"Know what?"

The white of Kebwe's eyes darkened with blood as capillaries burst. "What there are no words for. Kai, be not afraid. It is nothing to fear. Death is more natural than life. . . ."

His crimson eyes suddenly grew frantic, and he looked around the room, relaxing when he saw Makur.

"I . . . I cannot be taken," said Governor Pili. He hunched on the floor, wrapping his arms around his knees. Although the night was warm, he shivered. "They will torture me." And then added, almost as an afterthought: "And my wife."

Kai laid his friend's head on the ground, and fought his urge to break Pili's jaw. "We will do our best to protect you," he said.

"It is not enough!" said the Governor.

Kai's eyes grew cold. "You are not yourself. Find courage, man!"

Madame Pili glared down on her husband. "The Wakil is right. Be a man, can you not? If not in our bed, then on the threshold of death." Her scorn was searing, and enough to deflect Kai's wrath.

"He might prefer the grave to a life with that one," Makur whispered.

"Cowardice has infinite variety," Kai replied.

Pili *Hamam* approached them, and lowered her voice. "My husband is not well," she said, "but in one thing he is correct: the people who planned this will do anything to complete their plans. If my husband falls into their hands, many will suffer. Make no mistake: he will sign anything, *do* anything to avoid pain."

Although whisper, those last words dropped like acid. Shrew she might have been, but also a *feqer näf*, with all of the iron discipline that that implied.

"What would you suggest?" asked Nandi, looking back at the Governor. He seemed to be lost in his own world of ego and mortal fear.

Pili *Hamam* locked her gaze on Nandi, and then Lamiya. The three women stood as the three points of a triangle, as if the men were not present at all. "That he not fall living into the hands of the Hashassin." Pili *Hamam*'s voice was arctic.

Kai and Makur exchanged a startled expression.

"And you?" Lamiya asked.

"Let them do their worst."

Makur whispered to Kai, "I think Allah gave this one the balls of a camel."

Kai nodded. "And her husband those of a mouse."

"What do we do?"

Kai looked back at the vault door. He and Makur nodded grimly, understanding each other in an instant.

As primary shareholder, Kai possessed the combination opening one of the vault door's locks. The old caretaker provided a hidden key that opened the second, and the door yawned wide as the Governor, orphans, Babatunde, and both Kai's wives were ushered inside.

"There is air for some hours," said Kai. "Be quiet, that it not be too swiftly consumed."

Nandi shivered. "I do not like confined spaces," she said.

"I empathize more than you know, but cannot have you here, now. It would distract me." He kissed each of his wives, quickly. "Keep the children well. You and Lamiya protect each other. And if that idiot of a governor grows too obnoxious"—He shrugged—"strangle him."

He closed the door. Kai, Makur, and Fodjour put their backs to the vault door and waited.

CHAPTER EIGHTY-TWO

AT TEN MILES PER HOUR, it had taken almost seven hours for the Tortoise to enter the bay. As it did, the sea rolled over them as if their ship were a rock in the ocean, floating only a few digits above the water. Several times Aidan swore that they must sink and miserably drown.

The wheel had been temporarily rigged on top of the turret, where Chifi and the sisters now stood. From below he performed whatever tasks were directed of him: loading shells, stoking the boilers, or manning the pumps. Through a hollow copper tube he could hear the commands from up top, and every few minutes one or the other of them would climb below or back up again on one errand or another. Despite his fear, he exalted, as if after a lifetime of wandering he had finally found a home.

The Tortoise entered into the burning bay, so low to the water that in the early morning's darkness, the combating vessels on both sides failed to detect them.

They skirted the harbor, Chifi thinking to come in from the south, behind the crafts, trusting in the night, smoke, and storm clouds to conceal them.

When they reached open sea, the Tortoise was making very heavy weather, riding one huge wave, plunging through the next as if shooting straight for the ocean floor, and splashing down upon another. Her hull trembled with such shock that the crew was sometimes shaken from their feet. A wave would leap upon them and break far above the turret, so that if they had not been protected by a rifle-armor that was securely fastened and rose to the height of a man's chest, Chifi and the Dahomy might have been washed away.

When the pounding was at its worst, Aidan tried to remember that he had *volunteered* for this, and remembered something that a veteran had said to him at the Mosque Al'Amu: a man *always* gets into trouble if he volunteers.

Words to live by. If, indeed, he and his black companions were not all headed for the bottom of Djibouti Bay.

*   *   *

For a moment his mind had drifted to thoughts of the Ouachita crannog, of Sophia and Mahon . . . but then his attention was ripped away from such pleasant thoughts as he watched the water gush in through the coal bunkers in sudden volumes as it swept over the deck above.

In the engine room behind him, Sallah Mubutu screamed, "Coal's too wet to keep up steam! Pressure's dropped from a hundred debens to thirty!"

The water in the vessel was gaining rapidly over the small drainage devices. Chifi screamed for the engineer to start the hot-air pump. When the pumps began to churn, a stream of water eight digits in diameter spouted up from beneath the waves.

The Tortoise steamed ahead again with renewed difficulties. "Leave the wheel!" Sallah called. "The tube's blocked—need you to run messages up to Chifi!

"Tell her it's too wet. The coal's too wet," Sallah called again. The little man's warning had become a liturgy. "I won't be able to keep up steam."

Aidan climbed the ladder. Up top, the spray and the rain made the Tortoise's rolling more stomach-churning. Despite nausea, he related his message.

"Slow down," Chifi called in return. "Tell him to put all the steam he can spare into the pumps."

A heavy wave crashed against the deck, carrying away one of the Dahomy. To her credit, she screamed not a single time, as if concerned that, even in the midst of such a storm, she might be heard, and the element of surprise lost.

The fires began to die, and the small siphons choked up with water. "The pumps are drowned," Sallah reported. "The main pump has almost stopped working for lack of power."

Chifi climbed down to see for herself, and then turned to Aidan: "See if there is any water in the wardroom."

Aidan went forward, and saw the water gushing in through the hawsepipe, through which the anchor chain ran. Aidan guessed that dropping anchor had torn away the insulation.

He ran back up and reported his observations, and at the same time heard Mubutu report that the water had reached the ash pits and was gaining very rapidly. "Stop the main engine," Chifi called. "All steam to the pumps."

Almost miraculously, the pumps began working once again.

"Eight degrees right," Chifi said.

"I cannot breathe," said Yala, hand at her dark throat.

"It is your mind, Sister," Ganne replied. "There is air. It is these confined spaces that convinces you there is not. Irish!" she called. "How goes it?"

"I wish I could see better," he said, peering through the mirror device Chifi had arranged for him. "This contraption leaves much to be desired."

She grinned savagely. "You talk strangely for a pigbelly."

"And you act strangely for a woman."

Despite, or perhaps because of the circumstances, both laughed.

"Ready? Fire!"

Aidan and Yala had loaded shell and a gunpowder cylinder into the cannon. Aidan took a moment to sight, and then heard the scream:

"Thunder and lightning!"

Recoil slammed the Tortoise like a gong, and Aidan's ears felt as if they would rupture. The pumps continued to drain water, and for the moment, they were in the fight.

Chifi was watching through the mirror device. "Two degrees left," she said.

"Two degrees left." Aidan worked the turret's hand-crank until Ganne, sighting, told him to stop.

Again the ship shook.

They held their breaths, waiting, and then they heard the distant sound of detonation. Chifi threw up her arms, and gave a savage shout of celebration. "Excellent!" she cried.

Her hand cut the air again.

"Fire!"

The Tortoise fired again, and then again. Over the next hour they scored one hit for every three shots.

Then Aidan was thrown from his feet, the Tortoise reverberating as if a giant had taken a sledge to its armor.

"We're hit!" Yala called.

"Only a matter of time before they found us," Chifi replied. "Fire!"

"Dear Jesus!" screamed Aidan.

"I thought you didn't believe in the _Yahudi,_" said Yala.

"I didn't believe in metal boats either—ah!" Another shell slammed off the deck, rocking them.

Water began seeping in through some of the weld cracks. Aidan and some of the Dahomy women were set to bailing—bailing out the ocean, as it seemed. He was kept employed most of the time taking the buckets from through the hatchway on top of the turret. They seldom would have more than a pint of water in them, however, the balance having been spilled out in passing from one person to another.

*   *   *

Up on deck, he squinted through the rain, watching one of the damaged Djiboutan warships as it managed to return fire against the Alexandrians. The ball struck an enemy vessel amidships. In that instant it
seemed their luck had changed, for the powder magazine leapt into flame
and smoke with a roar that had to have been heard as far north as Dar
Kush. A wall of flaming air rolled across the water, and Aidan dove back
below before it reached the Tortoise.

Entranced by the violence, he peered back up to see the result.

The damaged steam-screw began to sink. As it did, its port cannon dis-
charged.

To Aidan's horror, sparks and flame exploded from the side of Bilal's
head. The statue resounded with an ear-pounding note, like a giant bell.
When the smoke had cleared, half that head had been sheared away, leaving but a single glowing eye to gaze balefully on the carnage below.

"Captain!" Aidan called down. "They hit Bilal!" With an oath, Chifi took
the scope, peering out through the smoke and flame to see for herself.

"*Muzawwars*," she muttered. "Unbelievable bastards."

"We'll make them pay for that," Ganne promised. "A hundredfold!"

"They want war?" Chifi screamed. "Then war they will have. Father,
guide my hand!"

She turned the scope back over to Ganne, and walked with unsteady
tread back to the captain's station.

"One of the ships is sinking!" Ganne called back. "They're abandoning
ship."

"If only we could kill them in the water," Chifi muttered.

"What?"

"Nothing," she said. "Carry on."

For the next two hours the Tortoise took a horrific shelling, but despite
the worst the Alexandrians could do, her armor held. Despite all odds or
expectations, Chifi's eye and nerve held, and they managed to sink two
more ships.

The crew was cheering when the greatest impact yet exploded amidships, throwing everyone from their feet. A rivet blew out of the side of
the Tortoise, striking Sallah Mubutu in the ribs with a bullet's impact. He
doubled over, crimson foaming from his lips as water gushed over his face.
Yala and Aidan carried him to a bunk, the little toolmaker screaming and
spitting blood every inch of the way. Aidan was uncertain what to do next.
"Should one of us stay with you?"

"Are you a fool, man?" Sallah said, eyes blazing. "Get back out there and kill them!"

When Aidan returned to the main cabin, Chifi was on the verge of losing control, trembling as she screamed. "Do you like that? How does it feel? You murdered my father, you bastards! I'll kill you all, kill you all—"

Aidan was aghast, feeling that he was witnessing a human being abandoning sanity like a snake shedding its skin.

"Chifi!" cried Yala. "Get hold of yourself!"

Chifi turned. Aidan guessed that if she had held a sword, the inventor would have slain her friend.

But she did not hold a sword, and the Dahomy woman gripped her shoulder, preventing her from turning or breaking eye contact. "A cool hand guides a steady spear," she said. "Calm yourself." Chifi struggled back to control, and clasped Yala's hand in thanks. The air compressed as another massive blow shook the Tortoise: a cannonball glancing off the deck. Another rivet blew, and water sprayed into the main cabin.

"We can't take more of this," said Aidan.

Chifi replied. "We'll take it until I say otherwise."

"We'll sink!" Ganne screamed.

"Do you know what this ship is capable of?" Chifi said fiercely. "Do you know the quality of her armor? What my father and I built the Tortoise to be? Do you?"

"Chifi—we are your friends. Get hold of yourself. We will sink!"

"No. No. I have to . . . I have to . . ."

"Wait," said Yala. "The smoke is clearing."

"What do you see?"

"I see . . . more ships coming."

"From where?" The air was deadly still. New Alexandrian reinforcements would be the end of them. Chifi took the scope.

"The flag . . . is Djiboutan! They're our ships, returning from Azteca!"

She swiveled the scope around as far as it would go. "The Alexandrian ships are in retreat!"

They cheered, hugging each other madly.

Another rivet blew, and now the water lapped about their feet. All eyes turned to Chifi.

She scanned at the vessel's iron walls, running her hand over it lovingly. "We'll build you again," she said, and then turned to her crew, speaking the two words they had prayed for:

"Abandon ship."

Sallah Mubutu lay injured in his bunk, a bandage tight around his midsection. His face was ashen, a terrible contrast to the crimson bandages. He watched the water as it grew deeper and deeper, already aware of what his fate must be.

"We have to get you to safety," Aidan said, and slipped an arm around him. Surely they could move him up the ladder to the deck, and from there . . .

Sallah screamed piteously, arching his back and clawing at Aidan. "Let me go! Ali's wounds, you're killing me!"

Aidan backed away in alarm. "There has to be a way . . ."

The toolmaker shook his head, and coughed blood. "No, Aidan," he said. "Try to get me out, I'll just drag you to the bottom with me. Let it be here, in this beautiful ship. Go tell your friend the Wakil 'thank you.' " Despite his pain, the little man managed to twist his lips into a smile. "Get out, boy. Go live your life."

"But sir—"

The toolmaker coughed up a trickle of crimson, and wiped his mouth with his sleeve. He looked up at the Irishman. "Get out! Or don't you know how to obey your betters?"

The flash of pain on Aidan's face must have reached the old man, whose countenance softened. "Go on. We did good work, didn't we?"

"We did," Aidan said. "They're in retreat."

"Good. Drown them all. Go on now. It's just me and the Tortoise, and that seems like the way it should be."

Still Aidan hesitated. Mubutu closed his eyes, a bright pink bubble foaming at his lips. The toolmaker gasped for air, then fumbled a hand under his coat, withdrawing a gold-plated pocket watch of Benin design. "Take this," he whispered. "Give it to my eldest son."

Aidan nodded, trying to find words, but the little man gave him no time. "Go," he said.

And finally, Aidan did.

As he ascended the turret ladder the sea broke over the ship and came pouring down the hatchway with so much force that it took him off his feet. At the same time the steam broke from the boiler room as the water finally reached the fires. At last it became viscerally clear that the Tortoise was actually going down.

As Aidan reached the top of the turret he saw a boat thrashing in the waves off the port bow, filled with men and women. Three others stood on deck trying to get on board. One woman was floating leeward, shouting in vain for help. Another woman hurriedly climbed the ladder and jumped down from the turret. She slipped, was swept off by a breaking wave and never rose.

The ladder had been washed away, so Aidan made a loose line fast to one of the stanchions, and let himself down from the turret. The moment he struck the deck the sea broke over it and swept him as he had seen it sweep his shipmates. He grasped one of the smokestack braces and, hand over hand, ascended to keep his head above water. It required all his strength to keep the sea from tearing him away. As waves swept from the vessel he found himself dangling in the air nearly at the top of the smoke-stack. He let himself fall, and succeeded in reaching a lifeline that encircled the deck by means of short stanchions, and to which the rescue boat was attached. Again the sea broke over the deck, lifting him feet upward as he still clung to the lifeline.

The Irishman thought he had nearly measured the depth of the ocean when he felt the turn, and as his head rose above the water he was somewhat dazed from being so nearly drowned. He vomited up what seemed a cubic cubit of water that had found its way into his lungs. He was then about ten cubits from the others, who he found to be Chifi and Tala; Ganne had been washed overboard and now struggled in the water. The men in the boat were pushing back on their oars to keep the boat from being washed onto the Tortoise's deck.

Evidently, the rescue boat was from one of the foundering ships. The leader in this one wore the emblem of first lieutenant, but Aidan didn't recognize him at all. "Is the captain on board?" the officer called, struggling to have his voice heard above the roar of the wind and sea.

"I am she," Chifi called, "throw a line to Ganne!"

Sailors scrambled to comply. The captain of the rescue boat helped Chifi across. "Women? All women?"

"Not all, but most," she screamed above the crashing waves. "Permission to come aboard."

"Granted."

The moment she was over the bows of the boat one of the Dahomy, eyes wide with terror, cried, "Cut the line! Cut the line!"

As the sailors bent to sever the connection, Aidan saw several Dahomy standing on top of the turret, apparently afraid to venture down upon deck, and it may have been that they were deterred by seeing others washed overboard while they were getting into the boat.

Chifi tried to reach them with a line, seeing that their grips were weakening. All on the lifeboat held their breaths, stunned by her courage, and were dismayed as another wave struck the Tortoise, tearing her feet from

beneath her. She slipped a foot, caught again, and with her last prayer—
"Allah forgive me!"—she fell back to the far side of the Tortoise, where he
could no longer see her.

"Get around! Get around!" Ganne shrieked, the wind drowning her
voice.

As they began to row, the ship rolled, and rose upon the sea, sometimes
with her keel out of water, so that he was hanging twenty cubits above the
sea, crashing down again with bone-crushing force.

Hands ripped and raw, Aidan still clung to the rope with aching hands,
calling in vain for help. But he could not be heard, for the wind shrieked
far above his voice. For the first time in his life, Aidan gave up all hope.
He thought of Sophia, who had blessedly told him to seek his sister, and
of Nessa, who, at least, he had delivered unto freedom. His children, who
would grow strong and safe in Donough's weathered hands . . .

While he was in this state, within a few seconds of letting go, the sea
rolled forward, bringing with it the boat. When he would have fallen into
the sea, it was there.

He could only recollect hearing someone say, as he fell into the bottom
of the boat, "Where in hell did *he* come from?"

Damn fine question, he thought. *Damned fine question indeed . . .*

And then he remembered nothing more.

CHAPTER EIGHTY-THREE

WITHIN THE SHADOWED CONFINES of the Lion's Blood holding company, the drama's final act was taking place. Seeing that Governor Pili threatened to elude them, and that the blockade was broken, the Hashassin had clawed their way up from under the street, girding themselves for one last all-out attempt.

"Kai of Dar Kush," rasped the Hashassin leader. His eyes gleamed behind his scarf.

"Your name," asked Kai, hoping that his voice sounded steady.

"Omar Pavlavi." His eyes darted to Kai's bloody arm. "You are wounded." There seemed genuine regret in the observation. "I am sorry— I wished you whole for the killing."

Kai managed to push aside both pain and fatigue. "What remains of me is still more than enough for the likes of you."

"Good," said the pale man, his smile a skull's. "Good. Let the dance begin."

And with a slight, respectful bow, never allowing his eyes to leave Kai's, Omar raised his sword and attacked.

Kai was wedged in, small battles raging to either side, no room to bring rifles into play even if they were so possessed. Kai fought against a rising tide of despair. He was exhausted in all but spirit, and mortal fear hammered at the door of his resolve. This place, a palace of gold and power, now threatened to become his tomb. The Hashassin leader engaged with him, and Kai immediately knew that his assessment of Omar upon the bridge had been accurate, and perhaps even overly optimistic.

Omar was a brilliant swordsman, and in the first ringing clash of their blades, Kai knew that Malik himself would have been sorely pressed. Malik was not here, and the man who held the breach was both wounded and exhausted.

Only the left arm could come into play, and if this was a disadvantage, at least Babatunde had urged Kai to practice on this side more extensively, claiming that it was a way to train his mind. There was an advantage to using the left hand: it was completely natural for Omar to have trained and fought primarily against the right-handed, who were infinitely more common in the Islamic world. A blade held in the left approaches from a fractionally different angle, and a man could easily make miscues attempting compensation. This placed Omar at a bit of a disadvantage, as well.

Still, the current situation was more than trouble. This was almost certain disaster.

But where Malik had taught Kai to be strong, to think of his mighty ancestors, to revel in the opportunity to expose himself to fortune and fate, Babatunde had prepared his mind for fear in another way: anxiety triggered the reintegration process, an increase in precision, a more intense awareness of angles and degrees, distance and cadence.

Fear triggered a deeper descent into the realm of the intellectual, where calculation replaced emotion as survival became more and more uncertain.

All emotion was quashed. No sentiment could rise through that, except . . .

Kai caught each blow, made each careful parry using the barest minimum of motion. Even now, his shoulder ached abominably. But something else lived beneath the fear, something even now beginning to shoulder aside the other emotions.

Your wives . . .

Omar's blade lunged for his heart, and surprising even himself, Kai effected a hairline deflection.

Your children were home *when the bastards attacked. . . .*

Kai's mind seemed to expand the moment, so that although he too was caught in the same torpid vortex, he saw everything with crystal clarity, and was able to make the proper choices, allowing a fractional tilt of blade to deflect a lethal thrust. . . .

They would endanger all that your father and father's father built. . . .

Omar grunted with pain as Kai found an opening and slammed his shoulder into the center of his enemy's chest, as Malik had taught him since childhood.

They kill for money.

And *there* it was, the thing that triggered Kai's deepest revulsion. To kill for self-defense was the right of any animal. To kill in defense of home and family was an obligation understood by all the world's peoples. To slay and die for one's country was the duty of any civilized man who would hold his head high in the company of citizen-warriors.

But to kill and die for coin? To skulk and strike from darkness? To rip apart families, endanger children for gold, and gold alone?

For the second time in a twelvemonth, Kai of Dar Kush went berserk.

Pain did not matter. Fear existed no more, all emotions dissolved to a magma driving the skill spent a lifetime in attaining, and despite his injuries and weakness, despite using his left hand, Kai pushed his opponent back.

Omar's eyes displayed shock as he found himself repulsed by a blur of thrust and parry, Kai's *shamshir* dancing like a willow-wand in a windstorm, something not wholly human impelling its quest for the Hashassin's heart and throat.

The killer's black eyes widened, and then narrowed, and the icy touch of terror filmed them. "To me!" he cried, and one of his men broke off his efforts to flank Makur and joined with Omar, turning aside a high-line thrust that might have torn his leader's throat.

The odds were now two to one, two blades against Kai's left. One step at a time he was forced to retreat, and under this stress his mind cleared and madness passed. Kai's carefully maintained focus fled, and the sheer overwhelming impossibility of his situation flooded over him

There was a *thump* at the door of the depository, men shouting, and a gunshot as the Djibouti militia challenged the lock.

Omar backed up a step, his eyes bright. "We conclude our game another time. Good-bye, Wakil." He whistled an earsplitting shriek, a sound Kai seemed to hear with his brain rather than his ears. His men broke contact and scrambled back through the floor as if they had practiced the maneuver a hundred times.

And indeed, perhaps they had.

Kai slumped back in utter exhaustion. "It is not a game. It was never a game," he said.

And collapsed, trembling so hard that his sword dropped from his numbed fingers.

CHAPTER EIGHTY-FOUR

SMOKE AND STORM CLOUDS roiled the sky above Djibouti Harbor, but amid the large-scale disaster, the human toll was revealed as less devastating. The rain began to temper its wrath, washing down upon them in waves rather than a steady wall.

Smoldering fires attempted to leap back to life, only to be repressed again, and finally, to die beneath the duel ministrations of man and nature.

Kai and the others were being treated for wounds and exhaustion. Slowly, the population of Djibouti Harbor emerged from the night-long bombardment. Anger supplanted fear as the survivors surveyed the devastation. Bilal's ruined visage loomed down on them, gazing through a single bright baleful eye. Whenever exhaustion or thankfulness muted Djiboutan wrath, a single seaward glance was all that was required to trigger it once again.

"Hold still, please," said Doctor Jimuyu.

Kai flinched as a bitter salve was slicked over his wounded right arm. "I . . . ow! Have you seen to the children?"

"Yes, Wakil," the Kikuyu healer said placidly. "As you ordered."

"And my wives?"

"Of course," the doctor said.

"And—"

"Will you please lie back? With wounds such as this, one has two choices only: medication or amputation. Might I respectfully suggest the former?"

Kai settled back. The door of the depository was open, and the shocked inhabitants wandered past, glancing in with glazed eyes. "Look at them," he muttered. "They never imagined."

The doctor paused in his ministrations to follow the Wakil's gaze. "They have not seen war."

For the first time, Kai fully appreciated the thin white line of a scar along Jimuyu's jaw, and needed no further clarification. From where he sat, he could just make out the bay, and smoke from Bilal's statue streamed to the sky.

"Great Bilal," said Kai.

"There will be blood, Wakil," said the doctor. "There is no avoiding it now. North against south. Pharaoh against Empress. Look at the children."

He had no wish to do so, but it was unavoidable. The young ones seemed completely shell-shocked. One small body was draped by a blanket.

"I can't believe that they intended this," Kai said.

"It matters not. Already, I have heard men speak of The 'Orphan War.' "

"Labels are not things," said Kai. "Men exploit tragedy for their own purposes. They would not act to protect the children, but will happily turn their tears into gunpowder. This grows worse every moment."

Governor Pili was, if possible, even more disoriented than the children. He had emerged from the vault round-eyed and shaken, possessed of a new nervous habit: the tendency to wipe at his face with the cuff of his coat again and again, as if trying to smear away imaginary blood. "I didn't . . . I really didn't think they would dare. I thought our interests were theirs. I see now. I see." Phil looked up at Kai. "Months ago, you warned me not to lower my sword. I reacted shamefully. How can I make amends?"

In that moment, Kai was too tired and disgusted to play the politician. This once, he would speak the truth. "I fear my father might wish me to answer such questions with platitudes. 'Win the war,' I might say. Or perhaps 'Your friendship is all I crave.' On this occasion I do not say that. We are entering pale times, and if you do not forget that which happened today, it may suit me well."

Pili had almost been overcome by his trembling. He gazed at his shaking hands and then back at Kai. His teeth clicked together nervously. Pili squared his shoulders and with an admirable effort, steadied himself. "I shall not."

"I have heard that the Governor's word is his bond," said Kai, taking the offered hand. It was not strong, but it was firm, and that was a beginning. "Let it be so."

CHAPTER EIGHTY-FIVE

IN TWENTY-FOUR HOURS, things began to settle again. The harbor was dragged. Amid the wreckage and loss, dozens of bodies were recovered, but not Chifi's, whom Aidan had seen pulled out to sea.

"We have lost her," Kai said to Babatunde.

"There is still hope," Nandi said. "I hear citizens have taken wounded into their own homes. She may be among them."

"I fear, young Wakil," said his teacher, "that the days ahead will be perilous."

"As we have known. At least her efforts were not in vain. The Tortoise proved herself. Its schematics are drafted, and I can place them before the Senate."

Babatunde gazed out at the horizon, and he dropped his gaze. "I promised Maputo that I would protect his daughter. I failed."

Rarely had Kai seen Babatunde in such a sour, foul mood. He draped his arm around his teacher. "We have done the best we could with the resources Allah gave unto us," he said. "More than that we cannot do."

"Perhaps not," agreed Babatunde. "But we can try."

Days passed in which life around Dar Kush threatened to return to something approximating normal.

Kebwe's military *janazah* was conducted on his father's estate east of Djibouti Harbor, attended by Kai's regiment. He was buried with full honors, and the posthumous rank of grand sergeant.

Kai had just returned from the funeral when bin Jeffar arrived, escorted by four members of Kai's territorial guard.

The Admiral was brought into the courtyard, and there Kai met him. The two men studied each other: both were in formal military uniform, Kai's the dress whites with gold trim of Djibouti Pride, the Admiral's a deep blue-green coat with white pants and silver-trimmed black boots shiny enough to serve as a heliograph mirror.

One of Kai's guards stepped forward.

"Sidi, we have not searched this man, and were not certain of the protocol. If you wish—"

"Until I have said otherwise," said Kai, "he is to be treated as an honored guest." He looked at the admiral sharply, and then back to his men again. "Until I say otherwise."

His men retreated, leaving the two statesmen alone. "I did not expect to see you here," said the Wakil.

"I was on . . . personal business," said bin Jeffar, "but with the outbreak of hostilities, my trip assumed a more official flavor."

"I think it is best that you serve in that official capacity. Tempers are high. 'Outbreak of hostilities.' What a polite way to phrase an unprovoked attack on a peaceful population. I trust you are a mediator."

"So have I tried to be. We wish only harmony, Wakil."

Kai laughed heavily. "Your people have a strange way of showing it. Our harbor is in ruins. The statue of Bilal, our proudest accomplishment, lies in pieces. I would gladly deliver you to the torturer."

"I am under the protection of Governor Pili."

"Who owes me a favor. Be careful, and hope that I choose not to request it."

Bin Jeffar turned his empty palms upward. "May I speak candidly?"

Kai nodded.

"I want independence for Bilalistan as much as you—for different reasons, yes, but I am sincere, nonetheless."

"Why should I believe you?"

The admiral sighed. "I understand. This is war, now, and no man can see the future. I offer you two tokens, which may convince you of my sincerity."

"And they are?" Despite himself, Kai was interested.

"First, my word that your sister is safe."

Kai tensed. "You know of this?"

"Of course. The Pharaoh crowed to the Caliph, and he could not wait to share the news with his circle. Egypt has done this before, and always the hostage is kept safe until all matters are concluded."

"Meaning war?"

"Or peace. She will not be harmed, Wakil, if the Pharaoh is not *personally* angered. Send him gifts, but do not allude to the imprisonment directly—this has worked in the past, and will again."

"My gratitude. And this second token?"

"Kai, if the south loses this war, Djibouti will not be safe for you. The Caliph knows that it was your man who stole a device—"

"Of your construction?"

"Not solely mine, but yes. How did you know?"

"I guessed," said Kai. And without elaboration, added, "My compliments."

Bin Jeffar studied him. "I had thought the cipher unbreakable. Apparently, we underestimated the men of the south."

"Just one very special man," Kai said, and added nothing more. He would not mention Babatunde's name—there had been too much death, and the concept of even marginally increasing risk for the Sufi was beyond endurance.

Bin Jeffar smiled. "Apparently that same thief disgraced the Calipha in a particularly . . . intimate fashion."

Northerner and southerner studied each other, and despite the fact that they were enemies, were unable to prevent repressed laughter from pinching their faces. Obviously, both men knew exactly what had happened, and neither would be the first to speak.

"What exactly have you heard?" asked Kai.

Bin Jeffar considered his words. "The Calipha was rumored to have a taste for pale flesh. This time it backfired."

Kai said nothing, but whether out of delicacy or wish to avoid self-incrimination, he would have been hard-put to say. "Your official business is clear. But you say you were on a *personal* mission as well?"

"Yes. The night the scroll was stolen, there was . . . upset in the capital. Several servants left their households. Most have been recaptured. One . . . member of my household left. A woman named Habiba."

"Escaped to the Nations?"

"I believe she went south."

"Why south?"

"I have sources, friends who saw the fight between the Caliph's wrestler and a gold-haired Irishman. This Irishman escaped with the cipher machine on the same night that Habiba disappeared. On several occasions she spoke to me of her twin brother, who had sworn to find her. It required little application of logic or intelligence to realize that this man was the childhood companion of New Djibouti's most notorious Wakil, and to surmise what had happened."

"With whom have you shared your suspicions?"

Bin Jeffar met his eyes squarely. The next two syllables were the most crucial. "No one."

"This female slave, this 'Habiba' . . . You came all the way here in hopes of finding her?"

"Yes."

"You hoped to take her by legal means?" This was said with deliberate casualness.

"No, nor by force of arms."

"What then?"

"That is between myself and the lady," said the Admiral. "I ask that you let me speak to her."

"As an officer of New Alexandria?"

"I ask as a gentleman." It was, given their situation, the perfect answer.

Aidan pulled himself groggily from a dream of restless, hungry waves, of pounding guns and drowning sailors. The waves clutched at him, trying to pull him back into dream, but then he heard a pounding at the door, and rolled over onto his side. He was breathing hard, as if he had swum a hundred cubits of angry sea, and it took a moment to orient.

"I'm coming!" he said as the thudding at the door began again. He had slept on the floor since Nessa's arrival, allowing her to sleep in their mother's bed. She was curled there now, mouth curled in a child's smile. Nessa had their mother's mouth, and a trace of their father's strong chin . . .

His, Aidan's face. His own soul, living a different life.

He answered the door.

The girl Tata stared up at him with her stubby nose and olive face. "Yes?"

The brown eyes watched him carefully. "The Wakil says that Admiral Jeffar is here to see Nessa."

He felt his heart race. God! Found already? Could Kai protect them? Could they flee . . . ?

"Tell him I will join him shortly," said Nessa, only a slight slur betraying the fact that she had, only moment before, been sound asleep.

He spun about. She had already sat up, had already begun to comb her hair out with her fingers. "Nessa," he said. "You don't have to see him. We can protect you . . ."

No, you can't, Nessa thought. "I must do this." She turned back to Tata. "Where is the Admiral?"

"Waiting in the garden," the girl said.

Her heart raced. So many emotions, so quickly: disbelief, fear, excitement . . . she tried to conceal some of the emotions, but Aidan seemed able to read them on her face.

"Nessa," he said. "War has begun. Bin Jeffar has no power here. Kai will protect—"

She rose, and took his hands in hers. "Aidan, Aidan . . . your friend can't be everything, protect everyone." She leaned closer to him. "And perhaps I don't need protecting," she said, and then turned to Tata again. "Sweetheart," she said. "Can you help me with my hair?"

The girl nodded eagerly.

It took Nessa a half hour to prepare. When she was finished, every hair was in place. Her face was clear of paint, but freshly scrubbed she needed none.

"You look beautiful," Tata said wistfully, and Nessa patted her head.

"Ready now?" Aidan asked in irritation.

"Yes," she said. "Now we can go."

Nessa walked the maze of flowers with Aidan at her side. A hundred varieties, a thousand shades and scents embraced her, their colors and fragrances shifting with every step she took.

Such beauty, she thought, heart still racing in her chest. *Even more than the Admiral's own. How plain I will seem in such a setting.*

They rounded a corner, and there bin Jeffar stood, resplendent in his formal uniform, slender and strong, erect as a bamboo shoot. In the late afternoon's light his skin was almost golden. His high cheekbones and slanted eyes made him seem as if he had walked out of an ancient Egyptian glyph.

Bin Jeffar bowed to her and then Aidan, and extended his hand. Her brother seemed nonplussed by the courtesy, but finally extended his own and shook hard. He was fit and lighter-skinned than most southerners.

Bin Jeffar's eyes never wavered, and the two men tested their wills before Aidan found control again and released his grip.

"Your brother has fire," the admiral said calmly, working the fingers of what must have been an exceptionally sore hand.

Nessa nodded to Aidan and Kai, and somewhat hesitantly, they left her alone with bin Jeffar.

"I came to find you," said the admiral to Nessa as they walked in Kai's public garden.

Her expression did not change. "So many miles for one small slave girl."

"I had hoped to have more time, but things have changed. Things always change. I cannot stay. I am summoned north again."

She stopped. "Then fare you well, sir."

Bin Jeffar paced. "Habiba, I am a man of position and power. You know that for men like myself, marriage is a state institution, and not a matter of the heart."

Quietly, she said, "Yes, I know. I've always known."

"Yet, be that as it may, I hope that I have ever been fair with you. Treated you as a man should treat a woman that he . . ."

She turned and looked at him, expectant. "Yes?"

"That he cares for," he said softly.

That response was less than she had hoped for, but more than she had expected. Nessa sighed. "What if the world were different?" she asked.

"Then there would be no greater pleasure for me, in this life, than sharing it with you."

Nessa dropped her gaze. "What do you see when you look at me? My flaccid hair? My white skin?"

"I see the first thing that has given me peace since my wife's death. I see a woman who, if she would come back with me, would have everything I could give her," he paused. "Save my name."

"And what of children?" she said. "What if there were such?"

He looked at her hard, "If you bore me a child, that child would be educated, taught a trade. That child would be free."

"And what if this country were no fit place for a pale child to live?" Nessa brushed her fingers along a rose stem, then sat on a narrow marble bench.

"There are other places," said bin Jeffar. "Along the Egyptian Sea, there are large settlements of whites who are literate and capable of self-governance."

"But you could never speak publicly of your feelings. You would marry a woman who might have me whipped or sold away from you . . . from my own child . . ." A pause. "If child there was."

Bin Jeffar looked at her strangely, suddenly guessing. "You are pregnant."

She nodded, a bit shyly. "If God is good, she will be dark. And even if not, she is still my own."

Bin Jeffar exhaled a long plume of air, and then sat next to her, taking her hand.

"What now?" Nessa said.

"Know that you, and our child, will have whatever protection I can offer, always."

"If . . . ?"

"No if. That I give to you, by the name of all that is holy."

"You mean it?"

"Yes . . ."

"But?"

"But understand that the farther away you are, the less that protection means." He paused. "Habiba, know that there are currents within my government favorable to emancipation."

"You have said these words before," she replied. "Nothing came of it."

"But never before have we been at war. Emancipation means that we can offer freedom to slaves who fight for us. It means we can offer freedom to slaves who fight against their masters. The south *needs* slavery—we do not. Emancipation would give us a clear advantage."

"How noble."

"Habiba, I do not live in Paradise, in a realm of pure ideas and heart. I live in a world of men and their objectives. I am a soldier, yes, but also a politician—that thing your benefactor seems to hate so deeply. If I cannot speak to men's self-interests, I cannot sway them."

Nessa turned to face him squarely. "Tell me, Amon, when you look at me, that you see a human being. Equal to you in the eyes of God. Tell me that, bin Jeffar."

He searched her face. "Yes. When I look at you."

"And my people?"

"I do not know why He cast your folk as the servants of Africa. Perhaps because you turned away from His messenger. I do not know. But I know that among your people, there are still those whose beauty and spirit fly as high as any in the world, and that I have found such a one."

Tears sparkled in her eyes. "Can I trust you?"

"Have I ever given you cause to mistrust?" He took her shoulders. "Come," he said. "Be my heart, through this deadly, precious time. Help me see the humanity in those who might be free, if only we can turn this page in history, be free to see what comes next."

"And who decides what happens next?"

"You are free to be whatever you desire, Habiba," he said.

"My name is Nessa."

He nodded, and leaned closer, whispering into her ear, "Nessa," he said, "Live in my house as a free woman. Be my love."

Aidan and Nessa sat in Aidan's old Ghost Town dwellings. In all his years at Dar Kush, only a handful of things had ever happened comparing in pain or intensity to the things said this day.

"You cannot do this!" Aidan said, but his tone was more plea than a demand.

"Please, Aidan."

"Please? Nessa! I . . . I gave up my freedom for you! I opened doors within my heart that no man should have to open. I was beaten to within a hair of my life . . ."

Miserably, she said, "I know. . . ."

"Nessa. Nessa. You, and my promise, have haunted my dreams for most of my life. I left home, and family, because you are the other half of my heart. We shared our mother's womb. You are the last thing left of the life I once had. I thought—"

"Shhh," she whispered. "You don't understand, Aidan. You came for me. I thought there was no one in the world I could rely upon, save bin Jeffar. I love him, for that and so many other things, but you showed me how wrong I was to think I was alone. You needed to fulfill your promise, Aidan. But please understand that just as you managed to save yourself, I saved myself as well. Would you expect less?"

"But—"

"Stop," she pled. "Think this through from my position."

"Why did you come with me?" he asked.

"I had to—for both our sakes. You needed to save me, and I needed to visit our mother's grave. And I needed to know I had a *choice.*"

Despite his pain and anger, Aidan's spine straightened a bit.

"You had never forgotten me," she said proudly.

"Never," he muttered.

"You seized the only chance you could find to find me. To save me, and because of that, I am free."

"If you go back . . . it was all for nothing."

"Look at me and tell me that that is true. Look at me, Aidan!" Her voice crackled at him, and at that moment, oddly, he heard not Nessa's voice, or even their mother's, but the aural component of their father's strength and will. "We're free! Both of us, despite the worst that life could offer. You have a family, a woman who loves you—"

"Who would embrace you as a sister."

"And I her. And *will.* Life is not over. It just begins. Aidan . . . war is coming. And when the dust has settled and the blood dried, our people might be free. I believe that bin Jeffar will be on the right side of that fight, even if for the wrong reasons."

"But he was your master! He's one of the black bastards—"

"Like your dearest friend, Kai."

"Kai is different," he sputtered.

"So are we all, when you see with your heart, Aidan. Do not make the same mistake the blacks make. Kai is different, yes, because he has seen who you truly are. As you have seen him. As I have seen Amon."

He paused, all words momentarily rendered useless. Slowly, painfully, Aidan abandoned his position. He saw his own strength, and the strength he longed for, in the woman who shared his blood. "And has he seen it in you?"

"Yes. Aidan, this is no game we play. Your crannog must survive. You have Kai's patronage, but what if the south loses? What will the Wakil's support avail you then? If I go with Amon, I can guarantee support. You will have safety from both sides, north or south. Our people will have a place to go, to build. It could be a beginning."

"Our own land," he mused, that vision hot behind his eyes.

"Here, in a new land."

"Oh, Nessa." He sighed, and sat heavily. "If I had ever dreamed that life could be like this."

"We were children when last we met, my sweet." She rested his hand on her stomach. "Now we have children of our own, and must put away childish things."

"How did you grow so strong?" he asked, gazing up at her.

"Remember our mother, and you will know."

CHAPTER EIGHTY-SIX

İN CELEBRATION OF AIDAN'S APPROACHING DEPARTURE, Kai hosted an intimate dinner party. Aidan, Nessa, Kai's family, Fodjour, and Makur were in attendance.

"So, Aidan . . . " said Makur. "I hear you are leaving on the morrow."

"More mango juice, Kai?" asked Fodjour.

"Yes. Your father keeps an excellent cellar."

Fodjour poured, hand very steady on the pitcher, but he seemed to fumble a bit when handing the glass to Kai. He watched very carefully as his old friend drank, and only seemed to relax when the glass was empty.

"A long trip lies ahead."

"And more onerous still, I think," said Kai.

"Why?"

"You will be weighted more heavily than when you arrived."

"I will?"

"Indeed." He threw a sack over the table, and Aidan snatched it out of the air. Heavier than Aidan anticipated, the bag almost slipped through his fingers. Aidan opened it and peered within, his confused expression becoming one of amazed pleasure.

"What did I say?" Kai said, grinning to his friends. "His reflexes are entirely adequate."

"We will see—come next muster."

"Muster?" said Aidan.

Kai stood. He clasped his hands, and two white servants entered, one carrying a *shamshir* on a pillow. Aidan's eyes widened.

"Is this . . . ?" asked Aidan.

"And well earned," Makur said, shaking his head. "I never thought I'd say such a thing, but . . . you've earned the right, my friend."

"Aidan. I, Kai ibn Jallaleddin ibn Rashid al Kushi, do appoint you to the territorial guard, with a rank of sergeant, attached to Djibouti Pride as a noncommissioned officer. This rank has all of the rights and privileges ordinarily pertaining thereto, including the right to create, train, and maintain a militia. And if your service be honorable—" A pause, and then a stage whisper: "And it had damned well better be—"

His companions laughed.

"Then the rights of full citizenship will be enjoyed by your sons, and their sons, in perpetuity, in gratitude for your service."

Aidan accepted the sword.

"Do you accept?" asked Kai.

"With all my heart."

They cheered, and in the middle of the cheering, Aliyah began to cry, her dear little face swelling with tears and pain. The cries grew to wails. . . . Then she began to choke.

"What . . . ?" said Kai.

Babatunde started up. He inspected Aliyah's eyes and then pulled back her lips to expose her gums. "Poison," he said, noting their color. "We must act swiftly. Bring the child to my laboratory!"

"There is a murderer in my house," Kai growled. "Guard! Fodjour!"

"Hai!" called Fodjour.

"Makur."

"Hai!"

"Be on guard. I want every inch of my house and grounds searched. That bastard Omar must be here. Lamiya! Nandi! To your rooms at once, with guard."

"Can you save her?" Kai asked Babatunde.

"I think so. I believe so." He folded his hands together, thinking hard and fast. "Send for Jimuyu, and the herb woman."

"You will stay with my daughter. You will save her life, if it is possible. I know this."

"*Insh'Allah.*"

Kai gripped Babatunde's shoulder, then released it before rage and fear transformed his hand into a claw. Trembling, he stalked from the room.

As if it had held its greatest wrath for just such a moment, the sky had opened, unleashing its fury. The search continued for an hour in the midst of the downpour, and then . . .

"*The Hashassin is found!*" cried a servant.

They rushed toward the barn, entering with drawn swords, and found Fodjour standing over a limp body.

The corpse was freshly dead. The body was dressed in a Zulu kilt, a spear still clutched in his right hand.

"What is this?" Kai asked, kneeling to see more closely. "I know this man, but cannot name him." Had he seen the man before? His head seemed muzzy, anger coursing through his veins with such a fire that it grew difficult to think.

"He is Zulu," said a guard.

"Yes," said Kai. "Not Persian. But the Hashassin adopt children from other tribes, and raise them to kill. We must assume nothing. Does anyone know him? Has anyone ever seen him?" His guards shook their heads. Kai frowned. "There will be a reckoning. Someone among my people may know something."

"Why?"

"Because he either entered the house, or had a confederate within. I want my servants brought to the barn. Now."

Conair stepped forward, wringing his hands miserably. "I, sir. I have seen this man."

"When? Where?"

"I dare not speak," the boy said, averting his eyes.

"Why?"

"I'm afraid."

"You need fear nothing if you speak truth. And everything if you fail to speak. I will have answers." Kai struggled with all his powers to keep his emotions under control.

"I saw him speaking to the *sitta-t.*"

"Lamiya?"

Conair shook his head.

"Nandi?"

The boy nodded.

"When?"

"At the birthday party."

"Where were they?" Kai's head was whirling, rage and pain combining to head-splitting effect. "Who else was there?"

"Sir. They were . . . alone."

Kai looked stricken. His eyes tightened and then opened. "Nandi. Who else has words for me? Speak now."

"Sir," said the cook. "I saw her put a powder into your stew two months ago. I thought that they were special spices, and watched her sample it herself, so . . ." He looked completely abashed. "I hope that I was not mistaken."

"Why said you nothing?" The rage in his voice was shocking, even to himself. It was not his voice at all; it was Malik's, and some deeper part of

Kai said, *Why not? See where your greed and lust have brought you? But I am here. I will guide your hand.*

Release me.

"Accuse the lady of the household, sir? Your new wife? If I was wrong, she would have me crucified."

Kai was as silent and still as the center of a storm. Then without another word he left the barn, and walked through the rain back to the house, making no attempt to shelter himself, barely blinking as the water ran through his hair and into his eyes.

Kai went to the third-floor nursery. Babatunde still hovered over Aliyah, who remained deep in her swoon.

"How is she?" he asked.

"Strong," the Sufi said. "With the grace of the Almighty, I believe she will survive. I cannot leave her side yet."

"I do not wish you to," said Kai. "I wish you to remain in this room for the next hour."

Those words broke Babatunde's focus, and he turned to examine his pupil. What he saw alarmed him. "Kai. You are not well."

Do not listen to him. "I wish you to tell me the truth, Babatunde."

"Have I ever done other than that?"

"Never have I asked you a question of such import."

They were both silent. Aliyah moaned. Babatunde mixed unguents from several jars, placed the resultant mixture of herbs and honey on a thin stick, and placed it on her tongue.

"The fit has passed. Danger remains," he said finally. "Your question?"

"What do you know of Nandi, and a Zulu warrior. Nandi, and herbal powders in the kitchen. The truth!"

Pupil and teacher gazed into each other's eyes, and Babatunde was clearly uneasy.

"Babatunde," Kai growled, in a tone he had never before used with his teacher. "Speak, damm it!"

"I know nothing of powders. I know that she collected Lamiya's nail clippings. The Zulus believe such tokens can be used to influence behavior, and I thought it a harmless affectation. I corrected her, and thought that would be the end of it."

"And the Zulu warrior?"

"She admitted to me that she had spoken to him, but that is all."

"And my daughter?"

"There is no evidence . . . no . . ."

Babatunde hung his head, tears sparkling in his eyes. "I am sorry. I fear I have failed you."

"Not yet," Kai said. Crimson clouds boiled at the periphery of his vision, but he managed to lay a gentle hand on his old friend's shoulder. "You may still do me service if you save Aliyah's life."

Kai left. Behind him, Babatunde looked absolutely haunted.

Kai stalked downstairs, to Nandi's room. His foot crashed against the door, just above the lock, splintering it inward.

"Kai?!" Nandi screamed. IziLomo, crouched at her side, growled at him and started forward.

Nandi reacted instantly, spitting out *"Kulungile."* As if he had run into a wall IziLomo stopped, trembling, whining, straining forward, constrained by iron bonds of discipline and love.

She turned back to Kai, saw her husband's hand upon his sword hilt, and felt her blood turn to water. "What is it?"

"Up, witch," he snarled. His voice seethed with rage, but for just the moment, he managed to control it. "Walk out of the room," he said. His eyes were locked on her, but she knew that his vision was taking in everything in the room, every detail. Knew also that if IziLomo moved, Kai would gut him.

Managing to maintain a semblance of dignity, Nandi turned to IziLomo, who was staring at Kai, a low, hungry moan in his throat. She spoke to her canine friend in Zulu. *"Ngizokubuya."* I will return. The dog did not know that she was saving his life, knew only that there was something terribly wrong, and that his mistress was in peril. Still, though IziLomo loved her more than his own life, discipline was stronger than will or instinct, and he remained in place.

Posture very erect, Nandi walked from the room. Kai closed the door, both of them startled as IziLomo crashed against the heavy wood the instant she was out of his sight. He began to howl.

"Kai—" she began, but got no further as the temporary dam Kai had placed upon his rage broke. His hand flickered out, slapping her across the face with shocking, contemptuous force.

Nandi stumbled backward, crashed into the wall and then reeled forward. "You would kill the fruit of my body, and then me, and think to take what my father and uncle spent a lifetime in building?" Kai threaded his fingers into Nandi's hair, and dragged her down the stairs.

His men had arrived behind him, stunned at the sight, but instantly grasping the enormity of the situation. Nandi's maids had appeared at the top of the stairs, and Kai's men blocked their way with drawn swords.

Kai saw none of it. The only thing in his heart was the sight of his poisoned daughter, struggling for her life.

Kai dragged her outside, Nandi holding his hand with hers, lest her hair be pulled out by the roots. IziLomo's howls echoed through the house like the cries of a lost soul.

He began to drag her toward the barn, and was barely aware that Aidan had run up behind him.

"Kai! No!" Aidan called.

Kai gazed at Aidan with eyes that were as black as the heart of hell. When he spoke, there was no shred of humanity in his voice.

"This is not your affair. Go."

Aidan started to extend his hand, but then stopped, frozen by the expression on Kai's face. Both of them knew that if Aidan touched him at that moment, Kai's sword would taste blood. Doubtlessly Kai would regret it later, but regret did not return men from the grave. At this moment, Aidan's boyhood friend was like a half-tamed wolf chewing a mutton joint at fireside. Do not touch the wolf while it eats.

Or avenges its pup.

Kai pulled Nandi into the barn, and pushed her face at Chalo's corpse. Then he dragged her back outside.

"Not in a building," he growled. "Not beneath a roof. I want your accursed ancestors to watch. Try as it may, all Allah's rain cannot wash away your sins, and where your accursed blood spills, may nothing grow for a generation."

Lamiya had watched, and whatever warring emotions might have lived within her breast, no one could say. She stepped forward, screaming "Kai!" in a commanding voice, and indeed, as mother of his child might well have been the only human being on Earth who could still his hand.

"Kai!" Lamiya called again. "Listen to me!"

"Out of my way, woman!"

"No! I have as much right to revenge as you. Look at me and tell me it is not so."

Kai stared at her. The rain coursed down his face. Nandi lay weak in his grasp, undone by struggle and terror.

"There is more here than we know," the Empress's niece said urgently. "Think!"

For an instant he stared at her, and there was momentary hope that her words might have struck home. Then Kai spoke slowly, as if the pronunciation of each and every word were an effort. "I think that I brought a viper into our home," he said. "I think that there is only one way that this can end."

He looked down at Nandi. "One minute."

He drew *Ruh Riyâh*. Once Soul Wind had been his father's sword. Carried onto honest battlefields, Soul Wind had cleft honest skulls and stilled honest hearts. And now . . . this. He would rather have faced a thousand foes with blood in their eyes and murder on their lips than one deceitful woman.

Rainwater trickled off its blade like blood after a battle. His chest was heaving as if he had just completed a race. "I give you one minute to pray. Pray to the naked sky, or whatever heathen devils burn in the depths of your Zulu heart. Pray that there is no hell to swallow a creature who would defile the home that welcomed her, betray the man who loved her, kill a child who trusted her."

She gazed up at him, perhaps seeking some sign of softness, some trace of hope. The rain beat into her face, pouring from a cold and uncaring sky.

Distantly, IziLomo wailed.

He leaned down closer to her. "My hand feels weak tonight," he whispered. "Pray that my blade needs but a single stroke."

Kai raised his sword.

CHAPTER EIGHTY-SEVEN

NANDI'S WORLD HAD IMPLODED. All honor was gone. All hope, all love, and now all life were ended. The fall of Kai's blade would terminate more than her life—it would end any chance for her people to find their homeland.

Her father would learn of this, and he would want revenge against Kai. Djibouti would defend its Wakil, marginalizing Cetshwayo and his men. War would tear the continent—all because she, Nandi, had failed.

In the depths of her mind, images flashed like falling stars, dying just as swiftly. She saw the day of her own arrival at Dar Kush. The days of sexual delay and anticipation, once thought delicious, but now seeming only the games of a wounded child. The attack that had claimed Kokossa, when she had placed her own body between the children and danger. An instinctive action, not even now, in the last instants of her life, regretted. Chalo sneaking onto Dar Kush. The deathly sick Aliyah. With impossible swiftness the images sailed past, and might have continued backward to her childhood had she not taken control, a tiny possibility burrowing its way into consciousness.

"Your eyes, Kai," she said. "You've been drugged. You are not yourself."

"Witch. I know what medicine I need. It will flow in but a moment."

"Kai," she said, wrestling mortal fear in an effort to steady her voice. "You saw Chalo fight at the wedding. You *saw*. Could Fodjour beat him?"

The rain beat against Kai's face. "Save your breath for prayer, witch. You profit nothing by slandering Djiboutan men. Soon enough, your kin will flinch from our steel."

"Kai! Who profits from this?"

"You thought to bear my only child, my heir."

She nodded in misery, realizing how closely his words struck. "I hoped to bear your son. I put herbs in Lamiya's food to make her child a girl, not to kill her. And into yours was only a love potion. I sought to win your heart. That was my only sin."

Kai lowered his sword. "And your meeting with Chalo?" he asked, no trace of softness in the words. He might have been a machine.

Chalo. Brave, handsome, foolish Chalo. Chalo, whom she had toyed with. And led to his doom . . . ? "He was a boy, taken with me. I met with him to tell him never to come again."

"You should have been more persuasive," Kai said with finality. "Bow your head."

Nandi broke into deep, wracking sobs, cries that even a lifetime of iron discipline were unable to repress. Rain and tears mingled as she stared into the mud. Lightning breached the sky above them. Reflected in the puddle she saw Kai raise his sword again. Holding it in his right hand. She closed her eyes and remembered Chalo, holding his spear.

Holding his spear.

"Kai!" she pled in desperation. "One last question. Please. If ever you cared for me. Just one, and then I die."

The sword had crested, beginning its downward stroke when she spoke his name. Kai's shoulders trembled with the effort to halt the lethal descent. "What?"

She turned her head to look at him. Was it rain? Or was Kai crying? What lived in his eyes seemed not one but two men: one an unyielding angel of vengeance, but the other . . . the other . . .

She spoke what she knew would either be the most important, or the final words of her life. "Why was Chalo's spear in his right hand?" she asked.

"What?"

"He was *left-handed*, Kai."

Kai remembered the day of the wedding. Chalo's prowess was more than impressive—it was astounding, expert clarity of line combined with a sheer physical exuberance that seemed a defining characteristic of the Zulu people. Kai had wondered what damage he himself might take in the killing of so superb a warrior, and was profoundly grateful that the experiment was not required.

He struggled to remember. The fire in his blood pulled at him, whispering release if he would but surrender to it.

As Malik had surrendered. No. He was more than that. Not more than Malik—but he stood on Malik's shoulders. To do honor to his uncle, he must see farther.

A moment. Just a moment to think.

Yes, he had seen Chalo, watched him. Yes. And Nandi was right: Chalo was left-handed. *Why then, had he fought Fodjour with his* umkhonto *in his right?*

Kai stood stock-still in the rain.

A succession of images and sensations, running backward in time, colliding until he fell to his knees, the world spinning around and around, everything that had happened in the last three years weaving together in his mind.

There were two families of answer. The first posited that for a reason Kai could not, and might never understand, Chalo had simply used his right hand. A possibility.

The other, though, was enough to freeze his breath in his chest. *Because if Chalo hadn't fought with his right, then Fodjour had* placed *the spear in his hand.* And that meant that to one degree or another, the scene had been staged.

Fodjour? But why?

Kai was not in the rain. Instead, he knelt in his meditation and exercise room, the image of the *Naqsh Kabir* on the floor before him. And as clearly as he saw the rain falling before him, each drop separate and floating through the air like a drifting leaf, he saw Babatunde speak:

Time is created by our minds. The seductive temptation is to assume linearity is a thing in and of itself, and the best way to order and interpret events. In other words: What caused this thing? What led to this thing? What has happened before that, creating a foundation for this thing?

But that is not the only way to interpret reality. Look at the Naqsh Kabir. *If one orders events around the outer rim, that rim represents temporal sequence. But note the lines within. Every connecting pair forms its own meaning, a meaning that exists outside of formal time, that looks both forward and backward in the same instant. We learn one set of things by accepting time, and another still by denying it. Before you come to conclusion, ask yourself: what does this mean, from either view?*

The linear: Kai of Dar Kush killed Shaka Zulu. Nandi was sent to destroy his house: first his heirs, and then, after producing her own child, by killing him and Lamiya. The Zulus inherit Dar Kush's wealth and influence.

Diabolically simple.

But what else was there? Was there someone who benefited not from Kai's death, but his *child's* death?

Perhaps.

What if his sword had fallen on Nandi's neck? All hope of alliance with the Zulus would end at that same instant. The Zulus would form alliance with the north . . .

No. The Zulus did not respect the "effeminates" of New Alexandria. If a peacemaker approached them, offering sufficient proof of regret and honorable intent, the Zulu might well continue to back the south. Yes. If it served their best interests, that was exactly what they would do.

What else? What would be both a prize and proof of sincerity in the eyes of the Zulu?

The office of Wakil, of course. Given to Kai's father Abu Ali in part for military service, and in part a political acknowledgment of his economic and social power, the office bore powers of high and low justice, and was ancestral—that is, would be passed from father to son.

What if Kai were disgraced? Already, there had been rumbles, efforts to remove him from office. This action, destroying Dar Kush's alliance with the Zulus and certainly feeding into the perception of him as an unstable, violent man, would certainly result in impeachment, such an action providing proof positive of Djiboutan regret. A grieving Cetshwayo thus satisfied.

And into whose hands would the office fall?

Which was the second most powerful family in New Djibouti? Who had watched the creation of dynasty from across the lake, with possibly envious eyes?

Who had discovered Chalo's body? And who did Kai know, in his heart of hearts, to have no chance of defeating the young Zulu in single combat? Who was a master drummer, but only a middling swordsman?

A fissure seemed to run from the front of Kai's head to the back, a crack that widened and widened until it engulfed him, a lifetime of images shattering and rearranging as everything that he thought he had known about his oldest friend was cast in a new light. Inevitably, that destroying light engulfed him as well, an entire universe of shattered mirrors reflecting him.

So many of them gone now: father . . . brother . . . uncle . . .

Oldest friend.

All gone, and the few precious connections to those who remained not enough to keep the entire structure from falling, his very sense of identity suddenly, shockingly, swept away, the entirety of his *self* crashing without sufficient support to sustain it, until in a glorious, terrifying, utterly unique moment . . .

A child you were, a boy of softness born into a world of strength. You have struggled with it, and excelled, but the armors you have donned, the weapons mastered, are not you. None of them you. They are what you learned that you might one day put them down.

You are not a warrior. Not a scholar. Not father, or husband, or sinner, or saint. These are merely masks that you have worn, attempting to hide from My light.

Kai existed in a world without walls, without symbols or sounds. *No Dar Kush. No earthly obligation. No politics, or father, or uncle. You are all these things, and more.*

And less.

Merely existence, as the thing itself. Nothing but Kai, and his soul, and his God.

And for the first time in his life, Kai heard His voice.

Tears fell from his eyes, and there, kneeling in the rain, he was made whole.

CHAPTER EIGHTY-EIGHT

KAI SAGGED KNEELING IN THE DOWNPOUR, head bowed. He looked up, his face relaxed, his eyes soft. In a curious paradox, he seemed at that instant to be both younger and older than his years.

"Kai . . . ?" said Lamiya.

Lightning crackled above his head. He looked down at Nandi. Kneeling in the mud, eyes still cast down, shivering, awaiting death. He shook his head. A sensation like fog dispersing in a chill wind wound through him. *Rage*, he thought, *was not all that clouded my senses. I have been drugged.* The calmness of the voice in his head surprised him. It was not his father's voice. Nor Malik's It was his own.

Then he turned and screamed into the rain. *"Fodjour!"*

"He is gone, sir," Ganne said.

"Gone where?"

"He said he would check the grounds for Hashassin."

"Yes," said Kai grimly. "I think I shall, as well."

He nearly killed his horse, but it took only fifteen minutes for Kai to circle Lake A'zam, his guard close behind him. The guard at the Berhar residence met him at their gate, and saw the Wakil and his coterie bearing down on them with pale and singular purpose.

"Who goes there?" they were asked.

"The Wakil, on official business." Those were his words, his voice. But the calm and strength in them was beyond crediting. "Stand aside."

They could feel that there was something terribly wrong, but had received no orders to the contrary, and opened the gate.

Kai halted his horse before the front door of the great house, and fired his pistol into the air.

"Fodjour!" he screamed. "Come out! Son of a pig. You ate at my table, and fought at my side. You have betrayed everything that you claimed to hold dear. Come out! I would have an ending to this!"

There was a pause, and then the front door opened. Moving gingerly,

Djidade and Allahbas Berhar appeared. Djidade Berhar looked as if he were already sleeping in a grave.

"Our son is not here," Allahbas said.

Kai felt as if he were watching himself from above. "Where is he?"

"He has gone away on business," Allahbas said.

Kai stared at her, suddenly, clearly seeing what he had not, ever before. "You were behind this, weren't you? Your husband is a corpse," he said dismissively. "Fodjour hadn't the brains for it."

Her gaze met his squarely, without explanation or apology. "As you haven't the heart to be Wakil."

Kai nodded. "This talk of hearts makes me thirsty," he said.

Fodjour's younger brother Mada appeared from behind her, lunging at Kai with a sword he could barely keep aloft.

"Mada, no!" Djidade screamed, as Kai took the boy down and planted his foot on Mada's neck.

"Please, Kai," the elder Berhar said from his wheelchair.

"Did you know?" Kai asked. "They poisoned my daughter. Attempted to induce me to kill my wife. *My wife!* Drugged me in my own house. Soon, Djidade, you will stand before Allah. Tell me the truth. *Did you know?*"

His sword hovered above Mada's face. Allahbas trembled, Makur's blade at her breast.

"Did you know?"

"Not all," Berhar whispered. "Some, not all. Mada was blameless. He knew nothing. Please."

With such speed that she hadn't time even to flinch, Kai brought his blade to rest against Allahbas's smooth throat.

"I am the Wakil," Kai whispered, yet his words were loud enough to be heard against the storm. He struggled with the fire in his veins. "I am the law. I will drag your house into the gutter and burn it. I will find your son and parade his severed head through the streets, his *zakr* sewn into his mouth. Do you hear me?"

She trembled, but did not reply.

"Arrest them," Kai said to his men, then turned and stalked away.

CHAPTER EIGHTY-NINE

WHILE KAI'S GUARD SEARCHED FOR FODJOUR, Kai began the ride back to Dar Kush, the longest of his life. Unwilling to meet so much as a servant, he slipped though a side door and took back passages to his rooms on the second floor.

He did not emerge until the following day. As the effects of the drug wore off he brooded, hovering on the edge of one of the massive depressions that haunted the men of his family, wanting terribly to reach out to Nandi, but simultaneously too ashamed to face her.

Stress. Anger. Fear. All disintegrate the harmony of your structure. Alignment, motion, and breathing for the physical, psychological, and emotional.

And for the spiritual . . . prayer.

Babatunde's voice. So, then. Malik lived within him, and always would. But so did his father. And so did the Sufi. And perhaps it took the three of them to make him human.

What is a man? Father? No. Malik had not been that, through most of his life. Babatunde was not, still. Politician? Again, the Sufi had no such leanings. The power of the external world was not for him. And Lamiya knew more about politics than Kai ever would.

Warrior? Then how to explain the Dahomy? They were superb, and yet women.

None of those things, then. Then what?

And did it matter? And if not, what did? If dualities did not matter . . . What did?

It was not until the next evening that Kai could bring himself to enter her rooms.

He dressed in white, the color of death, for he understood that there are acts one cannot undo. There was no coming back from the precipice: the marriage was over. Nandi would return home, and perhaps it would be best if, after bringing Fodjour and the Berhars to justice, he retired from his office. This was not his world. He could retreat into prayer and raise his family, and allow other men the dubious pleasures of authority.

But first, there was one last honorable action to perform, and it could no longer be delayed.

So he took the long, long walk along the second floor, past Lamiya's apartment and down the hall to the southeasternmost section of Dar Kush.

He raised his hand to knock on her door.

Even before he had knocked, he heard IziLomo's howl, a cry of rage and fear, and he heard the voices as they sought to quiet the monster.

Allah preserve him. How had he come to such a place in his life? He knew now: he had been a fool, a turtle in the midst of a fire, believing that it could pull into its shell and be safe from the flame. He saw so much now, so clearly. How sad that that clarity had come too late.

But so often, that was the way of the world.

Baleka, Nandi's nurse, opened the door. "The madam is not in—"

"No, Baleka," he heard Nandi say. "Admit him."

The door opened wider, and Kai entered. Three of Nandi's retainers, the stern Zulu women who had accompanied her to her new home, stood between Kai and Nandi, but they were not the ones who captured his attention.

IziLomo crouched at the side of the room, watching him carefully, teeth bared. Not growling. Not moving forward. Watching.

"You are dismissed," Nandi said, gesturing to her ladies.

"But *Nkosikaz*," one of them began.

"You question me?" Nandi said. "There are things to be said between my husband and myself. They are for no other ears."

"Princess—"

"Go!"

Glaring at Kai, the women began to file out.

IziLomo seemed to watch Nandi questioningly. Now, the smallest trace of emotion creased her face. "IziLomo may stay," she said.

The women filed past Kai, but at this last proclamation of their princess, seemed to take a grim and stolid satisfaction.

The door closed behind him, and now it was just Kai, and Nandi, and the Zulu ridgeback.

For almost a minute the three of them watched each other. Nandi stood by IziLomo, the dog still crouching, every muscle seemingly relaxed, only its brown eyes alive and burning.

"I know not what to say," Kai began.

Nandi was silent.

Cursing himself for a fool, Kai continued. "I made a terrible error, the greatest of my life. I have no reason to think that you could ever forgive me. Or trust me. But I can show you that I trust you."

"How would you propose to do that?"

"I will give you the means to destroy me."

Finally, he seemed to have engaged her attention. "Yes," she said. "I would like that."

Kai dropped his gaze. "Three years ago, at the mosque, my brother disobeyed Shaka's orders, and Shaka killed him. In vengeance, I slew Shaka in turn."

She stared at him. Whatever she might have expected him to say, this was one of the least likely. "You lie."

"It is truth. Fodjour and Makur were there as well. If you can find them, you can ask them."

"You . . . murdered Shaka?"

"I was in front of him. His spear was in his hand. His eyes were open, and he had just slain my brother. Call it what you will."

She said nothing.

"Under military discipline, I am guilty of the murder of a superior officer. There are witnesses. If you tell of my deed, I die."

He paused, and then continued, "I think perhaps that it is time for you to pay a visit to your family. I think a month will be sufficient, don't you?"

She stared at him, disbelieving. "You would let me from your sight carrying such a secret?"

"Yes."

"*Why?*"

"Because I love you, and do not wish to live unless you can find it in your heart to forgive me."

Nandi turned from him, and stared out of her window. Who was she? She had been raised from childhood to be the bride of a great man. . . .

And was she not?

"May I speak freely?" she asked.

"You are my wife," said Kai. "I would expect nothing less."

"So. I doubt I need to say that the events of the last days have been the most hurtful of my life."

"My sorrow and shame knows no bounds."

She held up a hand, as if to silence him. "And your mistrust of me, and near taking of my life, is more than hurtful: it is a dishonor that, if it ever left the confines of this estate, might well trigger war."

"I know."

"Nonetheless," she said, "under the circumstances you describe, suddenly everything makes sense. In fact, I would not wish as husband a man who would react in any other fashion."

She stood, moved away from him, wrapping her silk robes around the body that had embraced his so fervently.

"You are my husband, Kai. But more than that, I love you, and have since first I met you, fifteen years ago. I think now that I understand many things . . . including the fact that my father knew you slew Shaka, and intended to use me for his own purposes."

"What purpose would that be?"

"Vengeance," Nandi said. "Power. He wanted me to spy upon you, even as he would not tell me all that he knew, or suspected."

"I see."

"So. You avenged your brother, as you were honor-bound to do. As my father was bound to avenge his."

Her face twisted venomously.

"But he should not have whored his daughter to do it!"

"Nandi—"

"I am tired of being a tool. Abu Ali trothed us for politics. You married me from obligation. I was given to you by my father, who cared not in whose bed I lay, or what it might cost my heart to lie there."

"Nandi—"

When he tried to comfort her, she twisted away. She was shaking in a way that he had never seen before, the white heat of her passion, fear, and need melting her resolve. He could see to her core.

"I disown my father," Nandi said, "and I free you from any obligations to me. No longer need you fear me, or from such fear maintain pretense of love."

She looked at him, such searing longing mixed with her tears that it seemed her very heart poured from her eyes. Then she turned away.

"Go. Please."

He stood there, uncertain what he should, or could, do. If he left, it was ended. If he didn't . . . what?

And then the question was answered.

IziLomo's long dour muzzle pointed at his mistress, and then at Kai, and back again. He stood, and pressed his massive head against her leg. She did not move. The dog looked at Kai again, then back to his mistress, and then shook himself.

Then walked across the room toward Kai.

Kai could barely breathe, unwilling to disrupt the moment, unable to make a sound. IziLomo stopped in front of Kai, looking up at him. And very slowly, Kai lowered himself so that he and the dog were eye to eye.

He could see every vein in the eyes, the white hairs among the black on IziLomo's muzzle, smell the meaty wetness of his breath. The white teeth shaded to yellow at the gums.

Kai opened himself, went back to the place that he had found in the rain. Kai did not exist there, only his soul, his essence. The dog's head tilted sideways slightly, almost questioningly. Not knowing how he knew to do it, Kai extended his hand. IziLomo sniffed it, and made a whining sound deep in his throat. He looked back at Nandi, who was staring at them both.

Then the ridgeback licked Kai's hand. Once. Whined. Then walked back to his mistress's side.

Nandi stared at him, then down at her four-legged courtier, and exhaled. She drew herself up as if composing herself for a ceremony. Confused she might have been, but Kai thought she had never seemed more regal.

A queen without a country, perhaps, but a queen nonetheless.

"Nandi," Kai said. "There has been a terrible mistake. Many of them. Some have cost lives, and will cost more. I do not know what lies ahead for our people. But I do know one thing."

He paused.

"Once upon a time, you showed me the extent of your father's lands and cattle, and said they were yours to share with the man you married."

She tilted her head up, so that the light seemed to flow over her. Exquisite. "And you said to me, further, that a man would be a fool to turn you away, even if you were penniless, even if you were not the daughter of Cetshwayo, the niece of great Shaka."

The set of her jaw was firm. Kai came close behind her, and took her shoulders with his hands. Warmly. Softly.

"And I thought at that moment that I had never heard truer words in my life."

Her eyes suddenly softened; her cheek tilted down a fraction of a degree, as if to rest itself against his hand. Then she seemed to remember herself, and straightened again.

"I have been a fool," he said. "I married you because my father arranged it, and there was no safe and honorable way to retreat from that arrangement."

She stiffened.

"But if I had not been Wakil, and you had not been the daughter of Cetshwayo—if I had merely seen you on the avenue, had grown to manhood hearing your laughter, marveling at the clarity of your mind, thrilling at your utter vibrancy—I would have wanted you, but never dreamed that I could be your equal. I would have thought, 'Kai is a simple scholar' or, 'Kai is a herdsman,' and that a woman like you could never want someone without so wild a heart as yours."

Her shoulders tensed beneath his hand. "You hesitated to send for me because of what happened to Shaka?"

"Yes."

"And that is why you married Lamiya?"

"No," he said. "I love her, and always have. When all was lost, she gave me light."

"I would have healed you, Kai." Her voice was very soft.

He turned away from her, toward the window. "How could you want me?"

"If I were a man, I would have done as you did. If I were a man, I would wish to be as you are."

The silence between them stretched for an eternity. Kai felt as if his throat was closed. "If I were truly a man," he managed to say, "I would take you in my arms, now, and find a way to show you that all the stars of heaven have no light to exceed that I see in your eyes. That I would discard all I own if we two could start anew, and I could come to you with just my heart and my sword, pledging both to you for all my life. If only you would forgive me, and love me as once you did."

There, he had said it, and now there was nothing but to wait.

"I cannot give you that heart," she said finally. "It is dead and gone." She paused. "But I can give you the new one, born this day. I will be yours, Kai, if you will be mine. No Wakil, no royal daughter. No state, no contracts. Two souls. One heart."

Their eyes locked for a long moment, and then her lips pressed against his, and Kai felt as if his limbs had changed to both water and steel in the same instant.

Their clothes rustled as they fell to the floor.

Izilomo did not leave their room that night.

And although his warm brown eyes saw all that occurred, he made no sound at all.

CHAPTER NINETY

As THEY HAD SO MANY TIMES IN THE PAST, Kai and Aidan sat on the banks of the stream dividing the woods west of the main house. A thin breeze wove through the trees, rustling leaves, bringing with it a scent of clover and distant pine. Kai spun a rock out into the water, watched it skip and then sink. "This water has always been here," he said, "and will be after we are gone."

"Do you think it remembers us?" Aidan asked.

"I don't know," said the Wakil.

"Things were so much simpler when we were children, Kai," Aidan said.

"Men take the actions they do so that their children might lead simpler lives. More peaceful lives."

"My children's life will not be simple," said Aidan, "but they can be better than my own."

"Insh'Allah."

"I have another favor to ask you," Aidan said.

"Name it. Please."

"I wish to take Tata home with me as well. She and Conair . . ."

Kai exhaled, some inner knot of tension relaxing. "I had hoped you would say that, Aidan. I don't even know why I brought her here. But I can't look at her anymore. Every time I do, I remember how I found her." He tossed a rock out into the water. "I wonder if her grandmother was one of the slaves my father or grandfather brought here. I wonder how much she fetched. I wonder what toy of mine was bought with the money that paid for her rape."

"Kai," Aidan said gently. "You do what you can."

"No, I don't," answered Kai. "But I will. Take her, of course, with my blessing." He paused. "You asked me once if our men were stronger, or our women weaker."

"You remembered."

"Yes, and have an answer. The answer is neither. It's just custom, and cir-cumstance." Another pause. "Like too many other things in this world."

Aidan stared at him, perhaps knowing that Kai had just come as close as he could to saying *I'm sorry. For everything.*

"Farewell, my brother," Kai said. "Thank you so much, for everything. For every day that you've been in my life, even before I knew who you were."

"I won't say it's always been a pleasure," Aidan said. "But it's always been . . . extraordinary."

CHAPTER NINETY-ONE

AS OFTEN HAPPENED, Lamiya, Nandi, and Babatunde were gathered in the main library, enjoying warm after-dinner glow. The fireplace crackled with ginger-scented logs. Aliyah and Azinza were upstairs, watched by their Zulu nursemaids. IziLomo was out at the lake, entertaining and being entertained by the Dahomy, who would leave in another week, carrying with them gold enough to sustain their community for a year.

Kai disapproved of mercenaries but had found nothing to fault in their demeanor, loyalty, or performance. They were not Hashassin, striking from darkness. They guarded, protected, acted in daylight, faces exposed, lawfully engaged in honorable service. The Dahomy were women making their way in a men's world, and if he could not respect them on their own terms, perhaps he was not fit to be Wakil. They were not as he had been taught women were. But they were women, and that changed his view of all women. Aidan was not as he had been taught whites were. And that changed his view of all whites.

Nothing is as it seems, he thought. *But some things are even better.*

If their journeys brought them south again, there would be a place for them at Dar Kush.

For now, the pleasures of home and hearth were enough to engage him fully, and few were the times in his life when contentment had felt so complete.

"Aidan has gone?" asked Lamiya.

"Yes," Kai said. "But he will return in some months to train with my guard."

"That is good."

"Husband?" said Nandi.

"Yes?"

"Do you like the name UmNtwana?"

"I suppose." He looked at her curiously. "What does it mean?"

"Do you think a child born in Dhu'l-Qa'dah will be strong?"

AFTERWORD

I WOULD LIKE TO THANK THE READERS of *Lion's Blood* for their hundreds of letters and e-mails. Some chord was touched with that book, one for which the author cannot take complete credit. It is a world created from love and pain and hope. Both Kai and Aidan live in my heart, and it is joyous to know that others have found them as interesting as I. If life is kind, they'll be back.

Kai's eating patterns are modifications of the partial fasts observed by Muslims worldwide during the month of Ramadan. To learn more of its theory and benefits, consult Ori Hofmekler's *The Warrior Diet.*

Sharp-eyed readers will recognize, amid the chaos of the Djibouti Harbor battle, the narrative of Francis B. Butts, survivor of the sinking of the *Monitor.*

A very partial listing of the research works contributing to this volume: Tizita Ayele's *Ethiopian Cooking in the American Kitchen,* Yahiya Emerick's *Complete Idiot's Guide to Understanding Islam,* F. Steingass's *English-Arabic Translator Dictionary,* Neil Grant's *The Egyptians,* A. G. Smith and William Kaufman's *Life in Celtic Times,* Marc Frey's *The Civil War,* Cheikh Anta Diop's *Precolonial Black Africa,* and John Laband's *Rise and Fall of the Zulu Nation.*

The physical training techniques utilized by Kai and Aidan, and taught by Babatunde, originate from a variety of African, Asian, and European sources. I would especially like to thank Pavel Tsatsouline for information about muscular irradiation, synaptic facilitation, and the use of the Russian kettlebell. Information about this incredible man's work can be found at www.dragondoor.com. And thanks to Scott Sonnon for bringing the Russian and Slavic health systems to the West as well as for his theory of the Flow State Performance Spiral. More of his sophisticated thought can be found at www.ammeross.com.

The combat theory and motion presented in this novel is a mixture of Filipino Kali, Indonesian Pentjak Silat, and Zulu knife-fighting, perhaps

"The month of rest. Certainly. Why? Nandi . . . ?" Kai asked. "What is this?"

"He is a slow one, isn't he?" Lamiya said, smiling.

"Yes, but trainable." Babatunde chuckled.

"Ah. Well, perhaps we will have more luck with his son," said Nandi.

"My . . . son?"

"Yes," Lamiya said. "You know, Kai . . . small, helpless male creature. Trouble in a small package? Lock up your daughters?"

"A son."

"I believe," said Babatunde, "that *UmNtwana* means 'child of the king.'"

Kai stood, stretching himself. Then a sudden thought stopped him in his tracks, and he turned. "When did you know?"

"A week ago," Nandi said.

Kai's jaw dropped. "Why didn't you tell me?" he whispered. "I have—"

"It must have slipped my mind," she said.

"Did *you* know?" he asked Lamiya.

Lamiya continued with her sewing. Kai stood, and poked. Started to say something. Stopped. Looked out over the room. Nandi. Babatunde. And upstairs, his daughter Aliyah and Ma Azinza.

His family, save only for the man now on the way to his own man who had risked and won much because he trusted Kai. Kai trusted Aidan, and both, thank Allah, had proven worthy.

A vast sense of contentment descended upon him.

"Did you say something, my husband?" Lamiya asked.

Kai smiled. "No," he answered. "Nothing at all."

the most fearsome fighting technique I have seen in some thirty years of martial rigors.

And in closing, I would like to offer three deep bows to Vernon Turner, Kitabu Roshi, for insight into the experience of enlightenment. Your humble author has experienced many awe-inspiring things through the years, but not this.

Hope springs eternal.

Steven Barnes
August 26, 2002
Longview, Washington